CW00662956

About the Author

Richard Young grew up in Braintree, Essex, UK, before settling down with his wife, Mandy, and daughter, Rose. By day, he works full-time. He completed an online screenwriting course through Smart Majority for TV and film, which gave him the inspiration to create the first short story of *The Short Story Saga*. In his spare time, he enjoys gaming, writing stories, and spending time with friends and family.

The Short Story Saga

Richard Young

The Short Story Saga

Olympia Publishers
London

www.olympiapublishers.com
OLYMPIA PAPERBACK EDITION

A CIP catalogue record for this title is
available from the British Library.

ISBN: 978-1-80439-253-9

This is a work of fiction.
Names, characters, places and incidents originate from the writer's imagination.
Any resemblance to actual persons, living or dead, is purely coincidental.

First Published in 2024

Olympia Publishers
Tallis House
2 Tallis Street
London
EC4Y 0AB

Printed in Great Britain

Dedication

For my wife, Mandy, and my daughter, Rose, and my family, who believed in me and encouraged me to take my hobby further.

Acknowledgements

To begin with, I would like to thank the team at Olympia Publishers who took the time to read my book and give me positive feedback. I am grateful to the team who has worked hard to publish this book and bring the story to life. To the members of the Smart Majority writing course for helping me develop as a writer and giving me hundred per cent feedback on my course modules. Without them, I would never have created my first Short Story chapter. Next, I would like to thank my father, John, who has spent a lot of time reading my short stories and has given me honest feedback, and to my mother, Sylvia, who has listened to the ideas for the stories to see if they are strong. To my mother and father-in-law, Jan and Terry Trinkwon, who believed I could achieve my goal. Last, but not least, to my friend, Stephen, with whom I have been co-writing our own material as a hobby since 2002, and we are still writing stories to this day.

No matter who we are. What gender. What age. What colour. What race and what language we speak. We all have a story to tell.
-Richard J Young

FAITHFUL

1

LOVE, is what Matthew Cornwall lived for in his life. He sat in the back of the taxi with mixed emotions of excitement and terror. As he stared out of the window watching the dense green countryside pass him by, he thought back to when he was young. He had just left high school and got good grades in his exams, giving him the chance to start out on his lifelong ambition, to become a writer, by taking an English journalism study at Pentemy College.

Matthew had lived in Pentemy Village all of his life. The village wasn't that far from the College, which was just on the outskirts. Matthew couldn't believe the size of the building when he stood outside it. It was much posher and more adult than high school.

As time ticked by, Matthew found himself studying hard to achieve his goal. Then, one day in the library, a beautiful woman sat in front of him. Her name was Allison. They both smiled when they acknowledged each other and started to talk about who they were and what courses they were taking.

Allison told Matthew that she was taking business studies and hoping one day she would be working in the admin department for Foptix Industries. Towns-end City's leading computer and robotics company. Matthew shared what he was studying for and Allison took a big interest in the ideas, turns and twists for stories he would be planning to write.

Matthew and Allison started out as friends until Matthew asked her out on a real date. They became closer and were college sweethearts all the way till the end of getting their degrees for their courses. Matthew proposed to Allison not long after and by the end of the year they were married and were living in a little flat in the Towns-end City area.

Allison achieved her dream and worked in admin at Foptix Industries. But not everything went to plan as she hoped. Sure, she was working in her admin role but alongside, Jennifer, the receptionist's assistant.

Matthew on the other hand had sent lots of his work to publishers and companies to try and get noticed for his next step towards his writer dream.

As the months went on, Matthew never heard a single response from any of them.

Feeling deflated and disheartened, Matthew started to think realistically and give up on the writing dream and just get an everyday job to keep the rent paid. But Allison urged him not to give up and pushed him to carry on.

Then one day, while looking through the Internet, Matthew found a short story competition. So, he put the hours into creating a condensed version of his story.

Matthew felt really positive that the story was going to be a hit as no one would see the twist coming and was even more excited when he had confirmation that the story had been submitted to the right people.

As the months went by, the submissions had been read and the winner had been announced. Matthew found out that someone else had won the competition who had written a story about politics and depression. Matthew was upset and angry that people would rather read about bad and low points just to feel the same.

Allison felt sad for Matthew. She wished there was something she could do, to make him feel better, but Matthew wasted no time in looking for jobs. Then one day, out of the blue, Matthew received a phone call for a job interview. Matthew wasn't told what the job would be over the phone and had no way of knowing if it was a job he had already applied for.

Matthew attended the interview where he got his job orders and would be starting with immediate effect,

Matthew hurried home to tell Allison the news that was going to change his life, forever.

Allison had her feet up on the two seated leather sofa, in the small cramped living room while watching the TV game show *Playing 4 Real.* Allison was then startled when she heard the front door slam and footsteps hurrying towards her.

"Allison? Allison?" said Matthew, with excitement.
He sat down next to Allison on the sofa and took her hands in his and told her that he had been contacted by a woman called Madison Milburn. Allison was puzzled, as to who this mysterious stranger was.

Madison Milburn had won the Miss Towns-end pageant and had represented a short story seminar. She had come across Matthew's discarded story and taken it a TV producer. She told Matthew that they

16

enjoyed what they read and had offered him an opportunity to write a TV movie. He would be travelling to Pentemy Village where he would meet the team of writers and stay in a flat to write the material for a month.

This did not please Allison in the slightest. Being apart for an entire month would be torture and lonely. Allison didn't drive and with Pentemy Village being six hours away, it was too much of a journey to visit. She told Matthew about the financial difficulties they were facing. If he pursued his dream, then they would not have enough money to pay the rent and keep the roof over their heads.

"You don't understand. What I would get from this movie would help us with our finances. Besides, Madison is paying for the cost of the travel. It's not going to cost us a thing," Matthew explained.

Matthew took Allison in his arms and assured her that a month would go fast. She admitted that she was going to miss him as it would feel like she was single again.

"Promise me one thing before you go?" Allison insisted. "The bathroom tap is leaking again. Can you fix it before you go? The last thing we need is a high-water bill."

"Of course, I will – I love you," said Matthew, as he pressed his lips on Allison's.

2

When we marry the one, we love, we make a vow to love, honour and be with them for the rest of our lives. But what happens when the greatest challenge of a marriage, is to continue that vow of love, by being apart.

The memories of his childhood filled Matthew's head as he saw the familiar sights and sounds, he hadn't seen for years. The taxi passed *The Pink Snow* bar that he and Allison used to go to when they were dating. He passed the College where they first met and everything that started his journey to where he was now, came full circle. He felt nervous being back after all the years away.

The taxi soon pulled up outside a three-storey block of flats. Matthew peered out of the window to see the place where he would be staying for the next month. It was a run-down old building that didn't look a patch on the one he and Allison lived in, in Towns-end City.

Matthew took his suitcases from the taxi and made his way to the lobby doors where an attractive woman in a summer dress stood, stroking her short blonde hair.

"Mr Cornwall?" she asked. "I'm Ash Cartwright – Madison sent me to give you this," she said, as she dangled a small key between her fingertips.

Matthew examined the key, that had had the number three carved into it. "I thought Madison, would be here to meet me?" he assumed.

"Madison is unwell," Ash told him. "And she is a very busy woman with lots of preparation."

"Preparation?" said Matthew, puzzled. "Preparation for what?"

"Oh, you'll find out eventually." Ash smiled. "Your colleagues will be at Pentemy College, where you'll discuss the ideas of your work at nine a.m. tomorrow."

"Thank you," Matthew replied.

Ash turned to leave, but then stopped and gave Matthew another smile. "Oh, welcome back home." Ash then walked away, causing Matthew to shudder to how creepy she was to him. When Matthew entered the building, it looked worse on the inside than the outside. There were holes in the faded blue carpet. The white walls were faded with cracked plaster. Dirty marks had been smeared on the stairwell wall, as Matthew climbed the stairs to the next floor.

The first door he came to was the same number as the key he had. This was it. This was where he was going to be staying. As he unlocked the door, faint footsteps came down the stairs from the floor above. What followed was a slim attractive woman, with long blonde hair, wearing a white vest top, tight leather trousers and a red leather jacket. She stared at Matthew as she walked past him, pretty much ignoring his smile that he gave.

To Matthew's surprise, the flat was small inside. Not as big as he imagined, which made him appreciate the flat that he and Allison were renting. The living room had a two seated leather sofa, an old looking TV, bookshelf and a small glass coffee table. There was no table and chairs to sit at to have dinner and the kitchen was cramped and basic, with dim lighting coming in through the windows and a musty smell in the air.

When he opened the door to the bathroom, he had a shock, when he felt the coldness of the floor and a wetness that soon followed from small amounts of water that were in between the cracks of the floor tiles. The bedroom wasn't much different either. The room felt cold, causing him to shiver. It was dark and eerie with a single bed and not much else. For free accommodation, Matthew couldn't complain and wasted no time in unpacking.

When he opened his suitcase, he was greeted by a folded-up piece of paper. The note read *Missing you already, I love you always – Allison x.*

"I love you, too," he mumbled to himself.

Half an hour later, Matthew was sat on the sofa, with his laptop connected to the Internet and the Vidtex Chat app open. He let it ring for the full duration, but there was no answer from Allison on the other end. As he looked around the room, feeling lonely and comfy on the sofa, he found that he couldn't keep his heavy eyes open any longer. But it wasn't long till he heard a ringing sound in his ears and realized that he was being called on his Vidtex.

Matthew felt a lot better when he saw Allison on the screen, until her expression told him otherwise.

"It's so good to see you. I miss you, it was too long a journey."

"I bet," said Allison, abruptly, acting like she wasn't bothered to see or hear from Matthew.

"What's wrong?" Matthew asked. "Is it because we're apart – it's only a month."

"No, it's not that." Allison sighed and crossed her arms. "You didn't do what I asked you to do. It was one simple thing." But Matthew was puzzled. He couldn't remember what Allison had asked. "I asked you to tighten the tap – it's leaking more now."

Matthew bit his finger nails, annoyed and frustrated as he had other things to worry about than a leaky tap. The pressure that he might be under were more important to him.

"Look, we rent – call the landlord – tell him about the tap, I'm sure he will send someone out."

"You know I don't like him – he creeps me out – it's why I wanted you to do it," Allison snapped, but Matthew was at a loss as he was far away from her. "Fine, don't worry about it then, I'll sort it," she said with a firm tone. "Anyway, I'll let you get some rest, don't want to ruin your important day, do I?"

"I love…" but Allison cut off the call before Matthew could finish what he was saying "…you." Matthew closed his laptop and lay back on the sofa. He began to think that he had made a big mistake accepting the opportunity to work far away. The last thing he wanted to do was upset his wife that he loved so much. Not only did he feel distant from Allison, he also felt distant from his marriage.

3

The very next day, Allison made her way to work as normal, but was not happy as she normally was. To be a receptionist's assistant for the leading company in computers and robotics wasn't what she really wanted as she felt that everyone around her was doing better than her. The feelings that she felt had shattered her love and enthusiasm with Matthew so far away. She looked over to Jennifer, a hot looking twenty-year-old, who was speaking into a headset while she typed.

"Good morning, Foptix Industries, Jennifer speaking, how can I help?" On the other end of the call was an important client that wanted to speak to *Tracy Luna*, the CEO of Foptix. "I'm sorry. I'm afraid, she's in a meeting, can I take a message?"

A delivery man called Harry stood at the desk holding a brown box with fragile tape around it. He waited and listened to Jennifer talking.

"No, I'm sorry – how long will she be? I don't know I've never measured her," Jennifer replied. Both Allison and Harry grinned at Jennifer's amusing joke. "Okay, I will pass the message on, thank you, have a good day, goodbye."

Upon taking off her headset, she gave Allison a glare. "You do realise you can sign for deliveries as my assistant?"

"Well, you try and have a husband that swans off and leaves you for the other side of Towns-end then," Allison snapped, as she stood up and walked away.

4

Meanwhile in Pentemy Village, the taxi had collected Matthew and had taken him straight to the College. The memories soon flooded back when Matthew trailed the familiar hallways of his teenage years. The ghosts of him and Allison were all too familiar, hearing the faint conversations they had, like ghostly voices from the past.

When he walked into the library which was the first place that he and Allison properly talked, he was greeted by four other men. The oldest of the bunch who was in his thirties stood up and introduced himself. "Matthew, right? I'm Blue."

Matthew shook his hand and was puzzled by the name. "Blue? You must be the first person I have met to be named after a colour – so, who are you lot, Red, Yellow and Green? Just like a set of traffic lights."

"I can see we're going to get along just fine," Blue chuckled.

Matthew listened to what project he would be writing.
Blue handed him a biography book of Towns-end's sweetheart and loveable actress, Jessica George, and told him that he would be converting it to a script for TV.

"Does this have her consent?" he questioned. "I mean, she did disappear. Should you really be making a story about her while there's an investigation going on with her disappearance?"

"Mr Cornwall – Madison had spoken to her family. She told us we have full control to make this story," said Blue.

Matthew accepted his words. With her biography in his hand he got excited and couldn't wait to start writing. He knew that he was going to have a full blown evening reading up on Jessica to get the story the way he would envision.

The Taxi that had brought him was waiting outside when the time was over. As the Taxi took him back, Matthew noticed a new bar that had opened up called *the Keyholder* and decided he would check it out as his dream had finally come true, he felt like he deserved a celebratory drink.

Matthew was hit by the cool air when he entered. It was fully air conditioned with strange sexualized music playing from the jukebox, talking about mistresses, bondage, sexual moaning and other strange erotica things. Matthew couldn't help but wonder why that sort of music even existed. A long bar with bar stools stood in front of him with tables and chairs scattered all around and a pool table in the corner. Behind the bar stood a woman who looked familiar to him. When he sat down and got a closer look, he realized that it was the same woman he saw in the hallway where his flat was.

"Can I get a beer, please?" Matthew asked.

The woman looked at Matthew with interest. She thought the same as he did that he looked familiar but she never acknowledged it, instead she just smiled and said, "Sure, what beer would you like?"

"Oh, I haven't been here in a long time, I'm a little out of touch, you decide what's best for me," Matthew suggested.

"Coming right up," she said as she grabbed a glass and went over to one of the beer pumps. Matthew wasn't really paying attention to what she was pouring, but he couldn't help but check her out. She came back and handed him his beer. "That'll be four fifty."

He handed her the money and took a sip. "Wow," he coughed. "What percentage is this?"

"Nineteen percent."

"Okay, all it'll take is a few mouthfuls and I'll be pissed."

"It'll take more than that, sweetheart."

"What's it called?" said Matthew.

"Permanedge." As he drank some more, he noticed that she was biting her lip, like something was on her mind. "I'm sorry, have we met?"

"I was thinking the same thing. You don't happen to live in a flat block do you, not far away?"

"I thought that was you. I do." she smiled and held out her hand for a handshake. "Evelyn."

"Matthew," he replied, as he shook her hand. "Nice to meet you, I love your accent, I've always loved that Canadian accent."

Evelyn raised a smile and was impressed that he could tell what accent she had. "I've always had a thing for English accents – I love listening to it, so, I keep people talking as much as I can."

"Well, that's all right, I'm quite a chatterbox," said Matthew. "Besides, I'm the same, I love hearing the Canadian accent, I think it's pretty sexy."

Evelyn bit her lip again, causing her to blush. She then leaned over the bar. He couldn't help but take a quick glance down her top at her smooth curvy breasts before looking back into her pretty eyes before he made it too obvious. "So, what are you doing in Pentemy Village?" she asked.

"I'm here to write a TV movie – I've always wanted to be a writer and I finally got my big break."

"Wow," said Evelyn, taking a fascinating interest. "I could never do anything like that, you must have one hell of a creative imagination?"

"A bit too much sometimes as I can't switch off," Matthew replied as he sipped his beer. "So, how long has this place been here? It wasn't here when I was younger."

"You're from around these parts?"

"I used to be," Matthew replied, "in fact I used to go to college here."

"Say, I get off in a hour, would you like to go elsewhere and get a coffee? I really enjoy talking to you."

Matthew's heart then raced with a mixture of emotions. Part of him wanted to go elsewhere with Evelyn and get to know her more, like he did when he dated Allison. But the other part of him was scared, a guilty feeling of what Allison would think, of him going out with another woman. He knew he had to be honest.

"I'm sorry, Evelyn," said Matthew, as he flashed his wedding ring in front of her, "I'm married."

"Oh, sorry," she replied, as she looked and sounded disappointed.

"Hey," he said, as he reached out for her hand. "Don't be, I'm flattered – if I was single, I would go out with you in a heartbeat, but I could never be unfaithful to my wife, because if you and I were dating, I would never be unfaithful to you."

Evelyn understood and admired him for his honesty and faithfulness to his wife. She wished she could find an honest guy like him one day, as she had had some terrible relationships in the past. All the guys she'd been with had either broken up with her, tried to control her or even cheated on her. Matthew was sorry to hear that she'd suffered heartbreak and assured her that if he was single – he would treat her like a woman should be treated, with love and loyalty.

"Thank you. You are so sweet," said Evelyn. Matthew downed his beer.

"I better go. I need to call my wife."

"Of course – she's a lucky woman. See you around." Matthew got up to leave. Evelyn watched him go.

24

5

Minutes later Matthew has returned to his apartment, and Vidtex, Allison. It rings constantly but no one is answering. He begins to feel like she doesn't want to speak to him – a great weight is coming down on his marriage from being apart from her. The call ends. He feels frustrated, like he's trying to keep two things in his life but feels like he's only allowed to focus on one. He begins to think that maybe he should've spent more time at the bar and talking to Evelyn. But he knows in himself he would never cheat on Allison – as he loves her.

His attention soon focuses on the laptop when an incoming call, beeps. It's Allison. He is more relaxed and glad to finally hear from her. He answers the call, and that's when he wishes he never had.

Allison appears on the screen, dressed in her bra and knickers, hot, wet and out of breath. Behind her stands another man who is bare chested. Matthew goes through all the emotions. Angry. Sick. Heartbroken. Seeing another man with Allison showed why she hadn't answered the call.

"What's wrong, baby?" says Allison.

Matthew grabs the laptop and throws it across the room.
It hits the wall, smashes to pieces. He screams in anger. Loads of thoughts and doubts flood through his head. This is what leaving his wife for a month has cost him? Would she have still cheated on him if he hadn't have gone? He looks around the room – begins to feel dizzy. His breathing increases. He has to leave – he can't stay.

Evelyn returns to her apartment, slowly climbing the stairs to her floor. She yawns feeling tired after her shift at the bar. As she gets to the next floor she sees Matthew sitting on the stairs, crying his eyes out. It hurts her to see him upset, considering she likes him. She rushes over to him.

"What's wrong?" asks Evelyn as she sits down beside him. She puts her arm around him to comfort him. He rests his head on hers and cries.

6

A week passes. Matthew begins to feel like his old self after coming to terms with what happened. He had made a friend out of Evelyn. He had told her what happened. She was horrified to hear what he saw and thought that Allison was a right bitch to do that to him. She told him she would never have done that to him. She had been with many partners and had always been loyal to them even though they hadn't been to her. Matthew felt the same as her – he knows what being faithful to someone is like and would never dream about being unfaithful to anyone.

As Matthew had been working long hours at the offices to get his work done after breaking his laptop – Evelyn suggested that he have dinner with her that night in her apartment, if he wanted to. Matthew had no problem saying yes to that. He liked the idea of actually spending some time with Evelyn instead of seeing her in the bar.

That night, he makes his way to Evelyn's apartment. He knocks on the door. She opens it and stands there wearing a sexy red dress and looks pretty in makeup. She looks stunning to him.

"Hi – come on in," says Evelyn, smiling at Matthew.

Evelyn shows Matthew round her apartment. The layout of the rooms is similar to the apartment he's staying in – but more cozy, with better furniture and the walls are wallpapered.

"You look amazing – I got to say."

Evelyn bites her lip, smiles at Matthew. She goes up to him and holds his hands. She leans forwards and presses her lips against his. He is surprised that she made the first move. His heart races, as it begins to turn into a passionate kiss. He backs away, breaking their kiss. She looks concerned. She thinks to herself that maybe she shouldn't have kissed him – maybe it was too soon to be affectionate towards him.

"I'm sorry – it's just…"

"Don't be," says Evelyn. "I shouldn't have made a move."

Matthew assures her that he has wanted to kiss her ever since he met her. Her nice warm heart and soul. She is the kindest person he's met since he came to Pentemy. Evelyn says the same about him. She has never met anyone as nice and kind as him. Caring, loving and faithful.

"I haven't actually made dinner yet – are you hungry for food – or for me?"

Later, Evelyn is asleep. Matthew lies next to her – staring, admiring how beautiful she looks. He is happy – but something worries him at the back of his mind. He is still married to Allison. He should really concentrate on talking to her about divorce proceedings. He notices Evelyn's laptop on top of her chest of drawers. He leaves her bed slowly, making sure he doesn't wake her.

He opens up her laptop. The lights illuminates the room. A log in and password appear. He's stumped and doesn't know where to begin.

"What are you doing?" asks Evelyn, causing Matthew to jump as he didn't know she was awake. He explains that he was going to skype Allison – to talk to her about divorce. What he and Evelyn just did was amazing, but at the same time was wrong as he was still married. So going through divorce should be a priority so he and Evelyn could be together. She understands and would want Matthew in her life.

"My username is just Evelyn – my password, cheath8ter – replace the A with an eight."

Matthew inputs her details and unlocks her computer. As he searches for Vidtex, Evelyn turns on the bedroom light. She watches him from the bed. Matthew inputs the call ID for Allison into the skype, and calls it. It rings; Allison appears on the screen. She looks happy to see Matthew.

"Oh, thank god – I've been worried sick – I've tried to call you."

"I broke my computer – after what I saw – hot and sweaty, soaking wet, out of breath – barely wearing much," snaps Matthew making sure she knows how he feels about what she's done.

"Babe – you've got it all wrong – that guy you saw was a plumber – that tap I wanted you to tighten burst and we both got soaked – I was out of breath because I didn't want to miss your call."

Matthew feels sick, guilty and in a panic. He realizes that her story makes sense. She wasn't unfaithful to him after all. He looks at Evelyn, who looks horrified hearing what Allison said. Matthew was the one who was unfaithful to Allison by getting with Evelyn.

"Babe – who's this woman? – what have you done?"

We all make assumptions, the doubt of a truth that is certain to happen without proof – but when we assume the worst of someone we love. The one we have to blame – is ourselves.

EXTERNAL

1

Isn't it ever going to get easier? Ana – a late twenties busty blonde bombshell thought as she had such a hard life, especially when it came to dating. She had been on so many dates through her life that she didn't remember how many she had actually been on. Ever since high school, no one could ever get her or accept the person she is. She felt lonely, until she met her best friends – who could relate to what Ana had been through.

The reflection of Ana stared back at her as she stood in front of a mirror of the fashion shop, *Clothes-4-Me*. She saw herself with a look of uncertainty. Sure, she was pretty with her long blonde hair that hung past her cleavage in the vintage frock she was wearing. She turned to her side and placed her hands on her hips while posing.

"It looks good on you," said Madison.
Ana smiled at the beautiful shop assistant, then rubbed the scar above her right eyebrow. "You think so? – I just don't think I'm ever going to look right with this – I'm never going to be a glamour model."

"Why would you want to be?" Madison asked. "Not being able to live or eat the way you want. Vain and thinking about your appearance all the time. You look good as you are – you're real."

"Thank you," Ana replied. "It's just my scar makes my face look…" But she couldn't bring herself to finish the sentence.

"You shouldn't worry about that sort of thing. Scars can tell stories about your life. I've got one from my C-section and I have a healthy daughter because of it," said Madison folding her arms. "So, what's your story? How did you get that scar?"

"It was ten years ago – I had driven to the hospital as I was booked in for surgery. I was discharged and like a fool I got behind the wheel and decided to drive home instead of getting someone to pick me up or taking the bus. I felt groggy and I crashed the car. My head hit the windscreen hard, that's what I was told, hence the scar," Ana explained.

"Well, it could've been a lot worse – you're pretty. I'm sure your partner thinks so."

Ana laughs. "Chance would be a fine thing – I don't have much luck in finding a decent guy, they take one look at me and judge me."

"Well, I'm sure one will come along eventually."

"Thank you." Ana smiled. "I like this dress, I'll take it."

"Great – bring it over when you're ready."

Madison left Ana to get changed. She returned the dress to its hanger. Then put her grey leggings and white top back on. When she pulled the curtain open she saw a man standing at the other end of the store. He was dressed in blue jeans and a red checked shirt. Ana felt uneasy the way he was staring at her.

"What are you staring at?" called Ana. But the man never replied. Ana pulled the curtain back to stop him from staring at her. She didn't know what to do. "Madison?" She waited patiently for Madison to come to her, but she never did. She then heard footsteps slowly making their way to her cubicle before a shadow appeared through the curtain.

The curtain was yanked back causing Ana to jump out of her skin, but it wasn't the man.

"Are you okay?" said Madison concerned at the state Ana was in as she could see that she was shaking with fear and her breathing was erratic.

"That guy – he was creeping me out."

"What guy?" said Madison puzzled. Ana poked her head out of the changing cubicle to see that the store was empty and the only people that were around were Madison and her.

"But there was a guy – I saw him just staring at me," Ana insisted and then noticed a camera in the ceiling of the shop. "You've got cameras, he would've been captured on the footage."

Madison took Ana to a small cramped office that showed a security monitor that covered the shop. Madison wound back the footage but saw no sign of a guy in the shop. She looked at Ana. "I'm sorry, but there is no guy." But Ana knew in herself that someone was definitely in the shop who had taken an interest in her.

We all at one time want to change who we are, to be noticed more and to change our future. But what happens when a single thought of change – could lead to an appearance, that could be truly deceptive?

Ana had left the shop with so many thoughts in her head about what had recently transpired. She walked past tourists and commuters of the busy street of the city of Towns-end in a daze, accidently knocking her shopping

32

bag into them.

"Hey watch it," they yelled. But Ana didn't take any notice. She started to have a headache from a combination of overthinking things, the noise of the crowds and busy traffic passing by which caused her to drop her bag.

As she bent down to pick it up, she caught a glimpse of the man watching her through the busy crowd. Ana reacted, grabbing her bag, then weaved in and out of the people to try and confront them.

"Hey," she shouted. "Who the hell are you?" But by the time she had got to where the man was standing, he had disappeared again. The noise from the crowd was getting too much for her. As she fumbled about to take out her phone from her bag, she dropped it then bent down to pick it up. People didn't care as they bumped into her, snapping and telling her to get out of the way. She grabbed her phone and in an upset voice spoke to the only person she needed to talk to.

"I need you – help me, please."

2

Ana sat in a corner of *The Pink Snow* bar surrounded by alcohol fuelled customers that were laughing loudly over the hip hop music that was being played from a nearby speaker. Her friend, Missy, walked in and looked around past the shady characters, to spot where Ana was sitting.

"Hey – I got here as soon as I could," said Missy as she hugged Ana tightly.

"I'm glad you're here," Ana said with a crack in her voice. Missy could tell something was wrong. She had known Ana for a year ever since she had moved to the city and found her the bubbliest person she had ever met as she had never seen anything get to her or worry her.

"All right, sit down honey," Missy insisted. As they both sat down, Missy noticed Ana's clear drink on the table. "Now that stuff isn't going to do you any good."

"I know but the way I'm feeling I just…" Ana paused. "It's water."

"That's what I mean, you need a proper drink – I'll get you a vodka lemonade." But Ana stopped her and made it clear that she didn't want it. "All right, so what happened to get you in such a state?"

Ana told Missy what happened with the mystery guy that stared at her in the clothes store and from the crowded street.

"Is he stalking you?" Missy asked.

"Stalking? I never thought of it that way. Why would you say that?"

"Let's just say you're not the first one who has been stalked like this?"

"Look I know, Missy, a lot of people other than me have gone through stalking," Ana replied.

"I didn't mean that," Missy explained

"I know what the guy looks like. Five foot ten, medium build, black buzzcut and facial hair," Ana told her.

"About five foot ten?" asked Missy as she found it hard to believe that Ana could know for sure.

"Not about, I know he's five foot ten – I saw him," she insisted.

"Have you met him before?"

But Ana was unsure. She had a feeling this guy was familiar to her. But she couldn't remember and be a hundred per cent sure.

Just then Missy noticed a tall medium build guy with blonde hair smiling at them.

"Hey – twelve o clock."

Ana checked her phone. "It's a quarter to two."

"Not the time – guy checking you out at the bar – that's not your stalker is it?"

Ana looked over at the guy who smiled at her. His appearance was different to the guy she had seen. "No that's not him."

"Are you sure? This guy could be bald and have different wigs to make him look different."

"You're so suspicious, Missy – he had facial hair as well and his build was slightly different."

"I'm not suspicious, just cautious. I don't want my close friends to get hurt," she said squeezing Ana's hand tightly.

"Hi there," said the guy who had wandered over from the bar. "Can I get you ladies a drink?"

Missy looked at Ana whose eyes sparkled in delight. She knew that this would be her cue to leave the two of them alone, so they could get to know each other. "I was just going – are you going to be okay, honey?"

But Ana was lost. She looked the attractive guy up and down who was smartly dressed in a grey business suit.

"Call me later okay?" she told Ana.

"Sure."

The guy stepped aside to let Missy out of her seat, then left the bar.

"Are you going to sit down, Richie?" Ana asked

"Wait – have we met? How do you know my name?"

"It's on your name badge." Ana pointed out the badge that was clipped on his jacket. Richie was amused and felt like an idiot, considering the badge told her all she needed to know: 'Richie James – IT Manager, Vision Electrics'.

Richie sat down in front of her and they started to talk. Richie spotted the shopping bags and wondered if she was having a late lunch from her work. He didn't want to assume that she may not be working. Ana told him that she worked at Snow's convenience store which was three streets away. She had the week off and wanted to have some time to herself from the rubbish hours and minimum wage.

"Oh, sorry if I ruined your time to yourself, I know how important it can be just to wind down. Did you want me to leave?" asked Richie.

"No – please stay, I didn't mean it to come out like that, I like the company." Ana's phone began to vibrate.

Seeing that it was Missy, she was hesitant to answer it with her attention mainly focused on Richie. "It's Missy. I'll call her back later."

"No, that's okay, please answer it – I'll get us some drinks."

"Vodka lemonade, please," said Ana as she left for the ladies' toilets.

When she pushed the door open, her nostrils filled with the mixture of urine and air fresheners. For a bar that had a lot of attention to its four-star rating, the toilets were the only reason it never got a five star in hygiene. The mirrors were smeared and the wall tiles were cracked which allowed a slight chill to roam the air.

"Hey – what's the matter? Are you okay?" Ana spoke softly.

"Look I know I said contact me later, but I had to see if you're okay – the guy is a stranger after all, especially as there is someone stalking you," explained Missy.

"Don't worry, I'm fine," Ana replied.

"Good," said Missy, relieved. "So, all is going well between you and him?"

"Yes. It's still early, he seems nice, but…"

"But what?"

"You know my luck; I'm just hoping that this works out. I get to know him more and maybe we both end up in a relationship."

"I hope so, Ana – it's about time that you found your happiness." But Ana's attention wasn't on Missy, it was on the mirror as her stalker's reflection appeared behind her. Her stalker reached out to grab her causing her to freak.

She dropped her phone and went straight for the toilet cubicle, slamming the door and locking it. She backed away as the stalker banged on the door constantly.

"Leave me alone," screamed Ana in distress. And just like that, the banging stopped. Ana was shaking, scared to move and check if her stalker was still outside the cubicle.

"What do you want with me?" she called, but no one answered. She then knelt down to check if he was still there but she didn't see any sign of him, all she saw was her phone on the floor that she had dropped. She cautiously unlocked the door then peered out. She felt relieved that the stalker had gone.

Ana picked up her phone to call Missy back, but heard the word 'Andy' whispered to her. She turned around to see her stalker standing in front of her. She bolted for the door and knocked into Richie knocking him to the floor.

"Jesus," he said surprised. "What's wrong… with your eyes?" As Ana dropped to her knees and burst into tears.

3

Later, after her breakdown, Ana came clean to Richie about her stalker problem. She didn't mention it straight away when they started to talk in case it put him off her. Richie was sympathetic and wanted to help her, so he escorted her to the police station so she could report it.

Scottish Police Constable Sarah Williams, the newest recruit to the force, who had only been working there for two weeks, took the two of them into a small room with a two-way mirror and asked Ana lots of questions. She asked her what the description of her stalker was. She asked where the confrontations took place. Ana told her everything she knew, from the description to what took place in the ladies' toilets at the bar when the man whispered the word 'Andy' which she assumed was him telling her his name.

Sarah was a strong and determined woman for someone in her early thirties. She had always wanted to work for the police and had a goal where she would become a detective as she loved working things out and ninety nine per cent of the time, she was always right.

Once Sarah had her information to go by, she asked Ana and Richie to wait in the room until her return as she would make a few calls and look on the database to find any information that would match the description of Andy.

When Sarah left the room, an awkward silence fell between Richie and Ana. Richie was at a loss not knowing what he could say to Ana without making things worse.

Ana on the other hand felt terrible as it wasn't the greatest introduction to meet someone new and, within minutes, they were both down at the police station. She started to come to terms that once the police had helped her resolve everything, Richie would just leave and not want to see her again. But that doubt was quickly put to rest when she felt Richie's hand reach for hers to comfort her. She smiled at him, he smiled back at her warming her heart, a feeling she had never felt before around men.

"Thank you."

"For what, Ana?" said Richie.

"For being here so I didn't have to go through this alone."

"Well, I wasn't going to leave you after the state I saw you in," Richie explained.

"But you hardly know me. We were talking for what? Ten minutes?"

Richie took Ana's other hand in his and gave her strong eye contact as he suggested, "Look – once all this is done – how about we have lunch in the park tomorrow. I would like to pick up from where we left off – if you would?"

Ana couldn't believe her luck. Of all the men she had known in the past, she had never come across anyone who was nice and as kind as Richie. She was nervous to say yes to rush into things so quickly, but she knew in her heart she couldn't say no. "Yes, I'd like that."

After waiting about twenty minutes, Sarah returned to the room with her colleague, PC Bill Walker. She dropped a file on the table then both of them sat down in front of Ana and Richie. Sarah folded her arms, her face filled with thunder.

"So, did you find anything?" Ana asked.

But Sarah didn't answer. Instead Bill told them that they had called the bar she was in to check the camera footage of who went in and out of the toilets. They had confirmed that Ana went in ten minutes later came out, but there was no sign of the man she described.

"But I saw him – he tried to grab me; he was banging on the door," Ana insisted.

"Are you having a joke with us, Ana?" Sarah snapped as she opened the file and took out the picture of her stalker. "His name was Andy; this man no longer exists and you know that. So why are you wasting our time?"

"What?" said Ana in distress. "But I know what I saw. I saw him. I've never met him before."

"I think you both had better leave before we charge you for wasting police time," Sarah insisted.

Richie was outraged at the police's attitude as he could see how upset Ana was. He took her hand and led her out of the room. Bill turned to Sarah and said, "You didn't explain to Mr James, why her stalker doesn't exist?"

"It's not my place to. He'll have to find out by himself," Sarah explained to Bill.

4

Outside the station, Ana broke down into tears. Richie held her closely as her tears soaked his clothes. She felt she had been let down by the system as they didn't take her seriously. Richie assured her that he would help her. He gave her his number and asked her to call him if she ever needed him and assured her that their lunch meeting would still go ahead. This made Ana happy. She gave him a firm hug, then the two of them parted ways.

Ana returned home all happy and smiley. She messaged Richie to tell him she got home safely, thanked him for his support and told him she couldn't wait for their lunch date. He replied admitting he felt bad that he didn't escort her home and stay with her to make sure she would be safe. Ana assured him that she was going to be okay as her friend Missy was going to keep her company. This relieved Richie knowing that someone was going to be with her.

Even though it was early in the evening, Ana felt tired from all that had happened in the day and retired to bed.

But as she slept, images of her car crash flashed through her mind which caused her to sit up in a cold sweat. Her hands were shaking as the sweat dripped from her forehead. She sat in bed seeing the memories play in her head over and over again like she didn't remember them. The only thing she remembered was being told by the doctor she had been involved in a car crash and accepted it at face value.

But then the voice of PC Sarah Williams entered her head as she told her that her stalker no longer existed. This worried Ana as she started to put two and two together.

Was Andy dead? Was she seeing his ghost and that's why the cameras never picked anything up? Was she the one responsible for killing him? Was he the reason she had a car crash?

Ana turned on her bedside lamp then threw the covers back and got out of bed making her way over to her white dresser table. She sat down then used her tablet to look up any information she could find about Andy. She tried different descriptions from his name, height and the clothes he was wearing. Eventually all she found was the same photo that Sarah had shown her from the police file, but there was no solid information that would give anything away.

Missy then entered Ana's room, half awake and yawning dressed in a silk white robe. "Hey it's three in the morning – what are you doing up?"

"I couldn't sleep," replied Ana as she put her tablet down. She told Missy about her dream and the memories she had remembered.

Missy sat down on Ana's bed. "Do you think it means something?"

"I don't know. I feel the answer is there but I just can't remember it."

"Well, don't try too hard, sweetie. The last thing you want is a headache from overthinking all this. If there are memories that you can't remember, I'm sure they'll appear when the time is right." Missy smiled. "Come on – get back to bed okay? You've got a lunch date to go to."

5

The next day when Ana woke up, she felt like all the worry regarding her stalker had faded away. There had been no appearances through the night and she felt she could concentrate on the day in hand.

After she had breakfast, she took a relaxing soak in the bath. She dried and straightened her hair then applied her make up before finally getting dressed in the frock she had bought from *Clothes-4-Me*. She smiled at herself in the mirror and felt confident that this was going to be a good day.

The weather was grey and cloudy with a slight chill in the air when Ana arrived at the park just before twelve. As she made her way to the duck pond, where Richie had suggested they meet from a text, she passed two women who were talking on a bench while their children were playing on the swings and slide.

A jogger checking their phone that was strapped to their arm went past while an old man walked his dog. As she followed a winding path past the damp grass and bushes, she saw Richie sitting on a bench in front of the pond. He looked up and grinned with delight when he saw Ana. He couldn't believe how beautiful she looked.

"Wow – you look stunning," he told her.

"Thank you," she appreciated. "You don't think I'm a bit overdressed?"

"Not at all," he replied. Ana shivered from the chill, regretting that she didn't take a coat with her. Richie took off his jacket and put it round her to cover up her shoulders.

"Thank you, but what about you?" she asked.

"It doesn't bother me – I'm used to it."

Ana sat down on the bench. As her back was turned, Richie shivered then smiled at her hoping she didn't realize he was cold, but Ana could tell. She took her arm out and put some of the jacket round him to cover some of him up. Richie could see the kindness in her eyes and feel the warmth in her heart as she cuddled into him. Richie took his phone out and took a selfie of the two of them.

"I made cheese and tomato sandwiches – I hope that's okay?"

"Fine – I like that."

Richie took a plastic bag from his side and handed her the sandwich, then took a selfie of the two of them to look back on the highlight of his day.

"How did you sleep?" asked Richie.

Ana explained between mouthfuls what happened through the night. He listened as she told him about her car crash dream and the theory that it could be linked to her stalker. Richie admitted that he did a bit of searching to see if he could uncover any more information about this mysterious Andy that the police were reluctant to help with, but like Ana, Richie found nothing.

From that point she didn't want to talk about her problems, instead she wanted to focus on who they were.

Richie began to talk about himself. From his life in high school and what he wanted to do after he left. He studied hard, got A grades in IT and Science and wanted to work with computers. He loved curries and steak meals. He was interested in video games and his music interest ranged from the classic eighties to rock music.

Ana told him she loved the eighties music and curries and suggested that they should go out for one, one time. Richie agreed and confirmed that it would be a date.

He then asked her to tell him a bit about her. She started by explaining to him, that what she was about to tell him, came from other people she knew as she had forgotten a lot about her life since she had the car crash.

It began with the place she was born which was a quiet little town on the other side of Towns-end where she spent her childhood with her family and friends, where they would go for walks and spend time in Cyril's old-fashioned sweet shop. She was of the newer generation but she liked the old-fashioned ways that her parents grew up with.

"Sounds like you had a great childhood." Richie smiled.

"So, where do you see yourself in the future?" Ana asked.

"Settling down with a family – it's always the dream. I got friends around me that have already done that. I was always hoping that was going to be me. Is that where you see yourself?"

But Ana didn't answer. She looked upset and miserable then turned away from him as her eyes started to tear up.

"Sorry – did I say something wrong?"

Ana shook her head and wiped the tears away. She then took her bag and stood up to leave. "I should go," she said with a crack in her voice.

Richie jumped up and grabbed her by the arm to stop her from leaving. "Hold on there – look I know it probably wasn't appropriate to mention that sort of thing on a first date, but you did ask – I was just being honest."

"I know you were," Ana spoke softly. "I like people being honest, but I don't think we should see each other – you should see someone else."

"Why?"

"Because I can't have children."

Richie didn't know what to say, so Ana explained, "I was told that I was never able to have children since I was born. I lived with it all my life seeing people around me have kids with their partner. I was jealous and it always upset me – so please, don't waste your life with someone who can't give you what you want."

Ana walked away leaving Richie upset and lost for words. At that moment he didn't know what to do. He thought he would upset her more and she would shout at him and hate him if he pushed the issue and tried to stop her walking away.

6

The next day, Richie woke heavy eyed after a terrible night's sleep, the first thing that entered his mind was Ana and what happened the day before. He looked at his phone to see the selfie he had taken of them in the park and was sad that a happy moment could turn sour.

When he got to work, he struggled to focus. His colleagues noticed the mistakes he was making, the mood he was in and how quiet he was. During his break he looked up Cyril's old-fashioned sweet shop and took a screen shot of the address. That was when he decided to take the rest of the day off and drive to the other side of Towns-end which was six hours away.

After a long journey and a few stops at service stations, he arrived in the town that Ana had told him about. The place was small with many shops. There was an express off license, a charity and antique shop and of course Cyril's old-fashioned sweets. Richie saw Cyril, an old man wearing vintage clothing with white hair, closing up for the day.

Richie got out of his car and walked over to him. "Excuse me," he called. Cyril turned around to see the stranger approaching him, all smiley and confident. "You Cyril?"

"What makes you think I'm Cyril?" replied the old man. Richie pointed to the sign of the shop.

"Kind of gives it away." Richie grinned amusingly.

"I'm sorry, but if you want any sweets you'll have to come back tomorrow as I've just closed up for the day."

"I don't want any sweets – I just want to ask you some questions."

"What are you, police?" Cyril asked.

"No just an IT manager," Richie replied.

"What do you want?" Cyril asked.

Richie took his phone out and showed him the selfie he took with Ana. "Do you remember Ana? She used to come into your shop with her friends all the time, must have been over fifteen years ago, something like that."

Cyril shook his head. "No, I don't remember anyone like that."

"Are you sure?"

"Trust me – a pretty girl like that I would have remembered."

Richie then brought up the image of Ana's stalker. "What about him?"

"Blimey – I haven't seen him for a long time."

"You know him?"

"That's Andy, he was a quiet lad – always kept himself to himself. Hung round with lots of people so he wouldn't feel alone."

"Was he dangerous?" Richie enquired.

"Him? No, he wouldn't hurt a fly – why do you ask?"

"He's been seen stalking Ana; we both never knew he came from here."

But Cyril chuckled to himself. This annoyed Richie as he didn't find it funny. "What's your problem?" he snapped.

"Andy disappeared years ago. No one knew where he went. It's like he didn't exist. Sure, people enquired, tried to track him down. His parents were worried sick. It pretty much killed them when they never found him," Cyril explained. "I tell you something, boy – sounds like this girl of yours knows something about what happened to him."

"She doesn't remember him."

"Convenient," said Cyril. "Then you'd better ask yourself how well do you know her?"

Cyril then walked away leaving Richie with doubt about Ana. He sat in his car and wondered if maybe Ana was right about the car crash. Did she kill him? Was that why he was haunting her?

Everything with Ana from her problems and information he collected gave him a headache like it was a spin cycle from a washing machine. After three quarters of a journey he plucked up the courage to call her. The phone rang until it went to voicemail. Richie didn't want to leave a message so he constantly called her four more times until she finally picked up.

"Richie, please leave me alone," Ana spoke through the speakers of his car. Richie replied into a small microphone above the sun visor.

"I can't – I really need to see you. We need to talk," Richie insisted.

"No Richie – it's a waste of time."

"Then just see me one more time and if you don't agree with what I have to say then we will part ways." Richie paused. "Please – one last request."

"Very well," sighed Ana.

"I'm about an hour and a half away. I'll meet you at *The Chunky Pie* at eleven."

"It closes at half eleven."

"Just for a quick drink and it won't take long what I need to say, okay?"

"Okay Richie – I'll see you there – safe journey."

Ana cut off the call leaving Richie feeling satisfied.

7

The Chunky Pie was quiet by the time Richie arrived.

He parked up and went inside but didn't see Ana anywhere, all there was were two couples sitting eating the burger pie, the rest of the tables were cleaned and the seats were on top. Seeing the couples eating made Richie hungry. The burger pie was their signature dish. A burger meat patty inside a short crust pastry filled with rich gravy, served with green beans and creamy mash potato. Richie licked his lips just thinking about it.

He went up to the counter and ordered two coffees.

Richie left the coffees on the counter, took the seats off the table, then collected the coffees and sat down. He looked at the time to see it was five past eleven. Ana was late. He gave it another five minutes. Richie started to doubt that she was going to turn up. But his fears were put to rest when she walked through the door.

Ana sat down in front of him. "Well, I'm here – say what you've got to say."

Richie told her that he went to where she used to live as a child, that he met Cyril and he didn't remember her. Ana was confused that he didn't remember her, as he was her favourite out of all her friends that went there. Richie explained that he showed him a picture of her stalker which he remembered and then told her what he told him.

"He was there? All that time I had been going to that shop, oh my god," Ana said shocked. "How long has this guy been stalking me? I mean, all the time I've been growing up and now he's here."

"Ana, I'm not going to let him get anywhere near you because I want to date you."

"Huh?"

"The truth is I can't stop thinking about you. I took to you the day I met you. I like you," Richie promised her. "I'm not saying we could become boyfriend and girlfriend straight away – but if we did and we were in a long-term relationship, I would want to marry you and then we'd adopt a child."

Ana looked up surprise. "What? – you want to adopt? But wouldn't

48

you want to have one of your own?"

"I wouldn't want to if you couldn't have children. It wouldn't be fair on you. So, adoption would be a solution to the problem."

"You're sure?"

"Yes – I like you..." But Richie didn't have a chance to finish his sentence as Ana had already pulled him towards her lips and kissed him passionately.

8

A month had passed by since that night. Richie and Ana had gone out for their first date at his favourite curry house. They both had the vindaloo and went through two bottles of red wine. They then ended their date on a nice cool stroll through the night and kissed near a lake.

Their second date consisted of bowling. Richie wasn't a professional and Ana ended up beating him a hundred and twenty-three to forty-seven. She jokingly mocked him the rest of the night, but Richie didn't find it offensive as he liked the banter.

When they had their third date, they went to a music concert to see pop sensation, Megan May. When they left the concert, Richie took Ana back to his as it was the closest to the stadium.

When Ana entered Richie's flat, she was amazed how big it was compared to her tiny sardine tin flat. Richie showed her around every room, ending the tour with the bedroom. Ana didn't need much of a hint to know why he finished there. But Richie wasn't the type to assume that anything was going to happen on their third official date, he was just surprised when Ana wrapped her arms around him and started to kiss him all over.

Richie got excited as his hands, which were slightly chilly, felt every inch of her warm body. Ana couldn't take any more and pushed him down on the bed to get on top of him. She parted her legs then pulled her top off. Richie stared in amazement at her perky breasts that were pushed up by her white silk bra. She pulled the bra off, then took Richie's hands and placed them on them making him tease her erect nipples.

She leant forward, her breasts hovered above his face wobbling back and forward while her nipples flicked the edge of his nose. She kissed him with passion as he returned the kiss. He was turned on, his breathing getting faster as her taste and hot breath entered his mouth.

Ana helped him take his clothes off, then got off the bed, took her leggings off, followed by her panties. Richie noticed scars around her groin area and was about to ask her why she had them, but she stopped him by getting on top of him again.

She gasped as he entered her. It had been a long time since she had sex. It felt uncomfortable but pleasurable at the same time. As she began to grind back and forth the sensation stimulated the two of them. They couldn't get enough. As their motion got faster so did their excitement. They wanted to orgasm but it was too quick, so they paced themselves and tried not to lose the moment.

She held his hands down on the bed, dominating him so he couldn't move. She smiled as he couldn't touch her body. Her legs began to quiver. She was so close. She wanted to slow down, but couldn't fight the excitement.

Her back arched as she let out a soft moan trying to catch her breath. This caused Richie to lose control and follow suit.

Ana flopped on top of Richie. She rested her head on his chest, hot and breathless.

Richie struggled to catch his breath while he cuddled her tightly. Ana breathed in deep as her eyes became heavy. She was lost for words to say anything. As she closed her eyes to sleep, she was pleased that Richie came into her life and wanted to be with her.

9

Five months had passed and their relationship was getting stronger every day. They had kept to their traditional date nights ranging from a movie to a restaurant meal.

They had gone for picnics and bike rides when the weather was warm. Alternating to stay round each other's flats started out as a weekend tradition until they started to regularly stay in the week. Coming home to each other after work made their day. The time they didn't spend together made them unhappy. It was quiet and lonely when neither of them was in each other's flat.

Richie had got fed up by this point and suggested to Ana that she move in with him so they could live together.

"Are you sure you want to? Don't you think it's a bit quick? It's only been about five months."

"I want to. I feel that the time is right – we're in a good place – we click – and there hasn't been a single sign of your stalker."

She kissed him, then said the words he had been longing to hear, "I love you."

"I love you too," Richie replied.

All of sudden, Ana's eyes widened in shock as Richie bent down on one knee and held out a ring box in front of her. "Will you marry me?" he asked her.

She didn't have to give it a single thought. Finally, her time was now. She had waited to be happy for so long, to find someone to settle down with and now she could.

"Yes – I will," Ana replied excitedly. Richie grinned with delight. He took a white gold ring, with a small pink jewel, out of the ring box then placed it on her finger. She looked at it with admiration. "It's beautiful."

Not long after Ana was engaged and she had submitted her notice, the time came for her to move out. Richie helped her pack and move the furniture and boxes into a van. Ana struggled with the last two boxes that were on the top shelf of a cupboard. They were covered in dust and hadn't been looked at since she moved in. As she moved one, the box fell, spilling its contents all over the floor.

"Are you okay?" Richie panicked when he heard the loud bang as he came into her flat.

"I'm okay – box slipped out of my hands," Ana explained.

Richie began to sort out the contents which ranged from old jewellery and clothes, but then he spotted something under an old pair of leggings. It was a picture. He pulled it out and then reacted as he couldn't believe what he was seeing.

"What's wrong?" Ana asked.

"You tell me," said Richie in an annoyed tone as held up the picture of Andy. "Mind telling me why you have a picture of your stalker?"

Ana snatched the photo out of Richie's hands, confused, not knowing what the picture was doing in a box of her old possessions.

"You do know him, don't you? He's someone from your past? Who is he Ana?" Richie snapped.

Ana panicked as she stared at the photo. At first, she didn't know how the photo got into her possessions, but then a memory was triggered. She could see herself in the car crash followed by Andy on an operating table. It all connected the puzzle of why she was being haunted by him.

"Oh my god," she said as a tear ran down the side of her cheek and she began to shake with fear as she remembered it all. "I know who he is."

"Who is he, Ana?"

"He's me, before my surgery – before my sex change." Ana started to cry when she saw Richie's reaction to her.

Everything that Ana had told him all made sense from being followed by her former self, to the reason she had scars from her post op surgery on her groin area and couldn't have children. She was originally born a man.

Everyone wears a mask. To hide who we really are. But when we use this to deceive the honesty within ourselves – the hurt that is put on the ones we care about, is the price we have to live with.

53

NEED

1

A full stadium caused the atmosphere to be electric in the Snowdome Arena. Crowds of people sat in the darkness. The only light coming from the small stage lights. They are waiting for her. The anticipation of seeing her perform.

Music begins to build. The lights come on lighting up the stage. And there she was. Pop star sensation – *Megan May* – walks on. The crowd goes wild, cheering, screaming, and applauding. Camera lights flash from people's phones as she walks to the centre of the stage. She holds a microphone in her hand, wearing a black sparkly top with black leather trousers. Her short blonde hair reaches down to her shoulders.

"Hello, Towns-end," says Megan speaking into the microphone. The crowd roar, cheering at her. "We're going to start things off with my recent hit, 'I was born to love you'."

Coloured lights shine towards her as she begins to perform. She walks up and down the stage, her back up dancers appear and dance around her.

2

Two hours later, Megan walks through the corridor of the arena making her way to her room. She looks hot and tired. She is followed by her manager, Tyrone, an African man in his mid-forties. His assistant, Clarice, a half cast Mexican, stands by Megan's side telling her the upcoming tour dates she's got. Clarice was always a little jealous of Megan – she always wanted to live the life Megan had. She loved to sing from an early age. She was noticed through YouTube. Tyrone never really saw anything in Clarice apart from being a good assistant. She had become close to Megan who didn't see Clarice as an assistant – but instead saw her as a friend.

Megan interrupts Clarice. She isn't bothered about hearing about her upcoming dates. She was more concerned about where Mason is, her boyfriend. Clarice hands over Megan's phone. Megan looks at it and reads a text message that Mason left her. Tyrone and Clarice can tell that Megan is angry. They don't say anything as they don't want her to take out her anger on them. Megan shakes her head and storms off.

3

Megan enters her room – slamming the door behind her. She calls Mason. It rings but he doesn't answer. She gets angry, like he's ignoring her. She imagines what he's doing. He was always laid back, never putting that much effort into their relationship. She could picture him sitting in front of the TV, sucking on a beer watching sport. But Mason does answer.

"What the hell's going on Mason? – You break up with me by texting me?" says Megan, aggressively.

Mason explains he's had enough. He can't take this life with her. She has a status – so much media attention on her and he isn't exactly a celebrity. He hardly sees her with her busy life.

"Do you think, just because you're not a celebrity – I wouldn't like you? – I like you because you're not a celeb because their relationships never seem to last. I want just a normal guy."

But Mason's mind is already made up. He wishes her all the best and knows that she'll get someone else easily. He then cuts the call. Megan is outraged. She screams with anger. Upset. Feeling lonely. She goes over to a bottle of vodka – opens the top and drinks from the bottle. The burn of the neat alcohol soothes her. Her eyes water. She wipes away the tears. She thought her life was finally perfect – that she got her singing career and could finally focus on a future with her man. She takes the bottle of vodka over to the sofa, grabs her phone and starts writing a status for social media.

"Famous – but single again. What a surprise?" she mumbles to herself. She posts the status and begins to drink more. As the minutes pass, she begins to feel the effects of the alcohol. Her eyes feel heavy, she smells and feels the fumes coming off her breath. She checks her social media, only to be disappointed. Lots of her fans have commented, but none have read her status. They have ignored what she has said. Their comments were predictable as always – *Love you Megan – I'm your biggest fan.* This was a time when she needed someone to talk to. She reaches for the bottle, but before she takes another drink, something stops her. An inbox message on her social media. She opens the message up and reads:

"Megan – there is nothing wrong with you – if guys can't accept you for the beautiful woman you are – then they're not worth it – keep smiling. Writer 82 x."

Her frown turns to a smile like someone has touched her heart.

4

When we grow up – we all want to follow our goals and achieve the things we want in life. But what happens when we discover that not all is everything it appeared to be?

Would we continue our success that we worked for? – or would we find something else that we didn't realize we needed?

Crowds of people ranging from tourists and commuters are wandering around the city of Towns-end's square. A man dressed in a blue and black checkered shirt with grey trousers waits in the middle of the square. Megan walks down the steps and across to where the man is waiting. She is dressed in black trousers and a red and white check shirt. She wears sunglasses so she doesn't get recognized. But she should know it's how celebrities get recognized when they wear sunglasses especially on a grey cloudy day.

"Jason?" says Megan as she approaches the man that's waiting. "Or should I say, Writer 82?"

"Hi, Megan," Jason replies. Megan gives him a welcoming hug. She holds onto him tightly which surprises him to as this is their first meeting. It has been a week since they started talking to each other via social media.

It all started after Jason had sent Megan that positive message to try and make her feel better after Mason had broken up with her. To Megan, Jason was the only one that actually read her status. She was hurting and needed someone to talk to. As all her fans focused on how much they loved her and praised her success. She didn't want that – she just wanted people to see her, just like anyone else in the world. A woman with feelings and who can get their heart broken.

"Wow – it's really nice to meet you – I can't believe you wanted to meet me," says Jason, as he is overwhelmed to meet her in the flesh. Jason was a writer for *News-End*, Towns-end's local newspaper. He wrote short stories on a weekly basis. He had a strong positive feedback from the readers and was hired full time. He lived in the countryside far away. He had a little lodge. It was secluded and peaceful where he could concentrate on his writing.

Megan had found all this out when they started talking to each other through social media. She found it interesting. Jason had admitted that he was a fan of Megan's music and listened to it regularly. He said he found it helpful to write his short stories for the newspaper. He had been listening to her music that night Megan had put the status up. He had read the comments fans had posted and didn't agree with them. He knew she wanted something positive, a little bit of help to make her feel better and perk her up, and that's why he posted his comment. He couldn't believe she replied and they ended up messaging on a regular basis. A celebrity wanting to get to know him.

"Can we not think of me as a celebrity, please – I don't like that – I'm just a regular girl like everyone else."

Jason couldn't agree more. He liked that. As they had met, Jason wondered what she fancied doing. She admits she had never seen much of Towns-end City. Jason had – so he offered to show her around the sights. Megan loved that idea as she didn't have a lot of time to do that what with preparing for her performances. As Jason walks off she stops him and takes her phone out.

"Wait a second," she says.

Megan takes a selfie with Jason in the shot. She then uploads it to social media with a comment that says *Day out with my friend, Jason x.*

Jason is surprised that she wanted to take a photo with him. He thought she might not have wanted to – as the media would make a big thing of it. Wanting to follow her around and get the latest story of who he was, how long she has known him.

"They can keep their nose out of it – I'm still going to live my life like normal. I'm not going to hide from them and hide from who I want to see."

Jason can tell Megan is starting to get wound up, but there is something else too. He starts to think that not everything is okay with her. He doesn't say anything though just in case it upsets her. She then takes his hand and tells him that all she wants is to have good day out. She made the first move. As they set off, Megan tells him that there's no need to worry about the photo as she would be taking lots of photos as it's something she loves doing – not for attention but something to look back on. Good memories.

5

The hours of the day flew by and soon come to an end as they walk through the Park, hand in hand. But Megan's happy personality soon turns to misery. She looks saddened.

"What's up?" asks Jason.

"It's been an amazing day – it's been a long time since I've had so much fun – and now it's over."

"I'm glad seeing all the sights has made you happy."

"Not the sites – the company."

Jason feels good in himself that he's made her happy but at the same time is worried about getting close. Megan had been thinking a lot of what they had been talking about, finding out things about each other. She loved the sound of where he lived – in the middle of the country in a lodge peaceful and quiet. She admitted she would love to see it, if he didn't mind. Jason told her that it was quite far from the city. It was two and a half hours away, approximately a hundred and four miles.

"I don't mind staying – I'm in no hurry to get back," says Megan jumping at the chance – but she ends up backing down assuming that Jason would be okay with her staying at his place. Thoughts go round Jason's head, part of him loves the idea that she would come back to his place but at the same time he was scared. He asks himself if it's a bit quick to have her come to his place considering this is their first meeting. He doesn't want to disappoint her and at the same time he might discover why she's so reluctant to leave his side.

6

The sun had already set and darkness had settled in by the time Jason and Megan arrived at his lodge. Megan heard the sound of the gravel path as Jason drove away from the main road. They pull up outside a one story wooden lodge. Megan sees it more clearly as the headlights from the car illuminate the lodge. She looks out the window and smiles at the sight of it. She likes what she sees.

They exit the car. Megan shivers as the cold air hits her.
After travelling for two and a half hours in a car with the heating on, she soon felt the cold. The air smells damp like it had been raining recently, with the mixture from the grass of the countryside.

"I told you it was a long way," explains Jason.
Megan was fine with it. She enjoyed the journey. As Jason locks the car, Megan is startled when she hears a noise of an animal.

"What's that?" asks Megan.

"It's just the ducks – there's a duck pond nearby."
They both make their way to the porch of the lodge. Megan notices something covered up by a canvas. She can't help but wonder what is.

"That's my hot tub," says Jason as he opens the door, enters and turns the lights on. Megan raises an eye brow and smiles – she hopes to get a use out of that.

7

Jason and Megan stand in the hallway. It's slightly narrow. Jason explains that to the right of them are his bedroom and the bathroom. To the left of them is the living room, kitchen and dining room. Jason takes Megan to the living room.

Megan sees four chairs and a table to the left of her.

The kitchen is to the right of her and in front of her are two sofas and a TV in the right hand corner. She grins with delight – she thinks it's pretty lovely and cozy. Megan begins to yawn. Jason can see she's getting tired. Megan hopes he doesn't mind if she goes straight to sleep – it has been a long day. Jason is cool with that. He tells her he'll be right back. He leaves Megan in the living room. While he's gone she takes a closer look around. She loves it. She feels it's the type of home she'd like to live in.

Jason returns holding two pillows and a quilt. She is really grateful for letting her stay. Jason then explains that the pillows and quilt aren't for her – they're for him. He offers her his bed as he will sleep on the sofa tonight.

Megan feels bad and says that it's not necessary. The sofa will be fine for her as she is his guest. But as a guest, Jason thinks she should take his bed. It's what a gentleman would do. Megan puts her arms around him for a hug. She gives a strong squeeze to know how grateful she is.

"Thank you," says Megan. "Goodnight."

"Night," says Jason, as Megan leaves for his bedroom. He turns to her. "Oh… and sweet dreams."

"You too," she says as she turns and smiles at him. They stare at each other – like their urges for each other kick into gear. But they don't give in. Megan leaves for his bedroom. Jason hears the door close.

In Jason's bedroom – Megan slips off her trousers, pulls back the bed covers and gets into bed. She reaches for the lamp and turns the light off. She lies there in the darkness – the only light is from the moonlight. She lies there feeling relaxed. It is so quiet. No noise whatsoever. A lot different from the hotel she had been staying in. Jason's bed was less lumpy – it was cosier. The sheets felt soft on her skin and she was comfortably warm. Her eyes feel heavy – she closes them and within seconds she falls asleep.=

8

Megan's eyes blink open. The room is bright with the daylight from outside pouring in. She can hear the sound of ducks quacking and birds tweeting. There is something else that she notices. The smell and sound of cooking. She gets out of bed and puts her trousers back on.

In the kitchen – Jason is cooking scrambled eggs. Two plates are on the kitchen side, each with half an orange on. He puts the scrambled egg on the plate – then takes them over to the table. Megan enters the room – hair a mess and clothes all crumpled.

"Morning," he says. "Did you sleep well?"
"Best night's sleep I've had for a long time," says Megan, "you made me breakfast?"

"Of course – it's not a lot but it's a good way to start the day."

They sit down and eat. They discuss between mouthfuls what Megan would like to do for the day if she's in no hurry to get back. He suggests they could spend the day together, look around, do a bit of shopping, have a spot of lunch then – if she wanted to – go out for the evening to this little conservative club he knows. Megan reaches for Jason's hand and holds it.

"That would be lovely, I could do with some clothes – thank you."

9

Jason and Megan walk amongst the people. None of them recognize Megan. This time she's not wearing her sunglasses. Jason thinks this suits her better as he thought it hid her pretty eyes. Megan's heart flutters. She starts to have strong feelings for him. Of all the guys that have come and gone in her life – he was the one that finally touched her heart. She thought it was crazy – as they had only been talking for a week, had a day out and stayed over on their first meeting. Were things moving too fast? Does he have the same feelings for her as she does for him? The constant questions went round and round in her head. She wanted to ask them but she was too frightened in case he didn't feel the same about her. All she could do was keep quiet and not speak a word of how she feels.

The hours flew by. They had lunch at a little café, both had a chicken salad, and a glass of orange juice. After lunch they hit the shops. Megan bought clothes, not as fashionable as you'd expect, just casual everyday clothes.

They sat on a bus, making their way back to a park and ride where Jason's car was waiting – with shopping bags on their laps. Before Megan knew it – she was back at the lodge. She stands on the porch looking out at the countryside watching the sunset. Jason joins her, smartly dressed in a check shirt and grey trousers, with black shoes. He looks Megan up and down, dressed in a blue dress wearing black high heels. Her blonde hair tied back wearing dark red lipstick.

"You look stunning."

"So do you – so handsome," says Megan. She approaches Jason and holds his hands smiling at him staring into his eyes.

"Okay – come on then – I'll take you to the club."

He lets go of her hands. She is disappointed, hoping that he was going to hold her in his arms and kiss her.

10

The conservative club has the atmosphere of a holiday camp. People of all ages sitting at tables, laughing, talking, some with children and some without. Megan enters the club hand in hand with Jason. She sees children dancing on the dancefloor with someone dressed in a bear costume dancing to the music. He tells her that this is normal. They always have something on for the children before the adult disco. She thinks it's great.

Jason feels his phone vibrating in the inside of his jacket pocket. He takes out it out to see who's calling him. The name *Matthew* flashes on the screen. He looks at Megan telling her that he's sorry and that he should take this.

"It's fine – please, go ahead."

"Matthew – hey, everything okay?" says Jason quite loudly as the music is starting to drown his voice out. His expression tells Megan that not everything is okay. His cheery excited expression turns to shock. "…Wait – what do you mean you and Allison are going to get a divorce? You did what?"

"Sorry, Megan – I got to take this outside," he says covering the phone with his hand so Matthew doesn't hear anything on the line. "I'll be right back with some drinks."

"It's okay – go – I'll be fine."

Jason leaves the club. As Megan watches the kids show. A little boy bumps into her and ends up falling on his bum. His mother runs up to him.

"Oh god – I'm sorry about that – he just runs off…" She looks surprised to see Megan in the club and realizes who she is and gets excited. "Oh my god – you're Megan May."

Megan looks around the club – not wanting any attention or causing a scene so that others will notice her there. She places her finger on the mother's lips and begs her not to say anything. She doesn't want people to know she's there. The mother apologizes and understands completely, but asks a favour from Megan – she wonders if she could watch her little boy for her as he loves this show while she goes to the toilet. Megan doesn't really know what to say as she had never been asked by anyone before to look after a child. But, in gratitude for her not making a scene, she accepts.

While the mother disappears for the toilet. Megan bends down and talks to the boy. "You want to see the show?" The little boy smiles and nods. She takes his hand. They make their way over to the dance floor. The bear and the other children dance to the music. The little boy starts dancing while holding onto Megan's hands. She smiles, looking happy to see the joy in the boy's face. Jason returns to the club and sees Megan on the dance floor. Megan looks up to see Jason walking over to her. He smiles at her and she smiles back at him.

11

As the night came to an end, Megan found herself back at the lodge again. She stands on the porch looking out at the darkness of the night – feeling unhappy. It had been an amazing day to her – the most fun she had ever had for a long time – and she knew it was coming to an end.

"You okay?" asks Jason, joining her side. Megan admits she couldn't be happier. Looking after that little boy made her realize how good motherhood could be, seeing the joy on their little faces touched her heartstrings. She then gives a big sigh, and Jason sees her frown.

"I'm going to miss this – I don't want to go back."

Jason admits that it's going to be quiet again as he's just been getting used to the company. Megan confesses that she wants to stay. Jason would love her to stay but he's concerned that if she did stay, what would happen to her career, her fans, and her music? She wipes her eyes as she begins to tear up. She admits that she doesn't want it any more. For the first time in her life she is happy in herself, in the lodge and happy being with him.

"Will you just hold me already? Will you just kiss me now?"

Jason doesn't hesitate. The tension between them was real and now he had no reason to hold back. She wanted him as much as he wanted her. He puts his arms around her waist. She holds onto his arms, resting her head against his chest. She closes her eyes, enjoying the feeling of being held by him feeling his warm embrace. They then stare at each other looking into each other's eyes. Their lips then press against each other's. They hold their kiss for a few seconds and then part.

"First time kissing a famous singer?"

"First time kissing you, Megan – the real you."

This touches her heart. Finally a guy that actually sees the real her and not the celebrity that everyone else seems to see. She suggests that they go to his bedroom.

12

Megan lies down on Jason's bed with Jason on top of her. She pulls him towards her – they kiss passionately until Jason begins to kiss her neck. She breathes heavily, turned on by his passionate affections.

"I want you," whispers Megan.

"Wait – let me get a…"

Megan stops him. She says it's okay. She wants this to happen, that she wants to be with him – only if he wants to be with her. Jason knows that things are moving too fast – but at the same time he wants to be with her. The thoughts that some couples work at their relationship to find out whether they're compatible is a normal thing. But then there are tiny precious moments that couples know that they are meant to be. Jason knows that in his heart he is falling for her – even if it's way too soon to use the L word.

Megan pulls Jason towards her, kissing him. Jason slips his trousers off. Megan closes her eyes then gasps – her breathing increases as he begins to make love to her.

Minutes later. Jason is asleep. Megan stares up at the ceiling – smiling to herself. She looks at Jason – takes his hand and holds it.

"I love you," she whispers. He doesn't stir but she hoped he would have as she longs to hear those words coming from him.

13

Three and a half weeks pass by. It was the best time in Megan's life. She was happy and relaxed living with Jason. He had continued to write his short stories for the newspaper and the money had been coming in steadily but they had nothing to worry about with Megan contributing her fortune she had made. Jason felt it wasn't right that she should use her money towards expenses, but she wanted to as now it was their life – together. They had enjoyed days out together – going for walks, spending the day at the nearest beach. Her most memorable time was them sitting on the beach watching the sunset. An important and romantic moment for her. She loved life – even evenings in with a candlelit dinner. It was perfect – but one day, two familiar faces turned up to make her choose what type of life she really wanted.

It was a cloudy day. It was raining and there was a slight chill in the air. But the weather didn't concern Megan, she was lovely and warm as she sat in the warm bubbles of the hot tub. She wore a bikini while holding a newspaper – reading one of the short stories that Jason wrote for it. She was engrossed in what he wrote and loved his imagination that told a good story.

She is then distracted by the sound of car tires crunching over the gravel path that leads up to the lodge. Megan sees that it's a black car but can't make out who's driving it. It pulls up outside. Megan's happy feelings soon turn to dread when she sees Tyrone and Clarice exit the car.

"So this is where you've been hiding," says Tyrone looking up and down at the lodge, looking pretty disgusted. "You've been hard to track down."

Megan gets out of the hot tub. Her skin, wet, dripping all over the porch. She grabs a towel and wraps it round her. She is curious to know how they found her. Clarice explains from the photo of her and Jason in the conservative club. It took them all this time to track him down – who he was and where he lived. Tyrone had thought about contacting the Police and reporting Megan missing. They had left loads of messages on her phone – as it rang but no one ever picked up. Megan shakes her head then goes inside. Tyrone and Clarice look at each other then follow her inside.

14

As Megan goes to the bedroom to dry off. Clarice and Tyrone wait in the hallway. Clarice wanders off to the living room.

"Wow – this is really nice – cozy."

"Not bad," says Tyrone, "not exactly a palace."

Clarice shakes her head at Tyrone. He always thought that money and having posh priced possessions were more important. It presented an image and a status to him. Megan enters the room – now dressed in black tracksuit bottoms and a black and pink vest top.

"I don't know what kind of breakdown you're going through, Megan – but you've got to come back – you've got concerts to do – a career to focus on and money to make."

She looks at Tyrone fiercely. Her eyes glaring, and anger building. She snaps at him – assures him that she's not going through a breakdown. She's in love. Clarice's eyes widen. For a long time now she always wanted Megan to find someone nice and not another jerk.

"In love? – with who?" says Clarice with excitement in her voice.

"With me," says Jason, as he walks in on the conversation. Clarice notices Megan's facial expression change when she sees Jason. When they arrived, it was like Megan didn't want to know them any more – but with Jason, it looked like her world was complete and she looked and felt alive. With all the men that had come and gone in Megan's life – she had never witnessed this before. She could tell Megan was in love.

"You're the one that stole my talented girl away. Do you feel good about that – you're taking away her dreams that she's worked for – and who the hell are you anyway?"

"Jason – and be careful what you say as you are in my home."

"In our home," says Megan holding Jason's hand. "And for your information, Tyrone – he didn't steal my dreams away from me – he gave me them."

Tyrone backs down. He's disappointed – as he has worked closely with Megan and was always afraid of losing her. They built such a solid

73

friendship. She was his star, and then he thinks of something that maybe she has forgotten about. In Tyrone's own words, she had signed a five year deal with him – she was under contract to do this otherwise a sizeable chunk of her money would be taken from her. She would end up with pretty much nothing.

Megan explodes yelling at Tyrone, saying that she is fine with that – she doesn't care if all her money disappears because that is the problem with the world nowadays.

Everything is about money, it comes before anything else in life. People don't live in a world – they live in a bank – the biggest bank ever made. She would work in a shop if she had to as long as she is with the man she loves.

Jason is surprised to hear her say those words that she loved him. It made him realize that she was the love of his life too. He is about to tell Megan how much he loves her but is interrupted by Tyrone who explains that it's only five years and after that she can find love as much as she wants as the only way to get out of this is to become ill or be pregnant. Megan is upset – she feels sick – and ends up rushing towards the bathroom. Jason is getting angry at how Tyrone is treating her. He makes an example of Tyrone telling him that he can't force someone into doing something she doesn't want. Tyrone understands she's found a good friend – just because he has never found love he doesn't believe that it could be real. Clarice tries to calm him down while Jason begins to think about what has been said. Was he really stopping Megan? He begins to doubt himself – all he wants to do is do the right thing.

Clarice begins to wonder what's taking Megan so long and suggests to Jason to see if she's all right. Jason is about to leave for the bathroom when Megan returns to the room. She had just been sick. Jason looks worried – he thinks this whole situation has made her ill.

"Hey – don't worry – we're going to be fine," says Megan taking Jason's hand and placing it on her belly. "All of us."

Jason realizes what this means. Megan gives the biggest grin, then holds up a pregnancy test which confirms the word 'pregnant'. He begins to think when it happened. She tells him it was from the first time they made love – after he took her to the conservative club. He remembers as she told him she wasn't bothered about him wearing a condom. Jason doesn't feel scared at all – he feels excited – he's going to be a father and be a family with the woman he loves.

"I love you," he says to her.

"I love you too."

Tyrone hangs his head. He knows he's lost. She can get out of the contract now she's pregnant. He hints at Clarice that they should leave. He wishes Megan all the best.

"Wait – this isn't the end, Tyrone – you may be losing me but I'm giving you something better."

Megan looks at Clarice and smiles. She tells Tyrone that she's heard Clarice sing – and she will be an amazing star for him. She will blow everyone away and make him a lot of money. Clarice looks embarrassed but at the same time she loves the idea that she's finally going to get a shot at a singing career. Megan recommends her.

Tyrone thinks about what Megan has said. This is coming from his favourite. He agrees to give Clarice a shot – but if it didn't work out he would return for Megan.

"Trust me – you won't," says Megan.

Tyrone leaves with Clarice following behind. She thanks Megan for giving her this chance and in return Megan tells her to knock them dead. Megan hears the door go, and a sigh of relief soon follows. With Jason and Megan now alone in the lodge, she does something that surprises Jason. Megan gets down on one knee and takes Jason's hand.

"Will you marry me?"

He doesn't hesitate to say yes but is surprised that she asked him as he feels it should've been him that asks her. Megan gets to her feet. Jason hints maybe they should go to the bedroom. She thinks about it, but Jason is curious what she's thinking. Megan is only thinking about six words that she wants to say to him. The words are the title of her hit song.

"I – was – born – to – love – you."

When we live our lives – we all search for the things that make us the happiest – but sometimes we find these, not in the things we want – but in the things we need.

ENCOUNTER

1

Weapon, why do people use their emotions like one? I always hoped things would change – that I would find someone that wouldn't do that. My name is Nelson, and this is my story.

It all started in Kays Koffee shop that I go to every day on my work break. Regular as clockwork I go in there and order an iced coffee. But I didn't realize that the odd change can change your entire world.

I enter the coffee shop – while I'm on the phone to my best friend, Alex. The coffee shop is packed with people sitting at tables.

Mother Sunshine? I ask Alex as I join the queue.

'That's her name – she is amazing – it's the best sex I've had.'

I look around the coffee shop while Alex continues talking, and I see something that stops me. I see this beautiful woman sitting at a table. She wears blue jeans – a green jumper – has shoulder length brown hair and the most beautiful face I've ever seen. Her head hangs down and her eyes are closed. She has fallen asleep. Her handbag is on the table. I'm concerned that no one has tried to pinch it – considering we live in a world nowadays where some people just take anything that isn't theirs. I leave the queue and go over to her table.

Miss? Miss? She doesn't stir. I take her handbag and place it under the table near her feet for safety. I then return to the queue as she yawns. With the distraction I forgot about Alex.

'You still there?' asks Alex.

I am, and remember what Alex had said about this woman being the best sex he ever had. Of course she was – she was a professional prostitute and he paid for sex. I tell him that he should go for just a normal woman the old-fashioned way and I make sure he knows he's got issues.

He has to go to the doctors and get himself checked over as he doesn't want to catch anything from the prostitute with the amount of men she's probably been with.

'Sure – whatever – look I'll catch you later, okay?' He hangs up. Clearly, he's not going to take my advice.

It's my turn to be served – I order my iced coffee – wait and take it once it's given to me. When I turn to leave, the woman at the table bumps into me – the coffee goes all over me.

'Oh god – I'm sorry.' She panics.

I tell her not to worry – that it's okay – it's cold. She laughs at my little joke, a poor attempt at humour that others wouldn't find funny.

'Please – let me get you another.'

She really doesn't have to do that. She looks around for her bag – her face filled with worry when she realizes it's not on the table. I point to under the table and tell her that I was the one that moved it as anyone could've taken it. I thought it'd be better being safe close to her out of sight. 'Thanks – that's so sweet of you.'

She takes her bag and takes some money out – then joins the queue. I stand with her and ask her if she has a Canadian accent. 'I do – I'm from Berry Green Village, originally – I moved to the city area a year ago – I'm Mary.' I introduce myself as Nelson, not the best of names. 'I think it's pretty lovely,' says Mary, smiling at me.

She gets my coffee – we both sit down and start talking, finding out a little bit about each other. I discover she works as an accountant at Vision Electrics – they're the biggest electric company in the country. I tell her that I work at 'See Through Ltd' they're a Window manufacturing company that supplies window installation across the country. Mary recognizes the name of the company I work for. They did work for their building.

She's interested to know how long I've been there for – as she has been at her job for about six months. I tell her that I've been there for two years.

'So – you helped build the window frames for our company – considering Vision Electrics started a year ago. Have there been any other companies you've helped build?'

I had helped build the windows for the construction of the lobby of Foptix Industries. The CEO *Tracy Luna* had come in to talk to the project managers and get quotes from the estimating team. It brought a lot of money into the company. I can't help but wonder if Mary had dealings with Foptix Industries. She hadn't personally but they had a contract with them as they supply the electricity to them.

I mention that our contract with our electric company is over next month, and I would recommend them to our company to change over.

'That would be great – I'll try and help find your company a good deal.'

I had heard rumours that the CEO of Vision Electrics is a bit of a player. Trying it on with lots of guys. I couldn't help but wonder if that was true. Mary didn't really know she couldn't really give an opinion as she didn't really have much to do with her. But Liz Cooper was a great boss to work for.

Her phone then rings – she looks at it – her face drops with disappointment. 'Sorry – I got to take this.' She answers the call. 'Ah ha – okay – really?   Okay I'm on my way.' She puts the phone in her bag.

'Sorry – I've got to go to work,' she says, looking as disappointed as I was. I understood though. 'I really enjoyed talking to you – we should exchange numbers – if you want to.' I jumped at the chance. We exchanged numbers and arranged to meet the next day in the park for a lunch date. I was sad to see her leave but the thought of seeing her again made me appreciate that it's not like I was never going to see her again. She smiled and winked at me as she left the coffee shop. I smiled to myself looking forward to finding out who this woman really was.

2

When we meet someone new – we find the fun of asking questions to know more about them. But would we find it fun to get the answers to the questions we didn't want to discover?

As I finish my iced coffee – I get up to leave – but am surprised to see a familiar face walk in.

Matthew? – You're back from Pentemy already? How did the writing go?

He gives me the short version – that he's on the verge of a divorce – that he accidently cheated on his wife, Allison, with another woman called Evelyn.

I didn't know what to say. I thought Matthew was a real sensible guy and there is no excuse for what he's done. I can't feel sorry for him – all I hope is he's learnt a lesson through all of this.

3

The next day came. The date was simple and easy. We both sat by a duck pond eating our own lunches – throwing pieces of bread to feed the ducks. We talked about each other's lives – who we are and what we've done with our lives.

I discovered Mary had a hard life – her father disagreed with her life choices and threw her out of the house. She never went back to her family. She ended up living in a little tiny flat on her own – she lived all by herself. I felt sorry for her it must've been hard not seeing her family just because they didn't like what she was going to choose in life considering it was her life not theirs. Some families can be so cruel.

We were then interrupted again by her phone. Mary sighs, looks angry and frustrated. She answers the call.

'What?' she snaps but her attitude soon changes to like she was scared. 'No – no – please don't – I'll come right away.' She looks at me looking disappointed. 'I'm sorry – I've got to work – I understand if this annoys you and you don't want to see me any more.'

On the contrary – I would love to see her again every day. She holds my hand. 'Thank you for being so understanding.' We both stand. I then ask if she would like to see me the next night at my flat – I could cook a meal and that. She smiles at me – then nods. 'Yes – definitely – I have tomorrow off anyway – I can't wait.' She tells me that dating gets difficult for her, she's on standby all the time with her work as she had an important role. I understand what accountants go through – working long hours and working holidays. The money is big but their social life is little.

'Text me your address okay?' She stares at me – hesitant to leave. 'Bye.' She then walks away. Watching her leave – I felt lonely – but happy that I get to see her for the whole evening next time. She then stops and looks at me. She gives me a big smile and waves goodbye. I wave back. I can tell there is something between us – she must like me as she looked back to see me before leaving.

4

Later that night – I was laying on the sofa watching boring old TV. I couldn't wait to see Mary again, so I message her and wonder how she is – wonder how work is going. I wait a little while realizing that she will be busy and not getting an instant response. But I am surprised as a reply comes through. She is on a coffee break, work is tiring but she has been thinking of me and the short afternoon we spent together. She tells me she's looking forward to having a nice meal and seeing me again. She can't remember when she had a home cooked meal last – most of her meals always consisted of microwave dinners for quickness and convenience.

Another message comes through from her which makes me happier. She tells me that tomorrow night she will make sure we won't get interrupted as she will turn her phone off. At least we will be able to concentrate, and it'll be our first proper date. Mary tells me that she will be wearing a blue frock with a flowery pattern, how about me? I reply back and tell her that I won't be as my frock will look terrible on me especially with my hips. She texts back with a laugh out loud (LOL) and a kiss (x) – she tells me that I make her laugh. I like making her laugh and show that I can take banter and have a sense of humour. She likes that.

I had already thought about what I'm going to cook her. We will eat at the dinner table by candlelight with romantic and soothing music. I want to make a good impression and hope she doesn't think I'm trying too hard.

The truth of it all – I was rather nervous as I really like her and want to get to know her more. I text her asking her if she likes chicken pasta as that's what I want to make her along with my address that she asked for and what time to come round. I suggested about half seven – which seemed to be the best time for any dinner date.

I wait a few minutes – she doesn't reply. She must've gone back to work. A couple of hours pass by – there is still no answer from Mary. I begin to get paranoid – my mind says I may have said something wrong or come on too strongly, but my heart says she has a busy life – she likes you. That's the thing I've found when you meet someone new. We all have paranoid thoughts. You like them but they may not like you. It's natural. My phone then rings – I grab it as fast as I can, but I am disappointed to see it's only Alex that is calling me.

I answer the call but before I can say anything, Alex talks – sounding very distressed. He tells me he slept with Mother Sunshine again – he said I was right – that he should stop seeing her. He won't be seeing her ever again. He's on his way to the hospital to get himself checked out as he thinks there is something wrong, that he may have picked up something from her. I did tell him but he's done the right thing now in ending it and going to the hospital to get checked. I tell him to keep me updated with how things go. He cancels the call on his end.

I still have no reply from Mary. I text her again, tell her I can't wait for tomorrow night as I am counting down to it. I hope she gets home safely. Good night and sweet dreams. I put a kiss on the end of the message and send it. I then go to bed. As I get into bed and snuggle under the sheets my phone vibrates. I grab it and discover it's Mary. She had replied saying that she's looking forward to it too and hopes she sees me again. Goodnight. Kiss with a smiley face. I feel more relaxed now I've heard from her. I close my eyes and go to sleep.

5

The next day comes – I start preparing dinner – a healthy chicken pasta meal. I hadn't heard from Alex all day and am starting to get a bit concerned but at the same time if things were really serious, he would've contacted me by now. As I'm about to cook the chicken – the buzzer to the door goes. I leave the chicken cooking while I go over to the intercom.

'Nelson – it's Mary.' I tell her to come on up – I press the buzzer.

Within minutes she is standing at my door. She looks amazing – she wears a dark blue flower frock and smells of a perfume. I compliment her on how beautiful she looks and smells. She grins and then enters my flat.

She enters the living room – looking around seeing a TV – a small dinner table with two chairs. Two seated sofa. Bookcase. I tell her it's not much but it's home. 'I think it's pretty lovely,' she says.

I tell her that dinner will be ready soon. 'That's fine.' She smiles. She places her bag on the sofa then opens her arms out for a cuddle. We hug. 'I thought about you all day,' she says whilst hugging me tightly. The feeling was mutual, ever since I met her in the coffee shop – she was all I could think about.

Half an hour later we were sitting down at the dinner table with music on in the background – one of those greatest love song compilations. She loves the chicken pasta I've done. Even though I've known her for this short time I feel myself falling for her already. I then do something bold and ask her to dance with me.

She looks up at me and is surprised. 'But we're in your living room,' she says. I insist we dance. I get up – go over to her and take her hand – pulling her up towards me. We stand close – gaze into each other's eyes – and begin to slow dance. A romantic moment in anyone's eyes. She holds her gaze – leans in – this was the moment – our first kiss. We hold our kiss for quite a while. Her lips are soft and her taste is pleasant. 'Where's your bedroom?' she asks.

We go to my bedroom – we kiss each other passionately – our hands over each other. I then stop – forgetting myself. She wonders if everything is all right. I explain that I really like her but I feel that this is a bit quick. She understands – but she wants this to happen as she really likes me. No one in her life has ever made her think about someone all day. From the moment she woke up till the moment she goes to sleep. The feeling was mutual.

Before I know it our clothes are on the floor and we begin to make love. I kiss Mary's body all over which excites her. She gasps – breathing fast and heavy – she keeps her eye contact with me, never closing her eyes once. We both orgasm at the same time, then lay there hot and sweaty – out of breath – cuddled up.

'Wow – that was amazing,' she says trying to catch her breath. I was thinking the same thing. For the first time in my life I feel I'm in love with her – but I'm scared in saying that this early.

'I love you,' says Mary looking at me. I'm surprised – she was thinking the same thing. I love you too – I say it back to her. She has a big a smile on her face – we kiss again. She cuddles up to me. As we lie there – I begin to think what others would think of me and Mary. That they would see us rushing into things way too fast. Telling someone they love them pretty much straight away and sleeping with them when they don't know everything about them. But I didn't really care as it felt right to me. I did love her.

'I'm glad you think the same way – I don't ever want us to be apart. You're all I've thought about. Do you believe that you can meet the one you're meant to be with and feel so in love so early after meeting them?' she asks as she holds my hand, tightly. Absolutely – as I feel that way already.

There are some couples that have an instant attraction when they first meet. My mum and dad knew straight away. Not the most romantic of ways to be together. They met at a party – were both drunk. Woke up in bed with each other the next day with the mother of all hangovers. Then my dad asked her if they wanted to get married – and my mum said yes, and that was that.

We're then interrupted by my phone ringing which is charging on my bedside cabinet. It's Alex. 'Well – it's your turn now.' I apologize to her and tell her it's my mate. 'Don't be – it's okay.'

I answer the phone. 'Nelson – I'm on my way round to you – I really need someone to talk to after what the doctor told me.' I explain that I'm sorry but I'm on a date and I got company.

'It's okay – your friend needs you,' says Mary urging. I tell Alex it's okay and I'll see him soon.

About ten minutes later the buzzer goes. Alex has arrived. I open the door to him. He looks terrible.

Distraught. Worried.

'Thanks for seeing me – sorry to interrupt your date.' I tell him it's fine – Mary is the one that urged me to be there for you. 'She sounds great – really nice of her to be so understanding even though I haven't seen her yet.'

I tell Alex that this would be a good opportunity to meet her, so I call to Mary to come out. She comes out of the bedroom dressed in her frock with a big smile on her face. That's when it all goes wrong. Mary's smile drops when she sees me and Alex.

'Mother Sunshine?' says Alex looking shocked himself.

Now it all makes sense – Mary is the prostitute Alex has been seeing. An awkward silence fills the room between us. I feel sick – like I'm going to vomit. The thought of Alex having sex with Mary made me feel ill. I felt angry like I was going to explode like a volcano.

'Nelson,' says Alex. 'I had no idea that Mother Sunshine was Mary – it's not exactly like they give you their real name.'

I keep my cool – I tell him to get out. He doesn't listen to me, instead he just wants to explain himself. But I don't want to hear it – I feel betrayed. I shout at him, threaten him to get the hell out of my flat. This time Alex listens and leaves straight away. As I hear the door go, I turn my back on Mary. I can't even look at her. But I need to know everything about Mary – why is she a prostitute?

Mary begins to explain. She lied to me. She didn't really work at Vision Electrics as an accountant.

Prostitution was her job. When she had trouble with her family – she had no one to turn to and nowhere to go. She had made herself homeless. Wandering the streets, starving, a Korean man by the name of Jin found her and offered her shelter. He offered her a job as a working girl – gave her a flat of her own to live and work in. The money she made was more than any job she could go for. I began to understand why Mary's father didn't agree with her life choices as this is what she become.

Each one of Jin's girls went by a made up name. Mother Sunshine

88

seemed fitting as Jin thought she brought rays of sunshine in to the men's lives that she slept with. Then one day she had a new client. It was Alex. His time with her was the best sex he had ever had. The next day Mary had gone to *Kays Coffee Shop*. She was tired and exhausted – she began to doze off. That's when she bumped into me – and that's when she realized that she met a genuinely nice guy that didn't want her just for sex. After having a conversation with me, she felt something, she felt like she wanted to get to know me more and hoped that I would be the guy that would take her away from this disgusting life.

When the phone rang while we were talking on our park date and she snapped at who was calling, she had forgotten herself. She had stepped out of line with her boss. She was scared of him. She thought of him as someone from a dodgy Mafia. She had witnessed one of the girls telling Jin that she wanted to leave. Mary wanted to too – but she never could leave. She was trapped. The second the other girl said she wanted to leave – Jin's men held her down, raped and beat her, then dumped her body in a dumpster.

After she left the park – she had to get ready for her client. It turned out to be Alex. She was worried because that night I had been constantly texting her. She didn't want the client to see who was messaging her on the phone. She never realized that Alex was my friend. The next part she told me was the part that made me realize she was completely dead to me.

Alex was pretty drunk by the time he called on Mary.

She had offered him his usual, but this time he declined. He brought triple the money that he had paid the previous times and wanted to make this the last time, and try something fun. With three thousand pounds – he wanted an intimate night with her. Most offer the girlfriend experience. He wanted the wife experience. He wanted to have sex with Mary, unprotected – he wanted eye contact on the moment of orgasm. Mary was scared of him as there was a pregnancy risk, if he was unprotected. She didn't like the idea of having an emotional moment with a client. Alex blackmailed her into doing it. If she didn't go through with it – he would complain to Jin. She had to go through with it. If she didn't, she would end up in a dumpster.

This made me realize what kind of perverted monster her boss and my friend were. I feel like I've been betrayed and used by all. What's worse is that Mary had sex with me after all that's happened. She had no problem with it. She made me use protection. She could be pregnant right now with Alex's baby. She tells me no matter what I think of her – I must know that she loves me. The emotional time of making love to me was the best she had ever had. She wants to quit the business and leave. But she doesn't want to lose me.

I assure her she already has. No one can fix the damage that's been caused. I tell the whore to get out of my flat before I lose it. I can hear her crying. I close my eyes – then hear the door go. I'm all alone now. She's gone out of my life.

6

A month had passed and I'm still haunted by that day.

The way I feel hasn't changed. The next day after what happened – Mary constantly tried to contact me. She left me text messages and voicemails. I listened to them – her voice reminding me of what she sounded like. Part of me missed that accent of hers, but the memories of the good times tormented me. Alex tried to contact me too, but I couldn't bring myself to speak to him either. I eventually blocked both their numbers. I needed to move on and leave them both behind.

I had made a new friend over that month. His name was Jack. Yes – he was a whiskey. I got through three bottles in a week. I had missed days at work. My life had hit rock bottom. As I sit in my flat finishing another glass of whiskey – there is a knock on the door. I open the door and see Alex standing there. I close the door but he stops me by putting his leg in between the door to stop me closing it.

'Jesus – what's happened to you?' says Alex, more concerned to see the state of me.

I haven't shaved since the night me and Mary made love. I can't help but wonder what he wants. I tell him if he's here to talk to me then he's wasting his time.

'It's about Mary – she's in hospital.'

I look at him – not angry but concerned what's happened. He tells me that her body was found in a dumpster. She had been raped and beaten. I remember Mary telling me about one of the girls she knew that was dealt the same punishment. Now I know I have to see her.

7

I stand in the ward – with Alex by my side. Mary lays in bed hooked up to a machine. Her face bruised and swollen. She has a black eye and a cut lip. She wakes up to see us both watching over her. She looks relieved and happy to see me.

'Nelson – it's so good to see you – I've missed you.'
Before I can say anything, a nurse enters the ward to check on Mary. She wonders how they are both feeling today. This confuses me. Both?

'Her and the baby,' replies the nurse.
A cold shiver goes down my spine. Baby? I think to myself. I look at Alex and shake my head. His unprotected sex got Mary pregnant.

'It's not what you think – and before you think it – it's not her boss's either – she was pregnant before that.'

Alex explains that when he left the hospital, he was told that he can't have children as he has an extremely low count and he's already been tested. I am the father.

Even though I used protection – it must've broken as I was the only other guy that had sex with her.

I feel ill. I can't accept all this – I don't want to take responsibility for this. I was a good person, kind and loving. But I can't love someone who sold her body night after night just to make money. So I run away and leave them both behind. As I run – I hear Mary calling for me to come back, bursting into tears, screaming out my name telling me she loves me. My heart breaks to leave them behind – but I never deserved this hell.

We all make mistakes. The trust, the lies and fear that we find in love. Frightened of how good a relationship is – or frightened of what a relationship could be.

TEMPTATION

1

Love can be found anywhere – that's what Missy Lockhart thought, as she stood in front of the bathroom mirror – her thirty-year-old reflection looking back at her. She is wondering how her life ended up like this. Full of confusion and frustration. She wears a red silk nightgown – make up and red lipstick makes her look pretty with her long straight brown hair past her shoulders. With her attractiveness – the only thing that looked out of place was a frown – like she was miserable, unhappy. She looks at her finger – an engagement ring is on it. She takes a deep breath and leaves the bathroom.

She enters the bedroom – her fiancé, Will, lies on his side – bare chested with a smile on his face. She goes to her side of the bed and gets in, pulling the covers over her and turns her back on Will. She then feels his hands on her shoulders – he starts to kiss her back reaching up to her neck.

'No – no stop.'

She turns to face him and stops his urges. He looks slightly annoyed – he wants to make love to her, but she doesn't want to. Even though they're engaged, she wants to wait till they get married as it will make it special, she doesn't want the anticipation to be ruined. Will feels frustrated, as she hasn't even wanted to make plans to get married. She tells him that there's so much going on that she hasn't had time to think about it – but she promises that she will make time to start planning as she assures him that she loves him. She kisses him – then rolls on her side. Will rolls on his side looking unhappy.

2

The next night, Will and his work colleagues arrive at the *The Open Bar* – a small karaoke bar which is only a couple of streets down from where Will works. He felt happier when he saw his work colleagues and was never in a rush to see Missy. He was feeling confused and frustrated like Missy never wanted to get close to him or show him much love and affection, due to her religious beliefs of waiting.

He waits at the bar – ordering a round of drinks for his colleagues and thinks about his life. He was the manager of *The Chunky Pie* fast food restaurant, and was very creative at coming up with new ideas for food which was popular with a lot of people. He was pleased with his achievements and it was there that Missy walked into his life.

She had gone there one evening with her two friends Allison and Ana. Missy was impressed with Will's success and liked how he was kind and generous. As the weeks went by, she returned to the restaurant more and more.

They got to know each other and within the month they were dating. After dating for three months, Will proposed. Missy was a little shocked just by springing it onto her like that. She hesitated by not saying yes straight away – but she accepted his proposal. The thought of her hesitating made Will realize that maybe she doesn't want to marry him.

As he continues to wait for his drinks – a woman joins his side, wearing a sexy black evening dress. She wears lots of make up and has long blonde hair. The dress is low cut. Will can't help but notice her cleavage. She smiles at him noticing him staring at her.

'Hi – I'm Marcy,' she says, 'what do you say we get out of here and go somewhere quiet?'

She strokes his hand and smiles at him. 'And have some fun.'

3

When we are with someone – we make a commitment to be with only them. But how strong would we be when the temptation of another is in front of us? Would we give in to our urges – or be strong with the love and commitment that's in our hearts?

A lot of thoughts flood through Will's mind as he stares at Marcy. The temptation of taking up her offer – knowing that she wants him all to herself. The way she looked he'd be a fool not to. But the thought of being unfaithful to Missy – he couldn't go down that path. He wasn't the type.

'Sorry Marcy – if I was single, I so would,' he says, 'but I'm engaged to my fiancée.'

'Oh,' she says sounding disappointed, 'forget I offered – sorry,' says Marcy, walking away and feeling embarrassed.

Will is left standing at the bar feeling a little bad, but he knew in himself that he wasn't going be unfaithful to Missy. Will's work colleague, Quincy, goes up to him, while mainly being distracted by the gorgeous Marcy. Quincy was known for being a bit of a Jack the lad – trying it on with lots of women. Whether they were single or married, it didn't matter – the danger and risks excited him.

'Will – what the hell? – who was that?' said Quincy, who can't understand why Will wouldn't take advantage of a gorgeous woman like that.

'Just a stranger – she wanted me to go somewhere quiet with her and have some fun, if you know what I mean.'

'Why didn't you? It's a missed opportunity,' says Quincy hinting that he should have gone with her.

Will gets annoyed at Quincy. He snaps at him saying that he's engaged to his fiancée and he would never even consider cheating on her. Quincy snaps back saying a few truths about Missy – that she's avoiding being intimate with him deliberately. Who really waits till their wedding nowadays? Will knows what he means – to him it feels like Missy isn't interested. Frustrated as he is, he loves Missy and respects her wishes.

Quincy disagrees with the way Will is being treated. He doesn't understand why he's bothering with Missy as he feels she's hiding something. Like there isn't love there at all.

'Don't judge her, okay – just because you don't know when to keep it in your pants,' snaps Will. 'You think you're god's gift? You try it on with that woman.'

'I will,' shouts Quincy as Will storms away from him. Quincy takes a sip of his beer – walks through the bar and up to Marcy who is standing in a corner. She holds a glass of wine in her hand – takes a sip and watches Quincy walking over to her. She knows what's about to happen.

'Hey there gorgeous – fancy going somewhere a bit quieter with me?' says Quincy.

She looks him up and down, takes another sip of her drink.

'Get over yourself,' says Marcy as she rolls her eyes at Quincy then walks away. She leaves Quincy standing there, annoyed and shot down. He takes a sip of his beer.

'Whore,' mumbles Quincy.

Will makes his way down the corridor. Not looking to where he's going, he bumps into a guy.

'Sorry – I was just... Richie, hey, how are you?' says Will shaking Richie's hand.

'Will, it's been a long time. I was just popping in here for a good time. There are women, here right?'

Will is puzzled at his comment and what he meant. Richie explains that he's had a problem when it comes to women. He tells Will that he met this beautiful woman called Ana. He really liked her a lot. They went back to her place and began making out. She then acted strangely and admitted that she used to be a man before her operation. So he has a hard time believing if women are really women.

Will tells Richie this Ana sounds like a friend of Missy's as Missy had told him about this guy, she was friends with called Andy who had a sex change.

'The truth of the matter is – I haven't been able to stop thinking about her, Will – I like the person she is.'

'Love can be found in all shapes or forms – talk to her. You can be friends or more than that if you don't let external appearances get in the way.'

Richie sees Will's point. Ana is Ana now not Andy who she originally was. Will says he's got to go and wishes Richie all the best in talking to Ana.

4

The next day Will wakes up in bed. Hungover with a pounding headache. His eyes are barely open, and he feels tired and exhausted. Missy walks into the bedroom dressed in her bra and knickers. She sees that Will is awake.

'Wow – you look like hell.'

'I feel like it,' Will replies, yawning.

Missy can't understand why Will would get so drunk. He tells her that he did it because he's so frustrated. She gets annoyed – bringing up this conversation again. He knows the situation and she wishes he wouldn't keep on about it.

She is not going to be intimate with him until they're married. Will raises his voice – saying that she isn't doing any planning whatsoever. Most women would be planning it out once they got engaged.

'Will – if you're feeling sexually frustrated, then just have a self-release.'

Will doesn't want to get sexual with his hand. He wants to get sexual with the woman he loves. She assures him that it's not going to happen anytime soon. Will throws back the covers of the bed and leaves the room. Missy stands there shaking her head. She goes over to her bedside cabinet and takes her phone. She begins writing a new text message out that reads, 'I think I'm losing him.'

5

Will has returned to *The Open Bar*. He sits at the bar, a clear drink in one hand – his other hand over his head. He starts to doubt his relationship with Missy and thinks it was a mistake to propose to her, as he got thinking that this could be the rest of his life and wouldn't want to be trapped in a relationship with a woman that didn't want to touch him. He takes a sip of his drink and looks up at the TV that's showing the news.

The door to *The Open Bar* opens and Marcy enters.

Gone is the sexy dress – which has now been replaced by casual jeans, white top and checkered shirt. She sees Will sitting at the bar – drowning his sorrows in his drink. She shakes her head then walks over to him.

'Drinking alone?' says Marcy. Will turns his head to see Marcy sitting down next to him at the bar. 'That's not healthy you know.' Will finished his drink.

'I get so frustrated you know, I just...' Will realizes what she's assuming. He holds his glass out to show her '...It's water.'

Marcy feels embarrassed. She assumed he was drinking booze. Will isn't up for drinking any more alcohol after feeling the effects from the night before. Will stares at Marcy realizing who she is.

'You're the woman from last night, aren't you?'

'Not many men remember me,' replies Marcy giving Will a cheeky grin.

Will mentions that she looked embarrassed when she found out that he was engaged. Marcy admits she was a little bit. She just assumed he was a nice single guy, and it was nice that he was so honest about it. Not many men have admitted that they're with a partner, most she's met have just wanted a one night stand.

'So – are you going to tell me why you're frustrated or not?' she asks as she indicates to the barman to bring them a couple of glasses of tap water. Will admits he would like someone to talk to, but she's a stranger. Why would he talk to a stranger about his problems? She makes a point by saying that it would be no different to him talking to a counsellor about his problems. Will agrees she has a point. He begins to think that maybe she could help.

'I never thought of it like that before,' says Will.

The Barman brings two glasses of tap water and puts them on the bar. Marcy picks up her glass.

'Cheers,' she says as she raises it in front of Will.

'Cheers,' he replies as he toasts her glass. They have a drink. Marcy then notices how amused Will is.

'Something funny?'

Will had never known anyone that has toasted tap water

Champaign or wine but never water. He knows that she's just being friendly.

'Okay – so you don't want to talk about your problems with a stranger – well, let me tell you a bit about myself.'

Her name is Marcy Lingfield. She works temporary shifts as a receptionist for *Deluxe Waters*. She lives in a tiny little bungalow which she inherited from her mother who passed away just over a year ago. She lives alone. She's never married or ever stayed in a stable relationship. She has always put the effort in to please her men but they've always used her like a one night stand.

'I'm sorry to hear you've been through a rough time, Marcy.'

'Thank you,' says Marcy. 'Not many guys are that considerate – your fiancée is a very lucky woman.'

'I suppose,' he sighs. Marcy realizes that the frustration he has been having is to do with his fiancée. He doesn't seem happy in his relationship.

Marcy asks Will to tell her about his fiancée and tell her about his frustration as she suspects that the two are connected. Will gives in. He admits that Missy is his frustration. She doesn't want to be intimate with him because she wants to wait until they get married. She says it'll be more special when it happens. But Will suspects there is something more to it – as she doesn't like being kissed a lot. They have kissed about three times during their relationship. She doesn't like holding hands or cuddling. He begins to think he's made a mistake asking her to marry him. Marcy wonders why he did.

Will explains when they met, they clicked right from the word go. They laughed at each other's sense of humour – they had similar hobbies and interests in common. Will felt like he had met his perfect match and had fallen in love with her. She admitted that she loves him too. Everything seemed perfect and Will didn't want to spend the rest of his life without her. Marcy is understanding – but at the same time mentions that not everyone is meant to be. That's what she went through. The guys couldn't stand her taste in music. She was a big metal fan – not what everyone would expect when you first look at her.

Will smiles – he was a big metal fan too. They both start to talk about metal bands, and soon discover that they like the same bands. They can't believe the odds of it. They both have a great time talking with each other and surprisingly enough have more in common than Will expected. He finds that she is a perfect match for him. He starts to have doubts about Missy – that maybe she wasn't the one for him as he begins to think that Marcy was, and the difference was that Marcy actually wanted him.

They are then interrupted by the sound of one of the tables and chairs crashing. They notice a guy on the floor. Will rushes over to the guy to see if he's all right. The guy has his hand to his head – his teeth gritting like he's in pain. Will helps him to his feet then calls for Marcy.

'Call an ambulance.'

The guy pushes Will away from him and ends up leaving the bar. Will stands there wondering what that was about. Marcy goes over to Will.

'Some people just don't want to be helped,' says Marcy. 'Want to escort me out?'

6

Will and Marcy come out of the bar into the busy street with crowds of people walking past them. Marcy holds Will's hands.

'I had a great time talking to you – take care okay – I know things are going to work out for the better.' Marcy leans forwards and kisses Will on the lips. As she holds their kiss – a woman among the crowd sees them. She quickly fumbles about with her phone and takes a picture of them. She shakes her head looking disgusted. She then calls someone.

'Hey – it's Allison – I need to see you, right now – I have something to show you.'

Marcy let's go of Will's hands.

'Marcy – I think those guys that dumped you were idiots – you're a stunning catch.'

Marcy smiles. She takes out a card from her bag and hands it to Will.

'My address is on there – and my number's on the back. Call me okay – we can hang out as friends – see you,' says Marcy leaving Will standing amongst the crowd looking at the card. As she walks away, Will stares at her bum, wiggling from side to side.

'Nice,' he says, smiling and raising an eyebrow.

7

An hour later, Allison is sitting outside *Kays Coffee Shop*. She sits at a table watching people walking by. As she waits, she sees a Woman sitting at a table looking at her watch constantly. She is dressed in a blue frock with flowers on. Her belly is sticking out slightly. A small pregnant bump. The Woman looks up as a guy joins her.

Allison listens in on their conversation. 'Nelson – so good of you to come.'

'Mary,' says Nelson sitting down at her table.

Before Mary starts explaining herself, Nelson wants to confess something and get it off his chest. The truth of the matter was – he misses her and honestly loves her with all her heart. Discovering she was a prostitute and sleeping with all those men including his mate Alex was too much. The thought of touching her again made him feel sick. He had to run away.

Mary grabs Nelson's hand and tells him that it's his baby growing inside her. She's never going back to prostitution as all she wants is love in her life, that's all she's ever wanted. She is going to love this baby as much as she loves him. She doesn't expect him to forgive her for lying to him or expect any high commitment like living together. She just hopes that they can be there for each other.

Nelson doesn't mind the idea of living together. He just hopes she understands that it's going to take some time for him to heal while he's with her as he wants to love this baby as much as she does. Mary will give him all the time he needs and understands – as long as they're all together, it's all she wants. They tell each other that they love each other – then kiss. Allison shakes her head in disgust.

'Do you have to do that in public?' Allison moans.

Nelson and Mary look at her and wonder what's got up her nose. Mary holds Nelson's hand.

'Come on – let's go back to mine and start our life.'

'Okay.'

They leave the table. As they leave, they bump into Matthew. They apologize as Matthew sits down at Allison's table.

'Hi, Allison.'

Allison takes out some paperwork and slaps it down on the table with a pen. It's the papers for the divorce proceedings. Matthew is about to try and persuade her to not go through with it but Allison wants to hear none of it. She had found a good solicitor that pushed it through quickly. As he did the wrong, he gets nothing. Matthew looks distressed but knows that he can't say anything that will change her mind or make up for it. He takes the pen and signs the papers. She snatches the paperwork and pen back and puts it in her bag. Matthew is upset. He doesn't say anything – instead he just leaves.

Allison looks at her watch. She then looks up to see the familiar face that she's waiting for. It's Missy.

'Hi, Allison – sorry I'm late,' says Missy as she hugs Allison, then kisses her on the left and right cheek. They sit down. 'So, what's wrong – you sounded quite upset over the phone.'

Allison is upset for Missy, who doesn't understand what she means by that. Allison takes her phone out and shows the photo of Marcy kissing Will.

'I'm so sorry, Missy – I couldn't believe it when I saw this myself – I was walking by and saw Will with this other woman.'

Missy stares at the photo, not reacting at all. She then shakes her head.

'No – no it's not real,' says Missy, completely in denial.

Allison pleads with Missy – it is real, that Will is seeing another woman behind her back. Allison had a feeling this would happen. Guys are so impatient and all they care about is getting their end away. Missy smacks the phone away from her. She is still in denial and starts blaming Allison.

'This isn't real – you photoshopped this photo, made it up. Just because your marriage went down the toilet because your husband slept with that Woman in Pentemy – assumed you were cheating on him…'

Missy stands up to leave '…My Will loves me and I love him.'

Allison stands and snaps back saying that she is right – she knows what she saw and this has nothing to do with what happened between her and her Matthew – and that includes her losing her first boyfriend, Andy, who decided he wanted to change into a woman and be called, Ana. Allison takes her phone and sends Missy the photo.

105

'If you don't believe me – then find and talk to this woman – I'm sure Will has her details on his phone or in his wallet.' Allison grabs her bag and walks away, leaving Missy to think about things.

'Missy,' calls a familiar voice.

Missy looks up to see Ana walking towards her – hand in hand with a guy, looking the happiest she had ever been. Missy gives Ana a hug.

'This is Richie – my boyfriend,' says Ana, 'we had a rocky introduction but we talked things through and are going to see where our relationship goes.'

'I remember him, Ana.' Missy is pleased that Ana has finally found someone who is understanding about her situation. She's had a rough time of it. Richie explains his friend Will is the one that persuaded him. Ana and Missy look at each other in surprise. Missy wonders if it's her Will he knows, the one who's the manager of *The Chunky Pie*. Richie confirms it – they go back a long way ever since high school. Missy begins to look at Will anew. Why would a kind guy help a relationship with peculiar circumstances? He must've seen something in it. Richie and Ana part ways from Missy leaving her to think that maybe she should confront Will about the photo.

8

Later that day – Will came home to find Missy sitting at the dinner table. He can tell she is deep in thought as she doesn't even acknowledge him. Will goes up to her wondering if she's okay. She says she is, where she clearly isn't. Missy didn't want to talk about her day, and instead changes the conversation and asks how his day has been, where he's been – what he's been up to. Will comes clean and admits he was at *The Open Bar*, just drinking water helping him to sober up. He began chatting with this woman called Marcy. They had things in common and he told her the truth that he has a fiancée.

Missy looks up. She can't think the worst of him. He had been honest about it all and told her the truth. Will wonders what she's thinking – did she know about Marcy? Missy comes clean and explains that Allison saw him and Marcy holding hands and that they shared a kiss.

'Whoa – it's not what you think – that surprised me, I didn't expect her to plant one on me like that – and she knows about you – I had to be honest about that.' Will hopes that she doesn't think he's cheating on her.

'I believe you,' says Missy. 'You know, not many guys would be that honest – most would be trying to get in her pants.' Will tells Missy that would never happen – as they would look terrible on him.

Missy smiles and laughs, then hugs him. 'I'm so lucky to know someone like you.'

Will breaks the hug. 'I'm going to take a shower.' Will takes his wallet and keys out of his trousers and puts them on the table. He then leaves the room. Missy looks over at Will's wallet. She is curious that there may be a note from this Marcy in there. She looks around, making sure that Will has gone. She then takes his wallet. She begins looking through. There is a little bit of cash which is covered by receipts. She is about to close his wallet when something catches her eye. It's a business card behind his bank card. She takes it out and sees that it has Marcy's details on. Her phone number and address. She takes out her phone and takes a photo of the details. She then slips the card back into Will's wallet. Missy begins to write out a text which reads, 'You were right – I think he's going to have sex.'

107

9

The next morning, Will had left home early – he didn't even tell Missy where he was going. Will looks at the business card to make sure he's got the right address. He stands outside a small house in a suburban road. He goes up to the door and rings the bell. He waits – no one comes. He feels disappointed – he's been thinking about Marcy a lot and couldn't wait to see her again. He thinks about leaving. He rings the bell again. He waits but still no one comes. He begins to walk away – when the door opens.

'Will – sorry about that – I was on the phone,' says Marcy standing in the door way dressed in a white silk dressing gown. 'Are you okay?'

'I need to talk to you – can I come in?'

'Sure – come on in,' says Marcy. Will enters Marcy's house. She closes the door behind her.

10

Will walks into a living room with Marcy. He looks around – astonished at how nice her place is. The walls were cream. Flowers in vases spread around the room. A TV in the corner. A corner sofa in the other. A bookshelf with many books on. Will can't help but notice the titles of the books. *The Art of Sex, Kama sutra,* and *a Keyholder's Guide.*

'Blimey – you're a… a bit too kinky – I never thought you were that kind of woman,' says Will surprised that she was into that sort of thing.

Marcy ignores Will. She sits down and gets to the point, asks him what he's doing here. Will sits next to her and confesses that he has been thinking about her since they had a good time in the bar. He was honest with Missy and told her that he met Marcy in the bar. Marcy is curious at what Missy would think – most would get jealous about another woman in her man's life. Marcy sees that Will is a good man. She leans closer to him.

'I think we should go to the bedroom – don't you?' says Marcy. Will looks at her surprised that she wants him, but at the same time he wants her.

'I'm sorry, Marcy – I really want to, but I should get back to Missy – and break up with her as I don't think she is the one for me – but you are – if you feel the same way about me?'

'I do,' she says, holding his hands tightly. 'I know how frustrating this has been for you – and I can imagine her frustration with following her beliefs – you love her so much – so don't tell her – we can keep this a secret – why hurt her?'

Whichever way Will looked at the situation – she was going to get hurt no matter what.

'Now come to my bed – you'll always want to come back when I show you how intimate we can be – don't worry and don't feel guilty – everything is going to work out perfectly.'

Will and Marcy kiss. Marcy then drags Will to her bedroom.

A couple of hours later, Will comes out of Marcy's house – looking satisfied, happy and less stressful. She was right – he'd want to go back to her instantly as he didn't really want to leave her. As he walks down the road – he doesn't notice Missy watching him across the road. He is completely oblivious. Missy watches him go off in the distance. She then takes a deep breath and makes her way to Marcy's door, but collides with a pram.

'Oh god I'm so... sorry,' says Missy. She looks astonished to see who's standing in front of her. 'You're Megan May – the singer.'

'Was,' replies Megan. 'Now I'm just plain Megan with my husband Jason and my son, Mark.'

Missy is pleased that she has a family and has found love. She had been a fan of Megan ever since she started out. She was disappointed when she went to her concert only to discover that she had been replaced by another woman called Clarice. The reception wasn't good – lots of boos and ridicule. But when Clarice started to sing the atmosphere changed. Everyone loved her. She had a stunning voice.

'I recommended her to take over from me – I always felt that she should've had that break more than me – I thought I knew what I wanted but what I really needed was love and a family.'

'As did I,' says Jason.

Megan says they have to go as she is meeting Jason's mum and dad for the first time as they live on this estate.

She thanks Missy for the support as a fan and to take care. As they leave, Missy turns her attention back to Marcy's door.

She rings the bell. As she waits – her heart races. The door opens and Marcy stands there wearing her silk dressing gown.

'Oh,' says Marcy, realizing who this woman could be.

'We need to talk,' says Missy, as she pushes Marcy aside and enters her home.

12

Missy enters the living room. She ignores everything about the room – how it looks is no interest to her. She stands at the window and stares out, with her back turned to Marcy. She waits for Missy to say something, not knowing what to say.

'He's done it hasn't he? – he's had sex with you,' says Missy. Marcy confirms that they just have, and he's just left. Missy closes her eyes, takes a deep breath and keeps her cool. She says that her friend Allison saw them together kissing and holding hands outside *The Open Bar*. She denied it of course even with the photographic evidence that Allison showed her. The thing is – she had to deny it, as she knew that Marcy had met Will and come onto him.

'Because I'm the one that set you up with him,' says Missy, turning around to face Marcy. It was the only way to keep Will happy. He was the nicest guy she had ever met, she met Marcy and told her everything about Will, where he works, what his interests were like his music styles, and as he was so frustrated not being able to be intimate with Missy. The truth was she could never be intimate with him. She goes up to Marcy and holds her hands – she smiles at Missy, gripping her hands tightly.

'Men don't do it for me – but women on the other hand – I am in love with them so much.'

Missy had met Mary, one of her escort colleagues a while back and recommended Marcy to her.

'I love Will for being such a wonderful honest guy – which is why I wanted him to be happy – we can both be happy now.'

'By sharing me,' says Marcy. She strokes Missy's hair, holds her head from the back. They both lean forwards and press their lips together.

Men and women – we all have relationships with each other, whether it be men and women, men and men, and women and women. The lives we have lived – the mistakes and regrets we have made. The feelings we have for one another comes down to the same and greatest feeling of all

*– The feeling for L ♥VE.*_____

MONSTER

1

Is love something worth giving up your future for?

Voices are raised – doors are slammed – and tempers are flared, as Kirstie and Gordon enter their living room. Gordon slams the door making sure Kirstie can't leave. She passes a corner sofa – her feet knocking into the empty beer cans that are scattered on the floor from Gordon's slobbish ways. She tries to leave the room via the patio doors which are locked.

'There's no way out, bitch,' shouts Gordon with his alcohol fuelled temper.

'Don't you take that tone with me – he's still my son,' screams Kirstie, pointing her finger at Gordon.

'I never wanted him – he was never mine – I just wanted you.'

She turns her back on him. The thought of looking at him made her sick to her stomach.

'When we got married – you took on the responsibility for him as well – I gave him up – I'm paying for him to stay in my husband's house while I stay here with you – I'm giving up a lot and you think I'm selfish.'

Kirstie looks at Gordon – her eyes flaring with anger.

Her face turning hot and red.

'You know what – to hell with you – I'm going back to him – your children should always come first.'

Kirstie walks towards the door. Her arm is grabbed hard by Gordon.

'You're not going anywhere,' he shouts as he throws her down onto the floor. Her head hits a cupboard, hard, and pain shoots through her skull. Her body flops to the floor. She lies there still – not moving – not conscious.

SMASH – the glass of the patio doors – shatter. Gordon looks in the direction of the doors. A brick is on the floor surrounded by fragments of glass. He looks up to see a figure – their identity hidden underneath a hoody. The figure clenches their fist.

2

The unexplained and noises through the night can be regarded as the monsters that go bump in the night. But what happens if we actually meet one. Would we cower and hide in the dark – or would we see them, in their true light?

An hour later – Kirstie's living room is now a crime scene. An ambulance crew places Kirstie's body on a stretcher and takes her away. A forensics team examine the dead body of Gordon and take photographs.

Detective Inspector Russell enters the living room through the broken patio door. His footsteps crunch as he steps on the fragments of glass. He walks over to a Police Constable, who is just standing around.

'PC Foreman, right? – I'm Detective Inspector Russell – what have we got?'

'Dead male – brutally attacked.'

'Cause of death?'

'Blood loss – which is the strangest part.'

Russell wonders why it would be strange. He takes a closer look with Foreman – who points out two puncture wounds on Gordon's neck. Foreman suggests that it doesn't just look like blood loss – it looks like the body was drained of blood.

Russell looks unimpressed at what Foreman is suggesting. He is expecting him to say the V word, *Vampire*.

'You've been watching too many movies.'

Russell takes a closer examination of the hand print in the blood. He looks over at the body. He assumes it's smaller than the victim's – like a teenager.

'Were there any other victims?'

'Yes Sir, Kirstie Cook – she's not dead – she's being taken to hospital – head trauma.'

'What about next of kin?'

3

Tom Cook, Kirstie's son, sits by his mother's bed in the casualty ward. He holds her hand tightly, afraid she's going to die. Russell places his hand on Tom's shoulder – assuring him that she's going to be okay.

'What happened to my mother – was it Gordon?'

Russell regrets to inform him that his step father, Gordon, is dead. His mother is suffering from head trauma.

He wonders if Tom can help them by telling them anything that could help in their investigations, like his mother, Gordon, anything. So Tom begins to tell the story of what led up to this moment.

It was two years ago that Tom last felt happy with his life. His mother and father had celebrated their eleventh wedding anniversary and were looking forward to going on holiday. It was all they talked about – looking forward to visiting different locations. But the next day all those plans faded away.

Tom's father had collapsed. He was rushed to hospital and diagnosed with cancer. This hit Tom and his mother hard. The fear of losing him was going to destroy them – and it did. Within three months of trying to fight it – the cancer won and took Tom's father. All that happiness they shared as a family was gone in the snap of the fingers.

Weeks passed after the funeral – and they both felt empty with so much heartbreak and pain. The good memories made things worse as it hurt too much to remember what was lost. They didn't talk much – they just tried to carry on as normal. Tom felt detached – only half there – semidetached. As the weeks went on, his Mother started to go out once a week which eventually turned to three nights a week. Then one day, Tom came home from school and that was the day that changed Tom's life for the worse.

His name was Gordon. He loved his drink. He didn't work. He was scruffy – and he didn't really care much for Tom.

Tom lay awake every night in bed – listening to the moaning sounds of Gordon having sex with his mother. It made him cringe. He tried so hard to drown out the noises by covering his ears with the pillow – and wearing ear defenders. Then one night, it was the last straw – Tom couldn't take it any more. He lay there listening to music, the volume at maximum – but the noise was too over powering.

All of a sudden – Tom jumped at the sound of his mother screaming at the top of her lungs. He jumped out of bed – his heart racing as he ran to his mother's aid as it sounded like she was being attacked. Tom opens the door. His mother looks at him shocked as she lays there naked. She grabs the quilt and covers herself.

'What the hell are you doing?' yells Gordon – as he stands there naked in front of Tom.

His mother was shaking, hot and out of breath. 'I thought she was in trouble.'

'Trouble? – I just gave her the best bit of pleasure she's had in her lifetime – even better than the night you were probably conceived.'

Gordon walks up to Tom who backs away out of the room.

'Now stay out,' says Gordon who slams the door closed in Tom's face.

After that night – Gordon and his mother broke the news to Tom that they were moving out without him. His mother assured Tom that he wouldn't be homeless. They would still pay the rent – it was just that Gordon wanted him and his mother to have their own personal space. Tom already knew what that meant, so Gordon could do his mother more. He was furious with his mother. Being left alone like that. He felt that his mother died too after losing his father. He felt alone.

Russell shakes his head in disgust. He couldn't believe what this boy had been through. His mother had no right to abandon him like that – especially at a young age. She broke the law. But Russell's main concern was for her to make a full recovery.

4

As the days passed by, Tom went around school more distant than normal. The students asked after him – to make sure he was okay and hoped that his mother would make a full recovery. Tom didn't really take it in – he wanted to be alone.

He walked around the school grounds in a world of his own until he was distracted by someone sitting on a bench on their own wearing a grey hoody with their hands in their pockets. Their face was covered by the large hood. He approaches them, curious to talk to them.

'Excuse me,' he asks, 'are you okay?'

'I'm fine,' a feminine voice replies. Tom didn't realize that they were a girl as he normally doesn't talk to them.

'Why do you hide your face?'

She tells him she has her reasons. She hides it from the sunlight as it gives her bad migraines. She didn't wear her hood at night time – she always was more of a night owl so to speak. She's not much for hanging around with anyone because of her condition. Tom thought he had never seen her around before.

'You're the boy whose mother is in hospital – aren't you?'

'Wow – news travels fast,' says Tom.

'Kids talk – I'm sorry to hear about your mother.'

'Thank you,' he replies.

Tom begins to feel happy again. The last time he was happy was before his father died.

'I'm Tom.'

'Ashley.'

Tom longed to see what she looked like. He thinks no one should hide who they are – not the real them. But she was scared because of her condition. Tom remembers that she is more of a night owl and invites her round to his where he hopes he can see what she looks like. She doesn't have to be afraid – as she can be herself. He holds her hand tightly – it feels cold. She squeezes his hand and nods.

5

Tom looks at the clock as he finishes his dinner.

6.55 p.m. – five minutes to go before Ashley calls. He quickly finishes his microwavable lasagne meal and washes up his plate and cutlery. He was always a tidy person, quite mature and grown up for his age. He was forced to learn adult responsibilities to carry on living when his mother went to live with Gordon. The worry for his mother was on his mind all the time. For the last couple of nights, he had cried himself to sleep – fearing that she might die. He couldn't bear the thought of losing his mother as well as his father.

A knock at the door then distracts his train of thought. He opens the door to see Ashley. He gives her a big smile but he doesn't know whether she returns the favour as she still has her hood up. She walks into the house. Tom closes the door and asks her to remove her hood. She hesitates for a few seconds, but eventually flips her hood back revealing what she looks like.

Tom is thrown off guard by what he sees. In front of him stands a beautiful girl with short dark hair. She has violet eyes… and fangs.

'You're a… vampire?'

'It's my condition.'

Ashley turns the light off plunging the hallway into darkness. Her violet eyes glow in the dark. It looks creepy, like the glow a cat would have. Tom turns the light back on.

'I should go.'

Ashley attempts to leave but Tom stops and tells her to stay with him. He's not frightened of her as this is the real her and he can prove it. Ashley is curious how he could do that – and before she knew it, he holds her by her waist, leans forward and presses his lips onto hers. He holds the kiss – surprised at how cold her lips are. She kisses him back, caught up in the moment. Tom slips his tongue into her mouth, massaging her cold tongue. His tongue rolls back – lightly catching her fangs. It doesn't cut it but he can tell how sharp they are.

'Okay,' says Ashley, 'that's proof.'

Tom can't help but wonder what it must be like to be a vampire. He has read books, and seen movies and TV series, based on them. But Ashley disappoints him, as the films and books have just been made for dramatic effect.

She doesn't burst into flames and turn to ash when the sunlight hits her. She just suffers severe headaches, painful migraines. It feels like her brain is on fire. She does have a taste for blood – mainly animal. She prefers her meat rare so there is a little bit of blood which keeps her strength up. She doesn't drink human blood – as the taste seems different to animal, but the scent can draw her in depending on what meat they have eaten,

Her heart beats and she breathes. Garlic gives her an allergic reaction, and religious icons like crucifixes and holy water are a misconception. It doesn't hurt or scare her at all. But dying does. She can die just like any normal person. She can be shot – hurt – her skin doesn't regenerate by healing itself. It just scars like anybody's.

Tom is fascinated. He's never met anyone like her before.

'So do you always kiss girls on your second meeting?' she says, being cheeky and not minding at all.

Tom feels embarrassed that he made a move like that – but there was something inside of him that felt right. The phone then interrupts them. He picks up the phone and finds out that it's the hospital. His mother is awake.

6

Ashley stands outside the ward and watches Tom go up to his mother through the window. Her hood is back up – as she doesn't want anyone to see her. Her acute hearing listens in on their conversation.

'I'm just glad you're okay,' says Tom, holding his mother's hand in his.

Kirstie asks about Gordon. Tom tells her that he's dead – that he's not going to hurt her any more. Her reaction is a surprising one. There was no reaction. It was like after all she had been through, she was glad he was gone. She apologizes to Tom – breaking down in tears – ashamed of how she treated him and abandoning him. She didn't ask for forgiveness as she thought she didn't deserve it. He assured her that they can forget all this and move forward just how they were when his father was alive. Kirstie smiles – seeing how far her son has grown up full of compassion in his heart.

'Get some rest, Mum – I'll see you in the morning.'

'I never saw who they were,' she says, stopping him from leaving. 'I just saw them standing over his body.'

'I wouldn't worry about it, Mum.'

Tom joins Ashley by the entrance to the ward. He tells her he needs the toilet – then when he returns, they'll go back to his. Ashley has no problem with that as she feels uncomfortable. Tom left her standing at the doorway.

'Excuse me,' calls Kirstie. 'Can you come here, please?' Ashley slowly makes her way over to her.

'Haven't I seen you before?'

Ashley swallows hard, then removes her hood to reveal her face.

Kirstie thought she had dreamed of her. Ashley had been at the scene. Kirstie had come around – her vision slightly blurred. She could see someone kneeling over the body of Gordon in a puddle of his own blood. They put their hand in the blood and then licked their hand. They spat out the blood – it must've tasted vile. They then stood over Gordon's body and looked at Kirstie. They took out something from their pocket and held it to their ear.

'I need an ambulance – a woman's been attacked.'

Ashley stares at Kirstie wanting to talk to her but she doesn't know what she could say about her being there at the scene. Kirstie appreciates her being there and for saving her life. Ashley smiles but notices Kirstie's expression drop when she sees her teeth with her fangs revealed. Ashley steps back and leaves in a hurry.

7

When they return to Tom's house. Ashley sits on the end of his bed while he sorts out his clothes in his wardrobe. He thanks her for going with him to the hospital. She didn't mind but she admits his mother saw what she looked like and thinks that she was freaked out. Tom says she'll come around as Ashley may be what they call a monster – but she's just like everyone else – breathing and alive.

She smiles at his kind words, but something doesn't feel right to her. She begins to sniff the air. A strange aroma fills her nostrils.

'I'll be right back,' says Tom, leaving Ashley alone in the room. She smells the air again – the aroma is stronger this time and seems to be coming from Tom's wardrobe. Curious – she goes over to his wardrobe and begins to move his clothes aside to see where the smell is coming from.

She discovers a plastic bag and inspects the contents. She pulls out a grey hoody and a pair of trainers. To her surprise there is a BBQ fork in the bag. The hoody, trainers and end of the fork are covered in blood – Gordon's blood.

'You found it by smelling the blood – you really are a vampire,' says Tom, standing in the doorway.

Ashley is scared. She holds the BBQ folk up in front of Tom and asks him to explain himself. He laughs – not believing that she hasn't worked it all out yet.

Kirstie walks towards the door. Her arm is grabbed hard by Gordon.

'You're not going anywhere' he shouts as he throws her down onto the floor. Her head hits a cupboard, hard and pain shoots through her skull. Her body flops to the floor. She lies there still – not moving – not conscious.

SMASH – the glass of the patio doors – shatter. Gordon looks in the direction of the doors. A brick is on the floor surrounded by fragments of glass. He looks up to see a figure – their identity hidden underneath a hoody. The figure clenches their fist. They flip their hoody back – it's Tom.

'You – what the hell are you doing here – you're going to pay for that window.'

Gordon walks up to Tom like he's ready to hit him. He stands there ready to be attacked by Gordon. The second Gordon reaches out to grab him. Tom takes out a BBQ fork and stabs it into the side of Gordon's neck. He stands there stunned – looking into Tom's eyes was like looking into the Devil's. His eyes filled with anger – such burning rage – a darkness ready to be born.

Tom pulls the fork out of Gordon's neck. Blood spits out onto Tom clothes and trainers. Gordon staggers back. His hand over his wound trying to stop the blood pouring out of his neck. He staggers back in shock, and then falls to the floor. He lies there bleeding to death as Tom just stands there watching him as he dies.

Ashley cowers into a corner as Tom walks up to her, she shakes with fear at the discovery that he killed Gordon.

'You and I – we're very alike – both scary.'

Monsters. The things that scare us when we are young.

For the love of a loved one – it can make us do the most unspeakable of things. And sometimes, the Monsters can be scared – by the monsters – that live inside ourselves.

PLAY4REAL

1

An emotion can lead to the fantasy of love. Spicing up a loving sex life through extreme dares and risks. That's what went through Nikki's and Matthew's minds as they sat in the lounge with a couple of Vodkas in the Club of *Play 4 Real*.

They had both been through hell when it came to relationships.

When it came to Nikki – she had two sides to her. Her nice and wild side. Her nice side gave her a personality everybody fell in love with. She was a sweet little thing. A slender figure from eating healthy and going to the gym. She had just turned thirty but she looked twenty. She wasn't a religious person but she loved wearing a crucifix pendant that gave her, her own faith and compassion for forgiveness – something that everyone looks for.

When it came to her wild side – she loved trying new things when it came to the bedroom. She had a high sex drive. You would have thought that her partners loved the idea of it. Nikki got more frustrated than pleasured as they could never seem to keep up with her. She went through partner after partner trying to find the right one for her, but it was the guys that ended up breaking up with her as they got fed up with her mood swings through frustration and trying new awkward positions so love making wouldn't get boring.

Then one day, she had a nice surprise. She went to *Kays Coffee Shop*. It was a regular spot for her. The usual three times a week visit – same order, flat white, one sugar. As she was about to push the door open to enter the coffee house – the door was opened for her.

In front of her stood a Man – about her age. He was dressed in grey skinny jeans, white t-shirt and black leather jacket. She thought he looked like a character from the musical *Grease*.

'Thank you so much,' says Nikki. They give each other a big smile while their eye contact never breaks as Nikki enters the coffee house. He lets the door swing back and returns to the queue – now standing behind Nikki. She thought he was leaving and tells him that he can go in front of her as he was originally queuing, but he didn't mind waiting.

'I'm Nikki.'

'Matthew – Matthew Cornwall.'

'Cornwall? – Don't hear that surname very often.'

'So, what's yours?'

'It's Nikki Holliday.'

They start moving forward as the queue gets shorter. Matthew notices the crucifix she is wearing and asks if she's religious. She laughs and admits that she is anything but religious. But she has her own faith and compassion for forgiveness.

'I could use some of that – I made a big mistake not long ago.'

Nikki is intrigued and wants to know more. He hesitates to get the words out to tell her. She sees that it's difficult for him.

'Hey – don't worry about it – you don't have to tell me if you don't want to – it's none of my business.'

'I cheated on my wife,' he blurts out. Nikki is opened mouthed. She wasn't expecting that. Matthew can see how freaked out she looks – he automatically thought that she was disgusted. As the damage was already done, he explains what happened – that he cheated on her by mistake. She listened to his detailed story then took Matthew's hands and held them tightly. He looked down at the floor, not wanting to look at her expression which he assumed was disgusted at him. But again he was wrong.

'Look at me,' she says. Matthew looks up at her. 'Look – we all make mistakes – sometimes it takes time to forgive the one we love – but before that ever happens you have to learn to forgive yourself.'

Matthew took those words on board. She was right. For a while now he had lived with the guilt. Didn't know which way to turn. He looked at Nikki as his Angel.

'Thank you,' he said, holding Nikki's hands tightly.

'Look if I was in your shoes…' She pauses '…they would probably be too big for me.'

Matthew smiled in amusement.

'From what you told me I would've thought the same thing and assumed the same thing, it's a natural instinct,' she says, mesmerized by Matthew's brown eyes. Her heart skips a beat which told her that maybe this could be the man for her. But she was thinking ahead of herself as there was a secret past that he didn't know about her.

Minutes later they were sat at the table in the coffee house. Coffees on the table in front of them. Nikki held onto Matthew's hands.

'I have something to tell you – as you were honest about yourself – what mistakes you've made and honest feelings – I must tell you mine – but I am scared that you won't like it.'

'You can tell me anything.'

Nikki swallows hard and takes a deep breath. She tells Matthew that he wouldn't have liked her back in the day. She was a complete mess. Her parents divorced then abandoned her. She got in with the wrong crowd and nearly died.

She lifts up her sleeve. Matthew sees lots of holes on her arm. She injected herself with drugs as it was the only thing that made her happy. She's not perfect.

'So – who saved you?'

She tells Matthew – there was an man that found her in an alley next to a dumpster surrounded by empty syringes. The man was dressed in a long winter trench coat which looked like what a soldier would've worn in a war. He wore a trilby hat – and told her that she wasn't going to die. But his attitude soon changed as he looked at her closely.

He apologized to her and told her that she can't be saved. As he walked away – something fell out of his pocket. She goes over to the item in question. She picks it up – it's a crucifix necklace.

'So that's how you got that?'

She plays with it – indicating that it was her lucky charm. He may not have given her hope and faith – but she found her own by the necklace. She guarantees Matthew that she never touched drugs since that day. Matthew was glad to hear it.

It wasn't long till they ended up together. The first time they had sex – it was the best sex that Nikki had. Matthew could keep up with her no problem. But there was something at the back of his mind – something that he never admitted to Nikki. To him it wasn't the best sex he had. The best he had was with his ex-wife, Allison.

Allison was always on his mind. He liked Nikki a lot. He wasn't in love but he hoped that he could feel the same way one day like he did for Allison. With his ex-wife on his mind – it began to affect their love making. Nikki had no idea. She didn't want to break up with Matthew – for once he was the man for her and she loved him. With the troubles of their love life weighing down on her – she soon found something that she thought would save their relationship. It was an advert for a new club that had opened called

PLAY 4 REAL

It was a game that couples and single people could play to spice up their love life that featured, dares, and risks to excite the hormones.

They drink their vodkas. In front of them is a large circular table. To the side of them is a wheel covered with a cloth. In front of them is another sofa – where another man sits down holding his drink.

'I'm Dennis – So – Are you ready to play?'

2

Games – we all like to play them – for the challenge, the thrill, the fun and the excitement. But what happens when we throw our love into the game? Could the players make that love stronger – or could they be the ones to steal it?

Nikki and Matthew stare at Dennis. He is dressed rather smartly in grey trousers, shirt and tie. To them he looks like a mid-forties business man. Nikki notices he's wearing a wedding ring.

'You're married?' she asks. Dennis looks at his finger then takes the wedding ring off and puts it in his pocket.

'Separated – I forget sometimes that I still wear this.' His attention is distracted by a woman that stands in front of them. He looks her up and down. She wears long black leather boots with stockings, short skirt and a black leather corset. Her long dark hair hangs past her shoulders and she wears blood red lip stick on her pouty pierced lips.

'Welcome to Play 4 Real,' she says. 'I'm your hostess – before we begin, I'm going to tell you how this all began, why it's here, then the rules of the game so you can begin playing.'

The Hostess shows them a picture of a woman dressed in similar clothing to her – standing in a pink room – holding a rose to her lips. Her name is *Krista* – the creator of the game and the club. Krista had trouble finding love. Besides being three hundred pounds in weight she had her own personal issues but she never wanted to give up on people that were in love. She had seen so many people around her go through heartbreak from breakups and divorces. To her it seemed that the word love was dying and this was the only way she thought of keeping their love alive. So – for people that were struggling with their love life and stuck in a rut – her club was the place to go to refresh their relationship through love and fun.

As Nikki listened she nodded – agreeing with what the Hostess was telling them. She thought of Krista as the saviour of love. Even though the phrase is *Love Never Dies* – Nikki thought Krista's vision was kind of true. It was dying. What kind of world would we live in – in a world without love?

'Now you know about Krista's cause – I will explain the rules of the game.'

The rules were simple. The three of them would go into the play 4 real room. Inside the room was a double bed.

There would be a table with sex toys, handcuffs, pills, shot glasses, and a bottle of *Spyrtus Rektyfikowany Rectified Spirit (95%).* Not many people had heard of the drink. It was a rectified polish spirit bottled with the extreme alcohol volume of 95%. It was recommended never to be drunk neat. It was to be enjoyed diluted or with a mixer.

Too much consumption of the drink, neat, could cause inflammation and severe liver damage along with cancer of the organs. It was like Russian Roulette – but the bottle of drink was the gun.

On either side of the walls there were six touch screen monitors. The players' names would appear on them. A notification would let each player know whose turn it is on the monitor to see what dares they got and who with. Some dares would be tame – and some would go beyond the extreme.

'Are you all ready to play?' asks the Hostess. Dennis and Nikki confirm they're ready. But Matthew is unsure he wants to play. He is curious what these extreme dares are. The Hostess tells him that she cannot say – the only way he would find out is to play 4 real.

Nikki reaches out for Matthew's hand and holds it tightly. 'Come on, Matthew – it won't be as bad as you think – we need this.' She was right – but Matthew always thought there was another way to fix their love life. With Nikki wanting to play the game – he reluctantly agreed too. This made Nikki happy.

'Excellent,' says the Hostess. 'Now you're all in agreement – the three of you will sign a disclaimer before entering the room.'

The Hostess puts her hand down her corset which is tightly pressing against her breasts. She pulls out a folded piece of paper and a pen – unfolds it then passes it to Nikki along with the pen.

Nikki jumps right in and signs one of the six signatures.

She then passes it to Matthew.

'Can I read it first? I want to know what I'm signing,' says Matthew to the Hostess. Nikki rolls her eyes and sighs.

'Come on Matthew – just sign it – I want to play,' says Nikki who sounds bored of his caution. He can tell she's getting frustrated with him.

He signs the disclaimer then passed it to Dennis – who signs it straight away. Dennis hands it back to the Hostess.

'If you'd like to follow me – I'll take you to your room.'

Dennis follows behind the Hostess. Nikki takes hold of Matthew's hand. 'Come on.' As he follows – he feels uncomfortable, scared even – the thought of the unknown and what's going to happen.

The Hostess brings them to a pink door. 'This will be your room – you have sixty minutes to play the game and relax. Once the time is up – you will vacate the room – is that understood?'

'What if we want to leave early?' asks Matthew.

The Hostess smiles. 'No one leaves early.'

'That good is it?' says Dennis.

'The door is locked once you enter – it will unlock after sixty minutes. Have fun.' The Hostess walks away. Dennis opens the door and enters the room. Nikki and Matthew follow.

3

Inside the room was everything the Hostess told them. It was bright inside
– due to the pink walls. Nikki realized that it was a similar room to the one
that Krista was pictured in. They hear the door close and lock behind them.
When they turn around they don't see the door. The colour of the door has
blended in with the wall. Their sixty minutes has begun.

Three of the monitors light up. The names of *Matthew, Nikki* and
Dennis appear on the screen.

'So what do we do? – How do we start the game?' asks Matthew
looking around.

The three names on the screen then begin flashing, fast. They then start
to slow down until Dennis and Matthew's name stops. Nikki's name is the
one that flashes. She is the first player to start the game. Her name
disappears off screen. Words flash on her screen – too fast for her to know
what they say. The words then stop instantly. Nikki thought it was planned
– because if it slowed down they would know what other dares lie ahead.

'Take a shot,' says Nikki. She walks over to the table and picks up a
shot glass which is half the size or a normal sized shot glass. It was nearly
the size of a bottle top. She inspects the bottle of alcohol. The 95% is what
stands out to her. She opens the bottle and pours out a shot. As she puts it
near her lips – her heart beats fast as she is nervous.

She slams the shot to the back of her throat which slides down towards
her stomach. Her eyes widen as a burning sensation soon follows. She
smells the fumes of the alcohol coming off her breath. Her eyes feel heavy
– she's never known a sensation like it. To Matthew and Dennis she looks
like she's already drunk after one shot.

'I'm okay.'

Her body feels like it's shaking. Like she's anxious or panicking. She
begins to feel a little irritation from her mouth, throat and stomach.

The names on the screen flash again – slow down and then stops.
Matthew's name flashes – soon followed by more words flashing fast which
then stop. Matthew's dare flashes. *Kiss Nikki on the neck, seductively for*

twenty seconds.

Nikki looks excited as Matthew walks over to her. He holds her by her hips – leans closer to her. She raises her neck, tenses up as he begins to kiss it. He glides his lips up her neck then round to the side, leaving a little moisture on her neck. Her breathing increases rapidly as she is turned on. She wanted him to take her there and then – but she knew that he couldn't as this was part of the game.

An alarm then sounds. Their twenty seconds are up. Nikki opens her eyes looking disappointed – lost in the moment and feeling frustrated.

The names flash and stop on Nikki again. The words flash and stop on her next dare. *Strip tease and dance seductively for Dennis for two minutes.*

'Now that I like,' says Dennis, sounding excited.

Matthew glares at Dennis. The jealousy already kicking in.

The lights then begin to dim and sexy music begins to play. Dennis stands by the bed as Nikki begins to perform.

She creates an s-form, rolling her body to the music. She then lifts her top up and lowers her trousers slightly revealing her belly and her hips teasing Dennis but not giving too much away. She then goes over to the table – leans on it with her hand, arching her back aiming her bottom at him. Matthew looks away as his anger builds. He knows he can't stop it as this is part of the game.

Nikki takes her top off revealing her breasts supported by a black bra. She then wipes her top between her legs then throws it at Dennis which hits him in the face. She then pulls her trousers down – revealing black lingerie, then kicks the trousers away from her.

Matthew looks at the screen. There is still a minute to go. He wants the time to hurry up so that the dare stops.

But Nikki isn't even thinking about the time. She's too lost in the fantasy. She gets on her hands and knees and crawls along the floor until she reaches Dennis's trousers.

She gets to her feet and sits him down on the bed. She sits on top of him then removes her bra. Her breasts dangle in front of his face. He gets the urge to put his face in them, but this was a tease so he couldn't. She touches him all over – enticing him with her femininity. As she takes hold of her lingerie and begins to remove them – the alarm sounds and the dare is over.

Matthew is relieved that it didn't go any further. Nikki walks over to him leaving her clothes on the floor.

'You look like you enjoyed that,' says Matthew, his tone annoyed and angry.

'Don't take it seriously – it means nothing – it's a game, a bit of fun.' She looks down at his trousers seeing a slight bulge. 'See – you obviously like it.'

The names flash again – then stop on Nikki's. Words are randomly generated then stop on Nikki's next dare. Her expression drops when she reads, *Take three shots.* She worries as the effects of the first shot are still irritating her. 'I can't do that.'

'Of course you can – you're a team player,' says Dennis.

'Hey – back off,' says Matthew aggressively. 'You know how dangerous that stuff could be – why do you want to endanger her life?'

While Matthew and Dennis argue – they don't see Nikki walk over to the table. She pours three shots and does one after the other completing the challenge. She puts her hand over her tummy as it burns from the alcohol. She can barely keep her eyes open and the fumes overwhelm her from her breath.

'Whooze go iz ittt jnow?' she says slurring her words. She staggers around nearly losing her balance. Matthew is concerned for her health.

'Okay I think this has gone on far enough.'

'For god's sake, Matthew – this is part of the game – you signed the disclaimer so whatever happens this place isn't liable – can't you see she's having fun?'

'Yesh – stchop being boring,' slurs Nikki.

The names flash and stop on Matthew. His dare then comes up. *Give Nikki a two minute massage.*

She staggers over to the bed and flops onto it. Matthew gets on the bed and begins to massage her shoulders. She closes her eyes as the pressure of his hands massage her muscles. His hands wander down her back. She gasps. With the mixture of alcohol, strip teasing and now the massage she can't take any more. She grabs hold of Matthew and kisses him passionately.

They are interrupted by an alarm. They look at the screen. The dare has been cancelled with over thirty seconds remaining. The screen flicks to *Play 4 Real: Extreme Dare* on Matthew's screen.

'What does this mean?'

138

'Must be a punishment for not completing your dare,' says Dennis. 'You were supposed to massage her not make out with her.'

'But why do I get punished – she kissed me.'

'It was on your dare, that's why.'

The words randomly generate then stop with *Nikki and Dennis*.

'Oh come on – this is rigged,' blasts Matthew, 'why do you two get the extreme dare?'

The words randomly generate again. They all wait in anticipation to find out what extreme challenge they get. Matthew looks closely at the screen, he can make out one of the challenges that are flashing. *Drink 250ml of Spyrtus Rektyfikowany.* That's the equivalent of half the bottle. He hoped it wouldn't stop on that one as the drink might kill them.

The words stop. A cold shiver follows Matthew's terrified heart. He reads the extreme challenge. *Pregnancy Risk.*

They all look at the screen in horror. What they're asking is ridiculous and obscene.

'Okay – no more playing – we just wait until sixty minutes is up,' says Matthew, panicking.

'Look you can't be angry about this,' says Dennis. 'We knew what we were getting into – we signed a contract.'

The three monitors with their names on begin to flash random words. On each monitor he is prompted to touch the screen to stop the words to decide how the dare is going to be played out. Above the random words are the three questions to discover how the answers will play out for the dare.

Question 1: How will the challenge be prepared?

Question 2: What protection will be used?

Question 3: How many times will this be attempted?

He goes over to the screen. His hand quivers as he reaches out to touch it. Nothing happens when he does. He tries it again – but still nothing happens.

'Maybe you've got to touch the other two screens to stop them all.'

Matthew touches the other two screens. All three stop at once. He shakes his head to see what he reads, backing away from the answers. Nikki must take ten fertility pills, Dennis must have sex with her without any protection and the amount of attempts to get her pregnant will be the rest of her life.

Nikki takes the bottle of water and pops each fertility pill out. She takes them all with the water and swallows hard.

'You really want to hurt me don't you?' says Matthew, his voice full of upset and distress.

'We're under contract – come over here with me.'

She takes his hand. They make their way over to the bed. She gets on all fours and faces Matthew. Dennis get up on the bed and undoes his trousers. She leans forwards to Matthew as Dennis takes her from behind. She gasps – closing her eyes as he grinds her. She gets excited – her breathing increasing rapidly followed by her pleasurable moaning.

Her eyes then snap open – she grips Matthew.

'I love you for this,' she pants. It isn't long before her body quivers with Dennis injecting his seed into her.

4

Six months have passed since that night. Matthew sits on the sofa staring into space – haunted and reliving the nightmare over and over again in his head. Nikki then enters the room wearing a black see through robe.

She goes up to him – spreads her legs to sit on his lap and kisses him. She opens up her robe – takes his hands and places them on her pregnant belly.

'I love you, Matthew – I knew you'd like this – thank you for playing.'

We can all define love with more than one person.

Many people are happy sharing their love and relationships through the power of their fantasies – but playing with people's love and emotions – is like playing with fire – which can end in a hellish nightmare that we will live with, forever.

PERFECT

1

Emotion is used on an ordinary night that takes a single moment to change the happy life you have worked for. That's what Harry Perry thought, as he stood in the lift making his way up to the head offices of Foptix Industries – the number one leading company in robotics and electrical technology.

It was a month after that he and his wife Jennifer got married. They had problems with the people around them and had decided to go away. Somewhere peaceful, relaxed and laid back where they could make a start on their future for a family. They didn't really want to wait as they both wanted the same goal in their life.

Harry was driving at the wheel, concentrating, his eyes focused on the road through the blurriness of the rain obscuring the view, as the wipers washed the rain back and forth from the windscreen.

'I love you,' says Jennifer, as she stares at him from the passenger seat. Harry quickly glances at her, taking her hand in his – smiling at her, then kissing her hand.

'I love you too,' he replies.

Jennifer looks out the passenger window smiling to herself.

All of a sudden, another car crashes head on into the passenger side. The car spins out of control – glass shattering everywhere. The car goes off the road and crashes into a tree. Jennifer is thrown out of her seat into the windscreen head first, which shatters to pieces. Her body lies lifeless on the ground.

2

The lift doors open and Harry steps out. The managing director of Foptix Industries, Tracy Luna is waiting for Harry standing next to a young woman sitting at a circular desk. She looks sad the second she sees him. A broken man, head bandaged, with an expression of sorrow on his face.

'Please step this way, Harry,' says Tracy. 'Cynthia – hold my calls.'

'Yes, Miss Luna,' says Cynthia as she types at her computer.

3

Tracy closes the doors as Harry enters her office. She makes her way over to her desk while Harry looks around. It's decorated in vintage looking furniture – not what he was expecting. Computer. Desk. Stationery. Filing cabinet and bookcase with folders and books on.

'Please take a seat,' says Tracy, as she sits down behind her desk. Harry sits. Now that she and Harry are alone free to talk she tells Harry that she is as upset as he is as Jennifer was one of her finest employees. Harry noticed that it didn't take long for her to replace Jennifer's receptionist role.

'You mean Allison? – well, she had been assisting Jennifer for some time – besides Allison went through a bad divorce with her cheating ex-husband – she's suffered enough.'

Harry thought Allison wasn't really a suitable candidate after what he saw when he met Jennifer.

'Then why don't you start at the beginning?' says Tracy, wanting to hear his story.

4

When we want a relationship – we all want to search for the perfect partner. But what would we do when we find them? Would we see the perfect life we want to live with or would we see too much of ourselves in them?

Harry pulls up outside a large structural tall building. He looks up through the windscreen of his delivery van.

The logo *Foptix Industries* in large red bold letters can be seen at the front of the building.

'I wonder if they're compensating for something,' he mumbles to himself. He takes a parcel from the passenger seat – a small brown box with a logo on the parcel tape that reads *CL Petra*. They are an electronics, computer supply, company.

5

The lobby doors automatically open and Harry is greeted by the cool air from the large industrial air conditioning. He looks around at the scale of the reception area. A circular reception desk in the middle of the lobby with spiral staircases on either side of it leading up to the next floor where the lifts are. Two women sit at the reception – one wearing a headset, pretty, long brown hair tied back wearing a name badge that reads *Jennifer*.

'Good morning, Foptix Industries – Jennifer speaking, how may I help you?'

On the other end of the call is an important client that wants to speak to *Tracy Luna* who is the managing director of the company.

'I'm sorry, I'm afraid she is in a meeting – can I take a message?' says Jennifer. 'You really need to speak to her – how long will she be? – I don't know I've never measured her.'

Allison grins at Jennifer's amusing joke as does Harry.

'Okay – I will pass the message on – have a good day – goodbye.'

Jennifer takes her headset off then glares at Allison.

'You can sign for deliveries you know – you don't have to wait for me to do it.'

As Jennifer deals with Harry. Allison pleads her case – moaning about her husband going off to Pentemy and leaving her behind. Her head isn't even in this job and she doesn't want to do this for the rest of her life. She leaves the reception for the toilets leaving Jennifer annoyed.

'Sorry about that – I'm training her.'

'She's coming on really well isn't she,' smiles Harry, causing Jennifer to be amused by his sarcastic comment. He understands what she's going through – it isn't easy getting your heart broken by being cheated on.

'Really?' says Jennifer. 'Who did your husband cheat on you with?'

'No – guys don't do anything for me.'

'I suppose you've got to have the balls to go out with other guys.' She smiles, winking cheekily at him. Harry likes her banter – she had a good sense of humour which was something that was lacking from the people he knew.

He had a woman in his life… he pauses. Jennifer can tell that he doesn't want to talk about it. Knowing that it's difficult for him to think about his past – she touches his hand and assures him he doesn't have to talk about it.

Harry's attention is distracted by a book that's near her computer. The title reads:

HIS LAST STORY

'You like to read, huh?'

Jennifer looks down at the book. She loved to read. Every day and every night. She loved getting engrossed into a story. Absorbing and learning knowledge. She read all sorts of books. Romances, thrillers, kids fantasy novels. Biographies and factual. There wasn't a single book she didn't find interesting. She was over three quarters of the way through the book. It was a strange story to her as it was a mixture of different genres. She described it as a typical boy / girl romance story with drama and science fiction elements. She liked it because it was different to other romances.

Harry could relate. He didn't normally touch romance novels – but the science fiction element got his interests going. Harry was halfway through the book. Before Jennifer could say anything more – Harry asked her not to tell him any spoilers as he's trying to avoid them as he's enjoying the surprises as the story unravels.

He can't help but wonder why she reads every night and doesn't go out to see people. She tells him she's a bit of a loner and doesn't know that many people. He is surprised that someone this good looking wouldn't go out – not even for a meal.

'Is that what you would do?' asks Jennifer. 'Take me out tonight for a meal?'

'Absolutely.'

'Great – than I accept your offer'

Harry is surprised. He didn't really mean to ask her out on a date, but at the same time he was a single guy and he liked her. Harry suggested they meet at eight at his favourite steakhouse as long as she wasn't vegetarian.

'I'm an all-rounder – when it comes to food – I like trying anything.'

6

The waitress walks over to Harry's and Jennifer's table.

She has food stains on her apron and her nametag reads *Sandra*. She places the plates down on the table. Two steak meals with chips, peas, half a cooked tomato, and six onion rings.

'Is there anything else you would like?' asks Sandra.

Harry smiles at her and shakes his head. She smiles at them both 'Enjoy your meal.' Then walks away.

Jennifer puts some steak into her mouth and chews. Her eyes are widened by the surprise. It is like a taste explosion.

Medium rare steak juices electrifying her taste buds with the hint of a chargrilled flavouring that followed.

'Oh my god – this is wonderful.'

'Well, you can't go wrong here,' says Harry, tearing off a hunk of bread.

The ambience of classical music set a relaxed mood within the restaurant. People weren't too loud talking to each other which didn't mean that Harry and Jennifer had to talk loudly. The clanging of the cutlery hitting the plates while food was being cut was the only loud noise in the restaurant.

As they ate their meal, they talked about each other.
What other foods they liked to eat. Harry was always partial to curries and spicy foods. Jennifer had never had a curry which surprised him, so he offered to take her out for one for her to try which she was up for. Harry felt happy that there would be a second date and it was a good sign that things could develop for them.

Harry loved food – ever since he was kid. His favourite was red salmon sandwiches with vinegar and pepper – something that his mum used to make.

Jennifer smiled with delight. She loved that too. Harry couldn't believe it. What were the odds of finding someone with similar tastes he had when he was a child?

She then reached out for his hand and held it in hers.

She squeezes it tightly staring at him – until her attention is distracted by a middle aged couple leaning over their table, kissing. He looks over too.

'Is that how you're going to kiss me?' asks Jennifer.

Harry doesn't know what to say. He's been tempted to but was scared to make a move this early as it's only their first date.

Jennifer doesn't give him another second to think about things. She leans over the table and pulls him towards her –and kisses him. It takes his breath away, surprised she made the first move.

'Can we go back to yours, Harry?'

7

Jennifer falls back on Harry's bed while pulling him on top of her. They kiss each other with passion – their hands feeling and touching all the parts of their bodies exciting the senses. She forgets herself and digs her fingers into Harry's skin, hard.

'Ow.'

'Sorry,' she says 'I forget my own strength.'

But it didn't put him off as he wanted her as much as she wanted him. She sat up and took her top off revealing her slender figure and small perky breasts that were supported by a blue and pink flowery bra. She laid back and he began kissing her all over her milky soft warm skin –from her belly past her breasts all the way up to her neck. She gasped as he licked her neck.

'Take me,' she said, her breathing increasing with excitement.

After ten minutes of intercourse – they both lay back on Harry's bed – hot, sweaty and out of breath. Jennifer cuddles up to him – looking satisfied and happy.

'So that's how you make love to me?'

'Well, I certainly wasn't disappointed – you're perfect.'

Jennifer kisses him, until she is interrupted by Harry's phone. He looks who is calling.

'It's my friend, Dennis – I'll call him back.'

'It's okay – go ahead.'

Harry answers his phone.

'Hey Dennis…' says Harry as he sits up in bed. 'What? Whoa, slow down – what do you mean your wife left you? Come around now?'

He looks at Jennifer – not wanting to ruin the night with Jennifer. But she is understanding and tells him that it's okay as his friend needs him.

8

It isn't long before Dennis is sitting in front of Harry in his living room. Head hung with a beer in hand. Harry listens to Dennis's story and the more he told – Harry became more disgusted.

Dennis had problems when it came to making love to his wife. She, like Dennis, wasn't attracted to him any more as they both never achieved climax. Times had been hard and then, one day, he saw an advert for a club called *Play 4 Real*. This sparked his interest as it was for people who were struggling with their love life and a way to reignite the spark of the excitement.

He had met a couple called Nikki and Matthew who were going to play the game. Each person randomly did dares and played the challenges for real. There were mild dares from kissing, massaging, dancing, flirting and drinking to more extreme dares. When Nikki and Dennis had got the extreme dare – the players could never go back. The dare was the pregnancy risk and Dennis had to take Nikki and have unprotected sex with her.

Harry sat there – mouth wide open in horror as Dennis told him all this. His wife found out about the sex club he went to. Harry could understand why she left him. It was disgusting and degrading.

They both sat there silent. Harry didn't know what to say regarding Dennis's behaviour. Luckily for Harry the tension was broken by Jennifer entering the room. Dennis is surprised to see this attractive woman bringing him a sandwich.

'Red salmon – you remembered – you are perfect.'

'Of course, I remembered – it's my favourite too,' she says looking at Dennis who is staring at her. 'Did your friend want something to eat?'

'No that's okay – he's happy with his beer.'

'Okay,' she kisses Harry. Dennis watches her butt as she leaves the room. Dennis is intrigued how long ago he met her. He is surprised when Harry tells him that it was today.

'And you're already kissing?' says Dennis. He can see by Harry's expression and lack of response that they've done more than just kiss.

154

'You've already plugged her?' He begins to like how fast Harry has worked and suggests the best thing he can do is use her and lose her.

Harry then loses his temper – pointing his finger at Dennis and warning him that he won't ever speak about women or Jennifer that way again. Dennis slams his beer down and yells back at Harry thinking that he was his friend. They stare at each other in silence until Dennis grabs his beer and leaves.

Jennifer comes back into the room – tears in her eyes.

Harry goes up to her and comforts her in his arms. 'Why was your friend so mean to me?'

'It's not you okay – he's not worth it – I'm with you – I'm yours.'

'For the rest of my life?' she says, smiling while she wipes the tears away from her face.

'If you want to be – I know I want you to be.'

9

It was only a matter of weeks since Harry and Jennifer had met for the first time, that they decided to get married. It was a summer wedding in the late afternoon. Outside a church in the middle of the countryside – family, friends and work colleagues gathered to celebrate their marriage. Jennifer stood outside the church being photographed in a long white wedding dress with black criss cross patterns down the back. She smiled – holding her bouquet close to her as the photographer took photo after photo.

Allison, her maid of honour, goes up to her and stands by her side as the photographer takes more photos of the two of them.

'You look beautiful, Jen,' says Allison. 'I'm still surprised but honoured to be asked to be your maid of honour.'

'I don't have many friends – we work together – it seemed the easiest choice – and besides the next wedding could be yours.'

Allison shakes her head. After what happened with Matthew she has no interest in getting married again.

'Well, maybe – you and Matthew will try again – there's still love there I think.'

Allison shakes her head again then leaves Jennifer's side. She passes her boss Tracy Luna talking to a Frenchman. She overhears their conversation.

'Look, Pierre – you can tell your boss from me – we are grateful for the supplies we have ordered from you for business – but we will not be funding your experimental program – because just like their program – they're dreaming.'

Tracy walks away from Pierre. A look of disappointment fills his face – he shakes his head then leaves. Allison is curious to know what that was about.

Later that day as the sun had set – after the first dance and the cake being cut – they said farewell to their family and friends. They left in a black limo – courtesy of Tracy Luna as Jennifer was one of her close employees.

'Mrs Jennifer Perry – I'm so happy,' she says, cuddling up to Harry resting her head on his chest.

'So am I.'

'Now our days can really begin – every day filled with love – it's perfect.'

10

Two weeks have passed since their honeymoon and life has returned to normal. Monday morning comes and the kitchen is filled with the smell of home cooking. Jennifer takes out a tray of freshly baked muffins and places it on the kitchen side. She takes off the oven gloves as Harry enters the kitchen.

'Something smells good'

'I made this for you – take some to work.'

She grabs two off the tray and places them in his hands.

He drops them quickly as they burn his hands.

'Ow – jeez – they are still…' Jennifer picks them up off the floor and holds them in her hands '…hot.' She puts them back on the tray.

Harry grabs hold of Jennifer's hands and takes a closer look at them. They don't feel hot and there is no sign of burning.

'Didn't you feel that?'

'Feel what?'

Harry is puzzled. She kisses him and wishes him a good day at work. He wishes her a good day too. As he leaves for the door, he looks at her again. She continues to take the muffins off the tray while humming. She is happy – but Harry is concerned that she's acting a little strange.

It wasn't long after Harry left for work, that there was a knock at the door. Jennifer goes to the door – happy – smiling not having a worry in the world. But all that changed when she opened the door and Dennis was standing there making her feel uncomfortable.

'Harry isn't here.'

'I know that – I just saw him leave – aren't you going to invite me in?'

She doesn't know what to say – so he barges past her allowing himself in. She goes after him leaving the door wide open. Dennis walks around the room staring at her.

'What do you want?'

'When I was here last – Harry said you were perfect,' says Dennis, his hand creeping down to his trousers and unzipping his zipper. 'I want to see if that's true.'

He makes a move on her. Grabbing her hard by her arms. She panics – scared – struggling to get out of his grip. She manages to push him away. He retaliates by slapping her round the face hard causing her to stagger back. He attempts to hit her again but she grabs his arm, hard.

Dennis screams in pain when he hears a crack. He is then pulled away from Jennifer and pushed towards the door. Harry stands in front of her protecting her.

'You stay the hell away from her – I'm calling the Police.'

Dennis leaves in a hurry. Harry turns his attention on Jennifer. She is crying and shaking with fear. He wraps his arms around her.

'I was so scared – I'm glad you're here.'

'I'm glad I came back – I came to get those muffins that you made me to take to work – they reminded me of you.'

'I remind you of a muffin?'

'Just the love and thought you put into making them for me.'

Jennifer kisses him.

'Look – let's get away for a bit – just stay somewhere else for a break – get away from all out problems.'

'Yes, Harry – I love that idea.'

11

Harry was driving at the wheel, concentrating, his eyes focused on the road through the blurriness of the rain obscuring the view as the wipers washed the rain back and forth from the windscreen.

'I love you,' says Jennifer, as she stares at him from the passenger seat. Harry quickly glances at her, taking her hand in his – smiling at her, then kissing her hand.

'I love you too,' he replies.

Jennifer looks out the passenger window smiling to herself.

All of a sudden, another car crashes head on into the passenger side. It spins out of control – glass shattering everywhere. The car goes off the road and crashes into a tree. Jennifer is thrown out of her seat into the windscreen head first, which smashes to pieces. Her body lies lifeless on the ground.

The car door is pushed open. Harry falls out – blood dripping off him from the cut on his forehead. He struggles to get to his feet – staggers around losing his balance – looking around panicking to find Jennifer. With his blood dripping into his eyes – he wipes it away obscuring his vision but then notices what looks like Jennifer's body.

As he makes his way towards it – he stops in his tracks as the vehicle that collided with his pulls up and stops near her body. The door opens. Harry can't make out who the driver is as the headlights blind his vision.

The driver steps into the headlights. Harry can see who they are. It's Dennis with his arm bandaged up.

'I didn't want to do this, Harry – but I need to know what makes her so perfect.'

'You son of a bitch,' yells Harry running at Dennis. He throws out a punch which Dennis avoids. Dennis hits Harry in the stomach, winding him – then hits him in the face causing Harry to drop to the ground.

'You don't see it do you – there's something wrong with her – she's not normal. I had to go to hospital – she broke my arm.'

'People don't always realize their own strength – you idiot.'

'Well, maybe I'll use mine on you – so you won't be able to save her

– when I use mine on her.'

Dennis is then grabbed from the back of the neck and lifted up. His feet dangle in the air. To Harry's amazement it's Jennifer that's holding him up in the air. Her arm is cut open and an electronic structure is revealed underneath.

Her face is damaged revealing a metal skeletal structure underneath. She throws Dennis into a nearby tree.

As he lies there stunned – he looks up to see her coming towards him. She flinches and begins to spark. Her circuits shorting as he she walks.

'I knew it – you're...'

'Perfect,' she says as she wraps her hands around his throat tightly. Dennis struggles to fight against her. He can't catch a breath as the pressure gets stronger on his wind pipe. Harry then hears a crunch as Jennifer crushes Dennis's throat with her hands. His body flops to the ground, dead.

Jennifer's body then sparks more – she shakes violently and drops to the floor herself. Harry runs over to her and holds her in his arms.

'I'm so sorry – I should have told you.'

'You're a robot – I never even realized.'

Harry holds her tightly in his arms. He is scared at the thought of losing her. His love for her was true and real. All his life he was looking for the perfect female for him – even though she was a synthetic – she was more human to him than any woman he had met in his life.

'I don't want you to die – I love you,' says Harry – the teardrops falling from his eyes onto her face.

She blinks, her eyes watering and tearful. She may have been created but she felt the love for Harry in return.

'I'm frightened, Harry – I don't want to go – I love you so...'

Her power stops – her dead eyes stare at him. He shakes her body – desperate for her to move again or say anything to him. But she doesn't. She's dead.

He holds her tightly in his arms – rocking her back and forth. Her life stolen from him by a man once considered a friend. He lets out a loud scream. All his anger, all his love – all his hate, exploded with a ton of emotion from his broken heart.

12

Tracy stares at Harry who still has his eyes closed. Visually remembering the worst time in his life. She wipes a tear from her face as Harry opens his eyes.

'Why didn't you tell me she was a robot?'

'Harry,' says Tracy, 'you have to understand that Jennifer was one of our first creations. If the governments knew about this – then they would get us to turn them into weapons.'

He understood where Tracy was coming from. But he was fascinated how they were able to come up with the technology that showed all the mannerisms of a human being. He had witnessed all sorts of human emotions in Jennifer. She could cry, love, feel frightened. Her saliva tasted like a human and when they made love it was just right. He was fooled. But there was one thing that he did find odd that should have made him realize she wasn't normal. It was when she held the hot muffins in her hand and didn't get burned.

An alarm then sounds. Harry thinks it's a fire alarm.

Tracy's phone rings. She answers the call.

'Allison? What's going on? …Okay, get security down there now.' She slams the handset down.

Harry is concerned at what's going on. Tracy was panicking, explaining to Harry that there had been a break in downstairs in one of the labs. The intruder had just taken three babies in relation to the GravitE project. Harry is puzzled and has no clue what she is on about. Tracy realized what she just said and changes her tone – telling him to forget everything she just told him as it was confidential information.

'Wait here – I will be right back,' says Tracy leaving her office.

Harry sits in the chair looking round her office. He reaches for a photo frame that's standing on her desk and turns it around. It's a photo of Tracy and Jennifer. Harry's heart aches – seeing her image in the photo brought back his broken heart missing the love of his perfect female.

We all search for the perfect love. With technology advancing all the time to create the ultimate perfection. There will come a time when we won't be able to tell the difference of a love between a human and machine.

162

FAYMILL

1

That old farmhouse sits in the middle of nowhere on the outskirts of Towns-end. Surrounded by cornfields and gravel paths. The farmhouse is old. Faded wood with the odd spot of wood rot. The farmhouse has had many occupants live there but not for long term.

It was just under a month that most of the occupants stayed there. They grabbed their possessions and ran. They never had any trouble replacing the occupants as the price of the rent decreased the more people lived there and left. But now – a mother and her two children moved in. Six weeks passed and everything was perfect. Until late one night – something happened.

2

Caroline slides the lock of the door. She goes around Faymill, making sure everything is locked up for the night for the safety of her children. She then goes to the kitchen to do the washing up. She takes a knife out of the bowl, wipes it then puts it on the drainage board.

A noise then distracts her coming from upstairs. She looks up at the ceiling and listens carefully for another noise to follow – but no sound is heard.

'Kids,' she calls. There is no reply. She wipes her hands with a tea towel then throws it down on the drainage board.

As she stands at the bottom of the stairs – she looks up into the endless blackness. It creeps her out. She turns on the light then makes her way upstairs.

'Kids?' she calls again, as she creeps towards their bedroom door. She opens it and peers into the room. It's dark, the curtains are drawn and her two boys are asleep in separate single beds. She then closes the door and returns to the kitchen.

As she stands at the sink her hands are still wet. She reaches for the tea towel on the drainage board – but it's not there, neither is the kitchen knife. She looks around the kitchen and notices the tea towel is now on the kitchen counter. She begins to doubt herself that she put the tea towel on the drainage board.

3

Paul's eyes snap open to the sound of a creaking floorboard. He looks over to his brother, Mike – who is fast asleep. Paul's eyes look around the room quickly to see if he can spot anything making the noise. His eyes snap up to the ceiling as it creaks. He remembers his mother telling him that there's nothing to worry about. It's just an old farmhouse full of aches and pains.

The bedroom door then swings open slowly. Paul's eyes widen. He pulls the bed covers up – peering over them as the door stops halfway. Paul's heart pounds like crazy as he waits for someone to appear. No one does.

He waits – afraid to move or get out of bed.

'Mike – Mike?' he whispers calling over to his brother.

But Mike is fast asleep and doesn't stir. Paul throws back the covers – his bare feet land on the cold wooden floor. He creeps towards the door and peers into the hallway. He sees nothing. He then hears the creaking of the floorboards – like there's an invisible presence getting closer to him.

He closes the door and jumps back into his bed, hiding under the covers. He hears the bedroom door close. He shakes with fear – breathing becoming rapid. The sound of the floors and the walls creaking. It then goes quiet. It takes him a while before he lowers the covers and peers over them. There is nothing in the room.

All of a sudden, a pair of hands appear in front of him and a boy is face to face with Paul. The boy waves his hands in front of Paul who then screams at the top of his lungs.

Paul hears footsteps running up the stairs and before he knows it the door to the room opens. His mother stands in the doorway who looks horrified at what she sees. It's not the boy on top of Paul's bed, but another figure standing near Mike's bed dressed in a nurse's outfit holding the knife that went missing from the kitchen above Mike who is still asleep. Caroline screams.

4

The appearances of ghostly apparitions are normally linked to the life they left behind. But if we see one, are we really seeing their previous life – or are we seeing a message that's beyond our eyes?

Frank Mason packs his possessions into a box and takes one last look at his office in the natural history museum.

For a few years now, he assisted Mr Alan in investigating paranormal and strange phenomenon. He remembers his first case – meeting Mr Alan and his assistant, Lilly.

'Goodbye to history' he says shaking his head then leaving the office. As he makes his way past the fossils of dinosaurs and other items of historical nature that are kept behind glass cases and cabinets – a woman dressed in a black evening dress and high heels walks up to him. He takes no notice and walks past her.

'Frank Mason?'

They both stop and look at each other. Frank looks the woman up and down. She's rather attractive and has long dark hair that hangs past her shoulders with a fringe.

'Sharon Addy.'

'Great – good name.' He nods then walks away from her. Sharon didn't expect that greeting from him and goes running after him. She follows him out of the building, weaving in and out of people trying to talk to him. He unlocks his car and places his box of possessions in the boot.

'You are Frank Mason, aren't you? – the paranormal investigator?'

'Was, love – I quit,' he says slamming his car boot down. She can tell something is not right with him. A man built up on anger and frustration.

'Why did you quit?'

'Why do you ask?'

'I need your help – it's to do with Faymill Farm.'

'Never heard of it.'

Frank gets into his car to get away from Sharon. He fumbles with his keys trying to get them into the ignition. She pleads with him to hear her

168

out. All she wants is for him to listen to her so she can explain why she's here. He gives in and begins to listen to her tell her story.

'Faymill Farm isn't well known. It's out in the middle of nowhere – no one knows it exists. It's had multiple residents and they've all left. There were rumours of it being haunted.'

Frank sighs – huffs – then takes a deep breath. He stares at her – says nothing, until he gives in and tells her to get in the car and tell him where this place is.

'Mr Mason?' calls, Mr Alan, running up to Frank holding a camera in his hand. 'You forgot this.'

Frank takes the camera and thanks him. He looks at Sharon and asks her if she's getting in the car or not. Mr Alan looks to where Frank is looking.

'Are you okay, Mr Mason?' asks Mr Alan.

'Of course – just going to miss this place.'

'Oh... okay.'

Once Sharon is in the car, Frank drives off.

5

As they drive through what feels like an endless countryside, Sharon explains all the details that Frank needs to know.

'So – they just packed up their things and left without telling anyone?'

Sharon confirms. Frank asks her to tell him more about this haunting she mentioned and how she knows about this. She saw Caroline and her two children, Mike and Paul – they left the farmhouse after experiencing a paranormal event. There was a boy on top of Paul's bed waving his hands in front of his face. His mother saw another figure there – a nurse holding a knife above Mike's bed. She ran over to Mike and pulled him out, just as the knife went down into the bed. She grabbed Paul and ran out of the farmhouse. She never went back there even though their possessions are still there.

Frank takes more of an interest in what she's saying. He asks her about the occupants that stayed there before. Who they were – what they were like? Sharon can't really describe. But there was a woman that stayed there before Caroline moved in with Paul and Mike. She disappeared – no one ever saw her again.

6

The car pulls up outside the farmhouse. Frank and Sharon exit the car. Frank overlooks the farmhouse. Planks of wood cover the windows – the air has a slight stillness about it. No sounds from anywhere. Frank takes his bag of possessions and walks up to the door.

'Is there a key for this place, Sharon?'

'It was left unlocked – there's no need for a key.'

Frank finds it hard to believe. What if someone had come along, walked in and took everything? Sharon says that would be difficult as no one really knows that this place exists. Frank wonders how she knows about it and how the occupants who rented it did. He feels like he's getting himself into a big puzzle that needs solving.

Frank opens the door. It creaks open slowly. The daylight beams into the farmhouse. Frank can see the dust particles within the sun's rays. They walk in – Frank is hit by a musty smell. It's dark inside. He doesn't know where the light switch is – and takes out a mini torch. A beam of light illuminates the room revealing a hallway.

'In front of you is the kitchen – to your right is the living room and the stairs are to your left,' says Sharon.

He shines the torch along the walls until a light switch is revealed. He flicks it – nothing happens. Sharon tells him that the breaker box is outside. Frank asks her if she could see to it while he takes a look around, but she admits she won't know what she's doing and would waste time – she would rather have Frank do it.

It didn't take long for Frank to get the power on – even with Sharon's reluctance to help. After a quarter of an hour Frank takes out his possessions from his bag. He begins by taking a rubber ball and placing it on a coffee table. Sharon was curious why he did that. It was all to do with his tactical experiment as this is what he always does with every paranormal investigation.

Frank begins to take photos of each of the rooms. Shots of the coffee table – pictures and angles of furniture. He uses a Polaroid camera that develops the snapshots. He preferred going old school as using a phone camera never seemed to catch any paranormal entities, regardless of what movies or TV showed.

Sharon is concerned as to why Frank is taking photos.

Once they are developed, he shows her the photos – making their way from room to room. She still doesn't see the point of it. After ten minutes of waiting – they both go around the farmhouse again. Now Sharon understands. She looks at the photo of the rubber ball on the coffee table.

There she sees it. The ball has slightly moved

He had been to lots of places. Not all were genuine hauntings. As it was just the two of them at the farmhouse this was proof that something was here.

They then jump at what sounds like a falling saucepan crashing to the floor from inside the kitchen. Frank's heart is racing. They hear the kitchen door, the squeaking sound of the hinges as it swings open. Frank creeps along the corridor and into the kitchen with Sharon following behind him.

Frank looks around for what made the noise. To his surprise – there was nothing. All the saucepans were hanging up. He begins to check the cupboards thinking something must have shifted. But again… nothing. As he closes a cupboard under the sink and stands from kneeling that's when he sees it.

A shape – in the reflection of the sink tap. It's not Sharon as she is standing by his side.

'Do you see it?' he asks Sharon. She is about to turn around when he tells her not to as she might scare it. He tells her to look closely at the tap.

As she gets nearer to the tap, she sees something. The shape of a small boy.

'I see it,' she whispers, 'what do we do?'

'Stay perfectly still.' As Frank witnesses the boy making his way closer to them. His breathing increases rapidly knowing that it's getting closer, and the hairs on the back of his neck stand up. His eyes widen as he sees the boy's hand reaching out to him from behind.

He can't stay like that any more. He needs to turn around. As the hand is about to touch his shoulder – he spins around… but nothing is there. To Sharon's surprise the boy has gone.

A loud bang comes from upstairs. Sharon and Frank look up at the ceiling. They faintly hear the sound of what could be mistaken for footsteps.

They both make their way up the stairs cautiously. The stairs creak with every footstep that Frank makes.

As they enter the upstairs hallway – they hear a creak from a floorboard outside one of the doors. Sharon hangs back while Frank approaches the door. He places his hand on the cold doorknob. He felt the roughness of small amounts of rust as he turned it to open the door. But it wouldn't open. It was locked.

'You wouldn't happen to know where the key is?'

'No – this door was already locked when Caroline and her kids were living here.'

Frank peers through the keyhole to try and see what's on the other side. It's dimly lit. He can't make out a lot – apart from rays of daylight creeping through ripped curtains. A foul smell creeps through the keyhole into his nostrils. The smell of something rotting.

'Sharon – How do you feel about spending the night in a haunted house?'

The sun set over the countryside. A dark shadow of the night loomed over the area surrounding the farmhouse. As the hours passed through the night, Frank and Sharon had retired to Mike and Paul's bedroom and kept the lights on. Frank sat on Paul's bed while Sharon lay down on Mike's. Sharon had told him the story about what happened to Mike where the boy appeared. But Frank was more concerned about Sharon. She knew where this nurse was going to appear with the knife and deliberately took that bed so Frank wouldn't have to.

He didn't know much about Sharon and began thinking that her life must be a terrible one. Someone without a care in the world – who would throw themselves into danger.

He thought she might be depressed and maybe a little suicidal.

'Are you still awake?' whispers Sharon.

'Yes,' whispers Frank. 'Why are you whispering? – there's been no sign of anything.'

'Maybe it's because we're talking.'

A silence lingers between them. There is no noise – everything including the farmhouse is still. Frank looks over at Sharon.

'I can't sleep with the lights on,' says Sharon, feeling restless. She sits up. 'Why did you keep the lights on?'

'You'll see,' says Frank. 'Why don't you tell me about yourself? – Who are you? Who is Sharon Addy?'

Sharon was an ashamed lady. She had a sister, *Krista*, who was younger, twisted and crazy. Sharon never married as her relationships never lasted long. She was scared of introducing them to Krista who was hell bent on sexually teasing and torturing men.

Krista could never get a boyfriend. Sharon was always the lucky one even though they didn't stay around long.

She was attractive and had a slender figure unlike Krista who was three pounds obese in weight. Some of Sharon's boyfriends gave in and broke her heart, as some were seduced by Krista. She would get them into bed and make them play with her. And once they made her climax she would make sure they never had the pleasure of having sex with anyone for the rest of their remaining life.

Their family were wealthy which gave Krista the incentive to take things to the next level. With such a strong passion for destroying relationships – she opened up a club called *Play 4 Real*, where couples could play their darkest fantasies with singles and other couples.

Sharon was disgusted – as all that club did was destroy every relationship that went in there. Sharon's reputation was cursed with Krista's behaviour as everyone began to think that Sharon was as bad as her.

The one day – to Sharon's surprise – Krista was arrested.

Things had escalated in the club and it was shut down, through a deliberate pregnancy risk challenge. When the police arrived at Krista's home, after reports of people who had visited there and gone missing, the police uncovered the true horror of what she had done.

She was sent to Marwood Asylum – for the criminally insane. Sharon had gone to visit her, with the intention of seeing her one last time.

Sharon talked to her through the cell door. Venting all of her anger and disgust, ashamed that she was her sister.

'I don't have a sister – and I don't ever want to see you again.'

Krista laughed. She didn't care. All her anger had driven her to this as no man would touch her because she was big. This was her way of getting revenge on a shallow world.

Sharon shook her head in disgust and walked away.

'I'm not the worst one in here you know,' said Krista, causing Sharon to stop and listen to what she had to say. 'Patient 100582 – is in a high maximum-security wing. He wants to end it all – not the world – he just wants to destroy something that lives forever and he will succeed in changing the world. I want to be part of that world – so he can be mine, forever.'

'What will he destroy?'

'Love.'

'That's impossible,' said Sharon. 'No one can destroy love.'

'He will – there's a storm coming – love will die when the pink snow falls.'

Sharon could see that Krista was lost – completely crazy with her ramblings. She left the Asylum – then left her home behind and all the people she knew.

She moved about for a time – working here and there. She got close to a man but had to leave him behind as she couldn't accept that she fell in love and was finally happy as the damage from her sister had already been done.

Then one day, as she was travelling, she came across Faymill Farm. The rent was cheap and it was out in the middle of nowhere with not much sign of life or nearby neighbours which was perfect for her as she didn't want to see anybody after what had happened and the bad reputation that her sister gave her.

Frank takes pity on her. Feeling sorry for what she has been through. The things she lost and tells her that she shouldn't be alone – that love can be found anywhere.

'I wish I could believe that – but I think my sister was right – love, is dying.'

'I don't believe that – love can be found anywhere with anyone – I can see that especially after what happened that made me quit.'

'Why were you quitting – investigating hauntings?'

'I lost someone that I loved – in a way she reminds me of you.'

'Then tell me about it – tell me your story.'

It all began on Frank's first day at the natural history museum. He met his boss *Mr Alan*, who left him with his assistant to show him what he would be doing. Her name was *Lilly*. Her mother and father didn't pick that name for her – she picked it herself.

Two weeks passed. Frank and Lilly became close – working together and researching locations that Mr Alan was investigating. Some of the locations were fake but some were genuine hauntings. Working late and things developing, he and Lilly shared their first kiss. They could tell they had feelings for each other.

Weeks soon turned into months. Mr Alan took them with him. Nothing ever happened when Lilly was there. But when it was just Frank and Mr Alan, he witnessed the paranormal and picked up the skills that Mr Alan used.

Franks feelings for Lilly grew stronger and he wanted a relationship with her. But to his surprise she didn't. The thought of it scared her. He couldn't see why as she would never say. She didn't like to talk about her

176

past especially when it came to family.

Then things changed. Mr Alan took Frank and Lilly to Field Towers where a string of murders was taking place and sightings of a ghostly girl had been seen. Once the investigation had been resolved late that night. Frank drove Lilly back to the museum. He wanted to talk to her about why they couldn't be in a relationship. He admitted he loved her. Lilly couldn't say the same, as she was frightened. And then it happened.

As Frank turned a corner – passing fields of the countryside. Someone, ran out into the road. He swerved, hard – causing the car to crash into a tree. Frank had cut his head from hitting it hard on the windscreen. He didn't remember much in detail that night. The last thing he remembered was seeing Lilly's body – her face covered in blood from a wide cut on her forehead.

The person that ran out in the road came up to the car. A teenage boy. They were wearing a grey hoody which was covered in blood. They were holding what looked like a BBQ fork. Frank called out to them for help – but they didn't. Instead they ran away from the incident they caused.

The next thing he knew – he was in hospital, in recovery. The first thing that he asked was where Lilly was and if she was all right. They broke the news to him that her body wasn't there when the ambulance crew arrived and retrieved him.

Over three months had passed and the Police searched the area. Her disappearance made the papers and the news. But her body was never found. She was declared dead. It broke Frank's heart. Working was hard as he was haunted by the memories of Lilly – working in the same office. Remembering how he fell in love with her.

'And that's why you quit? – But doing what you do? Saving lives so people can sleep safely in their beds and not being haunted by bad spirits.'

'It's the only reason why I'm helping you – because you look like the spitting image of Lilly.'

Before Sharon can say anything – the lights in the room begin to flicker on and off. The shutters rattle on the outside. Something begins to bang loudly on the door.

Frank and Sharon jump off the bed and look around the room. To Sharon's horror, spiders and cockroaches come out of the cracks in the floor. They hurry to exit the room. Frank pulls the door open but before they can exit the room the door is pulled back sealing them in. Frank opens the door again and this time they leave.

As they come out into the hallway, they hear the sound of glass smashing from downstairs followed by a child crying.

'The kitchen,' says Sharon.

They hurry downstairs and jump out of their skin as a tree branch bangs and scratches across the window. When they reach the bottom of the stairs the door to the living room slams shut. The kitchen door is already closed. As they approach the door and Frank puts his hand on the doorknob… the noise stops. Silence fills the air. Frank tastes a sour flavour in the air. It causes his mouth to be dry from the dust that floats in the air with a salty aftertaste.

'Do you smell that, Sharon?' says Frank as the smell of perfume enters his nose. He presses his face closer to the door. The smell is a lot stronger. 'It's coming from inside the kitchen.'

Frank opens the door and he and Sharon enter the kitchen. They stop in their tracks as they see a woman standing at the kitchen counter prepping vegetables. She is dressed in a nurse's outfit. The boy then walks past Frank and Sharon. He creeps up behind the nurse and climbs up onto the kitchen counter. He begins to pull faces – waving his hands and sticking his tongue out at her. He knocks a saucepan that's hanging up. It crashes down causing her to jump.

She turns around aggressively holding the knife out at him.

'I will not put up with that behaviour,' shouts the nurse. 'You will listen to your mother.'

'Mother?' says Sharon. The nurse looks at Sharon then blinks out. Frank and Sharon walk around the kitchen wondering where she disappeared to.

'Don't move,' says Sharon. Frank stops in his tracks. A phantom hand rests on his shoulder. 'Do you feel that?'

'I feel the cold – and a slight heaviness – is it her?'

'Yes.' The nurse stands behind Frank. Her other hand reaches for the back of his neck. The hairs stick up as her hand gets closer to him. The boy then runs out of the kitchen; the nurse disappears.

'Come on, Frank – upstairs.'

'What is this? Hide and seek?'

They run up the stairs returning to the children's bedroom. They see someone standing in front of them covered in a white bed sheet. They hear

178

whimpering. Crying. Frank cautiously approaches it. His hand reaches out to grab the bedsheet off of them. But before he can touch it – the bedsheet flops to the floor.

'He's there,' says Sharon, pointing over to the bed. His head buried. His arms round his legs – rocking back and forth. The nurse appears standing over him holding the kitchen knife. She then slashes at the air cutting his arm. He screams out.

'You've been a very naughty boy – you must take your medicine.'

The nurse raises her arm up in the air then swings it down into the boy who blinks out. She looks at the knife she just used – staggers back at realizing what she just did. The knife falls out of her hand and it sticks into the floor as it lands. She then places her hand over her heart – something is wrong. She falls to her knees, then blinks out.

'What did we just see?'

'I think we just saw how they both died,' says Frank. The nurse had anger issues – causing her to kill her son. The shock of the truth caused her to have a heart attack. They both died in the farmhouse and no one knew what really happened. It was why their spirits never moved on.

No one stayed long enough to see the truth. Now they know, the house is no longer haunted. The house is clear.

8

Upon leaving the kids' bedroom. Frank closes the door. 'Thank you – for all the help you gave.'

He closes in for a hug but Sharon steps back. She shakes her head.

'I'm sorry, Frank – I can't do that.'

He is confused. But then something hits him. As he looks closer – keeping his stare on Sharon's eyes. He realizes who she is.

'Lilly?'

She looks at him like she can't keep a secret any longer.

She hangs her head in shame. She couldn't hide the truth from him and explains why she disappeared.

The truth was – Lilly was a name she used to hide her real name which was Sharon. After everything that happened with her sister – she was scared that someone would recognize her, and the hell she had been through would start all over again.

She needed to survive – to get a job and earn money. The natural history museum was the first place she came across and working for Mr Alan being stuck in an office hidden away from the rest of the world made her feel safe. She felt uneasy when she went out with Mr Alan for the first time – being among the public in the daytime just in case anyone recognized her.

Not long after that she was introduced to Frank. He was the first man she felt comfortable with. She didn't know she was going to like him. She never knew she was going to fall in love with him.

The moment in the car where Frank wanted to turn their friendship into a relationship sent Sharon into a state of panic. She didn't know how to respond or what to do.

That's when the crash happened. Seeing Frank injured – she called the ambulance. The second she heard the sirens – she walked away and left him there.

She felt bad. Upset and broken hearted from leaving the man she loved. She was injured too, from a cut on her head and the blood dripping down her face. She needed to find shelter. As she walked across fields of the countryside, she found Faymill Farm.

In her mind – it was the perfect escape, the perfect place to hide. Out in the middle of nowhere. No one would ever find her. And she was right. As the months went on with the police searching for her – she was never found.

'You saved my life – I never ever stopped loving you – and now I know your past – I can save you.'

'You already did – I love you so much for that,' says Sharon, smiling at him. They both lean in for a kiss. As their lips are about to touch. They hear the sound of a door unlocking behind them. Frank spins around to see the door that had the missing key, swing open slowly.

'I thought the haunting had stopped,' Frank says as approaches the door, cautiously. He looks back at Sharon. He can tell she is reluctant to go. 'I'll be right back – see you in a sec.'

9

As he enters the room – he stops in his tracks. He is hit by the foul smell from earlier and the sounds of flies buzzing. The howl of the wind blows the torn curtains and the plaster has peeled off the walls. He looks over to a bed to see a body. Flies are buzzing around the dry blood of a head wound. It's a body of a woman. Sharon's body.

He looks behind himself to look into the hallway.

Sharon is nowhere to be seen. He closes his eyes – upset when he realizes the truth. All those little signs he missed.

It began back at the natural history museum – when he first met Sharon – when she followed him to his car – and Mr Alan passed him his camera and asked if he was okay. He asked him that because he was talking to himself. Other signs were when Sharon was reluctant to help him – backing away when he tried to touch her. When she told him about Caroline and her two boys. She watched what happened to them as a ghost.

He approaches her body – inspecting it closely.

Sharon's hand is holding something. It's a key. The key to the room. It's why he couldn't find the key – she was holding it the entire time. The occupant who lived in Faymill before Caroline and her children moved in – was her all along.

'Goodbye Sharon … my Lilly – I'll see you soon,' says Frank as he leaves the room, pulling the door, closed.

The memories we have for one another last forever in us all. From the good times and everything we have been through. But the love we have for them stays eternal beyond life – after death.

FAMILY

1

We all at one point in our lives hit the struggle of keeping a married life strong.

Neil is sitting at the kitchen table staring into space – silent as anything holding half a mug of warm coffee in his hand. A look of unhappiness mixed with worry fills his face. Is this the last day he remembers his life being? Could tomorrow be the beginning of a different life he would live?

His wife Amy enters the kitchen – early thirties, medium build. Long brown hair tied back. She looks annoyed at him. She doesn't speak a word – then goes over to the coffee maker. Apart from the sound of the boiling water, an awkward silence fills the room between them. Amy looks at the wedding ring on her finger. She begins to think to herself that maybe it was a mistake getting married. Once the coffee is made – she grabs her mug and holds it in her hand.

'Don't worry – I've made my own,' she snaps, hinting.

'What?' says Neil, snapping out of his thoughts – not realizing what she's getting at. Amy explains for years he has always made her a coffee while she got breakfast ready. They were a team. Strongly bonded.

'Have you even thought about our talk?' asks Amy.

Neil takes a deep breath and sighs, then nods acknowledging he has.

'Seven years, Neil – some call it lucky,' says Amy shaking her head. 'It's unlucky for us – all we do is row – and I don't want to live like this any more – do you?'

'No – not really.'

She takes a sip of her coffee, but a small one so it doesn't burn her mouth.

'Then I think we should talk about, divorce.'

Neil closes his eyes. He didn't want to hear that. He tried not to think where the marriage was leading to. He never showed it, but on the inside he was upset – devastated. Amy's eyes begin to tear up. She didn't really want this – but it was the only way to save themselves from constantly rowing.

A bang on the front door distracts them. They look at each other puzzled wondering who it could be as nobody ever called for them. Neil gets up from the table and goes to the front door. Amy is curious and follows him.

The door opens – and to their surprise they see a woman with their back to them.

'Can we help you?' asks Amy.

The woman turns around. She is slim, attractive, in her thirties. She wears black leggings and a green jumper. Her brown hair reaches down to her shoulders – and she holds the handle of a suitcase next to her.

'Hi – I'm Gia – aren't you going to invite me in?' she says, smiling, in a strong foreign accent.

Amy and Neil both look at each other puzzled wondering who this stranger on the doorstep is – who has introduced themselves to their life.

2

We all at one time in our lives hit a crossroads and a struggle to keep a marriage stable. But what happens when a stranger, steps in between a husband and wife. Could they be the answer to their separation – or could they be the one, to save it?

Gia enters the kitchen pulling her suitcase behind her.

She looks up at the ceiling and around the kitchen – smiling – impressed with what she sees.

'You have such a beautiful home – I think I'm going to like it here.'

Amy and Neil look at each other and think, who does this woman thinks she is – just waltzing into their home? Before Gia can say anything else – Amy butts in.

'Wait – what do you mean you think you're going to like it here? This is our home – and why do you have a suitcase with you?'

'Well, for staying over of course – I'm feeling a lot of negative energy.'

Amy begins to get frustrated and angry. She threatens Gia to get out – otherwise she's going to call the police. Neil grabs hold of Amy to calm her down to stop her doing something she would regret.

'Look, lady,' says Neil.

'Gia – please.'

'Look, Gia – why don't you tell me why you're here? – What do you want with us?'

Gia offers to explain everything if they'd both take a seat and keep calm. Amy's attitude hasn't changed – she is still feeling angry, but Neil persuades her to calm down as he wants to hear what she has to say. They all sit round the kitchen table and Gia begins to tell her story.

3

It all began a long time ago – when Gia was a little girl.

Her parents had been happily married for years. Gia was nine when they celebrated their sixteenth wedding anniversary. She was an only child but she loved her life with her family. But weeks after – her mother and father were rowing constantly. This upset Gia as she always retreated to the bedroom and put her hands over her ears to block out the shouting from her parents as it scared her. They soon separated a month after their anniversary. Gia hardly saw her dad as her mother was being a bitch not allowing him to see her just out of spite. Gia could understand the reason why they divorced if they had cheated on each other – but the truth was they just got tired of each other.

Gia felt lonely. Not seeing her dad as he ended up going out with another woman – then her mother hit the bottle hard, preferring to be drunk all the time and paying no attention to her own daughter.

Her school life was just as lonely – she could never connect with anyone or make friends. Until one day a new girl called *Chastity* joined her school. Chastity was in the same boat and never had any school friends. She noticed Gia and took an interest in her. She felt sorry for Gia – what she had been through with her family break up. But at the same time she could easily relate. Chastity told Gia that she used to have a mum and dad, they divorced too. It upset Chastity a lot and she ended up running away.

Homeless and alone – she was approached by a man called Jin. He helped her get some food and drink. With nowhere to stay – he offered her to come back with him to his wife, son and daughter. There she would be safe, loved and cared for. Chastity had doubts – she was cautious as this man could be anyone – a possible psycho or molester. But with no one else to turn to she accepted his offer, and she was right to do so. He was a man of his word and she met the family. They accepted her as one of their own and showed more tender loving care than her own family.

Gia was intrigued – she always wished that she could have the love of a family once again. Chastity suggested that she should go with her, so she could meet them. Gia liked this very much – she jumped at the chance. The day came and this was where her life changed – for the better.

Gia and Chastity stood in an oriental type of dining room. Red, yellow and black oriental coloured symbols are all around the room – on the walls and furniture. They stand in front of an oriental half caste man, woman, girl and boy.

'Welcome – you must be Gia – Chastity has told us about you,' says Jin, who smiles kindly at her. Gia goes all shy.

'Approach, girl'

Gia approaches the Woman.

'Do not be afraid, child – my name is Mai – this is my husband Jin, our son Bence and daughter Ai.'

Gia smiles at Mai. She's beautiful. A slender figure, with oriental features – long dark hair past her shoulders, red lips and a small mole on her left cheek. Mai holds her arms out and gives Gia a hug. Gia closes her eyes and smiles. She feels happy.

4

Neil and Amy continue to listen to Gia tell her story. Gia explains that she lived and grew up with Jin and his family for years. Jin had a particular way of life that he liked to live. Jin was just like Chastity and Gia – he came from a broken family as did Mai. They were there for each other which helped them through their hard times. A year after they met, they married – had two children and vowed that their children would never know what it's like to have a broken family.

One day Jin and Mai took their children to the park and saw a married couple rowing in front of their child. Their child was crying and screaming. The married couple were too into their row to even stop and tend to their child. This broke Mai and Jin as they remembered what it was like when they were younger. Mai took the children home while Jin went over to the couple to intervene. The distraction of this stranger made the couple stop rowing with each other and take out their anger on him. This didn't bother Jin – as, surprisingly, he had a way of talking to them. He told them about his broken family – what it was like to witness his mother and father separate. This made them realize what they could be doing to their child. Jin invited them round for dinner to meet his wife and children. They accepted and became good friends.

'Well, that's an interesting story, Gia – but what has this got to do with us?'

'Yes,' says Amy. 'What has this got to do with us? – How did you find us?'

Gia explains that she saw them in town. She was handing out leaflets to, *The Family Home*. That's what Jin called it. The couples he's helped have joined their cause, become their lookouts to see couples struggling with their marriages – handing out leaflets and approaching them to help them. Gia left her post – she began to follow them to try and introduce herself to them, but she was stopped when she bumped into a man outside *Kays Coffee Shop*.

He had a name tag that read, *Zac, Vision Electrics – I.T Assistant*. Zac

190

noticed Gia following Neil and Amy – he was curious why she was. Gia asked him if he knew them. He confirmed he did as Neil works at the same company he does.

'Really?' she asks. 'Do you know where they live?'

Neil could understand how she found them. Amy looks annoyed that Zac gave them their address.

'So – now you know – what do you think? – Let me stay with you and help regain that love back in your life.'

Neil and Amy look at each other. They think the same thing.

'Can you give us a minute?' asks Amy.

'Of course.'

Neil and Amy leave the room and retreat to the hallway. Neil is curious to know what Amy thinks. She is unsure what to think – having this stranger turn up on their doorstep trying to fix their marriage to stop them divorcing. She thinks it's a kind offer – and she seems nice, doing it for a nice cause after she told them her story – but is she someone they can really trust? Neil agreed and shared her caution, but at the same time he thought the help was right in front of them and they should take it – because if they didn't, then maybe they wouldn't be able to find a solution to their problem.

Amy quietly nodded. She knew Neil was right in what he said. She takes a deep breath before returning to Gia.

'Okay – you can stay and help us? But how much is this going to cost us?'

'Nothing – just allowing me to stay and help is payment enough.'

Neil looks surprised but at the same time is impressed that it's not going to cost them any money, like it would if they had gone to a marriage counsellor. They both sit down at the table again.

'So – where do we begin?' asks Amy. 'Your wedding album – show me.'

Neil leaves to fetch the wedding album. Amy is curious at why Gia is starting with it. Gia explains that it will show those moments of true love as a wedding is a special day where two hearts are joined and eternal love between each other is born. Neil returns holding their wedding album.

Gia holds the album in her hands. A slight dust covers the top and the side of the album. She could tell it hasn't been looked at for a long time. The front of the cover had a picture of Neil and Amy – dressed in their wedding attire – standing on a bridge over a lake somewhere in the countryside. They had chosen a wedding venue instead of a traditional church. Amy looked stunning in her dress. Neil was dressed in a black suit with a grey waistcoat and white shirt underneath. Gia raised a smile when she saw how handsome he looked. She flicks through the pages of their album – she sees how much love there is between the two of them. She can't help but wonder why they could ever fall out of love with each other.

When she reached the end of the wedding album, she passed it back to Amy.

'There is so much love in those pictures. Tell me – what problems have you been facing?'

Amy and Neil confirm that it's all down to work. Neil works during the day and Amy works nights at Towns-end's airport. They hardly see each other with the jobs they do. They feel like they've grown apart and their marriage is only kept through talking to each other over their phones.

Most of the time they feel like they're single again and aren't happy.

'What about sex?' asks Gia. 'When was the last time you made love to each other?'

They both go quiet – like they're both embarrassed to talk about that sort of thing with her. Amy is uncomfortable to talk about their sex life – to her, Gia was still a stranger.

'If you want to discover what the problem is with your marriage – we have to look at every aspect,' says Gia, putting her hands together, ready for them to start talking.

Amy tells Gia that it has been four months since she and Neil last had sex. Their sex life had always been great but just out of the blue it all seemed to stop. Their work patterns were completely out of sync. When one finished work – the other would be starting work. It was like a single life to them. When they did see each other – they were too tired to go out or do anything together. They spent most of their time catching up on sleep. The last time they attempted – it was a complete failure. They began kissing and teasing each other but had no passionate feeling as their minds weren't in it – they were thinking too much about work and the things they've still got to do. Gia doesn't judge them – she understands that all this is to do with sexual frustration which is the reason they have rowed – and doubted their marriage.

'You two need to release this tension – once you do that, you'll see that the love you have for each other is still there – and there is no time like the present.'

Amy feels awkward at what Gia is suggesting – that they should go upstairs and have sex right now. They would be upstairs doing it and Gia would be downstairs listening. The thought of that was just creepy – but before Amy could look at Neil – he had already grabbed hold of her hand and pulled away from the kitchen. Gia sits there all alone – smiling to herself as she hears them go upstairs, thinking how easy that was.

Gia stands up. She takes her trousers off followed by her top until she is standing in the kitchen in her bra and knickers. She puts her hands on her hips looking down and admiring her slender figure.

5

Neil and Amy enter their bedroom. She is already caught up in Neil's passionate kissing. She reaches to close the bedroom door for privacy but Neil just grabs hold of her and they end up on the bed. He passionately kisses Amy's neck – then kisses her under her chin. She closes her eyes, her breathing increasing as she becomes turned on.

She grabs hold of him – kissing him back. As she kisses him, she takes off his t-shirt. Neil does the same by taking Amy's top off, exposing her bra. But their attention is soon distracted by something moving about the bed. They turn to see Gia getting under the bed sheets. She smiles at them while lying there in her green bra and knickers.

'What the hell are you doing?' screams Amy at Gia's strange behaviour. 'Get out of our bed!'

Gia doesn't understand what the problem is. She thinks that it's completely innocent and she is only trying to help them. Amy explodes – screaming at Gia making it clear that they didn't want a threesome. Gia sits up snapping back that it was never her intention to join in with them.

She only observes their love making to understand their love connection.

'I don't care how you see it – don't you know how creepy that is? – I want you out of our home and out of our life.'

'I think you'd better go, Gia,' says Neil who is calmer than Amy.

Gia swallows hard. The feeling that you get when you've done something wrong. With all the couples she's helped over the years – she has never come across a couple like that who have told her to go away. She doesn't speak a word, instead, she just leaves the room closing the door behind her. Amy sits on the bed, stunned by Gia's behaviour. Neil sits next to her and puts his arm around her.

'Of all the people I have met in my life – I have never met anyone that has creeped me out as much as her.'

He comforts her – telling her that Gia is gone now. It's just the two of them – no strangers to interfere with their life. She looks at him, feeling his warm heart of consideration like she used to years ago. He kisses her and they lay back on the bed.

6

Minutes later they lie on the bed – quilt over them, sweating and out of breath.

'Wow,' says Amy trying to catch her breath. 'Where did that come from?'

'Who cares? – Just be glad it did.'

Amy cuddles up to Neil. They both admit that their love is still there and they should never be in any doubt that their marriage is nearing its end.

A thought then enters Amy's head causing her to sit up in bed. Neil wonders what's wrong. She remembers Gia and thinks that she is still here as she never heard the door go. To put her mind at ease they leave the bedroom and make their way downstairs.

7

The living room and kitchen are empty. There is no sign of Gia or her suitcase. She has left their home. Amy is relieved but she notices something that has been left on the kitchen table. It's a business card. She picks it up and reads: *Gia Patterson – The Family Home*.

Even after everything, Amy feels that maybe they should visit there. After all Gia's advice – it helped them mend their marriage. Neil is curious as to what this Family Home is after Gia told her story to them about it. They both agree they should pay it a visit.

8

The next day, Neil drove to the family home. He pulled up to a pair of big iron gates. Through the railings of the gates both he and Amy saw the scale of the house. It looked more like a spa facility. People were walking around dressed in casual clothes not paying any attention to the car that's pulled up at the gates.

'They look a bit weird,' says Amy observing them from the passenger window. The iron gates then open. Neil is surprised as no one has greeted him or spoken to him.

Cautiously he drives into the grounds until he stops outside the family home. Neil and Amy get out of the car – the doors open and Gia stands there waiting for them.

'You came – you saw my card – I'd hoped you would come to see us – please, come in.'

9

Amy couldn't believe the grand scale of the main hall of the house. She stands in awe looking up at the staircases to the left and to the right of them leading up to a balcony that overlooks the hall.

'Follow me – I'll take you to meet Jin.'

They follow Gia to the back of the house through a pair of doors under the balcony stairs. They stand in the dining room which Gia described in her story – everything she had told them was true to its oriental look, to Jin, his wife son and daughter that sat down on a low sofa. Mai smiles at Amy.

'Approach,' says Mai.

'You must be Neil and Amy – Gia has told us all about you – please, sit down,' insists Jin.

As they sit down, Amy is too quick for anyone else to speak and apologizes to them for how they treated Gia. She overreacted over Gia's behaviour. Mai understands as some would look at it as a creepy thing to do and a lot would be cautious having a stranger turn up to help them. But it worked; Gia was able to fix their marriage.

Jin looked at Gia proudly. She was always his favourite girl ever since Chastity had left and joined another cause.

She had gone to a village where a woman called Regina was in charge of their community and had big plans for the entire world – but Jin saw these plans as pure terror plunging the world into a hell no one could escape from.

Neil and Amy were both puzzled as to what Jin was on about – all he could say was that it's going to happen when it begins to snow.

'You must be hungry – why don't you both look around this place – you can stay here – get involved with all the ones we have helped,' Mai says urging them to do so. Amy thinks it's a kind offer but they will be heading back home.

Mai looks disappointed while Jin looks rather offended. Amy and Neil get up to leave – thanking them again one more time. Jin shakes his head at Gia – she swallows hard like she's done a terrible thing, feeling bad about herself.

10

When Neil and Amy get outside, they see crowds of people walking back and forth. They are in their way of getting back to their car. They hold each other's hands – not speaking a word. Neil notices something odd about them. They all have scars at the left and right side of their forehead like something has banged into their skull.

They weave in and out of the people trying to get down the steps to their car. As they get to the bottom, Neil gets into the car – he fumbles about with the keys trying to start it in a hurry. He notices that Amy isn't with him. He sees her staring at a bench with a puzzled look on her face. The crowds of people begin to come down the stairs getting closer to her.

'Get in – hurry,' shouts Neil as he panics for Amy's safety. She gets into the car, closing the door. Neil speeds off as the crowd gets closer.

'Why didn't you get in the car?'

'That bench had a plaque on it – it was a dedication.'

'To who?'

'To love.'

Neil looks at her puzzled at what that could mean. 'Look out,' she screams. Neil slams his foot on the brakes stopping in front of more crowds of people standing at the gate. They leave the car. Looking around as both crowds of people close in on them.

A red headed woman pushes her way through the crowd. She has the same marks as everyone else on her head but she acts normal. She grabs hold of Amy.

'You should never have come here – you'll never leave you should have got out.'

She lets go of Amy then blends back into the crowd. Jin and Mai stand at the top of the steps. They nod to the crowd which begins to close in on Neil and Amy.

11

Three months have passed since then. Life continued the way they've always known it for Jin and Mai. They sit at the dining table finishing their lunch. Gia collects the dishes and takes them out of the room. A blank expression fills her face with two scar marks on her forehead. The lobotomy that every other couple had received that had visited the family home after being helped by Jin's people. It was Jin's way of keeping people's love together forever – they could never fight, never row, never split up from one another. Married and loving each other forever.

12

At the front of the house – on the bench dedicated to love – sit Neil and Amy in a lobotomized state. Amy's right hand in Neil's while her left-hand rests on her pregnant belly.

We all don't want to see love fall apart – to fight to keep the trials – the tribulations and the challenges that are presented to us from stopping us end a love we once knew. But the only things that will stop this from happening no matter how far we go – are the things we do for love.

NINE-MONTHS

1

Will I ever feel better? Kay hangs her head over the toilet bowl as she vomits. She feels nauseous – like she is coming down with an illness. Someone knocks on the bathroom door.

'Sis – it's Sandra – are you okay in there?' calls Sandra on the other side of the door. Kay looks up from the toilet bowl.

'I'm okay – I'll be right out.'

Kay listens to Sandra leave. How did she ever get to this? Her stomach churns, feeling the sick build up in the back of her throat. She vomits again.

2

Sandra sits at the kitchen table eating her bowl of cereal. She looks around the kitchen – washing up has started to pile up. She sighs, knowing that she will end up doing it again. Kay didn't do it very often – that's one thing about her sister that annoyed her. Anything she didn't like doing she would leave it to Sandra, ever since they were kids.

She continues to look round the kitchen and sees herself in the ceiling mirror in the corner. A woman who has just turned forty stares back at her. Her hair a blonde short bob. Her eyes looking heavy and tired. As she takes another bite of cereal – she ends up missing her mouth, and the cereal ends up landing on the blue and white checked table cloth. She is then distracted by Kay, not looking her best as she enters.

'Jesus – you look like hell.'

'I feel like hell.'

'Night out on the drink again with Billy?'

'No – just another row.'

Sandra shakes her head. She doesn't understand what Kay sees in him. She suspects that Billy is cheating on her – as he looks the type. Kay gets annoyed, telling her that she can't assume things about someone you don't know.

'Look – Kay – I have to be honest with you – there's something about him I just don't like – call it a sister's gut feeling.'

'Please don't mention guts,' says Kay as she puts her hand over her mouth.

Kay sits down at the table. She would prefer not to talk about Billy – she would rather find out what's wrong with her. She feels nauseous and sick but she doesn't feel like she's got any symptoms of a cold or the flu. Sandra looks worried – she's realized what it could be.

'Have you – taken a pregnancy test?'

'No,' says Kay realizing what Sandra is getting at. Kay hurries back to the bathroom. Sandra puts down her spoon. She is worried that Kay is pregnant with Billy's child.

That's the last thing she wants for Kay – to be tied down with a guy who treats her like rubbish.

As the minutes pass by – Sandra waits with anticipation and worry. Eventually, Kay emerges holding a pregnancy test in her hand. A look of horror fills her face.

'I'm pregnant.'

Sandra closes her eyes. An angry look fills her face.

She shakes her head in disgust.

'What are you going to do? – Are you going to keep it?'

Kay is shocked at her sister for even thinking that she would get rid of the baby. She makes it clear that she's going to do the right thing and tell Billy. This happening to her maybe the best thing to bring them closer in their relationship and make Billy realize that there is more to life than just going out drinking at his local bar.

3

The black eight ball falls down in the top corner pocket of the pool table in the bar.

'Yeah – beat that,' yells Billy as he throws the pool cue down on the table. He grabs his beer which is half full – and downs the drink without taking a breath. His opponent, *Mason*, notices Kay enter the bar looking around for him.

'Billy,' he says, pointing over to Kay. Billy turns around to see Kay. He doesn't look impressed to see her as she walks up to him.

'Billy – can we talk – privately?'

'We can talk right here,' says Billy as he sets up the pool table for another game. Mason looks at Kay – sees that she looks annoyed and feels sorry for her as he didn't agree with the way that Billy treated her. Billy wasn't Mason's best friend, he was just someone he knew that came into the bar on a regular basis.

'Billy,' Kay raises her voice. 'This is important.'

'Well, say what you've got to say – Mason won't mind.'

She looks at Mason, he can tell she feels uncomfortable and would rather be somewhere private to talk.

'I'm pregnant.'

Billy doesn't look at Kay, instead he concentrates on the pool table.

'Did you hear what I said – I'm pregnant – and you're the father.' He grabs his cue and aims it at the white ball. 'BILLY!'

'WHAT!' he yells. Everyone in the bar looks in their direction. 'So what – you're pregnant – what are you going to do about it?'

Mason can tell that Kay is getting upset. Her eyes build up with tears. She blinks and a tear runs down her face. She tells him that he should have said what are we going to do about it? He can't hide from this – he is a father and she is going to need him to bring the baby up with her – just like a family would do. She yells at him, telling him that he should've been more careful and used protection if he didn't want to be a father. Kay was on the pill, but nothing is 100% guaranteed to be safe.

'No – you should've been more careful and made sure you couldn't have children.'

Mason bangs his beer down on the bar. He glares at Billy. Kay doesn't say anything – instead she leaves the bar crying her eyes out. Mason goes up to Billy – then punches him in the face. Billy falls to the floor, looking up, stunned at what Mason just did.

'You lost her – your child – and me – I don't want to know you if you treat women like this.'

Mason walks away and leaves the bar. Billy stays on the floor. Checking his face over. He looks at his hand to see blood from his split lip.

4

Kay walks through the door. Walking along the hallway, the door to Sandra's bedroom opens and she steps out to see her sister. She can tell things didn't go well. Kay had been crying as her eyes are red and puffed up through tears. She opens her arms and gives Kay her hug.

'I'm on my own – I'm going to be a single mother.' She breaks with a crack in her voice. Sandra holds Kay tightly.

'You're not alone you've got me to help you,' says Sandra. 'And there are millions of women who are single mothers – they have so much strength and love in their hearts – and so have you – you can do this.'

5

The thought of spending a life alone affects us all.

Could having a child fill that loneliness – or could it create a love we didn't realize was to come?

A week had passed since Kay had found out that she was pregnant. She stood in front of the mirror every morning – regularly checking her belly to see if and when it began changing shape.

'Kay – can you come here, please – I need to talk to you,' calls Sandra.

She leaves the bedroom and makes her way to the kitchen. As she enters she sees Sandra sitting at the table with a laptop open in front of her.

'What is it?

'Will you just sit down, please?' says Sandra smiling and excited. Kay sits down, curious at why she is smiling. 'Okay – please don't hate me for this – but you know when you said you're not alone in your pregnancy – well I was right because there is someone that is going to be there for you just like I am.'

Sandra turns the laptop around. Kay looks at the screen. It shows a dating site – for pregnant single mothers. She's not impressed. She couldn't believe that her sister signed her up for a dating site without even talking to her about it.

'Look Kay – you deserve someone good in your life – after all what's happened with Billy.'

'You mean someone you approve of?'

'I was only trying to help you – besides one guy has already contacted you – arrange to see him or just tell him you're not interested and shut your profile down.'

Sandra is annoyed and storms out of the room. Kay goes onto her account on the laptop looking for a way to close her account down. Once she finds her settings – the arrow hovers over *Deactivate Account*. But she finds that she can't do it. The curiosity is getting the better of her; who could've contacted her inbox? She cancels the settings and takes a look at the message waiting for her.

Hi Kay – I came across your profile and you sound like a pretty interesting person, so I thought I would message you. Have you read the novel of Residents of War: Patriots*? I noticed on your profile you like the TV series.*

What others books and TV do you like? Regards, Alex.

Kay looks at his profile more in depth. His profile picture shows him smartly dressed with a striped white shirt and grey trousers. She raises an eyebrow and a smile. She returns to her messages and begins writing a reply to him.

Hi Alex – nice to hear from you. I haven't read the books of Residents of War *– I just watch the TV series. Are they better? I am currently reading,* His Last Story*, that romance story with science fiction elements. It's really good – have you read it? I recommend it. I've taken a look at your profile and I'd like to know more about you.*

Kay dropped her phone number into the message and then played the waiting game.

It was about midday before she heard anything. They swapped messages regarding how their days were. Alex didn't wait around as he admitted he preferred to talk on the phone and wanted to hear what Kay sounded like.

As they spoke on the phone – hearing their voices for the first time – they both agreed that they liked the way each other sounded. Hearing Kay's soft voice, made Alex felt relaxed. Kay felt Alex sounded like an adult – not a tough guy who wanted to get noticed.

Kay talked about work – what Alex did for a living – even though it was already on his profile. Alex worked in finance – the accounts department at Vision Electrics. He had been there two years after working at CL Petra. He had swapped one accounts department for another, but this one paid better than he was getting.

Kay worked in admin at *Deluxe waters*. Inputting data into the database, and chasing up customers. It wasn't a great job and the money was minimum rate but she felt relaxed.

They spent a good forty minutes talking to each other until Alex told her he had to get back to work as his lunch hour had finished.

'Oh – that's a shame,' said Kay, sounding disappointed as she got engrossed talking to him and finding out more about him. 'Say – I know it's really quick but how would you like to go out for dinner tonight? On a first date?'

'I'd love to.'

'Great – I'll message you a place and what time to meet.'

'I look forward to it – I've got to go – I'll see you later, have a good afternoon – bye.'

'You too – bye.'

Kay smiles to herself – feeling and looking a lot happier.

'Now was that a waste of time trying to help you?' says Sandra, looking smug that she did the right thing for Kay.

All Kay can do is smile back and not speak a word.

6

Alex puts the phone down on his desk, smiling to himself.

'Going on a date tonight?'

Alex looks up at the voice that was talking to him.

Across from his desk sits Richie James, his boss.

'Yes as a matter of fact – she sounds amazing – I'm looking forward to meeting her.'

'Well, isn't that nice,' says Richie. 'Just don't mess this one up – after what happened with the last one – just be honest – no secrets.'

'I won't make that same mistake – besides how are things with you and Ana? I'm not like the others in this office that are going to judge you.'

'Things are good – really good – sometimes things are a bit difficult as it plays on my mind – she's a person just like the rest of us – not many people get what transsexual pre-ops go through.'

Richie explains that it was awkward when they first tried to have sex. Considering she still had her manhood. He wasn't concentrating on that. At first she expected him to but she realized how difficult it was. He confessed that he loves her dearly and doesn't want to be apart from her.

Alex is curious to know if he ever wanted children as it's not like she's going to get pregnant. It didn't bother Richie – he knew he always wanted kids, but he and Ana had already talked about the idea of adopting as she had the same ambition and wanted to be a parent.

'Do you see yourself marrying her?'

'My heart and love for her is going that way – yes.'

Richie looks over to Zac – one of his younger employees. He goes over to him wondering what he's doing. He discovers that he's surfing the internet – on a website called *Life-Halfway*.

'Get back to work, Zac – your lunch is over – you can do this in your own time.'

7

The ambience of piano music plays in the restaurant. Kay and Alex sit in candlelight. Alex looks around at his surroundings. The restaurant is an old farmhouse. Old wooden beams go across the ceiling covered by a straw roof. Wooden chairs and tables with couples and families eating their meals.

'So what do you think of it? – I've been coming here since I was a kid with my sister and mum and dad – it's always been my favourite restaurant – trying others – I've never really been interested in.'

'I like it – it's cozy,' says Alex, drinking a glass of orange juice.

'You don't drink?' she asks.

He puts his glass down. Looking a bit uncomfortable.

She wonders if she said something wrong.

'Kay – I like you – my boss said that I should be honest with you – but I'm scared that this could change things.'

She looks worried, and a bit cautious of what he is about to tell her. Multiple thoughts began to go round her head. Was he going to be another Billy? Just someone that wastes her time?

Alex begins his story. He admits he used to be a drinker. Going out regularly with his close friend, Nelson, to the local nightclub *Ret-Row*. A club for all ages. In the daytime they hosted kids' parties and events. At night the whole place come alive with a mixture of music from the 1940s up to present day. It was something for everyone for all ages. Even people in their sixties came for a night out – which gave it its popularity.

But one night, someone changed his life. Nelson had left the club early. He wasn't feeling well. Alex stayed on for half an hour to finish his drink and check out the local ladies. He tried striking up a conversation with them but they were snobbish towards him. As he left he bumped into a man who was wearing a three quarter length black winter coat and trilby hat. He reminded him of what an old soldier would look like.

The man takes hold of Alex's arm, stopping him from leaving.

'I know you're going to need this,' says the man, placing a business card in Alex's hand then walking away. Alex is left confused as to what that was about. He inspects the business card advertising an escort service called *ProsEscort* at surprisingly cheap rates. He looks at the website address and raises a smile.

When he got home – he wasted no time and within minutes he was surfing the website. He couldn't believe what he saw. Loads of beautiful women that looked better than the ones that he had seen in the night club. There was one that stood out that took his interest. Her name was Mother Sunshine. He read what kind of service she gave – £100 for an hour. To him it was a bargain.

He arranged to meet her at her little flat. It was a cozy little place. Quite homely. She gave him the girlfriend experience which is what was rated the best by others on her profile – and to him they were right. He saw her more regularly – enjoying every moment with her – until it all went bad.

He was introduced to Nelson's girlfriend, Mary, which turned out to be Mother Sunshine. Nelson was broken to discover the truth and what made things worse she ended up being pregnant. Nelson ran away from his life after that and never spoke to either of them again. Alex knew that the baby was Nelson's as when he had himself checked at the doctors he discovered that he couldn't have children.

He made a decision after losing contact with both Nelson and Mary that he would never touch alcohol again. He went to therapy to make himself better than the mess he had become.

Kay just stares at him – not knowing what to say to that. Alex feels uncomfortable and suggests that he should leave. As he gets up – Kay grabs hold of his hand.

'Wait.' She pulls him to sit back down. 'Stay.'
Kay understands why he joined the dating site. She feels sorry for him as it isn't easy coming to terms with the thought that you're never going to have children.

'You must think I'm disgusting though – about my past.'

She holds his hand. She doesn't agree with what he did. But she's proud of him. It's refreshing to know someone that can admit his mistakes and has the courage to turn his life around.

She admits that she's not perfect. Especially with her life choices. She chose the wrong man to be with – someone who treated her terribly. She got pregnant and then ditched to be a single mother as he didn't want a child.

'Well, I do – that's why I'm here. And before you ask – I don't care who the father was – I just care about loving the child just like his mother will.'

She squeezes his hand tightly. A big smile fills her face as his words touched her heart.

8

The days turned into weeks as they flew by for Kay and Alex. They went out for more dates, shared their first kiss and their relationship grew stronger. Alex was introduced to Sandra who took a shining to him straight away. This made Kay feel really good after her disliking to Billy. She felt like she was treading on eggshells every time he was brought up around Sandra.

The weeks turned into months. Kay stood in front of the mirror checking her belly. Her baby bump was showing.

Alex was on his lunch break at work. Slouched back in his chair – his feet up on the desk. He was reading *Pregnancy for Men: The expectant dad's guide to the whole nine months.*

9

Kay lies back on a couch. She lowers her trousers to her hips and raises her top to her chest. The ultrasound gel is applied on her tummy and tissue paper is tucked around her clothing to protect it from the gel. With the gel making sure the probe makes good contact with the skin – the ultrasound passes the probe over her skin while keeping eye on the monitor.

A black and white image of a baby soon appears on the ultrasound screen. Kay smiles at seeing her baby. She reaches out for Alex's hand. He is lost for words. All he can do is smile.

'Can we have a picture?' asks Kay.

'Of course you can.'

10

Kay takes a pickle out of the pickle jar and bites into it.

Sandra sits at the kitchen table watching her as she eats one after the other.

'I thought you hated pickles.'

'I'm craving pickles – pickles, crisps and chocolate… all together.'

Gross – thought Sandra as Kay could tell by the expression on her face.

'You are so different now – so much happier – glowing even.'

'Glowing and fat – while wearing pregnancy pants.'

Sandra asks after Alex – to see how he's coping with all of this. Kay couldn't find any faults. To her, Alex, was really supportive and as excited as she was.

'Well, that's how a father should be.'

11

Alex and Kay sit among other pregnant woman and their partners. Alex holds Kay's hand and listens to what topics are involved – from health in pregnancy to the exercises to keep fit and active during. Labour in birth and caring for the baby, including feeding. There was lots to take in.

Later that afternoon – they went to the park and sat on a bench near the lake. Kay rests her head on Alex's shoulder while he has his arm around her.

'My mind is going a mile a minute – I never realized there was so much to keep a track of.'

'No one does, Kay, until it happens to them.'

She looks up at him and kisses him. She sits up and wraps her arms around him kissing him more.

'You know – we haven't actually done it yet,' she says kissing him all over his face.

'Are you just wanting to because you're hormonal?'

'Ah ha,' says Kay, winking at him.

12

They both lay back on Kay's bed. Hot, sweaty and out of breath.

'Wow – that was different.'

'Yeah,' says Alex trying to catch his breath. They lie on their side facing each other. Alex's hand under her hip while his other hand is on her pregnant belly. They gaze into each other's eyes. They were falling in love with each other. Alex knew what he wanted to do.

'Ooh,' he says as he moves his hand away from her belly.

'You felt it move?'

'Yes.' He smiles.

'Do you want to go again?' she says kissing him.

13

Time flew so fast. They both worked on the spare room for the baby. Alex set up the cot and helped Kay paint the room and when the ninth month came around they were more than prepared. Alex had spent a lot of time finding the best and fastest route to the hospital for when it was time for the baby to come.

Kay sat on the couch watching boring daytime TV. Her eyes were heavy through tiredness. Her hands rested on her belly. She was controlling her breathing through slight discomfort.

Meanwhile in the kitchen, Alex sat at the table with a small box open. Sandra entered the kitchen curious at what he was holding.

'Oh my god,' she says, startling Alex who snaps the box closed. 'Was that an engagement ring? Are you going to propose?' Alex puts his finger to his mouth urging Sandra to keep her excited voice down. He tells Sandra that it's been on his mind for a long time – but he was scared that it wasn't the right time to ask her.

'You really love her don't you?'

'I've never felt this way about anyone before.'

She takes hold of Alex's hand. 'I will be so proud to have you as my brother in law.'

'Alex – Sandra,' calls Kay.

They both hurry to Kay. A puddle of water is on the floor.

'My waters just broke.'

14

Alex opens up his car quickly – with Kay's bag in hand which he puts in the boot. Sandra helps Kay to Alex's car and helps her get in the back.

Further away. A truck pulls up. Billy watches them from a distance. He gets Alex in his sights and shakes his head looking angry. As Alex drives off – Billy puts his truck in gear and follows them.

15

Kay sits up in the hospital bed. Supporting her baby in her arms. Her forehead sweaty – looking and feeling tired. She smiles at the baby boy she gave birth to.

'Look at him,' says Alex, smiling. 'You're a Mummy – you've done it.'

Kay holds Alex's hand tightly. 'We've done it.'

Alex kisses her hand. He looks at Sandra – then looks back at Kay, fumbling in his pockets for the engagement ring. But before he can take it out – they are interrupted by Billy entering the room.

'Kay.'

'What the hell are you doing here?' says Sandra, furious at the sight of him.

'Billy – what are you…?'

'I need to talk to you – about us – about our son.'

Sandra looks at Kay who nods at her. She shakes her head wondering what Kay is thinking for giving Billy a chance to talk after everything that's happened.

Billy sits next to Kay who asks where he's been for the last nine months as there was no sign of him. He explains after his disgraceful behaviour in the bar his friend, Mason punched him in the face. Mason wanted nothing to do with him afterwards which made him realize that he needed to sort his life out. So he went to therapy – stopped drinking – stopped being so aggressive and selfish. He knew he had a baby and wanted to be part of its life – so he can show his baby not to make the same mistakes he did.

Kay didn't know what to do. She was stuck in a dilemma. To choose a man she had strong feelings for over the father of her child.

'Oh come on – you actually believe all that?'

Lots of things went through Alex's mind, but there was only one thing he could focus on – and that was to do the right thing. They don't notice him sneaking away as they are caught up in Sandra's argument.

'Alex has supported you through all of this – are you really going to choose Billy over him?'

'You don't think I know that. I owe it to Billy – he's the Father of my child.'

She then notices that Alex is gone. Now she feels worse, trapped – with things left unsolved without him.

16

Alex slams the driver door shut. Turns the key to the ignition and rests his hands on the steering wheel and foot on the pedal. His eyes fill with tears and his heart is breaking for leaving Kay after all they've been through. But with the Father back on the scene – it's the best thing for the child. He takes out the engagement ring from his pocket – opens the driver window and drops it.

As he closes the window – he takes the handbrake off and pulls away. Sandra comes running out to see Alex's car.

'Alex! – Alex!' she screams. But she is too late. As she is about to return to Kay, she spots the engagement ring on the ground. She picks it up and holds it in her hand.

We all have the capacity to do the right thing – to make the ultimate sacrifice. With the choices we make for ourselves – it can show people who we really are. From the goodness in our soul – and the love within our hearts.

RANCH

1

All he wanted was a better life. As the sun began to set on a long and winding road surrounded by fields of long blades of grass. Zac, twenty-five, walks along the side of the road – headphones in his ears listening to rock music – dressed in a grey t-shirt, blue jeans and teal coloured trainers. A backpack hangs over his shoulder – and a slight sweat is on his forehead from the heat of the sun. He takes out a bottle of water from his backpack – takes a mouthful – then returns the water to his bag.

He stands at the side of the road looking to the left and right of him. He sees no traffic about. He takes his phone out of his jeans and brings up the Maps app. He looks across the field in front of him to the distance beyond. He squints and thinks he sees his destination – a ranch. He is roughly ten minutes away. He looks both ways again then crosses the road and walks across the field. He thinks that taking a shortcut will be better than following the road. He just wants to get there quicker.

As Zac walks onwards he thinks about his life – thinks how he ended up here of all places. His life was simple – but others could easily see it as boring.

When Zac was in his last year at school – he and his best friend, Michael, met up every weekend at Michael's house, went to the town, got Fish and Chips – went to the cinema or played video games. They both left school and kept up the same tradition – but things began to change as Michael wanted to do new fresh things. Zac was stuck in a rut – in a bubble in his comfort zone which caused him and Michael to drift apart, where Michael made other friends and hung out with them more.

He spent nearly a whole year on his own – playing video games and going for walks to reflect on his life as he didn't really do anything else. He went to college, improved on his IT skills and got a job in an office as an IT assistant for Vision Electrics, but he never enjoyed it. He struggled to connect and make friends with his work colleagues as they judged his life and found it boring. Even his boss, *Richie James*, he couldn't get on with. He tried to do everything right but Richie seemed a stubborn man – always expecting everyone that works under him to know what they're doing straight away so they don't ask him constant questions about what they should be doing.

But one day on his lunch break – Zac was browsing the internet, looking for jobs, when he came across an advert that took his interest. It read *Life-Halfway.Com* where you worked in a totally different environment for six months.

Zac clicked on the advert which took him to the website. He browsed through the different types of jobs but nothing took his fancy. He put his name, date of birth and his interests and hobbies into the search engine then hit the random button. After processing all his interests it came up with a job that was the complete opposite to what was in his comfort zone. He took the plunge and signed up for it – clicking on the job that had come up. It was six months work on a ranch. There would be no video games – no waking up late in the mornings. Life would be different for him. The thought of the change was scary to him – but in himself he knew he wanted to change his life.

2

There is a saying that asks – does the walker choose the path – or the path choose the walker? But what happens when our life is held by a choice we never realized we wanted to make?

The field soon breaks on a winding gravelly path with tall grass on either side. His footsteps crunch as he walks on the gravel, getting ever closer to a ranch. He hears a noise like a tapping sound up ahead. As he gets closer he sees a man chopping wood with an axe. He wears jeans, and a white vest.

'Howdy,' says the man as he sticks the axe into the wood. 'You must be Zac?'

The man wipes his sweat off his brow then wanders over to Zac.

'You're Euston?' Zac asks shyly as he shakes Euston's hand who has rather a strong grip. Euston can tell Zac is nervous and puts him at ease. He walks him towards the house to show him where he will be sleeping. He points out cows and horses – some of his responsibilities will be to clean the pens and feed them. Zac is told that one of the female cows is expecting and it's only a matter of time before she gives birth.

3

A door opens to a bedroom. Euston enters the room while Zac stands in the doorway. He sees a small room with a single bed and a chest of drawers. Curtains drawn over wooden walls. The light is dim in the room and there is a slight chill in the air.

'You'll stay here – it's not very big but it's a place to rest your head.'

Zac looks around the room. He doesn't look that impressed. Already he's missing his own room.

'I suppose you're used to bigger rooms, hey – well this is what you signed up for – a change from the life you know.'

Zac puts his bag down on the bed. Euston let's Zac know that dinner will be ready in half an hour. The bathroom is down the hall so he can freshen up then join him and his daughter at the table. Euston closes the door behind him. Zac sits on the bed – thoughts go through his head thinking that he's made a mistake. He lies down on the bed.

It feels less comfortable than his own bed. The pillow is slightly flatter as his head sinks into it.

4

Minutes later, after freshening up, Zac enters a little kitchen area. Dimly lit – the smell of cooked steaks and wood fill the air. Euston is sitting at the table along with his daughter, Donna. She doesn't say anything just stares at this stranger standing in front of her. To Zac – she's gorgeous. A slender figure, long dark hair – cute innocent looking face. Dressed similar to her dad. A checked shirt and jeans.

'Zac – come sit.'

Zac sits at the table. Donna is quiet. She looks uncomfortable with Zac being there.

'Zac – this is my daughter, Donna.'

'Hey,' she says quietly.

'Honey bee – I think you can do better than that.'

An awkward silence feels the air, until it is broken by the sound of a truck horn. Donna's attitude soon changes.

'Thank god,' she says sounding more cheery and excited. But Zac noticed Euston's attitude change. Donna leaves the table and makes her way to the door.

'Sit down and have your dinner – you don't have to jump every time that Billy comes calling.'

'I'll have it later – I won't be out too late.'

Before Euston can say anything else – Donna has left, closing the door behind her. Euston looks angry which makes Zac feel uneasy. Euston sits back in his chair feeling his loss of appetite. He looks at Zac and tells him not to wait for him – just eat. Zac takes his knife and fork – he cuts into the steak. He is pleasantly surprised how tender the meat is. His knife cuts through it in one swoop. It has been cooked just how he likes it – medium rare.

As the steak enters his mouth and hits his tongue, it felt like a pleasant electric shock. The juices and the flavour of the taste.

'Oh my god – this is great,' he says whilst chewing a mouthful of steak.

'Good – I'm glad you like it at least,' says Euston smiling. Zac gets the feeling that all is not good between Euston and his daughter.

5

It wasn't too long till Zac was snuggled under the sheets of his bed. It took him a while to get to sleep – thinking of all this change. Not sleeping in his own bed and own room, it was all so different for him. Eventually his eyes got heavy and he soon fell asleep.

But he wakes up all of a sudden when the door opens.

'Morning – get up – let's get you to work,' says Euston standing in the doorway. Zac blinks multiple times, still half asleep. He finds it odd as it's still dark outside. He takes his phone out and looks at the time. It's four thirty in the morning. He never gets up this early. For work days he gets up at eight, leaves his flat at eight thirty to start work at nine.

Weekends he gets up at ten thirty to eleven after a nightly session of gaming.

It wasn't long till Zac was outside – the sun rose and it was a lovely hot day. He ended up helping Euston fixing fences, clearing brush, and feeding the cattle. Zac felt like he didn't do a lot that day when sundown came. Euston explained that this is what being a ranch hand is all about.

'Some days you won't able to get a lot done in the day – the hours go extremely fast as you're always on the go.'

Zac sees that as his day is the same old thing and the hours drag. Being a ranch hand was tiring but he liked how fast the hours went and some chores were quite interesting.

'What you did today – do you think that you'll be able to manage on your own while I do other things?'

'Course.'

Euston pats him on the shoulder. 'Glad to hear it – thanks for the help – you're gonna be all right here.'

They are then interrupted by a truck – its tires rolling over the gravel path. Euston looks up to see it.

'Oh shit.'

The truck pulls up and a guy gets out. Jeans. White vest. Brown cap. To Zac he looked very thuggish. The guy spits as Euston approaches him.

'Euston.'

'Mr Maitland to you – Billy.'

The passenger door opens and Donna gets out. Her hair covering half her face. Zac is concerned the way Donna looks as he already assumes the worst.

'Dad – don't start,' she says, then makes her way to the house.

Billy and Euston stare at each other. An awkward silence between them. Billy then notices Zac.

'Got ya self a lacky, huh? – Who's this streak of weed?'

'Just know this, Billy – I don't like you – I personally don't see what my daughter sees in you – now get out of here.'

Billy licks his lips then spits to his side again. He gets back in his truck and speeds off. Euston goes over to Zac.

'Asshole.'

Euston can tell that Zac looks concerned.

'Don't worry about him, son – come on – I'd say you earned yourself a beer.'

6

Zac is sat at the table. Euston brings over a couple of beers – hands one to Zac.

'Cheers.'

They both drink. Zac enquires what other responsibilities a ranch hand would have. Euston likes this as he can tell that Zac is interested in the position. Others in the past have been useless, showed no interest and have done very little work to quit early on. Most hated hauling manure – feeding and drying calves after birth, giving vaccinations and doing paperwork. There's more to it than people think. But Zac was interested and hints that he has never ridden a horse.

'Okay – we'll take you out tomorrow.'

After supper – Zac retires to bed. As he wanders through the hallway, Donna comes out of her room and bumps into him.

'Sorry.'

Zac notices her hair move revealing what looks like a black eye. Donna quickly covers her face again with her hair trying to hide it quickly. She tries to get past him but Zac gets in her way quickly to stop her.

'Wait – let me see.'

He moves her hair to the side. Her eyes looks swollen by the bruise surrounding it.

'Did that guy do this? – Who was it? – Billy?'

'It's not his fault – it's mine – I… just didn't do what he wanted that's all.'

'Do you hear yourself? – You're scared of him aren't you? – Do you want to be controlled like that – what would your Dad think?'

'You can't ever tell him.'

'I won't – but you should.'

'Tell me what,' says Euston standing in the hall wondering what they're talking about. 'Move your hair.' He walks over to Donna who is hesitant to do so. 'Now.' He moves it for her and sees the black eye. He doesn't say anything – instead he leaves for his bedroom. Donna looks scared as she knows what he's going to do. She begins to shake. Zac goes after Euston to see what had got Donna scared. As he gets to his room he comes out – double barrelled shotgun in his hand and two shells in his other, which he begins to load into the gun.

Zac had never seen a real firearm before. Donna runs up to her father getting in the way of him trying to stop him leaving the house.

'No, Dad – please – please don't do this.'

'He thinks he can hit my daughter – he needs to be put down like a dog.'

'I won't see him again – I beg you – I won't leave here,' she screams pleading with him to not do anything foolish. 'PLEASE.' She breaks down in tears and hugs into him.

Zac goes up to Euston holding his hands out to take the gun off him. He gives in and passes it to him. Zac feels the weight of the gun – it's heavier than he expected. He places it on the dining table while Euston comforts his daughter.

Zac decided to leave them to it.

'Zac.' He looks at Euston. 'Thank you.' He nods then makes his way to his room.

It hadn't been that long till Zac had closed his eyes to get to sleep after overthinking the situation that Donna got herself in and hoping things will be good between her and her father.

The bedroom door soon swings open as Euston rushes in telling him to come with him quick. As Zac jumps out of bed he looks at the time. It's only quarter past one in the morning. He puts some clothes on and follows Euston into the kitchen where he hands Zac some towels.

They leave the house and make their way over to the one of the barns. One of the cows is on its side and Donna is on her knees tending to it.

'Kneel down next to me – hand me a towel.'

Zac doesn't hesitate through Donna's urgency. He passes her the towels and kneels down next to her.

'Okay – I'm going to need your help.' Zac nods but feels nervous.

'Dad – I've checked the birth canal – she's ready,' says Donna, then looks at Zac. 'I'm going to need you to help me pull out the calf.'

Before Zac can say anything, Donna tells him that this is going to be a long process. It's not easy pulling out a calf. Active pushing and progress should be seen every –fifteen to twenty minutes. The calf will be delivered between one and two hours' time.

'Okay – understood,' nods Zac.

The time went by and before Zac knew it – he was holding the calf in his arms. Donna was feeding it colostrum milk which gave it an additional dose of antibodies. Donna and Zac smiled at each other. Euston couldn't help notice how happy Donna looked. He was happy to see her like her old self again and all thanks to Zac.

8

Donna leans up against the fence watching the sun rise over the ranch. Beams of light breaking through white puffy clouds over a red sky. She closes her eyes, smiles, while breathing in the fresh air.

'Zac's fast asleep – you should get some rest too,' says Euston appearing behind her.

'I'm okay.'

'The last time I saw you this happy was before your mother passed away.' She stayed quiet, not wanting to tell Euston why she was happy. But he could guess.

'You like him don't you? Zac?'

'I do.' But Donna's happy smile drops. 'But I know he's only here six months – and then he has to leave us – I'm just going to enjoy the time he's here.'

She walks away from Euston leaving him thinking about things.

9

It wasn't long before Zac was up and back working. He felt good about himself – that the change from his repetitive life had done him the world of good, and yet he felt sad – as he was going to miss this.

As he fixes one of the fences – he watches Donna from afar tending to the calf. He couldn't help it but all he could do was stare.

'Come on, son – you're going to learn to ride a horse.'

Euston told Zac step by step how to ride and look after a horse. Step one, was to tie, groom, and lead. It would help to understand, stay safe and enjoy riding. Step two, was to saddle up. He learned how to put on the saddle, bridle and how to do up the cinch. Once he learnt that he was ready for step three, to mount and sit correctly.

Zac struggled at first to get his leg over to mount.

Euston just stood there not helping him as he would have to learn how to do this himself. He eventually got up and had no problem sitting correctly. Euston was impressed and moved onto step four, walking, halting and turning. As the horse started to walk, Zac began to feel awkward and unbalanced. It took time for Zac to get used to the horse's motions and turning it using the direct reins. But Euston was patient enough. He told Zac that with time he would build the confidence to jog and trot.

Donna watched her dad from afar getting Zac to ride.

He fell off a couple of times causing her to laugh with amusement. She knew that feelings had started to develop for him – she couldn't explain or understand why. With what she had been through with Billy – Zac was like a breath of fresh air, just what she needed.

Her phone then vibrates in her pocket. She takes it out and reads a text message from Billy which reads, *Meet me at the bar tonight – I think we need to talk about how much of an idiot I've been. Please, I'm sorry.*

Donna felt torn between Billy and Zac. On one half – Zac made her feel happy but she knew he wouldn't be around forever. But the other half, she knew Billy, and he was always around. He may have treated her terribly but she believed that people could change. She knew she had to see him – even if it was just for closure.

10

As the evening came around, Euston and Zac were in the stables. Zac was learning how to dismount properly – caring for the horse after the ride and rewarding it with treats.

'You did well out there today, boy – you were made for this. How do you feel?'

'It was exhilarating.'

'Look, Zac – I know it's a bit too early to even think about this – but how would you like to stay on longer?'

Zac's face filled with joy. The thought of staying and not going back to his old life made him feel happy. But he couldn't help but wonder why he's asking for him to stay longer.

'How much do you like my daughter?'

He didn't know how to answer that, so instead, Euston answered for him. He could tell there was something building between them. The way they both looked at each other and felt happy around each other. It was obvious and Euston knew in his heart that he would never hurt her.

When they return to the house they discover Donna's not there. They check each room and find there's no sign of her.

'Where is she?'

'I think I know where she's gone,' says Euston, his face turning red with anger. 'Come with me in the truck.'

Euston grabs the keys to the truck then the shotgun. 'Do you really need the gun?'

'I'm not going to kill him, boy – just scare him enough to stay the hell away from my daughter.'

Euston puts the gun in the back of the truck – then he and Zac get in too.

'What if she's not with him? – What if you're wrong?

'Trust me – I'm not – there's only one reason she would leave the ranch – and that's because of him.'

11

Donna walks into the bar. People drinking beers – talking amongst themselves sitting at tables. Country and Western music playing in the background. Sports on the TV and people playing pool. Billy is sitting at the bar drinking a glass of neat whiskey. Donna takes a deep breath then approaches him.

'Hi – you made it,' says Billy, smiling, delighted to see her. She folds her arms – curious to know what he wants to talk about. He admits he misses her – the guilt of how he treated her was too much for him to bear. He doesn't want to be that monster. He wants to be the man she wants.

'You really hurt me you know – I don't know what to think – I'm happy.'

'What's with the new guy on the scene? – We've been seeing each other a lot longer – been through a lot – how long is he really going to be around for? And yet I'm here in front of you now.'

He was right – Donna had thought the same thing. She considers what Billy said but on one condition – that he gives up the drinking. Billy takes the glass of whiskey, then pours the remaining contents out which splash to the floor – then puts the glass back on the bar.

'You're cleaning that up,' says the Barman, passing by.

'It's a start.'

She reaches out for his hands. He holds her and admits that he owes her an apology but the main person that needs an apology is her father. She couldn't agree more, as she hoped that it would change things for the better making things less awkward. Billy leans forwards as does Donna and their lips press against each other's.

'Oh my god,' a woman's voice, interrupts their kiss.

They both see a woman with a baby carrier. 'Kay.'

Donna looks at Kay. She can tell she is full of mixed emotions – from anger and upset.

'So you've been seeing someone else behind my back – and neglecting your son – spending time here with her,' snaps Kay. She wipes the tears from her face. 'I gave up Alex for you – he disappeared and I will never find him again – he was more of a father than you ever were.'

She looks at Donna, who looks puzzled at what's happening.

'Oh my god – she didn't know.'

Billy gets angry – shouting at Kay letting her know again that he never wanted her to keep the baby, and coming forwards and saying that he really wanted to try and be a dad was the only way to get rid of Alex out of her life.

Donna saw his true colours which made things perfectly clear to her. Everything was a lie and she had just been saved by Kay.

'I'm so sorry,' says Donna as she walks past her to leave.

Kay stops her. 'It's not your fault.' Donna looks at Kay's baby who looks adorable sleeping in the pram. She walks out with Billy following her.

12

Donna steps out into the rain. Her hair and clothes are getting drenched as she walks away from the bar. Billy runs up behind her and grabs hold of her stopping her from leaving.

'Where the hell do you think you're going?'

She struggles to get out of his grasp. Getting the urge to hit him as he begins to scare her.

'Do you really think I'm ever letting you go – you're nothing without me.'

Kay exits the bar to see Donna in a panic. She takes her phone out and calls the police. As she does, a truck pulls up in front of Billy and Donna. The glare from the headlights blinds them to see who it is.

The driver gets out, as Donna pull herself away from Billy when she sees it's Euston. He grabs the shotgun and aims it at Billy.

'Come on then, old man,' says Billy, spreading his arms calling Euston's bluff as he walks towards him. Euston closes one eye as he looks down the barrel fixing Billy in his sights. His finger resting on the trigger.

Billy catches Euston off guard by pulling the gun out of his hands – then punches him in the face causing him to stagger back. Zac reacts by punching Billy in the face. Billy retaliates by grabbing hold of Zac – punching him in the gut winding him then pushing him back. Billy takes hold of the gun and aims it at Zac.

'No,' yells Euston, as he pushes Zac out of the way. The gun goes off and Euston falls to floor.

Donna screams as she runs over to her father. She drops to her knees holding onto his body. Billy turns the gun onto Zac.

'Now your tur…'

His body flinches three times as three loud bangs occur.
Billy's body drops to the ground. Zac looks up to see the Police – standing in front of blue and red flashing lights from their car – with their guns raised aiming where Billy stood.

Zac hurried over to Donna – her hands covered in Euston's blood as she pressed against the wound to try and stop the bleeding.

'Daddy – I'm sorry – it's all my fault,' screams Donna as tears from her eyes fall onto Euston's chest. She feels cold, afraid that she's going to lose him.

Euston struggles to get out the words. His hands shake as his body temperature begins to fall. He grabs hold of Donna's hands. They're slippery from the rain and blood.

'It's not your fault, Honey Bee – don't blame... yourself,' he says trying to catch his breath.

'I don't want to be alone,' cries Donna, as she clings onto him.

Euston looks at Zac and smiles – then looks back at Donna. 'You won't be.' He takes her hand and places it in Zac's. 'I just wish... I could be there... to walk you down the aisle.'

They both look at their hands, holding onto each other, knowing that Euston is hinting they should be together. As they turn their attention back to Euston they notice he is not moving.

'Daddy?'

13

ONE YEAR LATER

The sun begins to set far from the ranch. Donna stands over a gravestone – placing some flowers on a grave. The headstone reads – *In Memory of Euston Maitland.*

'See you soon, Daddy.'

Next to Euston's grave is another gravestone. *In memory of Isabella Maitland – wife and mother to Donna Maitland.* Donna smiles at them both. She picks up her cowgirl hat and puts it on her head then walks away through the dry grass.

Zac stands by two of the horses – wearing Euston's cowboy hat.

'It looks good on you,' says Donna smiling at him. As she gets nearer, Zac holds her hands. Both of them are wearing wedding bands.

'My wife looks good on me too.'

'Cheeky,' says Donna grinning. 'Come on – let's go home.'

They kiss – then get on their horses.

'Yah,' says Zac – as his jogs on. His confidence had grown as he made a strong bond with the horse he called, Euston. Donna follows Zac as they both ride off into the sunset towards the ranch.

We all at one time in our lives get stuck in a repetitive routine and wonder if this is what the rest of our life is going to be. By doing something different to refresh and restore ourselves – we can all discover what our life was always meant to be.

LAUGH

1

Use, are we all to be here for that reason? A line of cream emulsion rolls over a green wall. The green is covered all over with the cream spreading across the wall. Matt and Colin look around the living room. The walls are completely covered and their job is done. Colin and Matt take off their painting and decorating outfits.

Matt begins to tidy up while Colin goes to make the coffee. Within minutes – Colin brings the coffee out and sits down on a chair next to Matt in front of the wall they had just painted. Colin hands the coffee to Matt. They continue to watch the wall – just staring at it alone with their thoughts.

For thirty-seven-year old Matt, his thoughts are of his family and his second job that he's recently started. The normal worries in life – mortgage and money struggles. Matt had met his other half, Laura, when she was twenty-five. Laura came from a family with two other sisters – *Melissa* and *Megan*. They dated for eight months, then Matt proposed and they were married the year after. They tried for a family really early but nothing ever happened. Worries of whether they could have children followed. Matt and Laura decided to focus on their jobs and as the years went by it finally happened for them. They had a boy called Ant.

Colin on the other hand wasn't so lucky. He lived his life, single. He had a partner and a daughter – but things didn't work out and they ended up separating. He saw his daughter every now and then but not as regularly as he hoped as his partner wanted things her own way. Colin looks at Matt – whose eyes look heavy – and his head starts to hang. Matt struggles to keep his eyes open.

'How are you, Matt? – You look tired.'

'I am, Col – my boy's been keeping me and Laura up all night.'

'Oh yeah – you still haven't shown me a picture of Ant.'

Matt takes out his phone and shows Colin a picture of Laura holding a baby boy.

'As you can see – he looks nothing like me – he looks more like his mum.'

'What? – Small, and not much hair?' says Colin, grinning cheekily. He passes the phone back to Matt.

'I just wish I could get a decent night's sleep and sleep like a baby,' says Matt, yawning.

'What? By crying and wetting the bed?'

Colin was always the joker of the two of them. It's how he liked to live his life. With his own personal issues with his family, he preferred to laugh his way through life and hide all of his problems instead of facing them.

'It was quite funny the other day,' said Matt. 'When I went to the pub – it reminded me of when you and I went out for the night and I met Laura – I saw this girl, attractive, big cleavage. I was sure I saw that girl before – didn't you?'

'No – I'd have remembered.'

Matt slouched back in his chair – sighs and folds his arms.

'You watch much TV lately?'

'Occasionally,' replies Colin. 'I saw this bloody gory program the other day.'

'Ah, you saw a horror.'

'No – it was a period drama.'

Matt looks up in surprise while drinking his coffee.

Colin looks over to Matt. 'How's the diet going?'

'Not brilliant to be honest – I miss going to *Kays Coffee Shop*– cup of tea – bacon and egg roll – usual order.'

'I thought so – they were wondering if they were going to afford a holiday this year.'

With Colin talking about food. Matt takes his phone and begins a shopping list.

'So, Colin – how are things going with your ex?'

Colin mumbles to himself regarding the touchy subject. He moans that she makes things hard for him to try and see his daughter. She couldn't admit she was in the wrong – that her paranoia caused friction in their relationship.

'Toothpaste, soap, shower-gel...' mutters Matt as he writes his shopping list out.

'It would never have worked anyway – she was nuts.'

'Nuts.' Matt adds it to the list.

Changing the subject Colin wonders how the wall is coming on. Matt goes over to the wall and lightly touches it.

'Still wet – slowly drying.' He sits back down next to Colin. 'So how are things with your daughter? She's getting married, isn't she?'

'Yes – she had her hen do the other night? I got her a stripper.'

'I bet she loved that'

Colin's smile drops and shakes his head 'Not really.'

Everything was steamy in Jessie's room. She sat on the end of the bed – watching a muscly man in front of her getting hot and sweaty. She reaches for her collar – catching her breath. Her excited face then drops as he strips… the paint off her wall.

'So… aren't you going to take your clothes off?' asks Jessie.

'You got her a paint stripper?' says Matt.

'What? It wasn't a total loss – it still made her wall look nice.'

'You haven't had much luck with relationships have you, mate?'

'Not really – I thought Marcy was the one – but then I discovered her secret and had to say bye to her.'

'Well, of course, you said bye to her – she was bisexual,' said Matt. He tried to make Colin feel better – telling him that he will find the perfect partner eventually. He knows someone that's available. Her name is Melissa, Laura's sister, she works at *Kays Coffee Shop*. He thinks they would be good for each other, and he has been seeing quite a bit of her.

'Well, of course, you have – you spend your life in the coffee house,' Colin says, frustrated. He had seen Melissa. She was medium build, slightly older than him in her early forties – with scruffy hair. There was something about her that made him cautious of her. Like she was going to knock him out and kidnap him. To him she looked a little crazy.

Colin changes the conversation onto Matt. He asks him if he's going to celebrate his and Laura's anniversary at the same hotel, like he does every year.

'No – not after what happened last year.'

Laura flings the curtains open to the hotel room. An expression of joy and happiness fills her face as she sees the sun beaming over the lush green countryside.

'Everything is exactly the same as it's always been – lovely view – nice

253

comfy bed...' she says flopping down on the bed. She reaches over to a bedside cabinet and opens the drawer. 'Even the bible in the... oh my god.'

'What?' says Matt who sees Laura looking sick.

'There's a used condom in the bible,' she says, putting her hand over her mouth.

'Well, that puts a whole new meaning on – O cum all ye faithful.'

Colin holds his coffee in front of his mouth – surprised at what Matt just told him, and says, 'I've gone right off that coffee' then puts it down on the floor.

'It may seem like it but it's not all good between me and Laura.'

'Really?'

'There's always something she moans about – a lot of negativity, telling me that I don't pay much attention to her... I don't know, I wasn't listening at the time.'

'Example?' Colin asks.

Laura sits down in the driver's seat of the car, while Matt straps Ant into the baby seat. Laura gets the sat nav up.

'Hey babe – what is the post code for that Old Mcdonald's farm?'

'E-I-E-I-O.'

Laura rolls her eyes at Matt.

Colin giggles and then jokingly suggests that Matt should've got with the other sister, Megan. Matt admits that he still hasn't met her yet. It was difficult at the time with her being on her music tour. Then she gave it up and got married to a regular guy and had a kid of her own. Laura hadn't heard from Megan for months and was annoyed at her from not being invited to the wedding. Megan and Jason ended up getting married in Bright Light City just before she had their child. To Laura she felt it was a complicated situation and the only sisterly contact she had was Melissa.

'I suppose if I had got with Megan – she wouldn't have me work two jobs.'

'Where do you work?' asks Colin.

'CL Petra – biggest computer, research and supply building in Townsend.'

'You work in computers?'

'I work in security.'

Matt is escorted into a small room by his boss. A Frenchman by the name of Pierre. Matt looks around the room. There is a swivel chair in front of nine monitors that shows the interiors and exteriors of the rooms of the building.

'This is you,' says Pierre. 'You'll monitor the area – respond to calls and do the occasional paperwork.'

Matt looks around nodding.

'I run a tight ship – get on the wrong side of me or fall out of line and I'll make your life painful.'

'I promise that won't happen,' says Matt. 'Besides I already know the meaning of pain – haven't you heard the music charts lately?'

Colin chuckles. 'Ooh that's harsh… but true – music nowadays it all sounds the same – like someone took the longest song ever made, cut it up into pieces and gave it to multiple male and female singers.'

'Society nowadays – like zombies – their heads buried in the phones.'

'I know what you mean,' said Colin looking at the news on his phone. 'Blimey – the things you learn – a woman has been arrested for trying to poison her husband by putting eye drops in his dinner.'

'Bet he never saw that coming.'

Matt notices Colin looking at Christmas present ideas.

'I can't believe it's Halloween tomorrow and it'll soon be Christmas.'

'I can't believe the way some people look at Halloween,' says Colin. 'I saw someone the other day that was scary looking?'

'What – yourself in the mirror?'

'Cheeky git.'

Colin gets up and checks the wall. He puts his thumb up to Matt. They then hear the front door go. Laura enters the room holding bags of shopping.

'It looks great – haven't you got to get ready for work?' says Laura, hurrying to the kitchen.

Matt checks the time and says, 'It's fine – it's not like I'm running late.'

255

2

Matt and Colin come out of the house and pack up their painting and decorating equipment in the back of Colin's van. Matt is now dressed in a shirt and tie. Colin shuts the van doors while Matt straightens his tie.

'Thanks for the help today,' said Matt smiling at Colin.

'That's all right – we've always made a good team decorating.'

'I don't mean the decorating – I meant thanks for cheering me up – having a laugh is just what I needed.'

'Any time,' says Colin. 'At least Laura can't give you a hard time about decorating that wall.'

'Anyway, I got to go to work – catch you later.'

Matt and Colin part ways. As Matt crosses the road to his job at CL Petra. Colin goes home to the house next door to Matt's.

Laughter – an expression of merriment and amusement. When life gets us down, when times are hard. Resorting to this emotion is one of the three words that can get us through – to Live, Laugh and Love.

CHRISTMAS

1

Forever, that's how long it felt like the snow had been falling outside the window of my car as I drove through the snowy countryside making my way to my parents' on Christmas Eve. The sun was setting in the distance which made the snow and ice glisten. It was like a portrait someone had painted. But something was strange about the snow. It was white – but there was a hint of pink within the snowflakes.

I didn't know why – but it did make it pretty.

The sun had started to set. Night time was approaching fast. I was still half an hour away. My parents always rented this log cabin in the middle of nowhere on the outskirts of Towns-end. It was always a family event with me and my two sisters. I was the first to be born – I was the oldest, a Woman of forty-two years. My two sisters *Laura* and *Megan,* were both twenty-eight, who were born weeks apart.

Laura was married to Matt – a guy who did painting and decorating on the side. He worked nights at CL Petra as security. They had a boy nine months ago and named him Ant. Laura phones me on a regular basis in the evenings – moaning about Matt that she feels like she's a single mother. But I always took Matt's side as he was working hard to provide for them as CL Petra paid good money. Matt worked so she didn't have to – she could just stay at home and look after Ant. I got annoyed at Laura as nothing seemed to be good enough for her when it came along.

For Megan on the other hand, she had all the luck. She loved to sing. At a young age she began to write her own songs and post them up on YouTube. She hit over a hundred thousand followers within the first few weeks which soon went into the millions not long after. She was approached by a music manager called, Tyrone, who took her on board and made her a pop sensation.

But things soon changed for her. Every time that I and Laura met up with her – she was unhappy. We were always introduced to a new boyfriend every time we met up. It wasn't her – it was them that did the breaking up. She never wanted a celebrity boyfriend as celebrity relationships never seemed to last – she just wanted an ordinary guy and she never cared what they did for a job – even if they worked at a supermarket. She wasn't shallow. But they could never accept her success, being a star – always on the move – so seeing her was limited.

The last boyfriend she had, Mason, was tired of her life.

She ended up going through a breakdown and she hit the bottle. But there was light at the end of her story. A fan gave her a positive comment on social media. They met up and she fell in love with him. They both have a child now and she's a lot happier after giving up her career. She told me that singing wasn't the life she wanted – but it was what she needed.

'Eh – what…'

I look at the passenger side. There is a man – a stranger, he looks slightly younger than me – his face is pressed up against the passenger window. He must feel the chill of the glass. He sits back – looking groggy – looking around like he doesn't know where he is. He looks at me. I see a bump on his forehead.

'What's going on?'

I apologize to him – tell him that I'm really sorry for all that's going to happen. But I need him. He is still confused at what I'm talking about. I explain to him that I'm driving him to my parents' – that we're only staying for the big day tomorrow and then I will let him go.

'Big day?' he asks. 'Who are you?'

I tell him, I'm Melissa. I need him to pretend to be my boyfriend as tomorrow is Christmas Day. He looks scared as I give him a big grin and wish him a merry Christmas.

2

When we gather at Christmas – we share the love and thoughts of what gifts we can give each other. But would we feel the same when that gift comes from a stranger we don't even know?

The lights from a log cabin are the only visibility I can see up ahead. The snow falls more heavily in the pitch black night and the headlights from my car don't give much away from the road ahead. With the car gaining distance to the cabin I begin explaining to Shane what's going to happen – that we have been going out for six months, we met in the summer, and struck up a conversation by the lake.

He was confused at what I'm talking about. I explain that my parents are going to ask lots of questions about us. If he says what I have thought of – we can both get through this.

'Okay – stop,' snaps Shane as he puts his hands up in surrender. 'Melissa was it? – You've obviously got issues with your parents and are obviously afraid of them – but why drag me into this? – How did I end up in this car anyway?'

I didn't tell him how he ended up in the car. But I confirmed that he was right – I do have issues with my parents ever since I was young. But he would be helping me out if he just played along. I slow the car down – not far away from the cabin and come to a stop. I lean over to him, he is defensive like he's scared of me. I open the passenger door and tell him if he wants to leave – here's his opportunity.

He stares out at a forest covered in a wasteland of snow and ice. The road disappears into the blackness of the night. I ask him how long he could last out in the cold. We're in the middle of nowhere and nobody lives nearby.

Shane closes the passenger door. He looks at me and says, 'I'm your prisoner then – that's the only choice I have?'

I promise that I will take him wherever he wants to go on Boxing Day if he does this for me to get through Christmas Day. He will stay in the warm – have a nice meal and drinks. Be better than walking in the cold wasting the day away just getting back to wherever he came from.

'Okay, Melissa – let's do this.'

I am so happy he accepted. I continue to drive to the log cabin and park outside. The cabin is covered in snow – icicles hang from the roof. Christmas decorations and lights illuminate the cabin giving it that Christmas feel.

As I attempt to leave the car, Shane grabs hold of my hand.

'Wait,' he says, stopping me. 'I don't know anything about you – aren't you going to explain, who you are – where you work? – What if your mum and dad bring up the topic of if you and I are having sex?'

I hold his hand and assure him that they wouldn't ask something that personal. I feel him shaking. I can't help but wonder if he's nervous or scared at meeting my mum and dad.

'Not nervous – just really cold.'

I see his point. So we leave the car and go to the log cabin.

3

We stand in the hallway – greeted by the warmth. My mum, Trudi, greets us. She gives me a hug and I introduce her to Shane. She shakes his hand and tells him that it's a pleasure to meet him. As I begin to take my coat off – Shane grabs hold of it and says, 'Allow me, dear.'

He catches me off guard for being so polite. But even I know he's only acting in front of my mother. He stares at me – holding my coat not moving. I wonder if there's something wrong. He tells me that I look gorgeous.

Wearing blue jeans and a bright red cotton Christmas jumper with a reindeer on.

'Your father's in the other room – go on in and I'll be in with the drinks,' says my mum as she leaves for the kitchen. I take a deep breath, nervous at entering. Shane can tell that something is wrong with me. My hand shakes as I reach for the door handle, but I can't seem to do it.

Shane opens the door for me.

'Are you okay?' he asks. He then takes my hand and leads me into the room.

4

The fire crackles as my dad, Jack, stands by the fireplace. A double barrel shotgun hangs above it – with a family photo on the mantelpiece. He leans up against it – a drink of brandy in his hand. The room is decorated with Christmas decorations and lights with a tall Christmas tree in the corner of the room.

'You're late – by a minute and a half,' he says in a strong tone. He finishes his drink then turns to me looking annoyed. I explain that it didn't matter if I was late as I was taking my time driving safely as I didn't want an accident what with the roads being icy. Dad did everything by the book, always being punctual. I and my sisters had suffered this all through our life.

Dad places the brandy glass on top of the fireplace next to the family photo of us. He reaches out his hand and greets Shane – asks him if he must be the latest boyfriend as I bring a new one every year. Shane looks at me and I can't help but hang my head in shame.

But then something surprised me. I was expecting Shane to tell my dad everything – that he was being held against his will and he wasn't really my boyfriend. Instead, Shane grabs hold of my dad's hand and shakes it. Dad always had a strong grip which caught my other boyfriends off guard.

'Wow – that's a nice strong grip you've got there,' my dad says looking impressed. Shane then takes an interest in the family photo. He takes it off the fireplace and takes a closer look.

'Great picture of you all.'

I explain that it was the first family Christmas photo we took – six Christmas's ago. Mum, Dad, me and my two sisters.

'Wait – is this, Megan May – the pop star?'

I nodded, rolled my eyes and sighed. Predictable as ever. Everyone always asks that when they see the picture of her – then follows the constant questions of what it's like to have a famous singer in the family. Shane could tell I didn't want to get into a major discussion about her.

'Megan won't be joining us or Laura – they've got their own

264

Christmases planned with their partners and kids – so it'll just be us,' says Mum as she enters the room with four drinks on a tray. 'Shane – do you like egg nog?'

Shane tells her he's never tried it and happily accepts. I didn't really like it. I was always the one that finished drinking it the last. Mum and Dad drank it like water – necking it back like it was shots.

'Lovely to have you here,' says Mum as she raises her glass. We all toast and drink then take a sit down. It doesn't take Dad long to ask Shane the details of how we met.

Shane tells him everything that I thought of to make it sound convincing. My heart was racing the entire time they were talking – watching Dad's expression and reactions to see if he could see through Shane's story. Luckily he believed every word of it.

'So, Shane – what's your opinion on what Melissa does for a living? You think she can do any better? It's not exactly a good future – financially.'

'I support your daughter whatever she decides to do – it's her life after all,' says Shane as he smiles at me. It was the nicest and most supportive comment I had ever heard. But I could tell by Dad's face – Shane annoyed him by not taking his side.

'DAD – STOP IT,' I yell. This topic always wound me up. I always had to justify why I liked my job. For Shane who didn't know me – I tell the story of who I am.

I have been working at *Kays Coffee Shop* for nearly a year now. It was a coffee slash bar – that sold coffee, meals and alcohol. As a waitress I find it a job that I enjoy. It's not giving people what they've ordered but I find the people fascinating. I overhear their stories of their day and how their lives are going. It's like a real life soap opera.

So there I was in the coffee house – wearing reindeer antlers on my head to get into the Christmas spirit – while the radio played 'Christmas May Holiday' by my sister Megan.

My day began with my very first customer. He comes in regular as clock work when we open. Orders the same thing – white coffee with sugar. His name is Colin – he's a painter and decorator. He used to come in with his friend, Matt, who is married to my sister, Laura. But I know the real reason why he doesn't come any more as Laura made him go on a diet, no more bacon and egg rolls for him.

'Cheers, darling – Merry Christmas – have a good one,' says Colin as he grabs his coffee to leave. I wish him a Merry Christmas in return. He's a nice kind guy. Matt and Laura thought I should go out with him but there was one thing stopping me from doing that. He had a daughter and there was too much baggage with his ex.

As I stood there waiting for the next customer to come through the door – I watched two men sitting at a table – already on the booze. They looked like they had given up with their lives – holding a glass of whiskey in their hands looking unhappy. They toasted their drinks, necking back the alcohol.

'How far we've both come – eh Matthew?'

'What happened with you, Will? It can't be as bad as what I've been through.'

Will and Matthew talked amongst themselves. Will's heart had been broken. He had been manipulated into having an affair by his fiancé, Missy, with a woman named Marcy. Missy hadn't taken any interest in getting intimate with Will. Then one day the truth came out. He paid a visit to Marcy. The door was ajar. When he entered, he saw Marcy with her legs wrapped around Missy's head giving her oral sex.

They were both shocked to see Will. He felt sick to the stomach. Missy confessed everything – that she was a lesbian, that he was the nicest guy that she's ever met and she didn't want to hurt him. That's why she set Marcy up with Will – someone they could share. Will understood that it must be difficult coming to terms with her sexuality. But what she did was evil – and she should've been honest with him. She didn't want to hurt him – but she did.

Will can't help but wonder how things could be worse than what he had been through. Matthew explains that Karma set in. After he ruined his marriage to Allison with him assuming she was cheating on her when in reality he cheated on her with another woman. After his divorce he met someone new – her name was Nikki. Their relationship suffered through their love life. To rebuild it they went to a club called Play 4 Real. A game for introducing others into their love life. Things went bad and Nikki ended up getting pregnant through another man. As the months passed by, Nikki teased and tormented Matthew until he just upped and left her.

Will understood why Matthew did what he did.

Matthew went through a psychological breakdown – he eventually

266

turned to suicide and overdosed but he was surprised when it didn't kill him. Something wanted him to stay alive and he didn't understand why he was still here.

'Maybe I can answer that for you.'

Matthew looked to see a Woman standing in the doorway. She had been listening to their conversation.

'Allison?'

'Hi – can we talk?'

Will gets the hint and gets up to leave. Allison sits down in front of Matthew and says, 'I heard what happened to you – I'm so sorry – I can't imagine what it was like.'

Matthew tells her that it was probably like what she went through. Betrayal, pain – constant reminders of torment. Allison couldn't deny it – but she has had time to heal. She explains that the reason why Matthew is still here is because that his time on giving up on love isn't over. She admits that she still thinks of him – there hasn't been anyone else and she still loves him. Matthew couldn't deny that the feeling was mutual. He thought about Allison when he was with Nikki which was what made their love life difficult. Allison reaches out and holds Matthew's hand in hers.

'Look – I don't want to be alone for Christmas – this was always one of the best moments of our lives that we shared – the thought of not having that upsets me.'

Matthew pulls his hand away. He would love to spend another Christmas with her. But he didn't feel like it was the right thing to do after what he did to her. She pleads with him – after what they have both been through – she would like to work at trying to rebuild who they were – she can see it working as lessons can be learned from the mistakes that have been made.

'Okay – let's spend Christmas together – see how things go.'

'Will you just kiss me now?' she says looking delighted. They share a quick kiss on the lips. She takes his hand and leads him out of the coffee house.

I couldn't help but feel happy for them. A couple who broke up working things out. Christmas was always a time for bringing people together.

I make my way over to their table and collect the glasses that Will and Matthew were using. As I make my way back over to the counter I noticed the news. Police had raided a place called *The Family Home* and arrested a man called Jin. He and his wife, Mai, had been luring married couples there and performing sadistic experiments on them.

They had lobotomized them. It was like something out of a horror movie. I then noticed two people who I hadn't seen for months, Neil and Amy, I used to serve them regularly every Saturday. The last time I saw them was when they were having a row in the town. I had wondered what happened to them, and now I'm seeing them on the TV – the Police are trying to move their dead bodies off a bench. I feel sick when I see that Amy was pregnant.

Another news report scrolls at the bottom of the screen. There is talk about a teenager who got arrested. His name was Tom – he killed his step father. He was trying to plead his case that he was a monster and he saved his mother from him. A girl named Ashley had reported him to the Police after discovering what he did. It made me realize that I was glad not to have children as I wouldn't want to bring them into such a terrible world.

As I return to the counter, my boss, Kay, joins my side. I like her a lot – she is great to work for. Full of energy and passion. She had built this coffee house from the ground up, no coffee pun intended. But all of her drive and ambition had faded away a few months ago.

At the beginning of the year she found out she was pregnant. Her boyfriend Billy was an awful guy – I didn't like him one bit especially the way he treated Kay. After he dumped her – her sister Sandra had set Kay up on a single mothers' dating site. She met Alex, a nice guy, he treated her right and supported her all the way through her pregnancy. Alex had a past which I witnessed. He used to meet up with a prostitute called Mother Sunshine. His friend, Nelson, saw her too but under her real name Mary. Alex had turned his life around by then after things ended terribly between the three of them. But Billy came back on the scene to be the dad he should've been. Kay went back with Billy and Alex left. I couldn't believe she was so stupid letting Alex go who had been so supportive going to classes and helping her prepare for the baby like a dad should.

Not long after that, Kay went to Billy's old hang out. A bar he was always in. She suspected he had gone back to his old ways but she got more than she bargained for when she saw him with his girlfriend. Donna was a young thing – I knew her and her father as I was a close friend of her mother's. Billy went mental and killed Donna's dad – but at the cost of his own life when the Police arrived and shot him.

Kay witnessed everything. She had lost Alex through choosing Billy and now he was dead. She lived every day full of regret – wishing she could see Alex one more time and make things right. But he was nowhere to be found. He had disappeared.

She never got over it. As she stood next to me I noticed that her eyes were red. She had been crying again. Every day since then.

'Melissa – are you okay to take over the rest of the day? I can't be here – I'm going home to my son, to see Mark. Give Sandra a break.'

I wasn't really all right with the thought of it. I would be late to my parents to spend Christmas with them. I didn't like the idea of being moaned at but I did it for Kay. I reach out for and give her a hug – rubbing her back to try and make her feel better. The door opens and Sandra comes in holding Kay's baby in her arms.

'Are you ready to go?' asks Sandra.

Kay looks up at her – nods – then thanks me for consoling her and being there for her. She wishes me a merry Christmas, then leaves with her sister and son. Now I'm all alone. It's quiet for Christmas Eve. Normally there's loads of people coming in – having a hot drink to keep the cold out – while they do their last minute shopping.

I then jump with the sound of my phone vibrating near the till. A message comes through. I look at it – and my face drops with disappointment. It's a text from my sister, Megan, saying that she, Jason and her son Henry, can't make Christmas as they want to spend their first Christmas to their selves.

The door opens. Missy walks in shivering. I knew her when she went out with Will – but she mostly came here when she wanted a girly meet up with Ana and Allison. I assumed that's what she was doing.

'Can I get a Latte, please?' says Missy as she takes a seat. But I hear raised voices coming from outside as the door swings closed. It sounded like Kay.

I make my way outside. The cold air hitting me with a sharpness as I leave the warmth of the coffee house. I see Kay – slightly distraught – trying to get Alex to listen to her. He tells her he left doing the right thing. Billy was the real father of her child and that's who she should be with.

'Billy's dead,' yells Kay. Alex looks surprised. Kay explains all that happened – he killed someone – the police killed him – all this happened

269

after she discovered him cheating on her with his younger teenage girlfriend. With her wiping the tears from her eyes – she grabs hold of him, pleading that she made a mistake by getting back with Billy and she's regretted losing him. She always hoped to see Alex again – because she always loved him with all her heart and she can't bear the thought of her life without him. She then bends down on one knee and takes out a ring box from her coat pocket – the ring box he left behind.

'Sandra found this when you drove away – she showed me the day you left – and told me you were going to propose to me,' says Kay opening the ring box. 'So I'm going to ask you… even though you will have to put the ring on my finger – Will you marry me? Please – I love you so much.'

I could see Kay shaking – with Alex not knowing what to say or react to Kay's proposal. I was scared for her. I didn't want to see her rejected and have her heart broken.

'Yes I will – I love you too, and I have missed you so much.'

He kneels down in front of her, places his hands on her face, leans forwards and presses his lips onto hers. I smile as he holds their kiss. He then takes the ring – then takes her hand – and places it on her finger. Sandra looks ecstatic. It made my day to see Kay finally get what she always needed. A good man in her life. And the upside was there was a wedding to go to. Kay introduces Alex to Mark who he begins to get acquainted with like he was his father. They look so happy.

As I return to the coffee house – I wish that could be me as I was sick of being single. I knew what I wanted. A good man and a baby so we could be a proper little family.

I look over at Missy – she looks annoyed while waiting.

I go and make her coffee. The door goes and her friend, Ana, walks in.

'Hey,' said Missy. But Ana stopped her before she could say anything else.

'Sorry, Missy – I can't talk right now. I'm meeting someone,' Ana interrupted. She took a seat across from her just as a handsome guy came in.

'Richie – over here,' Ana acknowledged.

He sat down at the table and said to her that he was glad that she wanted to talk. He had given a lot of thought to what happened and realized that in his heart that he loved her with all his heart. He had come to terms that she was a post op transgender and as proof that he wanted to commit his love and his life to her, he took out an engagement ring.

Ana looked overwhelmed. Tears of joy. From all the waiting that she had done to find a decent guy, she finally had him in front of her. But I could see that she was more upset than anything.

'What is it?' Richie asked.

'I can't marry you,' Ana explained. 'My post op surgery has gone wrong.' Richie was puzzled. 'I have a growth. Where my vagina was has formed back into a penis.'

'What? Is that even possible?' Richie questioned.

'There are lots of people who have had this abnormal growth. I was told that there was one woman who won't stop growing. So, I'm sorry.' Ana was upset.

Richie returned the ring to his pocket and took Ana's hand in his. 'Then let's just date for now and see how things go.'

'But I have a penis – sex will be awkward,' Ana explained.

'We'll see how it goes. Besides it's an extra part of you to play with.'

Ew – I thought, but Ana giggled. The door goes and Mary and Nelson enter. Mary holding her baby and Nelson loaded with shopping bags full of Christmas presents.

'Hi, Melissa – can we get two cappuccinos?'

I nod to her. It was good to see Mary again as it had been such a long time. The last time I saw her was when her and Nelson met for the first time. I was pleased to see her with a man and a baby boy – and to get away from the prostitute game. Nelson had fixed her life – and he seems to have fixed himself after discovering the truth.

I call over to Mary – asking what they called their baby. 'His name is John,' replies Mary.

As the day went on – the time went fast. This was the only day I wanted the time to go slow. I locked up the coffee house – not having to be back here until a couple of days' time.

'Melissa,' calls a familiar voice as I make my way over to my car. It was Laura and Matt with Ant in the stroller.

Matt looks tired but I know that's because of all the night shifts that Laura's been making him do. I ask her if she got the same text I did – that Megan won't be making this Christmas. She confirms she did – then tells me that she's not going to make it either. Matt would prefer to have a relaxing Christmas after all the work he's been putting in. I'm annoyed – as it's better when my sisters are with me.

'Well, sorry – but you don't get everything you want – we have our own lives too you know – things change, not everything stays the same – I'll see you – Merry Christmas.' Laura walks away from me – I can see in Matt's eyes he looks sorry for me after her outburst.

Before I start making my way to Mum and Dad's – I pay a visit to the cemetery and place some flowers on my nan's grave wishing her a merry Christmas and wishing she was still here.

I shiver due to the cold air – my smoky breath visible in front of my face. Not far away from me – a man is placing flowers on a grave.

'I miss you so much,' he says.

As I walk past him I take a look at the grave. It reads, *In Memory of Jennifer Perry.*

'Harry?' another voice calls. I stop in my tracks to see a woman, slim, attractive. Red lips. Blonde hair tied back – dressed in a blue tracksuit. I think she's crazy as it's freezing out here. It's like she doesn't feel the cold.

'Jennifer?' replies Harry. He looks her up and down. Like he knows her. 'You look like – you sound like...'

'Tracy Luna sent me – my name is Cynthia – you've seen me before outside Miss Luna's office – I was designed just like Jennifer was, from the same model.' She approaches Harry and places his hands on his face. 'So you wouldn't be alone for Christmas.'

I didn't understand what she meant by design but my jealousy began to get the better of me. Everyone who has lost someone gets to be with someone this Christmas.

I then hear a baby crying. I see a familiar face pushing a stroller. It's Nikki – the one who was going out with Matthew, who got pregnant by another man.

'Alexis – stop your whining,' shouts Nikki, her venomous tongue spitting at her poor baby. To me she was a disgusting human being. The devil's bitch. I had a bad feeling that kid is going to grow up an evil man who is hell bent on destroying lives just like she did.

After leaving the cemetery I began to make my way to the log cabin that my parents always went to for Christmas. It was the perfect family getaway. The sun had already begin to set and the snow was falling. As I drove through the middle of nowhere I noticed an old farmhouse. It was a derelict abandoned old place. Faymill Farm was rumoured to be haunted but I found the paranormal thing very difficult to believe.

As I turned a corner I slowed down. Donna was riding her horse with a guy that I think I had seen before. I wind my window down and acknowledge her.

'Hey, Melissa – are you off to your parents?' I nod. I offer my condolences with the loss of her father after what happened with that Billy. I used to serve her when she came into town with Billy. She introduces me to her husband, Zac. I realize where I have seen him before. He came in and ordered coffees for Vision Electrics. We wish each other a merry Christmas and then part ways. And the rest of that story we're up to date with.

My dad shakes his head. Mum keeps quiet as always but Shane nods and smiles. He sees my point why I like my job. The people I see and get to know. I like talking to them and getting to know their lives. I would rather that than be stuck behind a desk not interacting with anyone.

'Where's your toilet?' asks Shane.

'Upstairs – second door on the left.'

Shane gets up and leaves the room. Mum smiles at me and says, 'He seems nice – a lot better than your other boyfriends – especially that... Dennis – wasn't it?'

I tell Mum to stop bringing up my exes – especially Dennis. I don't want to be reminded that when he was going out with me – he was secretly married. And then he ended up at that sex club and got Nikki pregnant. We all sit in quiet and wait for Shane to get back. But he doesn't return. Five minutes have gone by. Dad amusingly thinks that he's got lost. So I go and check.

As I get out into the hallway I look towards the kitchen. The back door is wide open – letting the snow in. Shane's done a runner. I go outside – seeing footsteps leading off into the night. I look around but I see no sign of him. How am I going to explain this to my parents? I turn to return to the kitchen and bump into Shane causing me to jump. I hit him in the arm – wondering what the hell he was thinking.

He tells me that on the way to the toilet he felt a draught and saw the back door wide open. He found it hard to believe that my mother would leave the door open so he decided to have a look around just in case anyone is snooping about. I already explained to him it would be doubtful as we're in the middle of nowhere and we've never ever seen anyone in all the times we've been here.

'Do you really think I would abandon you?' he asks me. I didn't really know. I just thought if he had the chance to escape he would. He puts his hand on my cheek and rubs it. 'Ye of little faith,' he says, winking and smiling at me.

As we return to the living room – Dad can't help but ask what Shane has done to his forehead, noticing the bump. A box fell on his head as he was moving it. He works at CL Petra in the warehouse area. Dad looked convinced at his story. Before Dad started grilling Shane with the constant questions I yawned making out I was tired and was ready for bed.

'Okay beautiful.' He looks at my parents. 'We'll see you in the morning.'

'You don't want to stay with us while Mel has an early night?' asks my mother. 'Have another drink with us.'

Shane holds his hands up in surrender. 'Thanks, but I could do with an early night too.'

'Suit yourself.'

Shane looks at me surprised at Dad's comment. I take his hand, shaking my head hinting to just leave it. We go upstairs to my bedroom.

5

The room is a fair size – with a big double bed – a wardrobe and dresser. I am grateful to get through this night and thank Shane for being so convincing.

'It's okay.'

Shane grabs a couple of pillows – puts them on the floor and lies down. I tell him that he doesn't have to sleep there. He can sleep with me in the bed – keep warm.

'Isn't that a little weird, Melissa? – We hardly know each other and already you're inviting me into your bed.'

I didn't want him to have an uncomfortable night, and get cold – that was all. I never meant sex when I said sleep with each other. He gets up off the floor then looks out the window watching the snow fall. He tells me that he never imagined he would be here on Christmas Eve.

I apologize for doing this to him. But I'm really grateful considering he could've turned me in anytime he wanted.

Instead he chose to play along.

'Listening to your story earlier – about your job – it sounded fascinating – all those people's lives – I hope you get your happy ending.'

Hearing those words coming from him warmed the only part of me that didn't feel the cold. He warmed my heart.

'I thought you said you never see anyone here.'

Like I already told him – I don't. He points at the window and says, 'Well, who's that?'

I flip the covers back – jump out of bed and join Shane by the window. He was right. I see someone – faintly in the darkness near the entrance to the woods. They are staring us – until they disappear into the woods.

'Come on – let's have a look'

6

We sneak downstairs – luckily Mum and Dad are passed out in the living room from all the booze they've had. As we step out into the cold night, we use the torches on our phones to light the way through the woods. Our footsteps crunch as we step through the snow. It's an eerie atmosphere. There is no sound of any wildlife or noises around us. It's completely dead.

I consider on turning back the further we venture as there's no sign of the stranger and I didn't relish the idea of getting lost. But Shane spots something up ahead. I follow him and now I see it. It's a cabin – another log cabin. I never even knew this was nearby. I see through the window a flickering light. Someone must be inside.

Shane knocks on the door but there's no response. He tries the door and it opens. He is about to step in when I stop him – shaking my head not agreeing with what he's about to do. But he doesn't listen – he enters the cabin and I reluctantly follow.

7

Inside we are greeted by the heat of a crackling fire.

There isn't any furniture around – just two backpacks in a corner. We don't understand. I don't feel comfortable – I feel scared not knowing what we're about to discover and plead with Shane to return to our cabin. As we turn to leave we see a dog in the doorway. It slowly creeps towards us – growling. Shane gets in front of me as it snarls and barks. I'm scared – my heart racing at the thought of it attacking us.

'Easy boy,' a voice calls. The dog stops. In the doorway now stands a man who looks to be in his forties.

'Who are you?' asks Shane.

'My name is Mr Geoffries – I'm surprised you didn't know that.'

We both look puzzled at what he meant by that. Mr Geoffries tells us to get closer to the fire – stay warm and he will explain all.

As we go to the fireplace – Shane comments on what the two backpacks are for. He tells us that they're his and his nephew's.

'Well, where's your nephew?'

'Nearby,' says Mr Geoffries. He puts his hands in his pockets and begins to explain who he is. He told us that life set him on a path that he never expected – it made his life more adventurous but terrifying at the same time.

After being wounded in the civil war against the government – he was sent to Foptix where he received a medical operation.

Debris from an explosion had lodged into his head. Suffering damage to his brain – he would've died – but due to funding by Foptix Industries – they were able to save him by putting a chip inside, keeping his brain healed and working. He owed his life to that company for saving it.

But one day – many years later – he was having a drink in *The Open Bar*. He was listening to a man and a woman talking about music in the bar. I ask him who they were.

He tells me that their names were Will and Marcy. As he stood up to leave – he came over dizzy and began to see random images that he didn't understand. Snow. Pink snow changing the world forever and turning it into a world without love and replacing it with kinky terror. Will went over to him to see if was okay. But he didn't answer Will, instead he pushed him away and left the bar. The images kept on flashing in his mind. He made no sense of what it was about.

Not long after that he went to Foptix to see if they knew what it meant – was the chip malfunctioning? Doctor Cyrus checked him over and found no problem with his chip. As Mr Geoffries left the lab – he noticed something interesting in a glass jar. It was a pink snowflake. He felt that this wasn't just a coincidence. As the weeks passed the images faded away in his mind. He thought it was just a hallucination. But then he saw something new.

He saw himself going into a club called Ret-Row – walking up to a man called Alex and handing him a business card to an escort agency. Then finding a woman called Nikki – who was homeless and living as a drug addict. He didn't know why – but he found these people for real. He set Alex on his path but could see it in Nikki's eyes that she couldn't be helped. He thinks that he lost something that was precious to him that night. It was a crucifix necklace that his brother's wife used to wear. His brother Mr Alan gave it to him to hold on to.

Then the last image entered his head. He saw himself and his nephew travelling on the road on Christmas Eve.

So that's what he did. He made his nephew leave just to see what the vision was trying to tell him. As they walked a lonely road they heard a whining. Mr Geoffries left his nephew at the side of the road while he went to investigate. He found a dog wandering on its own which looked to be abandoned.

He then heard the sound of a car screeching. He took the dog with him and returned to where he left his nephew. He saw a woman dragging his nephew's body into the passenger side of her car. As he hurried over to the car – she had got back in and drove off as fast as she could. He followed the road – took a shortcut through some woods and found this place.

He then glares at me. He asks Shane how he got that bump on his head – does he remember much before coming here. Shane didn't. Because of me.

The guilt had hit me like a sledgehammer to the stomach. I had been running late – scared of Dad criticizing me for punctuality. I was driving a bit fast – I knew it was dangerous. So I put my foot on the brakes and lost control of the car. I saw someone standing at the side of the road – my car clipped them. When I got out they were unconscious taking a blow to the head. It was Shane. I didn't know what to do. I needed a boyfriend so I took him with me. He didn't remember the accident.

'You're my nephew, Shane,' says Mr Geoffries.

'You're my… uncle?'

I can't stay here. I feel sick to my stomach for what I did. Lying to my parents. They need to know what I've done and how I feel. I sneak out – they don't even notice me going.

7

I walk into the cabin – my mum and dad stir as I enter the room. Mum yawns – rubbing her eyes like they're stinging from the alcohol.

'I thought you were having an early night – why are you wearing your coat?' she asks.

'Where's Shane?' says Dad firmly. That's when I tell them the truth. Shane is with his uncle – where he belongs. I took him – pretending to be my boyfriend just so that my parents could have their approval of me. I didn't even want to come here – especially on my own. I have always needed my sisters to be here just so that I wouldn't suffer alone. I admit that Christmas time is supposed to be a time when we all come together – feel the love and the warmth of family. But there is no love and warmth in this family. All there is – is criticism about how we should live our lives through what my parents approve.

'You selfish bitch – without us you wouldn't even have been born – we gave you life – now it's your turn to give us something in return instead of wasting your life on what you want.'

Dad grabs hold of the shotgun hanging above the fireplace. He opens it up to check that it's loaded. I ask what he's doing and where did he get that gun?

He tells me that he got it cheap. It was originally a piece of evidence. The killer had shot a girl's father then got shot by the Police.

I realize it was the gun that Donna's Dad owned. Billy got it off him and used it against him.

'That Shane comes back – I will be ready to use this.'

I panic – he's acting crazy. I need to go back to Shane and warn him. I attempt to leave but Dad stops me – grabbing my wrist tightly so it hurts. I scream not being able to get out of his grip while he holds the gun which waves about. I'm scared that it's going to go off.

Then the lights go out. The cabin is thrown into darkness. Dad lets go of me. We then hear a growl. Something in the doorway. I know it's the dog that Mr Geoffries rescued.

'Now is that anyway to treat your daughter?' Mr Geoffries voice travels in the room. I take my phone out and turn on the torch – I flash it at the doorway to see the light reflecting in the eyes of the dog. Dad aims the gun at the dog. It barks at him.

'I give everyone the benefit of the doubt.' Dad swings the shotgun round the room not being able to see where the voice is coming from. 'I've seen this world change – it's people turning into monsters just like that boy, Tom, and then there was Nikki – a woman homeless – I looked into her eyes and saw that she was beyond help – the terrible things she was going to do – and she did them without a care of consequence in her heart.'

'Where are you?' yells Dad.

I aim my flashlight at Dad. Mr Geoffries stands in front of him. He grabs hold of the gun barrel which goes off – then pulls it out of Dad's hands. Dad backs away as Mr Geoffries stands there.

Shane stands next to him and holds out his hand to me. 'Come with me.' I don't hesitate – I grab hold of his hand tightly and he leads me out of the cabin away from my parents. But then he stops – waiting for his uncle who hasn't gone with them. We overhear my dad and Mr Geoffries talking…

'Nothing we do matters you know,' says Dad. 'You can take my daughter away from us – love is already dying and soon it'll be gone forever – the love between me and her mother died a long time ago.'

Mr Geoffries then joins us. He walks past us and says, 'Come on – we're leaving.' So we do – we leave my parents behind.

8

I stand outside the log cabin. For the first time in my life I feel relieved – not sad that I have lost my parents as I felt I lost them a long time ago. I close my eyes and breathe in the cold fresh air.

'Are you ok?' asks Shane. I look at him – feeling so happy that I took him. He saved me.

'You know all this time I thought I was your prisoner – but I wasn't – it was you all along.'

I take hold of his hand and thank him and his uncle for the help he's given me.

'What will you do with yourself now?' asks Shane.

'What anyone else would do? Just enjoy myself at Christmas – return to my job and look for love.'

'You won't have to look too hard, Melissa – love will find you in the New Year – I can see it,' smiles Mr Geoffries.

I believe him too. Those images that he saw came true. So this has got to be true. He tells me that I will make the move that will set up the rest of my love life. It's like he's hinting that I will be the one that asks them to marry me. Whatever it means – I'm excited to find out.

I look up at the roof of the cabin to see mistletoe. Shane notices too. After everything we have been through – and as it's Christmas I think it's a perfect moment. Shane holds me by the waist. We lean towards each other – closing our eyes until ours lips press together. We hold the kiss and are lost in the moment, until Mr Geoffries clears his throat to make us stop.

Mr Geoffries stares up at the sky. Shane joins his side and looks up too. 'What is it?' he asks.

'There's a storm coming,' says Mr Geoffries 'Is it me? Or do you feel like someone is watching us?'

Christmas – a time for family, friends and loved ones to come together and celebrate the spirit of good will and most importantly – the spirit, of love.

WALL

1

I don't know where I am. All around me is an endless blackness. I don't see much apart from images, like my mind is playing tricks on me. I can't speak – I don't know if I am a man or a woman. All I know is who I am.

So, what did I see? Snow. But no ordinary snow. The snow was pink. It began to fall after the bombs fell onto the world. Someone had launched them – hell bent on destroying the most powerful need and emotion. LOVE.

I know what people would think. How can you destroy love? Love never dies. But it finally did. It was like a vision. But not of what happened – of what was to come. These visual images are in my imagination. I saw it all.

How all this began. The pieces of a very large puzzle.

It all started with a couple. Their names were Allison and Matthew. They were married and in love. Their love seemed so strong. But Matthew made a mistake – he assumed his wife was cheating on him. It turned out his assumption was wrong and he was the one that cheated on her. I felt that broken heart – like it happened to me but at the same time I felt like it hadn't. I didn't want that to happen to me but there's always doubt in the back of your mind that it could.

Sometimes finding love was a struggle – especially if you're hiding a secret. That's what happened to Ana. She had lots of bad dates then one night she started to be stalked everywhere she went. But through all of that she found a decent guy until her secret was revealed. The stalker was a guy that was originally her before her operation. Being a transgender and trying to find love is a difficult situation.

But it can work out – there are some people out there that just like who they are no matter what they look like whether they're a man or woman. We all have feelings – I knew that myself and no one likes getting hurt.

We've all wanted things in life, love, family a career.

When we get them, it seems like all your dreams come true. But it doesn't last. You realize to yourself – that it's not what you want. Sometimes the things we need are what we really want. That's what makes our life stable and we finally find our happiness. It worked for Megan – a pop star who threw her entire career away. She got married and was a mother with the man of her dreams.

When it came to starting a relationship. You must always be honest no matter what secrets you hold. I saw that in Mary who fell in love. She kept her prostitution hidden from him and ended up getting pregnant with his child. She lost him when he discovered what she really did and what made it worse was one of his friends was one of her clients. Being honest in love is the only way to keep things strong. As break ups and heartache are caused by the lack of honesty.

Although some secrets are difficult to be honest about.

Missy Lockhart discovered this. She was engaged to the kindest man she had ever met. But she could never be intimate with him. She was a lesbian who had an affair with a bisexual woman who she secretly got to hook up with her partner to share her. She didn't want to hurt him – but you can never hide a secret – as the months went by Will went to see Marcy and discovered her in bed with Missy. The truth came out. Will felt destroyed and Missy felt bad. She wishes she had been honest with him from the day she met him. From that day onwards – she never kept anything from anyone. She learnt her lesson.

Love can do all sorts of things to us. It can also turn us into monsters. Ashley discovered this. She wasn't normal like anyone else. She was classed as a vampire – she drank blood – was sensitive to the light. She even fell in love with a boy at school that took an interest in her. Then school never knew who she really was as she would be classed as a monster. But Tom had a strong love for his mother who was in a dangerous relationship. He became a monster when he killed his mother's partner. Who was the real monster at the end of it? That's what I thought and I realized it was the monsters that are born inside us.

Monsters can also be part of games and fantasies – but the fantasy of love is the worst way love can go. It can destroy you. It happened for Nikki and Matthew. They struggled with their love life with Matthew still clinging on to the love for his ex-wife. They played a game called play 4 real and introduced a third person to their relationship.

The game was extreme but they signed a contract to agree to play the dares of the game for real. Matthew lost; he had to pick a sex risk challenge for Dennis and Nikki to play out for real. She got pregnant through it and

286

Matthew was left with a woman that teased him with another man's baby inside her belly. He thought it was his karma. I could see the dangers of bringing someone else into a relationship that's struggling and it isn't the answer.

Fantasies just want them to be perfect – but perfecting lies in all of us for just being ourselves. It worked for Harry; he found the perfect woman. Jennifer was loving, beautiful with a good sense of humour and lots of emotions. Things moved really quickly for them especially after their first date. They loved each other enough to get married quickly. Their friends had no problem with this as they could tell they genuinely loved each other. But love doesn't last – as tragedy struck. His friend Dennis attempted to kill her after such a bitter attitude to love. His wife had left him when he got another woman called Nikki pregnant. He couldn't come to terms with the mistake he had made. Jennifer killed Dennis but the damage she had sustained caused her to malfunction. Yes – she was a machine. With technology advancing all the time even machines need love too and, in the future, we won't be able to tell the difference.

It was proof that love could be found anywhere – like sometimes it can be right in front of you and others wouldn't see it apart from yourself. It's what happened to Frank. He was a paranormal investigator who lost Lilly, the love of his life. He quit the profession after that but took to it once more when a woman called Sharon turned up. The only reason he did it was because she looked like Lilly. Working together they solved a haunting and it turned out that Lilly was always Sharon who had a troubled life and couldn't tell him the truth until now. He discovered her body long after that. Even in death their love remained which means it has to last forever no matter what has been said.

There have been doubts – people believing that love is going to die out. I think that's what Neil and Amy believed. Their marriage was on the rocks – getting closer to separation – and divorce was inevitable. Then one day – a Ukrainian woman called Gia turned up at their door to help them. She came from a place called the Family Home where the people that she helped went to meet her boss. But they soon discovered that there was something more sinister going on and they were lobotomized – like brain dead zombies. The horror of how far people would go for showing love.

But things aren't all that bad. Where there was love – there was life. Kay discovered this as a life was growing inside her. She got pregnant with the wrong man called Billy who treated her like she was nothing. He didn't want anything to do with the baby and she found herself alone. The only support she had was from her sister Sandra who secretly signed Kay up for a single mother dating site. It didn't take long for a man to get in touch with her. Alex was perfect even though his mistakes with prostitute Mary was always on his mind. He was honest with Kay about that and supported her through the nine months of her pregnancy. They became close and Alex considered that he was going to propose to Kay – but he had a change of heart when Billy turned up at the birth – wanting to be a dad to improve his life. Alex walked away, as he knew that the baby should be with the real father. Some call it making a noble sacrifice – if you really love someone then you should let them go. I saw it as foolish. He should have done what he originally intended and stayed with Kay. If something feels so right – why would you let it go?

As the years go by – you begin to think is this what your life has come to. You can be in your forties and think that love won't happen to you and your life is going nowhere. But Zac was only twenty-five – and he already began to think that. Through an endless repetitive routine he was single and stuck in a job he didn't like. So he decided to change it. He changed everything about himself. The hours he woke up – the chores he did. And then he found love in the ranch hand's daughter, Donna. But at the time she was with Billy – Kay's old boyfriend. Zac and Donna's bond grew. Billy was controlling and jealous – then Donna found out he was still with Kay who he had a son with. She felt like a fool. But tragedy struck, her father was killed by Billy – and he was shot down by the police. She married Zac, and Kay felt like she had made the biggest mistake by letting Alex go.

I always hoped they would get together – so after everything they've experienced, one day they could laugh about it. Because when you're down and troubled, having a laugh can perk you back up and boost your spirts. It worked for Matt. He was going through a rough time with his wife Laura, tired of working two jobs and being kept up most of the night with his son. It was all getting too much for him. But having a talk and laugh with his friend Colin made him feel better. The love in laughter can turn a bad day into something good.

As the year came to a close, Christmas arrived. Everyone I had seen came together, like their stories through the year came to a conclusion. Christmas was always a time for love, joy and merriment. It's also a time to see how far we will push ourselves. Melissa had done the craziest of things. She took a guy and forced him to pretend to be her boyfriend as she was frightened of being alone with her parents for Christmas. They always gave her a hard time, never happy with her life choices. They always went on at her and told her she should be working here and you should have a boyfriend with a high paid job.

To Melissa they were very shallow. Shane witnessed this with his own eyes when he pretended to be her boyfriend. He felt like a prisoner being taken against his will and pretending to be someone he's not. But he realized that she was the prisoner all along – and together with his uncle, Mr Geoffries, they saved Melissa from her parents. Even at Christmas time – love still bloomed. But Mr Geoffries was concerned that a storm was coming.

Through all those events – there was always a hint of someone watching them – observing their stories. And there was. It was me. I was the observer. I saw their lives unfold like words that were written down on a page of a story. This story – the one I'm holding in my hand right now.

Everything I had experienced wasn't just telling a story. It was a moral lesson. Things that we all have experienced ourselves at one time in our life – things we could relate to and things we couldn't explain.

There looked like moments where love died out between couples – and some that were hell bent on keeping it alive – that never gave up the fight. And that's when I realized – there was a key to this story – hidden in plain sight all this time. The key was *fourteen words* – it was the first word highlighted at the beginning of every chapter of this story. It made a sentence. So I stopped reading this story and looked at the first word of every chapter.

Now I have returned to this story – and now I see it all. Those fourteen words are something that everyone will have to remember. I couldn't imagine a world without love – but it terrifies me to see what it could be. But as long as we have those fourteen words with us. Love will never die – as we will fight every obstacle and trial that stands in our way. And we will prove that *The Power of Love* can last forever.

PRICE

1

Matthew escorted Allison towards the dance floor where other couples were dancing to a slow romantic song. She placed her hand in his and the other on his waist. She gazed into his eyes, smiling as that old-fashioned feeling of love flooded through her body. The feeling was mutual for Matthew, his eyes widened at how beautiful she looked as she sparkled in the light coming from the glimmer ball.

"You know I've been thinking about everything that's happened this year between us, and…" But Allison put her finger on his mouth.

"Can we not talk about the past right now? We only have minutes before midnight – let's begin the new year as a fresh start, that's my new year's resolution," said Allison as she pulled him closer.

Matthew felt her warm breath down his neck, her smell that came from her mouth and skin that always excited and aroused him.

"Matthew – can I ask what your new year's resolution is?"

"My resolution is not to make the same mistake twice and to make up for the past – starting with this." Matthew bent down on one knee, took Allison's hand and presented an engagement ring in front of her. "Will you marry me, Allison?"

Allison grinned like a Cheshire cat and wiped the tears of joy from her eyes. "YES," she screamed. "I'll marry you." Matthew placed the ring on her finger, the small diamond sparkled in the light. She looked up, pulled him close and pressed her lips on to his. But their special moment was interrupted by the countdown as the people evacuated the dance floor to find the person they want to kiss at midnight while others rushed to the bar to get a drink as the countdown to the new year appeared on a big projector screen.

"Ten, nine, eight…" the people began to chant, "seven, six, five, four, three, two, one – HAPPY NEW YEAR," they yelled.

Confetti rained down upon everyone while noise makers sounded and people sang and danced to Auld Lang Syne while others were locking lips with strangers, loved ones and hugs were exchanged with friends.

"Come on," said Allison grabbing Matthew's hand. "Let's go home and start working on our future." But as she pulled Matthew, she found that he didn't budge. A look of sadness filled his face. "What's wrong?"

"Sorry," he said wiping a tear away from his eye. "It's just…" He paused. But Allison knew how he was going to end the sentence. When they were together, they had talked about working on their future before. Years had passed and then Allison discovered she could never conceive a child. This hit them hard and made things difficult between them for a whole year but over time they had moved on and continued with their lives.

"Hey," she said placing her hand on the side of his face. "I know it's hard living with this – I have to every day – but we can still work on our future – it's just you and me, okay?"

"Yes." Matthew nodded. "We've still got a wedding to plan."

"And quickly – I want to get married in two weeks from now – I don't want to waste any time." Allison pulled Matthew through the crowds of people towards the exit. As they left, Allison knocked someone's drink out of their hand. "Oh god, I'm sorry."

Melissa wiped the damp patch of her blue evening dress. When she saw who bumped into her, her reaction wasn't that of anger. She was delighted to see her.

"Allison – Matthew – what are you doing here together?"

Allison looked at Matthew then held her hand out in front of Melissa revealing her engagement ring. Melissa was open mouthed with excitement and joy and then wrapped her arms round Allison giving her a big squeezed hug.

"So, Christmas worked out for both of you then?"

"How do you know?" Matthew asked.

"I'm sorry – I work as a waitress, I overheard you both talking on Christmas Eve, that after all you've been through and instead of being apart, you didn't want to be alone for Christmas. I take it that worked out well."

"Well, in the bedroom it did," Matthew joked.

Allison hit Matthew on the arm. "Stop it." She smiled cheekily. "It's going to be tight – but we're planning to get married in the next two weeks – you'll come, won't you?"

"I wouldn't miss it for the world." Melissa smiled with joy.

"Bring your partner," Matthew suggested. "I take it he's here."

"I don't have a partner."

"So, you're here on your own?" said Allison.

"What I mean is, I do have a partner – I just can't find him yet – I was hoping he would be here, that's what I was told."

"By who?" Matthew asked curiously.

"A lovely man called Mr Geoffries, I met him at Christmas time and he told me that the man I am meant to be with is looking for me – that's why I'm here to make it easier so he can find me."

Matthew looked at Allison who thought the same thing. Melissa had always been one to overthink things in her life and people had noticed calling her crazy. To avoid any awkwardness, she said to Melissa that they had to go and she would get in touch with her to discuss wedding plans.

When they left Melissa found herself on her own again.

She made her way past the booze fuelled people that spilled their drinks and staggered around which caused one to knock Melissa to the floor, but she was soon helped to her feet by an attractive man in a grey suit.

"Are you okay there?" he asked.

"I am now," Melissa replied reading his name badge "Charlie Bradshaw." Melissa held on tightly to his hands. "Are you him? The man who's looking for me?"

"Sorry, love," he replied holding up his hand to reveal his wedding band. "I'm happily married."

Melissa frowned and looked disappointed. "It's not my night is it? I give up." She pushed Charlie aside and walked away.

Charlie made his way to the bar. As he was about to order his drinks someone grabbed his shoulder then patted him on the back. A man took his hand in his and shook it.

"Congratulations, Bradshaw – a new year and a promotion to kick things off with – you must be proud."

"Thanks, Mr Reed – but I already know what my wife is going to think, that it's not enough to get us out of our debt," Charlie explained.

"You're a hard worker and I like that; I wish I could offer you more but everyone knows what Liz Cooper is like."

"I know – she's very picky with her staff."

"Still – have a good new year and we'll see you bright and early, and it's Carl by the way – no more Mr Reed."

Charlie smiled in amusement as his boss walked away. He ordered two beers then noticed a blonde-haired woman dressed in a black and grey dress sitting at the bar on her own.

"And whatever the lady is having," Charlie acknowledged Steve, the barman, who he had gone to the same school as.

The woman rolled her eyes at Charlie, scowling at him in annoyance. She looked him up and down then spotted his wedding ring on his finger. She shook her head then snapped, "What would your wife say?"

Charlie could tell that she was assuming he was trying to chat her up and found that there was only one answer he could give her. "She would say you are so kind and that is why I married you." The woman just stared at Charlie making him feel uncomfortable. "What's your name?"

"Madison," she replied.

"Well, Madison," said Charlie taking some money out. "Enjoy the drink, and Happy New Year." Charlie put the money down on the bar in front of Madison and collected his drinks. As he walked away, Madison looked him up and down and then smiled to herself.

2

Two days had passed since then. Charlie and his wife, Robyn, had enjoyed New Year's Day together. They didn't get much time to spend with themselves with him working days and her working nights. As Charlie drove himself to work to start his first day in his new role, Robyn called him on the Bluetooth.

"Morning, Pumpkin, what's up?"

"I just wanted to wish you good luck in your new role and to tell you that I love you."

"I love you too."

"You're so kind and wonderful – however did I get so lucky to have an honest and faithful loving husband?"

Charlie chuckles to himself and thinks back to New Year's Eve. "I wish you could have told that woman that."

"Yeah I didn't get that – what's up with that? It's like she had a real distrust in men." But their conversation was interrupted by the door buzzer. "Look I have to go – call me later, love you."

Robyn hung up and threw her phone down on the sofa.

When she got to the door, she could see a slim shaped figure through the glass. When she opened the door, she saw a woman standing in front of her.

"Can I help you?"

"I'm Madison."

"And what are you here for?" Robyn asked curiously.

"Your husband," replied Madison. "I'm here to buy your husband."

Robyn just stood there going through a range of emotions, from confusion to anger.

"Excuse me," Robyn snapped. "You want to what?"

"I want to buy your husband – so I need to come in and discuss how I'm going to do this."

Robyn was about to explode with her anger, she took hold of the door and slammed it shut, but Madison stopped it from shutting with her leg.

"No – I'm not leaving until I get what I want," she insisted.

"Fine," Robyn snapped. "Then I'll call the police."

Robyn went to get her phone, when she started to dial the police's number, Madison took the phone out of her hand and threw it at the wall smashing it to bits.

"You don't really have a fucking choice in this – now shut up and sit down so we can discuss terms and conditions."

Madison pushed Robyn down on the sofa, but Robyn put up a fight against her struggling to get out of her grip. Madison than slapped her round the face. Robyn screamed and was afraid of what this strange lunatic was going to do to her.

"Hear me out – I just need to convince you to let me buy your husband – okay?"

Robyn was shaking, then nodded. "All right – we'll talk."

Madison sat down on the sofa, crossed her legs and put her hands together. Robyn placed her hand on the side of her face which stung where Madison had slapped her.

"So, tell me about your husband, Charlie."

"What is it you want to know?" asked Robyn.

"What your marriage is like? What he's like to live with, his personality?"

"Why do you want to know?"

"Because once you tell me your side of the story – I can tell you why I'm here."

An awkward silence filled the air between them. Robyn didn't know where to begin, but Madison never pushed her to start talking. She waited patiently for Robyn.

"I need a drink," insisted Robyn.

Madison smiled and nodded. "Just a water for me please."

Robyn went to the kitchen while Madison didn't move from the sofa. Robyn took two glasses from the cupboard above the sink and filled them both with water. "Come on Charlie, can't you sense something is wrong?" she spoke softly trying not to let Madison overhear.

When she returned to the living room, lots of thoughts went through her head. She could throw the water in her face and run out of the flat to escape Madison. She could drop the glasses to break them so she could take a piece and cut Madison to wound her then run. But she didn't, instead she handed her the water then sat back down. What she really wanted to know is why this woman was interested in her husband.

"Are you now ready to talk ‚sweetie?" Madison asked as she took a sip and listened to Robyn's story.

Robyn met Charlie when he was admitted to the hospital after injuring himself when he fell down the stairs at his job. Robyn was a nurse who tended to him. As Charlie's time in hospital was boring as there wasn't a lot he could do, he found the only bit of excitement to his day was talking to Robyn. She was a pretty little thing, five foot five with shoulder length brunette hair with a mole above her right eye. Charlie became Robyn's best part of the day when she found out they had a lot in common – they loved going to concerts, reading about politics, which became a very heated conversation as each had a different opinion.

When it came to their first date, they went to a bar called *The Pink Snow*. It wasn't the best place to have a conversation due to the noise from the alcohol fuelled people that were there mixed with the booming drum and bass music. Robyn drank her way through most of the night of their date as Charlie proved he was a bit of a light weight as he did drink but not to the extent of what Robyn put back.

With Robyn being tipsy she pulled Charlie onto the dance floor. She danced sexily in front of him but soon discovered that he wasn't a very good dancer. She was about to call it quits when Charlie did something unexpected and planted one on her lips. Something changed in her. She was excited and found he was a great kisser.

Robyn and Charlie ended up back at hers as she dragged him into her bed and after all the guys she had ever been with, found out that Charlie was the best sex she had ever had and she knew she didn't want to let him go.

Within the month Charlie proposed and two months after that they were married and living together. It was a whirlwind romance between them which their parents didn't agree to as they hardly knew each other

They both felt strong in their choices, were happy and in love and that was all that mattered to them. But rushing into it played on Robyn's mind more as time went on.

Happily married turned into a nightmare at first, as they started to find out they had very little in common. They rowed constantly, disagreeing with each other interests and tastes in food. Robyn was always working late night shifts and Charlie felt lonely in the flat every night he got home from working days. This caused more rows as neither of them would find common ground to change jobs so they could see each other. The marriage felt like they were single again and their sex life was non-existent.

Robyn was on the verge of a breakdown and cried herself to sleep when she came home in the morning from work and on top of it all they struggled to pay the rent. She made more money than Charlie and always pushed him to better himself so he could make more money and keep them financially stable.

They had talked about separating which made them both upset, but Charlie being a good lover as he was, persuaded Robyn, she didn't want to lose a good thing. After the passionate night Robyn's faith was temporarily restored but weeks turned into months and they were both back to square one. As time went by it looked like all was lost between the two of them, until Robyn came home one morning and saw Charlie still at home. It was that moment when he gave her the good news that he was getting a promotion and his wage would be increasing. It pleased her until she found out the money still wasn't enough to cover the bills as they had started to get into debt. Charlie convinced her that he would do everything he could to provide for them and if they lost their home, it wouldn't stop him working to get another as his love for her was too important and that is where Robyn finished telling Madison her story.

Madison sat quietly for a minute thinking about everything that Robyn had just told her and then came to a logical conclusion when she put her glass down on the coffee table.

"Thank you for telling me your story – I am ready and more than willing to take your husband off your hands."

"What? – You're really serious about this aren't you?" Robyn asked.

"You have just sat there and told me all the things that aren't making you happy. You don't have things in common and you're not willing to try new things. One of you has to give in," Madison insisted. She leaned forward and grabbed hold of Robyn's hand. "The money I can give you will set you up for life, no more debt, a clean break, a chance to start anew and find the stable love and common interests you deserve – isn't giving it up worth that price?"

Robyn thought about all the possibilities. Madison was right, she hadn't been happy for a long time and holding on to someone who's only

300

good at sex was wasted time.

"Before I give you my answer – tell me why you are insistent on buying him?"

Madison crossed her legs and told her, "The night of New year's – I made a wrong judgement. I assumed he as a married man wanted to cheat with someone else to get his sexual kicks, but I was wrong. I saw a pure heart, someone kind, loving and who stays loyal. That's what I've always wanted as – when it came to relationships – I made a bad choice and have suffered ever since. This is my chance to be happy and in love."

"What happened to you to make you suffer?" Robyn asked curiously. But she could see Madison's eyes tearing up as she looked away from her. Robyn realized that the subject was too upsetting for her to tell. Robyn quickly stood up and left for the door. Madison reacted and tried to grab her. But stopped when she realized Robyn went to the bookshelf for a box of tissues then held them out for Madison. She hung her head in shame knowing all too well that this was another wrong judgement she has made.

Madison took the tissues and dried her eyes. "Thank you," she said with a sniffled voice.

"So, how much are we talking?" Robyn asked as she held her hand out. Madison smiled with joy, then shook Robyn's hand.

3

The hours of the day passed and Charlie made his way home from the office. When he got home and walked in, he was greeted by something he wasn't expecting. His two suitcases in the hallway, all packed and ready to go.

"Robyn," he shouted, his anger building up wondering what the hell she was doing. When he walked in the living room, Robyn was dressed in a black dress looking stunning with a new hair style and full make over holding a glass of wine in her hand, smiling like a Cheshire cat. "What the hell is going on?"

Robyn sipped her wine. "I've come to realize that we are just not meant to be."

"What the hell are you talking about?' Charlie snapped.

"Charlie – we both know that we're not meant to be with each other. We're two different people who are looking for different things."

Charlie was confused and couldn't believe what he was hearing. "Look I know that we have different things in common but opposites attract."

"Not all the time. Thanks to her I've come to realize I'm using you just for sex and a relationship isn't just about that. It's wrong, surely you must understand that?"

But Charlie's emotions were all over the place, a mixture of anger and upset causing his heart to break. He wiped the tears from his eyes and couldn't find the right words to say.

"Don't be upset. I'm saving you. It's my fault as I am expecting too much and I want money to keep me stable so I don't have to worry the rest of my life," Robyn explained.

"The divorce proceedings are already finalized. She's got amazing lawyers to take care of it all."

"Who is this bitch?" Charlie snapped.

"That would be me," replied Madison as she appeared from another room. Charlie was lost for words when he saw the woman from the New Year's Eve party standing in front of him smiling with a big grin. "Hi,

Charlie – so good to see you again."

But Charlie aggressively lunged towards her. His fist clenched ready to attack her but Robyn stood in the way and stopped him from making a mistake. "Charlie stop, please." She pushed him back to get some distance between them.

"You're listening to this arrogant bitch – this is the woman I told you about," Charlie yelled.

"I know – she's already explained."

Madison pushed past Robyn and approached Charlie. "I'm here for you and you're going to come home with me. Of all the men I have ever met – you are the kindest, most faithful and loving man around. Robyn is not happy being with you, but I would be and I would love you forever. You wouldn't have to push yourself or try to impress me. You could just be yourself and we would both be happy."

Charlie starred at Madison. Her beautiful looks were more stunning than Robyn's and to him it was the first time he felt at ease. He had tired himself out emotionally trying to impress Robyn.

"I don't work, Charlie, and you won't have to either as I'm financially stable. We would wake up with each other in bed every day. Do fun things, have an amazing sex life and live like a husband and wife should do – doesn't that sound nice? Isn't that what you've always wanted?"

Charlie couldn't deny that what Madison was offering was too good to be to true. Robyn takes Charlie's hand in hers. "We both know this is how it should be – how often does someone come along that wants you?"

"But I don't even know anything about this woman."

"That can be the first thing we can do when we get to mine. We can sit down, have dinner and talk," Madison explained. She takes Charlie's hand out of Robyn's and squeezes it firmly. "Just give me a chance."

Charlie looked at Robyn who agreed, then Madison told her that payment should be in her account. Charlie pulled away from Madison. "Wait – what fucking payment?"

Robyn showed him a seven-digit number in her account. "You sold me out, you bitch."

He walked away and grabbed his bags then stormed out the flat. Madison and Robyn looked at each other for a second then Madison went after Charlie, leaving Robyn alone now wondering what to do with herself.

4

Charlie's emotions were all over the place. As he passed people in the street weaving his suitcases in and out of them, his anger got the better of him causing him to want to punch someone the more people that looked at him. He wanted to scream out loud but he wasn't the type of person to do that. All of a sudden, a hand grabbed his shoulder.

"Charlie," Madison called. Charlie backed away when he saw Madison. The woman that ruined his marriage was standing in front of him. He pictured himself getting into a car and running her over. He felt like he had nothing else to lose and killing her was optional.

"Fuck off," shouted Charlie aggressively.

"Charlie please," Madison pleaded. "Calm down."

"Okay – fuck off, you bitch, before I kill you."

"I understand how angry you must be feeling. It's not easy when someone betrays your heart," Madison explained. "But I am not the bad one here. I have just saved you from a terrible mistake."

"Mistake? You flashed money around, she sold me and you bought me. What am I? A fucking toy?"

"No – you're the best man that anyone would be proud to marry and spend the rest of their life with. If Robyn really deeply loved you, she would've fought for you and turned down the money. But she didn't. Now do you understand by what I mean when I say you were betrayed?"

Charlie couldn't argue. Madison's logic and explanation made sense. With being angry, upset and confused he began to think crazy thoughts. With the traffic rushing by, he could step out into the middle of the road and get killed by a car, then the pain and heartbreak would be over.

But Madison knew what he was thinking and grabbed his hand to be sure he wouldn't go through with it. "No," she insisted. "Don't even think about it – it would be such a waste." He looked at her with tearful eyes. He wanted to break down and cry. "Please, honey, come home with me. You have a place to stay and we can get to know each other more, come on." Madison took Charlie's car keys, then helped him sit down in the passenger side. She then got in the driver's side, closed the door, started the car and drove away.

5

Charlie stared out the window as Madison drove them to the countryside. He was still in disbelief of how the day had turned out and this stranger had replaced Robyn who he had been with for a long time. Their journey took them further and deeper, to places that didn't know existed.

Charlie took notice of an old car that looked like it was gathering rust outside an old farmhouse with a sign next to it that read 'FAYMILL'.

"That's Faymill farm – no one lives there now because of its history. But now it's going for sale."

"What history?" asked Charlie.

"It used to be haunted," Madison told him.

She continued to drive through the narrow roads passing a woodland area where an old log cabin stood.

"You live here?"

"No," Madison chuckled to herself. "This place is the May's – Megan May's family own it. They use it for their Christmas getaway every year for their family."

"Megan May? The pop star?"

"Ex pop star," Madison told Charlie firmly.

"So, what happens to it the rest of the year?"

"Oh, it gets used in the summer," Madison explained.

"So, where are we going? Where do you live?"

"You see that place at the top of the hill in the distance." She pointed. Charlie couldn't really make it out. "It's only five miles away. We'll be there soon."

6

Madison drove the car up the hill until she pulled up outside an old bungalow. Charlie was in disbelief at what he saw. The old house had large cracks in the wall and the roof was out of shape as it sloped in on itself. The windows were jagged and cracked and the grass grew long like it had been un-kept.

"This is your place?" Charlie asked.

"This is my little home," Madison confirmed.

"But it's so run down – I thought as you had lots of money being rich and all, you lived in a large posh house."

"Appearances can be deceiving, haven't you heard that expression?" Madison said with an aggressive tone. "I'm sorry – it's just I love this place, no one knows about it and it's a good place to relax in peace."

Charlie agreed with Madison. There was no noise.

Gone was the sound of traffic and people that plagued the streets outside his flat where he lived.

"Come on – I want to show you something."

As she stepped out of the car, Charlie felt uneasy like he didn't know what he was about to get himself into, staying in this stranger's place that he didn't know anything about. The nerves grew stronger until he had the courage to leave the car. But he didn't follow her. Instead he got back in the car to turn the ignition and drive away. But he couldn't – when he realized the keys weren't in the ignition as Madison had taken the keys with her. Reluctantly knowing that he couldn't leave as she could drive after him if he walked away, he made his way to the back of the bungalow to see Madison sitting on an old rusted swing seat. And that's when he saw the most beautiful view he had ever seen.

"Come sit next to me," Madison insisted.

Charlie sat down and stared out at the view. The peaceful surroundings made him feel content and relaxed around Madison. She didn't force him to talk, she just let him take in the surroundings. Charlie noticed buildings down below in the distance. He pointed at them and asked her, "What's that over there?"

"That's Pentemy Village – it's a little community that keeps itself to itself."

"Do you visit there much?"

"No," she whispered.

"Have I upset you?" Charlie asked, curious as to why Madison didn't want to talk about it. "Sore subject?"

"Just a little," Madison replied feeling uneasy. "I've been there once just to leave something there, let's just leave the conversation at that, shall we?"

"Okay," agreed Charlie.

"Let me show you the rest of the place." Madison got up and went inside. Charlie took one more look at the village, then followed behind.

10

Madison showed Charlie around her bungalow. The living room was vintage. Full of old furniture and vases like an older person would have lived there. It didn't fit Madison's style which Charlie found suspicious. She showed him the kitchen that had a small wooden table and two wooden chairs. When he saw the bathroom, it was vile. The smell of urine filled his nostrils and he saw black mold in between the cracks of the stained wall tiles. The bedroom however was the tidiest room of them all. It was oriental in style with a four poster bed. Madison sat on the bed smiling at Charlie while she stroked the bedsheets.

"So, what do you think, Charlie?" smiled Madison as she bit her bottom lip.

"I think this place needs a lot of work," he said looking unimpressed.

"Well, there is a reason why I haven't done anything with the place. I've been waiting for the right man to fix it up and design a home together to live in," Madison explained. "Haven't you ever wanted to have a home of your own design and decision?"

Charlie thought about when he moved in with Robyn. Every room of the flat was how she wanted it. He had no say in the matter as when he suggested changing one of the rooms it would always spark a row. In a way he was glad to be away from Robyn and this made him see Madison as a joint partner where decisions would be discussed instead of made one sided.

"Take my hand," she said holding it out in front of him. Charlie held her hand where she gave it a strong squeeze. "I know all this must be overwhelming and you must be confused at what's going on – but I wanted you and one day I hope you may say that you love me."

Charlie pulled his hand away. "Madison, you seem like a lovely woman, but if that's ever going to happen, it's going to take a lot of time me to get over Robyn."

"Of course, whatever you need," said Madison who sounded disappointed. "How about I cook us a nice dinner and we'll open a bottle of red wine, we could talk and get to know each other more?"

It was at that moment that Charlie saw her understated side and couldn't say no to her. "Okay – that would be nice – I like red wine."

11

Later that evening, the table was laid out with a blue and white squared table cloth. Two plates of homemade chicken in breadcrumbs, garlic green beans and steamed potatoes were on table mats with silver cutlery accompanied by two glasses of red wine.

Charlie didn't have much of an appetite. Instead he just drank his wine while listening to Madison share her ideas of how she would like to fix up the bungalow and asked for Charlie's input of what he would like to do.

"I don't know – I don't actually care," Charlie snapped.

His attitude upset Madison. "I'm trying here, Charlie; I didn't go through all this for you to upset me."

Her outburst made him feel guilty. He was acting like an asshole to her. As the two of them sat in silence, Charlie decided to make the first move and apologized to her by holding her hand. He then took his fork and ate the garlic green beans. The surprise flavour caused an explosion in his mouth which ignited his taste buds. "Wow – this is really good," he told her.

"Thank you." She smiled at the compliment. "It was just something I quickly threw together."

"It's been a long time since I've had a home cooked meal. I've mostly been living on convenience foods and takeaways."

"Well, all that's going to change now." She grabbed hold of the empty wine bottle. "I'll get us another bottle."

"Please." He put his knife and fork down. "I'll do it – I've got to learn my way around this place."

"NO," she outburst, which caused Charlie to sit back down in his seat "I said I'll do it."

When Madison left the room, it made Charlie feel uneasy at why she reacted the way she did. That's when he made a decision to call Robyn but found out that her phone was switched off. As he waited for Madison to return, he looked around the kitchen at the blue walls which made the room look dark and cold. When Madison returned with an open bottle of wine,

Charlie made a suggestion.

"What about magnolia?" Charlie asked.

"I'm sorry?" replied Madison, puzzled.

"The kitchen walls. I don't like it. I feel magnolia would brighten up the room that we eat in."

Madison smiled with delight when Charlie began to talk about all the plans and vision he wanted for their home.

Most of the rooms Madison agreed with until they came to discussing the basement. Madison insisted that it was her domain, her little study area she liked to go to think and create her plans of what she would do the rest of the day.

Charlie looked disappointed as he had always wanted his own game room. But Madison didn't rule out his idea as if it was what he wanted then he would get it and suggested that they extend the bungalow to add on his game room. Charlie was happy at this decision as Robyn would never compromise. What she said would go and that was how their marriage was.

With the hours ticking by, mixed with the flows of the wine and their plans, they both began to feel tired. Charlie felt awkward not knowing how the sleeping arrangements would work.

"I'll take the sofa. You sleep in the bed to get used to how it feels then one night, hopefully, you'll invite me to bed." She kissed him on the cheek then went to get some pillows and a duvet cover. Charlie's heart warmed to Madison's understanding nature. He couldn't understand how someone like her has remained single all this time.

12

The next day they left the bungalow to pick up painting and decorating supplies to start making their new home.

When they returned home, Madison laid out some old bed sheets on the floor where they would be painting. She turned the radio on and then started to paint with Charlie. His favourite song came on as he painted, he forgot himself and started to sing along with the song. Madison did the same which turned into a duet between them. Charlie couldn't believe his luck that someone else liked the same music as he did, as Robyn always told him off when he started singing as it annoyed him.

As the time passed, Charlie smiled happily at the efforts that he and Madison put in to the home they had built together. Freshly painted walls with the scent of new carpets and furniture filled the air.

"You've done amazing, Charlie," Madison complimented.

"We've done amazing Madison," Charlie corrected her.

Madison was happier than she had felt in years. She threw her arms around Charlie and hugged him tightly. "I love you," she told him. They stared into each other's eyes for a few seconds, then Madison closed her eyes and leaned forward to kiss him. But Charlie backed away. "What's wrong?"

"It's been just a week – I'm not sure I'm ready to say those words yet," he explained.

"But I've given you plenty of time – haven't we had fun this week? You can't tell me that we don't click – we're meant for each other." As Charlie thought about her words, she left the room then hurried back holding a rose in her hand. "I got this for you."

Charlie held the rose in his hand, puzzled that she would get him it when in his mind it should have been the other way around.

"Red roses mean passion and love – it's how you make my heart feel." Madison pleaded. "I was hoping by now we would be sleeping in the same bed." But Charlie didn't know what to say and caused Madison to leave the room.

With the two of them separated, Charlie couldn't understand why he couldn't bring himself to open up his heart to her. In front of him was a woman that wanted to be with him, someone with common interests and who would compromise to work at a relationship. That was when he decided to put all of his past behind him and make things work with Madison. He started by going down to the basement to fetch a bottle of red wine even though she never wanted him to go down there.

The basement was just like how he expected it to be.

Dimly lit light bulbs in a cold, damp musty area of the bungalow. Two wooden wine racks had a wood rotted appearance to them with the five remaining bottles of wine that remained in them, along with the sound of a leak dripping from a ceiling pipe. As Charlie took the bottle of wine out of the rack, he noticed something in the corner of his eye. There was another door.

He curiously took a closer inspection, knowing that it was Madison's little study room, but discovered it was padlocked. With no means of access, he was about to leave when he saw something else. He knelt down to see a red dry patch in the floor. He scraped it with his nails and was in disbelief when it looked like blood. He was stuck. He couldn't ask Madison what it was considering he shouldn't have even have been down in the basement. His curiosity uncovered a secret that Madison wouldn't tell him. But as he turned to leave, he jumped out of his skin when he saw her standing in front of him, with her arms folded and face filled with a look of thunder.

"What the hell are you doing down here?" Madison snapped.

"To get a bottle of wine. I thought it would be a good idea that we could have a drink and discuss our future."

"So, you're committed to us? We do have a future together?"

"Madison – if we are going to have a future together, you need to tell me everything – no secrets."

"What do you need to know?"

"The room down here – what's in there? And by the door, there is a stain, it looks like blood."

Madison walked up to Charlie and took the bottle of wine out of his hand. "Let's have that drink and I'll explain."

13

Charlie sat at the kitchen table while Madison pulled the cork out of the wine. He sat with his arms crossed patiently waiting for her to return. As the time passed, he couldn't help but wonder why she was taking so long. Madison soon appeared holding two glasses of red wine. She sat down in front of him and passed his glass to him.

"Cheers," she toasted. Charlie toasted his glass then took a mouthful.

"Okay – when you're ready," Charlie insisted.

"I was hoping that I wouldn't have to tell you. It's my personal room. Can't you just let it go? Please?"

"No, I can't," he snapped. "If I am ever going to say, I love you, there should be no secrets between us."

Madison closed her eyes, then wiped a tear away as she began to get upset. Charlie was getting impatient, and finished, gulped down all of his wine, then slammed down the glass. "Tell me," he shouted.

"It's where I do all my thinking, all my planning, privately. I've only taken my previous partners to end our relationship with them because once they've seen the room. It's over," Madison explained.

"Show me," Charlie asked.

"Please," Madison begged. "Don't go in there. I don't want our relationship to end."

"I said…" Charlie slurred his words, "…no secrets."

But his eyes became too heavy to stay open.

"Charlie? What's wrong?" Madison asked. Charlie lost his balance and fell on the floor, unconscious.

14

Meanwhile, Robyn was walking around the shops – looking for things to buy. Most of the clothes and jewellery stores were boring to her. She could buy any of those and not feel like her money had been worth the purchase. After an hour of looking around, she was about to give up until she came across an old antique shop.

The bell rang when she walked in. The air was filled with a musty and old scent as she wandered around looking for something to buy. There was old furniture, china vases and brass ornaments, but again nothing caught her eye, until she spotted it – covered by an old dusty blanket. A mirror. It wasn't the most ordinary looking mirror she had seen before. Robyn pulled the blanket off and took a closer look at it. The mirror was damaged with a crack running down the top over Robyn's face in the reflection. The side circular frame felt strange as the texture was smooth and bumpy in its brass colouring.

Robyn jumped when she heard someone clearing their throat and looked to see who it was. The shopkeeper was an old man in vintage clothing, with a name badge that read 'Thomas'.

"Can I help you miss?" Thomas spoke softly.

"Yes – I'm interested in buying this mirror."

"An excellent choice."

"How much is it?" she asked.

"Six thousand pounds," Thomas replied.

"Why is it so expensive?" Robyn asked with a surprised tone. "It's just a mirror."

"It's because it has quite a history – dating all the way back to the eighteen hundreds."

Robyn looked at it and felt a strange sensation the longer she stared at it. She rubbed her shoulders, licked her lips then bit them. She began to feel hot the more she stared at it, until she snapped out of it and looked at Thomas. "I'll take it."

"Good." Thomas smiled.

Robyn felt satisfied with her purchase. Normally she would never have been able to afford something so expensive, but thanks to Madison, she was now in a position to buy anything she wanted. What Robyn didn't expect was what was going to happen next. When she used her card, Thomas looked up with a concerned look on his face.

"I'm sorry, miss, but it says you have insufficient funds."

"What?" said Robyn. "Try again."

Robyn tried the transaction again and still the same thing occurred.

"It looks like you won't be buying this today."

Robyn used her phone to log into her banking app. When her funds appeared on screen – she felt cold and scared when she saw £0.

15

As the time passed by, Charlie regained consciousness as his eyes slowly opened. He blinked multiple times to clear his blurred vision and took in his unknown surroundings. He found himself in a small room where the walls were covered in a red canvas with a dim light that shone from the ceiling. He had been stripped of his clothes and his arms and legs were stretched out, tied up and sitting up standing upright. He tried to move but he couldn't. Something felt different. He felt aroused and stiff. When he looked down. He could see his manhood standing to attention.

The door to the room opened and Madison walked in now dressed in a black leather latex gown. She stood in front of him looking sexy and seductive with heavy make up that had been applied to her face.

"Madison – what the hell did you do to me?"

"It was just a sedative mixed with a blue Viagra pill. You're not the first man I've done this to," she explained as she undid the gown and let it flop to the floor. She placed her hands on her hips as she showed off her slender figure, while the image of her erect nipples of her busty cleavage tingled Charlie's senses down below.

"This is rape, Madison – you're not forcing me to have sex with you," Charlie shouted.

"You've got it all wrong, Charlie – I've never had sex with any of the men I've brought down here," she told him.

"What the hell is wrong with you?" shouted Charlie as he continuously struggled to get free. "How did you end up so messed up in the head?"

And so, Madison started to the tell her story. She began when she was twenty-three. Her mother was a volunteer for an experimental drug, but had died from the side effects of it. Her father had been hit hard with the loss and took to drinking. Then one night, drunk, frustrated and surfing the Internet, he came across an advert for a club called *Play 4 Real*. He took Madison along for fun to make her join in instead of sitting at home grieving for her mother.

Madison felt uncomfortable sitting among the alcohol fuelled strangers. The host, Krista, appeared before them and went through the rules of the club. As she talked Madison couldn't believe this three-hundred-pound woman was the owner while all her dominatrix looking employees were under half her size.

Her father took her into the room with two other guys.

They played the game from drinking shots of alcohol to dancing sexily, until an extreme challenge occurred and the two strangers took Madison against her will while her father didn't do anything to stop it.

The next day, Madison felt traumatized by what had occurred which made her ill over the course of the weeks. It was then she discovered that she was pregnant by one of the strangers. Her father didn't react or care and she didn't know the name of the strangers. She was alone. Madison saw her pregnancy through to the end; she wasn't the sort of person to get an abortion and terminate the life of a baby. With her father becoming non-existent to her, and her baby daughter's future now to consider, she left home and took to the road. She got lifts from kind strangers until she was miles away from her past.

She was dropped off in a little community called Pentemy Village and that was when she made the hardest decision of her life and left her daughter behind. Upon leaving the village she spotted the bungalow on the hill in the distance and made her way to it. She discovered it was abandoned and decided to stay there on her own. There she was at peace and constantly kept a watch over the village she had left her daughter with. But she knew she could never see her again as she knew she would hold onto the hatred of being abandoned. To her, her daughter was the future that the world would look up to.

As time passed even more, she searched for men, someone kind and loving to settle down with. They started out nice but they always turned into someone that was distrusting. That's why she thought that Charlie was the one for her. But she was wrong.

"You've got a daughter? What was her name?"

"I named her after the last lady I met, the owner of the club – Krista," she told him.

"So, this is revenge on men? After what they did to you in that club, what your father allowed to happen?"

"It's a test – to find the right man for me," she explained.

Madison knew that when he met Robyn she would give in to money –

like most of the women she had met in the past. They sold their lover for a seven-figure number just because they knew they could find someone else with ease and not worry about their financial future. But what they didn't know, was after Madison had given up Krista, she turned to working with computers and learned how to hack. Robyn had shown her bank account and she had taken it all back including the money that Robyn had. To Madison she looked at it as a punishment for selling or buying someone's heart.

All this led to the final test that Charlie and so many men before him had failed. Madison told him that her biggest issue with a relationship, was trust. Knowing that she had a secret room down in the basement she was always asked by men what was inside. When she told them that it was a secret that she didn't want to share, she wanted them to accept it and never ask again. That way she knew that they trusted her and never assume that she was hiding anything. She had been looking for the perfect man that would love her and trust her completely as Charlie failed, she knew that her search would still continue until she succeeded in her goal.

As Madison finished her story, she walked out of the room then entered seconds later wheeling in a guillotine. She wheeled it towards Charlie until his manhood poked through the hole where the sharp blade would come down to chop it off. Madison took hold of a remote control, then sat down in front of him with her back arched back and legs spread open in stirrups.

"Madison please." Charlie panicked. "You can't do this, you crazy bitch."

"I can't let you go – you've seen my room – you didn't trust me – you must be punished." Madison made herself comfortable and held on tightly to the remote. "I lose control when I climax and that is when I hit the button, it won't take long."

Madison began to play with herself. Charlie struggled to get free. He tried and tried with all his strength to pull himself free from the straps that held him up. Madison began to pant quicker and louder as she got close. Her hand quivered and shook as it wrapped round the remote tightly until the button was pressed in. Charlie screamed as the blade fell.

PRISONER

1

At the end of another year, two headlights illuminated the surrounding snowy area of the old log cabin. Its sight was familiar to Melissa as she drove down the gravel pathway and pulled up outside.

Melissa had prepared herself to return to the cabin from her nightmarish experience the year before as her cold breath floated in front of her face making her see the ghosts of her mother and father.

When she stepped out of the warm vehicle, a cold shiver down her spine soon hit her from the icy temperatures outside. Her footsteps crunched the snow under her feet as she walked around the dark cabin. To her surprise, the Christmas lights were still hanging while the icicles hung from the roof. She knew that her dad always took them down before they left, but due to what happened the year before, this proved that there was trouble in the family circle.

Melissa shivered even more as the cold froze her bones. With her hands already in mittens, she stuffed them in her coat pockets to try and warm them up. She then walked away from the car and past the cabin – going deeper into the woods. Any normal person would have gone inside the cabin to keep warm. But Melissa had another agenda up her sleeve.

She brushed aside the snowy branches and logs which looked like black creepy claws that illuminated in the bright moonlight, with the eerie silence in the woods, knowing that she was the only one around. It made her heart race through the fear of the unknown, that's when she stopped when she heard the snap of a twig up ahead. Her heart raced faster and her breathing became more erratic as her body shook with fear and the cold. Her mind told her to run back to the car, but her curiosity told her to go on to get the place she needed to get to.

Melissa followed the path through the dark woods until she came across something familiar which was revealed up ahead. Melissa smiled to herself, as the memories came flooding back. A small abandoned cabin stood in front of her, the place that she and Shane found along with the mysterious Mr Geoffries and his dog.

321

The little time she spent with the two of them was the highlight of her previous Christmas and to come back to remember those previous memories was going to be the highlight of her current one. The voices of Shane and Mr Geoffries echoed around her head like ghosts and her heart ached as she missed them and wished they were there.

It was cold inside the cabin when Melissa stepped in. The fire was out and the windows were frosted over. For a place that hadn't seen any life for a year, she was surprised to see some logs left on the fireplace. At a closer inspection, they looked like they had been freshly cut. Had someone else been there? Melissa found it suspicious. With the cold settling in on her, she lit the fireplace and began to tidy up.

After an hour, Melissa was sitting by the fireplace feeling more toasty than she had done. She stared out the window at the endless snowy woods, thinking about how she and Shane were talking to Mr Geoffries where they discovered the truth about him.

"Where did you guys disappear to? I need you now," Melissa mumbled.

Her eyes started to become heavy from the continuous staring and heat coming from the fire. Her head hung down as she nodded off for a split second, until she fought it and forced herself awake.

Just then, she shook her head in disbelief. She saw one of the branches bobbing up and down, like someone had knocked it. As she took a closer look, she saw something moving in the distance. There was something out there.

Melissa doesn't know if it was a person or some of the wildlife.

Bang, bang, bang. Melissa was startled when the thing was banging on the walls of the cabin. She moved from window to window to try and see who or what it could it be. Melissa was too scared to find out, so she hurried over to the door to lock it, but was too late when the door opened and a handsome man stood in front of her.

Melissa was shocked. She looked the man up and down with lustful eyes. He was handsome and quite a looker. He entered the cabin and wondered to himself who the mysterious beautiful lady was standing in front of him.

"Well, now, top of the evening," the man said in an Irish accent. "And who might you be?"

"I'm Melissa," Melissa replied. "And you are?"

"I'm Thomas – Father Thomas of St Michael's Parish."

322

"Father? Aren't you a little young to be a Father of the church?"

"In the eyes of the Lord – age is just a number." Thomas chuckled as he closed the door behind him. "I see you've already made yourself at home."

Thomas took his heavy winter coat off and hung it up over a chair. He rubbed his hands by the fire to get them warm while Melissa explained that the old cabin was a memory that she needed to visit. She didn't understand why Thomas was here and how he discovered it.

Thomas explained that he came across it by accident. He had broken down some miles back and had decided to go through the woods to find some help. He came across the cabin but found no sign of life. As it was getting late he got some fresh wood and was going to hole up for the night.

"So, how is this place a memory for you?" Thomas asked. "Care to explain?"

The minutes ticked by as Thomas listened to Melissa's story. She told him about the Christmas she had spent with her parents the year before that ended in disaster. She told him about Mr Geoffries and Shane, two strangers that had saved her life from her manipulative parents.

"The Lord works in mysterious ways, wonders to perform – sounds like this Shane was your Angel."

Melissa then confessed that Shane was an innocent as she had dragged him along to the log cabin against his will. She wasn't exactly a good woman back then, but thanks to Mr Geoffries she saw the right way of doing things.

"Confession is good for the soul," said Thomas as he held his cross tightly round his neck.

"Mr Geoffries told me a couple of things that kind of stuck in my head all that time ago."

"And what was that?" Thomas asked.

"He told me that he saw a future – that one day love would die when the pink snow falls."

Thomas looked puzzled. "Love will never die, that's quite a silly assumption and snow isn't pink."

"The second thing he told me was that one day I would meet the man I'm supposed to be with. That he was going to find me."

"God has a plan for all of us – a path where we meet the ones that shape the rest of our lives."

Melissa smiled at Thomas's words of wisdom. In a way he reminded her of Mr Geoffries. She then noticed a change in him. Thomas didn't want to keep hearing about a Mr Geoffries like it was against the law. For someone that assumed that love was going to die, he got quite aggressive against the notion. Melissa found out that Thomas was more worried about something else. He could see a time that the world would end. Melissa thought it was the typical religious apocalypse delusion, but Thomas made it clear that there had been less stars in the sky and that the time of the stars would be on its way to destroy all life.

She couldn't help but feel amused at his ramblings and burst out laughing. Feeling mocked, Thomas smiled and laughed along with her.

Melissa and Thomas talked and talked through the night where they discovered they had quite a lot in common.

Both of them liked similar foods from Italian to good wholesome warm British meals. They both liked the arts, watching theatre productions and listening to classical music. Melissa warmed to Thomas more and more and began to think that maybe he was the man she had been waiting for all the time, so that's when Melissa made her move.

"I'm cold." Melissa shivered. "Will you hold me?"

Thomas being the gentleman he was, wasn't going to ignore the fact that Melissa was secretly coming onto him. As he sat by the fire, he wrapped his arm around her and held her close to his heart.

And then it happened. They both stared into each other's eyes. Melissa leaned close and pressed her lips onto his.

Their kiss was soft and became passionate. Their hands were all over each other and their breathing became erratic by being turned on by one another.

"Sorry – sorry," Thomas apologised.

"No, don't be," Melissa urged. "Don't stop."

"Melissa, we hardly know each other," Thomas insisted.

But Melissa held onto Thomas's hand and held it close to her heart. She told him that she felt like she knew him, with lots of things they had in common that helped her see that they had a secret bond with each other. She had been waiting for far too long and felt that her search for the perfect man for her was over.

Thomas didn't know what to think. He was confused that everything was happening way too fast around him and felt that he was about to make the biggest mistake of his life.

"Mistake? What's that supposed to mean?"

Thomas was insistent about what he could foresee. His fascination with the stars made him constantly worry that the world was going to end. He didn't know why, but all he could see was tragedy ahead. Thomas was scared that getting close to a woman would break his heart and it would be the biggest mistake of his life.

"But I'm throwing myself at you – I'm not going to break your heart – I'm not the type of person to sleep around with just anyone I meet – there has to be a connection – it's what we have."

Thomas agreed that there was a connection. But he didn't know what type, if it was a good or bad one.

Melissa then made another move. She was tired of waiting and wanted to see if Thomas was going to go for her. She stood in front of him and slowly unzipped her winter jacket to reveal a thick Christmas jumper underneath which she pulled over her head and threw it on the floor.

She placed her hands on her hips. Thomas's jaw dropped by how sexy and stunning she looked. Her medium sized breasts bulged out of her silky grey bra and the soft warm skin of her waist looked untouched. Melissa then slipped her trousers off revealing her silky panties.

"Do you like what you see?" Melissa asked. But Thomas didn't answer as he was just blown away by gorgeous she looked.

Melissa then unclipped her bra and let it fall to the floor. Her breasts were perky while her erect nipples stood to attention from the cold air. She took Thomas's hands in hers and helped him to his feet. She then placed his warm hands on her breasts causing him to feel aroused while he massaged them.

"Your body is amazing." Thomas breathed deeply.

"It tastes good too." Melissa grinned as she bit her lip.

Thomas couldn't resist. He had to kiss her. To taste her all over like a rabid dog. Melissa moaned as he sent her pleasure senses through the roof. Thomas took hold of her panties and slipped them off past her ankles. He threw Melissa down on the floor gently in front of the roaring fire place and went down on her.

Melissa closed her eyes and gasped. The feeling of the sexual ecstasy she hadn't felt for years was overwhelming to her.

"Please," Melissa begged. "Please don't stop."

She could feel Thomas's tongue penetrate her deeper inside twirling like a propeller. Melissa pulled Thomas's head against her while letting out a soft yelp as her orgasm began to build. But as Thomas flicked his tongue on her top, Melissa screamed as her orgasm exploded.

"Oh my god," said Melissa trying to catch her breath. "Where did that come from?"

But Thomas was too excited and wanted to get inside Melissa. He unbuckled his trousers and let them drop along with his underwear. Melissa had a wow expression when she saw the size of his stiff manhood.

Thomas's senses felt all electric when he inserted himself inside her and felt how wet she was. Thomas gripped Melissa's hands as she pinned them to the floor. She closed her eyes and came two more times as it was the best sex she had ever had. But then something changed.

Thomas stopped and looked worried.

"What are you doing, don't stop?" Melissa panted. "I don't have protection," Thomas warned.

Melissa pulled Thomas towards her and pressed her lips against his. Her soft kiss felt so good and to his surprise Melissa slipped her tongue inside his mouth and massaged his tongue with hers.

"It's okay – I trust you, just don't hold back, Thomas."

And he didn't. Thomas didn't take long to cum inside her. Melissa was blown away by how good it felt as Thomas fell on top of her as his face rested between her sweaty breasts.

Half an hour had passed. Melissa and Thomas were cuddled up by the fireplace with an old dusty blanket over them. Thomas looked in Melissa's pretty eyes while she grinned like a Cheshire cat and stroked Thomas's chest.

"What are you thinking?" Thomas asked.

"I'm thinking that I can't believe Mr Geoffries was right. You found me. I'm the happiest I've ever been."

"You know I should get back. I don't think it's wise to be stuck out here."

As Thomas flipped the blanket back, Melissa pulled it back over him to stop him leaving.

"Why the rush?" Melissa asked "Let's just stay here and enjoy this moment."

Melissa didn't know it. But Thomas was severely worried about something. He knew that it wasn't good and felt that there were going to be consequences to come.

2

Two days had passed by and Melissa had returned to work constantly thinking of the memories she had spent in the trailer cabin with Thomas. Her boss and friend, Kay, had come out from the back room and checked the money in the till. That was when she noticed that Melissa was a little different than normal.

"You look happy," Kay complimented. "Did you wake up and bang?"

"Sort of the other way around," Melissa giggled.

"Really?" Kay screamed. "Who's the guy? Do I know him? About time you met someone."

"No, you don't know him," Melissa replied. That's when she told Kay the details of her trip to her parents' old cabin over Christmas and met Father Thomas from St Michael's Parish in Mr Geoffries' old trailer cabin.

Kay remembered what had happened with Melissa the previous Christmas and couldn't believe that a strange old man's prediction had come true.

Just then, Melissa vomited all over the counter. "Melissa," Kay panicked.

Melissa bent over and vomited again. Kay quickly helped Melissa to the toilet while she continued to vomit. As Kay didn't understand what was wrong, she grabbed her phone and called an ambulance. That's when a look of worry filled Kay's face when she saw blood in Melissa's vomit.

The very next day in St Michael's Parish, Father Thomas's footsteps walked across the wooden floor down the aisle past the benches either side of him. When he got to the end he walked up three steps and knelt down in front of a large cross and made the crucifix sign with his hand.

His attention was then distracted by footsteps echoing towards him. When he turned around he saw a worried Melissa walking up to him.

"What's wrong?" Thomas asked.

The news he got while sitting in the confessional was what he expected.

"I have sinned. I should have stopped," said Thomas feeling guilty.

Melissa pressed her face up against the grill and said, "I wanted this.

This is a wonderful thing and we should be happy."

But Thomas made a point of mentioning that they hardly knew each other. A one night meeting that led to a pregnancy. Thomas's reasoning made Melissa believe that he didn't want to be a dad and began to feel that she was going to be a single mother.

"I knew there would be consequences. I saw it in the stars." Thomas believed.

Melissa closed her eyes and wiped a tear from her eye. "How can you say it was a consequence? You're a father, who believes in love and faith – love was what made our baby between each other."

"We still don't know each other," Thomas insisted.

"Then let's take the time to know each other," said Melissa as she left the confessional.

Thomas knew that Melissa was right. He wasn't going to be the type of person to abandon a pregnant woman and in his way he did care about her.

3

So, after a month had passed, Melissa and Thomas had become an official couple. At first they started going out on dates. A casual meeting in the park where they had lunch and talked and then going out in the evening to a restaurant and enjoying home cooked meals together. Their most memorable date was where Thomas had bought tickets to the theatre. As they sat amongst the crowd while two operatic singers were performing on the large stage, it was at that moment that Thomas's hand slowly crept over to Melissa's bump. Melissa smiled and placed her hand on top of his. That was the night that they announced they were a couple and expecting.

As Melissa's pregnancy went on, they both stared to plan out getting the essentials, from baby clothes to bottles. For two of the happiest people in Towns-end, they were the only ones who hadn't got a worry in the world.

Even the sex was electric. The bigger Melissa's bump got, the more horny and hormonal she got. Thomas discovered that she couldn't keep her hands off him and wanted sex constantly. As she got heavier, Thomas found it awkward to keep up. Melissa would get angry when her sex quota wouldn't get achieved which would cause her to get sexually frustrated.

Thomas was concerned about her mood and the way she was behaving. He thought it was his fault. Getting Melissa pregnant triggered something inside her to become a sexual wildcat.

Eventually the mood swings began. Melissa took all her anger out on Thomas and blamed him for her anger as he didn't hardly touch her or want to be with her.

"We should go to the doctor," Thomas suggested. "This isn't the Melissa I met at the cabin. What's our baby done to you?"

"There may be one person that could help. Mr Geoffries."

Thomas had got sick and tired of hearing that name. Most conversations he had with Melissa always ended with his name being brought up. He felt like he was living in the shadows of this stranger she had only met once.

"Fine. Do you know where he lives?"

"No. Not really. I think he moved around a lot."

"Well, how does that help us?" said Thomas in frustration. But Melissa could only answer that question with a splash.

"Oh my god," Melissa panicked. "I think my waters just broke."

Travelling from Melissa's home to the hospital didn't take long. This was it. It was really happening. Thomas knew it was going to happen but nothing quite prepared him for it. The doubt of his consequences had disappeared over time and he was happy with the way things had turned out. He held Melissa's hand all the way in until he had to say goodbye to her to wait for them to find her a room.

Minutes ticked by and turned into an hour. He constantly watched the clock hoping that someone would come and inform him where they took Melissa. Eventually a young looking doctor approached him and sat next to him.

"Father Thomas?" asked the doctor in a German accent. "My name is Doctor Arden."

But Thomas saw the look on Arden's face and he knew that something wasn't right.

"What's happened?" Thomas asked with worry in his voice.

"There has been some complications with Melissa and your son," Arden explained.

"Son? It's a boy?"

"Oh, I'm sorry I assumed you knew."

"We were going to wait to find out."

Thomas listened to what Arden had to say. That's when a cold shiver went through his body. He felt sick. Like he was going to vomit. One of them wasn't going to survive the pregnancy and Thomas had to make a choice of who to save. With faith in his heart and belief, all that went away in an instant. This was the consequence that Thomas would have to live with forever.

"I know it's hard, Father – but which one will you choose to save?"

It was then that Thomas made his decision. So, he stood up and looked at Arden then walked out of the hospital.

"Father Thomas," Arden called. "Come back – where are you going?"

4

One month later, the sun was casting shadows over the worn gravestones, shining through the green tree leaves.

Bright yellow flowers pushed up through the ground. A rusty pair of gates opened to the cold shallow place as a man in a long trench coat entered holding a bunch of colourful flowers in his hand. He walked past the gravestones of the cold withering cemetery which had been leftovers from the years of sorrow.

The man placed the flowers on the grave and then took his hat off and held it over his chest as a sign of paying his respects.

"Did you know them?" another man's voice called. The man looked behind to see the father of the church.

"I did," the man replied. "Last Christmas. She was a reckless girl. But only because of how her parents were to her."

"How do you mean, reckless?"

"She captured my nephew. She pretended that he was her boyfriend just to impress her parents. She should have stayed single – that was her path," the man explained.

"How would you know what path she had to take?"

"Because the last time I saw her – I told her that a man would find her. Love her for the woman she is. That wasn't a prediction that she would meet the love of her life. It was a warning. That man was going to be the one that killed her, Father?"

"Thomas," he replied. The man began to walk away. "And who are you, sir?"

The man put his hat on and smiled at Father Thomas. "You can call me, Mr Geoffries."

Mr Geoffries left the cemetery, leaving a raging fire burning in Father Thomas's soul. The man that Melissa praised was now all Thomas could think about. This was the beginning of a rival battle between the two men and Thomas would stop at nothing to destroy the man that had played a deadly game of chess making him the one to kill the love of his life. This was the day he would seek his revenge, no matter how long it would take. Thomas looked up at the sky where he knew in his heart, that the stars were going to be answer to destroying Mr Geoffries.

CRASHER

1

The new year's ball was in full swing for the employees of PharmCorp, Towns-end's newest addition to rival the more successful companies such as Foptix Industries, CL Petra and Vision Electrics.

For a company that hadn't set the bar in the millions, they had planned their Christmas party as a new year's ball as the cost for treating all their employees to a special do was cheaper.

Set at the end of January, the event was set in a large hall with six chairs round multiple tables, each one decorated with gold and silver confetti, silver cutlery, roses in a vase, bottles of wine and jugs of water. A dance floor was nearby with two large speakers where the DJ would play the music they would dance to. Everything had been laid out to perfection with a long table on the side with trays of glasses of prosecco ready for people to take once they arrived.

The employees arrived, all smartly dressed from colourful sparkly dresses, glamorous looking hair styles, jewellery and over applied make up to men smartly dressed in suits and ties with some wearing posh watches. One by one, glasses of prosecco, beers and cheap wine were enjoyed by all. They all talked about their personal lives and what they had recently been up to. But, surprisingly enough, not a single employee discussed their job. It was strange that not one person did, but they were on a night away from work and stress and just enjoying themselves.

After they had their three course meal, some took to the dance floor, starting with the classic music of the eighties until it changed to a rubbish playlist that not many people knew, along with selfies being exchanged with one another. It was a great night, but the party had only just begun, when a woman with long blonde hair dressed in a black evening dress holding a small handbag in her hand walked in. The party looked up slightly puzzled at the stranger that stood before them. Some started whispering to each other at who they were, while others just sat in confusion.

The woman smiled at them all, then looked around for the head table where the boss of the company sat. She walked over then sat at the table, helped herself to a glass of wine then toasted everyone's good health. The boss, Liz Cooper, a woman in her late twenties gave her a puzzled look.

"Excuse me?" Liz asked. The woman gave her eye contact and smiled. "I'm sorry – I think you have the wrong party."

"No I don't," the woman replied as she drank her wine.

"You don't work for me – this is for PharmCorp employees only – I think your party must be on the next floor."

"There's no other party on the next floor – I'm in the right party," the woman insisted.

Liz began to get agitated. "Who are you?" she snapped.

"I'm Rachel and I'm here to discuss business."

"What business?" Liz asked.

"Your business," Rachel replied as she smiled smugly to Liz.

Liz couldn't believe what she heard come out of Rachel's mouth. Her colleagues that sat across the table glared at her with booze filled eyes.

"Will you get the hell out of here?" Liz shouted. "Call the police, now."

But all Rachel could do was giggle. Liz and her colleagues couldn't believe how calm she was being and not taking them seriously as she gulped down her wine.

"Why don't we start talking about exponential growth with the pink pills?"

Liz choked on her wine the second it entered her mouth. She couldn't believe what came out of Rachel's mouth.

"What do you know about that?" Liz asked with curiosity.

"I know that it's an experimental drug and the secret that it holds because of it." Rachel smirked. "And of course there was that consignment that disappeared too."

Liz and her colleagues looked at each other with worry.

"What do you really want, miss?" a middle aged man across from Rachel asked. "Are you here to blackmail this company, because I'm telling you now, it won't work."

"I don't need to blackmail." Rachel giggled "But you did when you wanted earlier retirement didn't you, Roger?"

Roger looked sheepish and didn't know how to react to Rachel's comment. Liz looked guilty in front of her colleagues who were interested to find out the truth.

"Isn't that how you got that gold watch as your retirement gift on your wrist?" Rachel asked.

Roger looked down at his wrist. An imprint of a watch was visible on his wrist but the watch wasn't there, Roger got himself into a state. He looked under the table to see if it was on the floor, but there was no sign of it. He then moved the plates and his colleagues' drinks but it didn't appear.

"You've taken it haven't you?" Roger snapped at Rachel.

"In front of everyone while I've been sitting here the entire time? That would be quite an achievement," Rachel joked.

"The ice is melting, miss," Roger threatened.

"Well, I'm lucky I learned how to swim." She smiled. "Can I get another bottle of wine, please?"

Liz became infuriated with Rachel's attitude towards her colleagues and ended up losing her temper. She shouted out for someone to call the police, so Rachel would be arrested and dragged away.

"I don't think that's a good idea," Rachel insisted.

"And why not?" Liz snapped.

"Because I know PharmCorp's darkest secret – you know what I'm talking about, remember?"

Liz didn't know what Rachel was talking about, until something made her change her mind to have the police called to the scene. A feeling inside her told her that Rachel had something on her company, but even though she tried to think of what it could be, she couldn't remember.

"I thought that would get your attention." Rachel smiled. "Now are you ready to let me talk?"

And with that, Liz was ready to listen to Rachel. She began with Liz, how she knew her story, that her mother Elizabeth Cooper was the CEO of Vision Electrics and as the years went on and Liz became of age, she saw a future CEO in her and a successor to take over the company that she had built from the ground up. But Liz wasn't interested. She wanted to make her own choices and put all of her skills and talents into making a company of her own.

With electricity, water and robotics established, Liz saw a future in pharmaceuticals, a growth in creating drugs and cures for illnesses and something rewarding. The profits and shares were high in the first year. She was the youngest boss of Towns-end, being only twenty-one years old and getting the woman of the year.

Her success drove a wedge between her and her mother.

They didn't talk for a year and a half and it took another year before Elizabeth decided to mend their relationship. Liz saw through this as she knew what her mother was like and, lo and behold, a proposal was offered to join both companies to share profits and expand their financial growth. Liz was one that always thought big and she could see an advantage in the offer.

"How do you know about this?" asked Liz. "That's highly classified information between me and my employees."

"Look, Liz – what I'm about to say to you next is for the benefit of your company," said Rachel. "You should refuse your mother's offer."

"And why should I listen to you?"

"Because you know you can find a better offer. One that will set your entire future. And what do you think that is?"

Liz thought hard. At first she couldn't think of anything, until a thought popped into her head. It was a word. One word. "Foptix?"

"Yes." Rachel grinned. "Foptix Industries is the number one robotics and electronic industry in Towns-end, currently they are working on a new watch."

"A watch?" Roger laughed. "Just like every other smart watch in the world."

"Rumours are that this one can control time."

Everyone on the table looked at each other and started to laugh. Rachel's words amused them. But the only one that wasn't laughing was Liz. She felt that Rachel was telling the truth and was intrigued in what she knew. Liz was an ambitious woman, full of drive and passion. All she could concentrate on was where her next job would be and upping her salary. She didn't have time for a relationship and she hated stopping to think about whether she was missing out on love. She acted like a strong independent woman, but what people didn't know was she was lonely and unhappy.

"I think we should talk in private," Liz suggested.

But Roger, frustrated and confused at what was going on, slammed his fist down on the table. "I've had enough of this – what the hell is going on? All this mystery, all these secrets."

"Roger," Liz snapped. "Don't you think I want to know the answer to all these questions?"

"I was enjoying this party. But I have to say this is the worst new year's ball I have been to and on top, this party crasher – I'm going to call the police and get her thrown out."

Roger went to take his phone out of the inside pocket of his jacket but was surprised to discover it wasn't there. He checked all of his pockets. He then snapped at Bridget who he was sitting next to and insisted she give him her phone.

"Roger, that's enough," Liz blasted him to calm him down. "I think you should leave."

"Me?" hc replied. "Are you kidding me? I'm not the party crasher here Miss Cooper."

"He's right," Rachel interrupted. She put her wine glass down and stood to leave. "I know this company's darkest secret and you're to blame, Roger."

"What is that supposed to mean?" said Roger.

Liz grabbed hold of Rachel's arm to stop her from leaving. She insisted she stay and tell her everything that she knows. Rachel smiled, satisfied at her little trick. She knew that if she said the right things, they would want to find out everything she knew. She sat back down and took hold of her empty wine glass shaking it from left to right.

"The tide is out – where the hell is that bottle of wine I ordered?"

Liz put her hand up and acknowledged a venue staff member to bring them more wine. When the bottle was placed on the table, Rachel grabbed it and topped up her glass then started to tell them what she knew.

She began by telling about the success of the company that started with the standard pills, such as antibiotics.

Their version was the fastest selling as its formula had been tweaked that resulted in a fast instant cure. The news of this attracted the attention of the media, even though some were suspicious that there could've been something dangerous in the formula. When they couldn't discover anything and the company were in the clear, the profits and success rose even higher than Liz expected.

Liz took on more staff to expand her business and looked into new drugs to try her hand at. That's when she overheard one of her employees, Leighanne, talking to Liz's assistant that she had had problems performing with her husband as her sex drive was low. That's when Liz got the idea of taking the pink Viagra pill and improving it. She called Leighanne and her assistant in her office and told Leighanne that she wanted to help her and made her an offer if she would agree to be a test subject for the drug that she would call 'The Pink Snow'.

With how Leighanne was feeling from the strain it was putting on her marriage, she instantly accepted. Her test results went through the roof showing her hormone levels explode like five nuclear bombs. She ravaged her husband like an uncontrollable animal until she had some fatal side effects and died.

Liz's company was in trouble. The evidence that Leighanne had signed was destroyed and her husband never knew about what transpired. He got a large pay off of course with enough money to tide him over that it turned out he spent on booze and became an alcoholic. The memory of Leighanne became PharmCorp's darkest secret that they lived with. But this didn't stop Liz from carrying on the research to improve the drug. She wanted it to be a success so that Leighanne didn't die in vain.

Once the tests had ironed out all the side effects that had killed Leighanne − Liz told her assistant that she would test out the drug on herself. Her assistant and Roger who was retiring would be the only one who knew what was going to happen. Roger received a gold watch for his retirement gift and gave Liz's assistant his watch to keep it safe on the day of the new year's ball.

"I'm your assistant, Liz," Rachel explained as she took out Roger's gold watch and handed it to him. "The side effects of the drug made you all lose your memory, that's why you all don't know me − that's why I know everything about your company."

They all sat in disbelief, but something at the back of everyone's mind made them believe Rachel. Liz looked ashamed that she tested the drug on her staff to see if there were any side effects. She hadn't learned from her lesson that another employee could've died the same way as Leighanne.

"You only did this for a reason − the one thing that you found out that you wanted desperately to forget − do you remember what that is?"

Liz closed her eyes to think and that is when it hit her.

She met Leighanne's husband and her young daughter. "Her daughter's name, was Madison Milburn."

CHEAT

1

Ben Parsons, a man who had just turned forty sat in a dimly lit game show studio, in front of middle-aged game show host, Jim Greene. The lights came on and Jim looked into a TV camera across from the audience.

"Welcome back to Playing 4 Real, the number one game show where contestants have the chance to win, one million pounds." Jim takes a deep breath. "Before the break, we had Ben Parsons, who had just answered the £250,000 pound question – How do you feel, Ben?"

"With my hands normally, Jim." Ben laughed. Jim smiled as the audience laughed along with the joke. "No but seriously, it's a great feeling."

"Excellent." Jim smiled. "So, you have no life lines left and can still walk away with £250,000. Do you want to walk or play on for the £500,000 question?"

"I'd like to play on," said Ben, confidently.

"Very well, then let's start, playing 4 real," said Jim. The lights dim followed by a tense music as Jim reads from a question card, "1982, 1988 + 31 is the answer that's missing to complete this three coded number, is it (A) 2000, (B) 1995, (C) 2019 or (D) 2009?"

Ben smiled. He knew the answer. He was always clever at mathematics and science. He enjoyed puzzle solving and quizzes. "The answer is C, Jim – 2019."

"You've just won, £500,000," said Jim, excitedly. "You now have the chance to walk away, or gamble it all for the million pound question."

"I've come this far, Jim, let's go for it." Ben nodded.

Jim held the million pound question card in his hand and read aloud, "Which British King, was married to Eleanor of Aquitaine? Is it (A) Henry the first, (B) Henry the second, (C) Richard the first, or (D) Henry the fifth?"

This was the moment that Ben feared. History was never his strong point. His heart was pounding as he wiped the sweat from his brow. He looked into Jim's eyes who was patiently waiting for an answer. He had no lifelines to help him and he had agreed to not walk away. He took a deep breath and said, "My gut instinct tells me that it's Henry the first."

Jim looks down at the ground, keeping a straight face not to let on whether it is the right or wrong answer. He could see that Ben was anxious to find out if he had won. "It's the wrong answer." Jim saw how Ben's heart sank when he told him that he had just lost all his hard earned money. "It was Henry the second."

But then, things changed. Ben was smiling. He was happy. "Thanks, Jim, for telling me the right answer." And with that Ben looked at his smart watch and rotated the dial anticlockwise. His whole surroundings then changed as time reversed for just a fraction.

Jim held the million pound question card in his hand and read aloud, "Which British King, was married to Eleanor of Aquitaine? Is it (A) Henry the first, (B) Henry the second, (C) Richard the first, or (D) Henry the fifth?"

"Henry the second – final answer." Ben grinned confidently. Jim looked at his card. He still kept a straight face not letting on the answer. "Oh come on, Jim, you know I'm right."

"You have just won, one million pounds."

The crowd screamed and applauded as Ben sat in the winner's chair with a smug grin on his face.

Everybody wants to be rich, on the journey and struggle for achieving that wealth. But what happens when we get what we want? Would we live the life we always wanted?

Or would we continue to want more?

2

The casino was alive with gamblers coming from afar with desperate people wanting to win millions. Their ages varied from young to old and was one of Towns-end's most popular places to visit.

Ben wandered past people playing the slot machines who were looking disappointed when the reels stopped rolling and beeping, only to discover they hadn't won anything. The rattling exchange of coins made the place noisy, which began to grate on him. He noticed the public bar over in the corner. Finally, somewhere it was a bit quieter. As he made his way over to the bar, he was startled by the sound of alarms going off. A man had just won, a silver Aston Martin Vantage.

He entered to hear the chilled out sounds of piano music. A very jazzy sort of vibe. Seats and tables were scattered around a neon lit area, with a long black bar that curved around the room. The barman was dressed in a waist coat and a non-creased white shirt. At either end of the bar sat two women minding their own business with a drink in one hand and a phone in the other. They were both dressed in slender evening dresses, one wearing red the other wearing black.

Ben felt out of place and underdressed in his tatty blue jeans and grey hoody. Not looking glamorous and sophisticated as the two women looked. He thought that his luck would be in tonight as he didn't want to be in his hotel bed alone. He smiled to himself, thinking back to his favourite film *Groundhog Day*, the way Phil Connors could manipulate the day and get with a woman. With the power of his smart watch, sure enough he could make this happen. But which lucky lady would he be taking home?

The one in the black dress looked elegant with her bob blonde hair and lots of make up. The one in the red dress was more to Ben's taste. Long brunette hair that hung past her shoulders of her red dress, which bulged out from her 36HH natural breasts. Ben was always a breast man, the bigger, the more aroused he got, as his manhood stood to attention.

He wandered over to the bar and acknowledged the barman. "Pint of lager, please, and whatever the lady is having."

Linsey looked up to see the scruffy looking man that stood before her. "In your dreams," she said, unimpressed.

Ben wasn't going to give up and insisted on wondering why she would turn down the offer of a free drink. "Come on, have a drink on me."

"I wouldn't have a drink on you if you were the last man standing," Linsey snapped. "Look at you – who taught you how to dress? The poor people's home?"

Linsey meant business. Her reference to being poor made Ben realise that she was interested in men who have lots of money. So, with the twist of his smart watch, he went back to try his luck again.

Ben wandered past people playing the slot machines who were looking disappointed when the reels stopped rolling and beeping, only to discover they hadn't won anything. The rattling exchange of coins made the place noisy, which began to grate on him. He noticed the public bar over in the corner. This time, he was dressed in a posh navy-blue suit with a white cotton shirt and silver tie. He then remembered the man who won the Aston Martin car and quickly hurried over, stepping in front of the man before he could get there. When he spun to win, the alarms went off and all attention was now on Ben for winning the car.

Minutes later, Ben went to the bar and saw that Linsey and the other lady were still sitting at the bar. When Ben went over to the bar and acknowledged the barman, Linsey finished her drink and grabbed her bag to leave.

"Finest bottle of Champagne and whatever the lady is having." Ben smiled.

Linsey stops in her tracks. She looks Ben up and down raising an eyebrow at him. She gives him a big smile and says, "I'll join you for some Champagne." She holds her hand out and Ben shakes it. "I'm Linsey."

Ben and Linsey drank the rest of the night away until they both felt tipsy. The other woman had finally decided to leave after spending most of the evening looking envious that Ben had picked Linsey instead of her.

When they both left the casino, Linsey was surprised to see Ben's Aston Martin that he won. Ben would have given Linsey a ride in his car but instead he called an Uber as he was over the limit after all the Champagne that they ingested.

The Uber driver dropped them off at a posh hotel just on the outskirts of the city area of Towns-end where it overlooked a large lake that reflected the lights of the tall buildings in the distance. Linsey stood on a balcony of the penthouse suite and admired the view.

"It's beautiful," said Linsey, who wrapped her arms round herself to protect her from the cold chill in the air. She entered the warm bedroom, while Ben closed the doors. "You must have millions to afford a hotel room like this – the penthouse suite, that's impressive."

"I got enough – let's just say that." Ben smiled to himself.

Linsey fell back on the large soft bed and told him to come to her with her finger. Ben knew this was moment – it was that easy to get her to have sex with him.

Ben got on top of Linsey and pressed his lips on hers. It wasn't very passionate as it felt like he was kissing a fish. As that was a failure, Linsey got him to concentrate to kiss and lick her neck which turned her on dramatically as she let out a light moan.

She pushed Ben off her and slid her dress off until she was in her bra and panties. She then undid her bra and exposed her 36HH breasts. Ben was excited. He couldn't wait to get his hands on them. But then Linsey did something unexpected. She grabbed his face and smothered it with her breasts. He kissed her nipples till they were erect.

He helped her slip her panties off. Initiated oral sex. But Linsey didn't want that. "You have a condom – I just want you now."

Ben slipped his underwear off and put a condom on.

When he entered her, he was surprised that she didn't moan. She held him tightly as he grinded. Not once did she look at him. With her large breasts wobbling about, it didn't take Ben long to cum. Linsey gasped and tried to catch her breath as she wanted him to get off her. She quickly cuddled up to him.

"That was amazing," Linsey panted.

As Ben lay there, he didn't know what to think. He knew that Linsey had faked the orgasm and hadn't cum. He began to think that she was a one night stand, but to his surprise, she met up with him every day.

From going abroad, fancy parties and dinners, Ben's life became busier than it ever had been. It got to the point where he no longer needed to rely on the watch. His sexlife was passable, as he came lots but she still never did and it was over in minutes. Ben was hoping that things would improve on that front, but soon found that she delayed having sex constantly, leaving him unhappy and frustrated.

Then one day, Ben decided to break up with Linsey as he wasn't happy, but before he could, he noticed a happier change in her. Linsey spoke of a new friend she had met. She didn't really like men, but supported Ben and Linsey's relationship after what Linsey had told her.

So, Linsey got down on one knee in front of Ben and took his hand in hers. "Ben Parsons – will you marry me?"

Ben couldn't believe it. That she would be the one to ask him. She loved him enough to marry him even if their sex life wasn't that brilliant. Ben hesitated. He didn't know what to say. After everything that he'd been through he was ready to break up with her.

Linsey looked like her heart was about to break with how long Ben was taking to answer her. "Okay," Ben replied. "Yes, I'll marry you." She was delighted and got to her feet, throwing her arms around him.

To Ben's surprise, he discovered that she didn't want a church wedding or wedding venue. She wanted to get married quickly and arranged for their wedding to be held at the casino. She didn't want witnesses or family and friends. Ben thought it odd, but as she asked him, it wasn't going to cost big.

3

So, weeks went by into their married life and Ben soon discovered how lazy Linsey was. She didn't cook him any meals and was messy, leaving dirty clothes all over the floor. The sex between the two of them became distant and disinterested, until one day, Ben came home and discovered the truth, when Linsey was naked in their marital bed with a muscly guy cumming inside of her without a condom on.

The image smashed Ben like a sledgehammer to the gut. He felt sick and couldn't shake the image out of his head.

"What?" Linsey smiled. "You loved it just as much as I did." She giggled at him.

"Get the fuck out of my home," Ben yelled.

"No." Linsey giggled. "You get the fuck out of my home, when we married, your home, money and assets became mine. I'll give you your divorce, but you'll end up with nothing."

Ben was crestfallen as she told him the truth, that from the day she saw him, all she wanted was his money. Her friend that she had met later, she would have met that night at the casino, if Ben hadn't intervened. So, when she met up with her later, she made her an offer that she couldn't refuse as she was annoyed that Ben got to her first and became a target on her radar.

"The offer to hurt me, obviously," Ben snapped. As he looked away from Linsey in disgust, he saw his smart watch on the table and knew that it was his saving grace. He smiled. Amused at what he could do to fix all this.

"You think this is funny?" Linsey's face dropped with annoyance.

"For me it is." Ben grinned as he grabbed his watch. "For you – you won't even remember any of this."

And with that, he twisted the dial and went back to the moment he met Linsey.

Ben stood in the lobby of the casino. The familiar sounds of the gambling machines and exchange of coins was all too familiar. Ben discovered that he was in hoody and jeans. No suit this time. As he made his way through, he saw the guy that won the car. This time, Ben didn't change things. He wanted the guy to win the car.

When he entered the bar he saw Linsey and the other woman sitting there as always. Not once did Linsey take notice of him.

"Bottle of champagne, please." Ben acknowledged the barman. He looked over to Linsey who finished her drink and grabbed her bag to leave. As he watched her walk away, he saw the woman approach her and listened to their conversation.

With Ben not on her radar, he felt he could relax more, knowing that he wasn't a target any more. The barman brought over a bottle of champagne and a glass.

"Drinking alone?" said the woman in the black dress. "That's not a good sign."

Ben looked across the bar feeling amused. "Care to join me?"

"I might just do that," she replied softly. "Yes." She grabbed her bag and drink and sat next to Ben. She then introduced herself and held out her hand. "Sasha Dawson, by the way – journalist."

"Ben Parsons – millionaire," he replied shaking her hand firmly.

"Ben Parsons?" Sasha questioned. "Of course – I saw you on TV – you're the first person to win the top prize."

Ben took out some money to pay for the drink. Sasha also got her money out. "Please allow me," she insisted.

"That's very kind of you – but I can afford it." Ben smiled.

"Why don't we split and go halves?" Sasha replied. "That's very gracious that you're offering to pay for it – I may not be a millionaire, but I still like to pay my way and be fair."

Ben was impressed and accepted her offer. What he had been through with Linsey, made him realize that he should have picked Sasha to get to know.

They both sat in a corner of the bar sharing drinks and getting to know each other.

"I work as a small-time reporter. It's not a big paid job and I barely have enough money to pay the bills. But I love my job all the same. I was really lucky."

"What do you mean by that, Sasha?"

"My boss, Michael Patterson, had to choose between me and India Johnson. Both of us had excellent qualifications, but only one of us was

350

going to be picked for the job. I gave him a couple of reports – the delayed opening of Towns-end's, wax work, Chamber of Horrors and a bizarre weather report – black clouds that were forming over a house. Lucky for me. Michael chose me," Sasha explained.

"Well, I'm sure in a parallel reality somewhere, she got the job and you didn't," Ben joked.

"I never thought of it like that." Sasha smiled. "Besides, money isn't everything."

"I used to think like that. I was on the verge of being homeless. I didn't have enough money to pay the rent. Tried all sorts of ways to get the money together."

"And look at you now." Sasha raised her glass. Her keen eye then spotted, Ben's watch.

"Fop-tex? Is that a smart watch? I've never heard of that brand before," Sasha questioned.

"It was made by Foptix Industries. Only one of a kind. I saw it on their website. It was a gamble to buy. I suppose you could say it was my lucky charm." He drinks. "So, are you after money? You're struggling?"

"No, that wasn't a hint earlier. I'm not after your money. It's been a struggle all my life. But I'll bounce back. I always do," Sasha replied.

"How do you mean, a struggle all of your life?" Ben asked.

"Daddy left when I was a kid. Mum was poor. I always hoped my luck would change, but it never did." Sasha sighed.

They were then interrupted by the sound of cheering as a man had just won £25,000 on a slot machine.

"Some people get all the luck." Sasha sighed.

And with that, Ben made a bold decision and reversed time by a couple of minutes.

"I never thought of it like that." Sasha smiled "Besides, money isn't everything," she repeated.

"Take this," said Ben, as he took a coin out of his pocket and placed it in her hand. "I have a feeling that your luck is about to change." He dragged her over to the slot machine just as the man who originally won the jackpot walked over. The man looked annoyed and then walked away.

"These things are such a waste of money. The only ones that win are the casino owners," Sasha referred.

"Trust me – I have a strong belief that you're gonna win," Ben insisted.

Sasha hesitated at first, but with Ben's words, she wanted to believe him. So, she took the coin and placed it into the coin slot, then pulled the lever. The reels spun furiously and slowly began to stop. To Sasha's surprised, three bars matched and the alarm sounded to acknowledge that she had just won £25,000.

"I don't believe it." Sasha was shocked "I've just won £25,000." She hugged Ben. "Thank you."

4

Sasha's apartment door flung open, as the two of them entered the living room with their hands all over each other and their lips locked in a passionate moment. She reached out for the light switch and hit it, revealing more of her apartment that was hidden in the darkness. The kitchen was integrated into the living room next to a three seated sofa, which they fell onto.

Sasha helped get Ben's shirt off and then took her dress off revealing a black cotton bra. She pulled his face into her cleavage as he began to lick and kiss her skin. She panted more and more as he licked up the side of her neck and then nibbled her ear.

"I want you now." Sasha gasped.

Minutes later, Ben fell at the side of Sasha. Hot. Sweaty. Exhausted and out of breath. "Wow," he struggled to say. "That..." He paused "...was amazing."

Sasha cuddled up with him and struggled to say, "You... are my perfect guy."

But not all first meetings have a happy ending. As the weeks passed. Ben and Sasha fell in love with each other. Their relationship was strong. He knew that he wanted to propose and marry her, until one evening while they were getting fleshy in bed, something, changed.

"Ow," said Sasha in pain, as Ben grinded her pelvis. "Wait – stop."

But Ben didn't. He was so close to climaxing, that he didn't want to stop. So, Sasha pushed him off. Ben was annoyed, but he could clearly see that she was in pain.

Doctor Redma's diagnosis was what Sasha didn't expect. The reason why she was in pain was because she had come down with endometriosis. She was told that it would cause pain, nausea and tiredness. It would be difficult and painful when she ovulates. Her stomach would become bloated, tight and uncomfortable.

"So, you're saying that I can't have children?" Sasha wept as Ben held her hand.

The endometriosis could grow from the womb into the ovaries and fallopian tubes. Sasha would suffer pain every time she had sex. This was something that Ben didn't want to hear. He loved making love to Sasha as she was everything that he had been searching for in a woman. That thought alone kept going round and round in his head as he drove her home. Not once did they speak, not knowing what to say to each other. He looked at her. He could see her eyes were red from all the crying she had done.

"What did Doctor Redma say, when he wanted to talk to you privately?" Ben asked, curiously.

"I shouldn't tell you. But I love you and I don't want to hide things from you," Sasha replied. "He said that if I hadn't have had all that sex with you, then this would never have happened."

Ben let go of her hand. The realization that he was the cause of her condition, her not being able to have children, was like a nail in the coffin for their future. So, he decided to go back and try again. This time, not to have sex with her as much as they did. But Sasha being the wild cat that she was wanted it more and they ended up rowing because she thought that he didn't want to touch her. When she broke up with him it made him realise that he couldn't go through life without her and that he loved her with all his heart. So, retreading his footsteps and making her ill was the only way to keep her.

At first when it came to their love, he suggested that they could still play with each other and only let him have release. But Sasha didn't want that. She couldn't go on with her life being sexually frustrated and not getting any in return.

As time went by, Ben became more frustrated. He started staying out late and spending time drinking at a bar. This made Sasha angry as she would sit home alone waiting for him to come back in his drunk state. Until one day for Ben, he made a choice that he knew he shouldn't have.

As Ben sat at the bar with a glass of whiskey in his hand, a gorgeous woman by the name of April sat next to him and ordered herself a glass of Champagne. Ben smiled at her with his alcohol fuelled heavy eyes and admired her beauty. She was a slender woman with long brown hair that hung past her shoulders. She wore tight leather pants and a black vest top and had tattoos of flowers all over both her arms.

The exchange of words and drinks between the two of them sparked off a connection and Ben quickly felt aroused. April asked him if he would

354

kindly walk her home. The thought of Sasha didn't even enter his head and Ben accepted.

He soon found himself lying on her king-sized bed in her flat with just his underwear on. Ben's eyes nearly popped out of his sockets when April stood leaning up against the door frame wearing green laced and black stocking underwear.

Ben's heart raced as he couldn't wait to get his hands on her.

"I'm going to rock your world," April purred. "Take off your underwear, lay on your front and close your eyes."

Ben did as he was told. He loved her dominance over him, something he had fantasized about before he had met Sasha. Something that she was lacking.

"Ow," Ben screamed as pain shot through his body. When he looked behind, he saw April taking him from behind with a strap on dildo inside his butt.

"Relax," she said nibbling his ear. "We've got the whole night together – I get to do you and then another night you can do me."

Ben didn't know what to think at first being taken from behind. But the pain soon turned into sexual ecstasy. He loved how she started off slow, only to speed up by pounding his butt checks with her pelvis and smelling the mixture of her perfume and hot breath on the back of his neck.

As the hours passed, they soon both became exhausted. Ben held her in his arms as she lightly snored. And it was only then that he thought about Sasha. He should have felt guilty about cheating on her. But he didn't.

When he left April's place, she quickly stopped him outside and arranged to meet up with him later that night at the bar. She kissed him goodbye and he left for home.

5

Sasha was sitting at the kitchen table with a cup of coffee in her hand when Ben walked through the door.

"Where were you all night?" Sasha screamed. "You should've called; I was very worried."

"I'm fine, okay, I just needed some time out," Ben replied.

"Oh really? Time out with her I take it." Sasha held up her phone to reveal a picture of April kissing Ben outside her place. "One of my friends saw you – how could you cheat on me when I need you the most with my condition that you gave me?"

Knowing that Ben had been caught out didn't worry him as he twisted his watch and went back in time.

When he was with April, he stayed with her longer than he did last time, just to avoid Sasha's friend who caught the two of them.

Ben returned home with flowers and an apology. He used an excuse that he had stayed over with a friend with frustration of how things had got him.

"I love you and I'm sorry," said Ben.

Sasha smiled and smelled the flowers. "They're lovely – I love you too."

Weeks soon turned into months with Ben manipulating time to hide his indiscretions with April. But not all secrets can be hidden as mistakes can always be made.

Ben was frustrated. He searched high and low for his watch but he couldn't find it.

"What is it, honey?" Sasha enquired.

"Have you seen my watch?"

"Not since yesterday," Sasha replied.

"Damn it," Ben snapped, stressed. "Could you help me find it?"

They were then interrupted by Sasha's phone ringing. "Hey boss – what's up?"

Michael Patterson was on the other end of the line. "Sasha, I know things aren't good for you at the moment, but I got no one else. There's a story I need you to investigate – single mothers in Pentemy – all their men have gone missing."

Sasha notices Ben's watch under the sofa and picks it up while Ben continues to look. "Well, it's a bit awkward, boss."

"I take it you're still with the gambler – you could have given up work, but he used your winnings, didn't he?"

"As an investment – we share our money and I love my job still."

"You found my watch – give me," Ben insisted.

"Wait – I'm on the phone," Sasha whispered. Ben was impatient. He tried to grab it off her but Sasha backed away. "Will you stop that," she said, annoyed. "I'll call you back, boss." She threw the phone on the sofa. "What is wrong with you?" And then it hit her. A strange funk in the air. The smell was all too familiar. "Oh my god – have you been with someone else – perfume – smell of cum?"

Ben knew that he had been rumbled yet again. "I can explain – just give me the watch and I'll tell you everything."

"No," Sasha screamed, upset. "You're gonna tell me everything now."

A struggle then takes place as Ben takes hold of Sasha and tries to grab the watch off her. Sasha accidently hits the button on the watch and freezes Ben like a statue.

She backs away. Curious at what just happened. She inspects the watch further and then slowly rotates the dial backwards to see Ben walking back a few steps. Sasha summed everything up. The way Ben manipulated time to get his millions and how many times he could have cheated on her without her ever knowing.

The answer was clear to her. She knew what she had to do. So, she unfroze Ben so he could see the watch.

"Give it to me," Ben insisted.

"Oh I'll give it to you – give you everything you deserve," Sasha threatened.

"No," Ben screamed, as she gave the dial an almighty twist and disappeared in front of him.

6

Ben was now sitting in front of his laptop in a dingy cramped messy flat. Scruffy looking. Unshaven. He was looking at his finances which were low. He was struggling to keep the roof over his head until an advert popped up. It was a new smart watch that Foptix Industries had made. He clicked the ad which took him to the site. The price was just about everything he had left. It was a gamble, but Ben decided to buy it, but before he could get his payment details, the page refreshed and said 'Sold Out'.

He felt gutted that he missed the opportunity to buy the watch and couldn't help but wonder who did.

Weeks had passed and Ben found himself on the street homeless and alone. He had barely enough money to pay for the rent and was kicked out.

Just then, a pram with a new born baby in was wheeled up to him. "Here," said Sasha, as she took out the same coin that he used to win her money. "I think you need this more than I do." Ben noticed that she was wearing the watch that he wanted to buy. The only difference was he did not know who she was as he had never met her. Sasha gave him a big grin as her life was now happy and complete with her baby in her life.

They say with great powers comes responsibility. But when we abuse that power to get everything we have ever wanted – that power can turn on us and leave us with nothing.

HEROES

1

Once upon a time, there was a kingdom. The kingdom of Alcina. It was a happy place where King Dragula and Queen Alcina lived happily. Surrounded by love and happiness, they lived their life without a worry in the world. Every morning, they would stand on their balcony and overlook the kingdom, surrounded by its bright green forests and blue coloured lakes and waterfalls.

Then one day. Out of the blue. A star shone bright, high up in the sky. King Dragula thought it was an omen. A star, that was easy to see during the day. King Dragula took some of his loyal men and rode out to get closer to the star. It was that moment the star exploded, knocking him off his horse. The shock wave it caused killed his men and travelled towards his kingdom.

When Dragula returned, his world had come crashing down. His people were slaughtered and his castle and Queen had disappeared without a trace.

Upon losing everything, Dragula's Vengeance grew and all he could think about was gaining power to start again and take another kingdom by force.

He went on a quest following the path, hoping it would lead him to his goal. Dragula arrived at Marwood, a small village with its inn and steel mill. When he rested and had the local ale, he overheard stories about two powerful gauntlets that would grant him the power he sought.

The stories took him to a tower. The dark tower in the lands of death and sorrow, plagued by the tormented souls that were trapped there. Dragula climbed the tower, working out its puzzles, riddles, tests and traps until he reached the highest point.

The gauntlets were now in sight. They were black and rusted with dried specks of red blood. When he put them out, they burned him. He screamed at the top of his lungs as they fused to his skin. The gauntlets engulfed him. Beefing him out as black spiky armour burst out of his skin and became a towering muscular dark knight that wielded a gigantic heavy looking jagged sword.

Dragula took his new power back to Marwood, decimating the locals that lived there. He explored different ways to use his power and resurrected the locals to become a small army of his own.

From a distance he could see his goal. The kingdom of the red mountains would be perfect, a kingdom that rivalled his own when Alcina stood tall and proud. So, Dragula marched his army towards them. A kingdom that had been at peace since all kingdoms banded together to fight the fatality wars.

Two guards, who were posted outside the gates to the kingdom stood proud and stiff. The sun cracked through the clouds making them hot underneath their suits of armour.

Their attention was then distracted by a large army marching towards them with Dragula leading the charge.

The guards drew their swords ready to defend the entrance to the kingdom, but were soon shot down by Dragula's archers.

"No gate will hold me back," Dragula threatened, as he clashed both his gauntlets together and unleashed a beam of energy that vapourized the two guards and caused the gates to explode into a thousand pieces.

Princess Shabetha and Prince Whitestone stood on the battlements, watching Dragula's army enter the market.

Shabetha watched in horror as she saw the innocent civilians get slaughtered at the hands of his army. But all was not lost, when a magical explosion occurred scattering his army all over the market. The mage, stood proud holding his metal stick with its glowing crystal ball charging to attack.

"Ascuda," the Mage shouted and unleashed a beam of energy at Dragula, who absorbed the energy in his right gauntlet and fired it back with his left. The mage disintegrated to atoms.

A ninja in black clothing wielding energy nunchucks runs through Dragula's army, hacking and slashing her way until she reaches the dark lord himself. Dragula punches the ninja, causing her to fly across the bridge and smack back into the foundations. But she didn't give in. She got back to her feet and put her nunchucks together to form an energy staff that she spun around her head.

A roar then startled everyone, as a dragon in gold plated armour flew towards them and unleashed an energy beam from its mouth, destroying the ninja and the walls of the castle.

Princess Shabetha watched in horror from the tallest tower, as

Dragula's army entered the castle grounds and slaughtered her people.

A nearby tower then exploded and fell from the deadly dragon's beam. Her people below, screamed as they ran for cover.

Shabetha entered her chambers to see the white knight, the leader of the Hall of Heroes barricade the door.

"The kingdom is falling," said Shabetha. "You should leave this place, my love."

Prince Whitestone, held her hands in comfort. "I will not leave you. We will stand our ground and then we will have our wedding."

The doors were then bolted as the army tried to break through. The white knight drew his sword as the doors buckled under the pressure and gave way.

Dragula's heavy footsteps thump as he strides into Shabetha's Chambers. "Princess Shabetha." Dragula drew his jagged large black sword and pointed it at her. "Your kingdom is mine."

"For the Hall of Heroes," the white knight shouted and charged at Dragula. Their swords got locked in combat, trading continuous blows with each other. But Dragula had the upper hand and shattered the armour, destroying the white knight.

Prince Whitestone swung his sword, once Dragula was distracted, but Dragula defended himself. "Fool – your heroes are gone – this kingdom is mine."

Dragula was then hit with a bolt of energy. He looked up to see Shabetha holding a staff with a crystal ball. "Leave my kingdom, before I destroy you." He was amused and raised his gauntlet in the air. A pink snow flurry formed around it and then flew towards Shabetha. She gasped. Feeling an exciting sensation, she had never felt before. She panted. The arousal of the snow was intense. She flung her arms out and dropped her staff. Her clothing changed to a pink shredded dress and her eyes turned the same colour. A new crooked staff formed in her hand and she gave Prince Whitestone a sinister smile.

"Shabetha – no." Prince Whitestone felt heartbroken, losing the woman that he loved.

"We're all here. Everyone who has died. Everyone who is responsible. It's your turn," Shabetha cackled.

The Prince had only one chance left. He took hold of Shabetha's old staff and held it against the wall.

Dragula changed. He held up his gauntlet in caution. "No," he warned. "You shatter the crystal and the energy inside will be unleashed – you could send us into another reality."

"That's right – maybe everyone who is left will have a chance."

"Wait," Dragula warned. "How do you know that the other reality will be better than this?"

"Because it has to be," he insists as he smashes the glass ball – and a pink light explodes out hitting Dragula, Whitestone and Shabetha. But the story was far from over.

2

In the town of Towns-end on a gloomy cloudy day – the large lake which had become a tourist spot was peaceful and still – until a rumble of thunder occurred from the sky and a bolt of lightning struck the waters. The water boiled and bubbled, then a green scaly hand came out of the water and reached up at the sky.

Further away from the lake was the school field of Towns-end High School – where three girls were standing in a lane of the one-hundred-meter track. Their PE teacher, Mr Lingfield, stood on the side lines in tracksuit bottoms, sports shirt and a whistle that hung from his neck. The girls were dressed in white t-shirt and shorts.

The three girls knelt down. They leaned forward and pressed their hands into the cold grass. Jessica looked up – fixing her sights on to the end of the track.

'On your marks – get set…' calls Mr Lingfield as her heart pounds with the anticipation to run. 'GO.'

But Jessica is slow off the mark as the two girls either side of her get ahead of her. She pushes herself hard – picking up speed, her breathing and heart race faster. As she catches up with the girls, she begins to get hot and her chest begins to hurt. She passes the girls and gets ahead of them. Before she knew it she had crossed the line. As she slowed down and stopped – she caught her breath.

'Well done, Jessica – that's a great run.'

Jessica looks up at him and smiles – proud of her achievement. 'Thanks, Mr Lingfield.'

'Thanks, Mr Lingfield.' Bianca, the high school bitch and her girls giggle as they give Jessica a nasty look.

Jessica scowls at them shaking her head.

3

The students are crowding the corridors inside the school. Headmistress, Rachael Benson walks in and out of them looking around. Mr Lingfield walks up to her.

'Mark,' she calls. 'Have you seen the caretaker?'

'About an hour ago – he's around here somewhere but I haven't seen him lately.'

'Well, if you do see him, can you send him to my office, please? – Thank you,' insists Rachael as she walks past a boy hanging by a locker.

'Xander?' calls Jessica as she walks over to him. 'How come you never watched me run?'

'Sorry I was in the library catching up on some studying,' Xander apologized. 'How did it go?'

'I won – as always – annoyed the girls but Mr Lingfield was proud of me.'

'That's great – well done,' said Xander, happily as he closed his locker. Jessica stops herself from laughing. 'What?'

'Nothing… Miss George,' laughs Jessica.

Xander looks at the name on his locker which read Jessica George. 'I can't believe they gave me her locker – she left years ago.'

'You should be honoured – you've inherited a famous actress's locker – at least that's one thing that this school's reputation can keep hold of,' replied Jessica.

She and Xander were then distracted by the sound of a thud on one of the lockers. They looked up to see one of the students being pinned up against one of the lockers.

'Isn't that Cullum?' asks Jessica. Xander walks over to the scene as three boys surround Cullum.

'Next time – do as I say. I wasn't asking a lot.' The boys then walk away from Cullum who is embarrassed and keeping his head down. Hoping not to draw attention to himself he walks away in the direction of the gym.

'What was that about?' wonders Jessica.

'I don't know – come on let's find out,' Xander urges.

Jessica looks at her watch. 'Shouldn't we get to class?.' Xander doesn't listen and walks away from Jessica who shakes her head. 'Guess not.'

4

Cullum is sitting on a wooden bench in the gym.

Surrounded by gymnastic equipment from vault horses, ropes and climbing frames. Two basketball hoops are on either end of the hall and the varnished wooden floor has a basketball court pattern on it. The doors to the end of the gym open – Xander and Jessica enter and go over to him.

'Cullum, right?' asks Xander. 'Are you okay?'

'Fine,' says Cullum shyly, lowering his head not to look at Xander or Jessica, who sit down either side of him.

Cullum felt uncomfortable, as they don't speak a word. 'Aren't you going to go?'

Jessica smiled at him and shook her head. 'Not until you tell us what those boys were doing around you.'

Cullum sighs. 'His pen ran out – I had a spare – I didn't lend it to him.'

'You know – what they did was wrong – but at the same time – sharing, is a good way of making new friends.'

Cullum knew Xander was right and regrets that he didn't share. 'You're right – I'll remember that next time.'

'And here's me thinking they were picking on you because you're a science geek,' says Jessica, amused.

A sound coming from the doors then startles them. 'What was that?' asks Jessica.

Xander jumps up and goes over to the doors. He tries them and discovers they're locked. 'We're locked in,' says Xander, as he looks at Jessica and Cullum who both stand up and hurry over to try the doors themselves.

Through the window they see Rachael Benson walking towards the doors. Jessica panics, and bangs on the window. 'Hey – Miss Benson – We're locked in.' Rachael peers through the window and looks around, then begins to walk away. Xander and Cullum look puzzled as Jessica continues to try and get Rachael's attention. 'She didn't see us – she looked straight through us – Why would she do that?' Jessica says, turning to Xander.

'It was like her perception was shifted? Making us invisible to her,' said Cullum, intrigued.

A rumble causes them to look at the centre circle of the basketball court. Xander cautiously approaches it – then stands in the circle. A vibration goes through his body as there was something underneath the floor. Jessica cautiously approaches the circle as Xander holds his hand out. She takes it and stands with him. 'What is that?' she asks.

Cullum approaches the circle but doesn't stand with them. Instead he feels around the edge. 'It's a platform.' He stretches one leg out and steps onto the centre circle. The second he steps onto it with the other leg – the platform jolts into life and begins to descend with the three students.

The lift stops at the bottom underneath the school and the three students step off into a dark damp cave. Along the walls are rows of flaming torches that lead off into the dark distance. Jessica shivers from the damp walls that cause a cold chill in the air.

'Let's explore, shall we?' Xander says, already leading the way. Jessica and Cullum look at each other, then cautiously follow behind Xander.

After walking for a couple of minutes, the three students soon come to a pair of medieval doors that look like something from a castle. Without hesitation, Xander pushes the doors open which creak as he enters a large room with a long table and large crystal ball, old-fashioned chairs and four metal looking cylinders with a man standing in front of them at the end of the room.

'What's the caretaker doing here?' asks Jessica.

'I'm not the caretaker,' says the man approaching them. 'I am Prince Whitestone of the Red Mountains – welcome to the Hall of Heroes.'

5

The castle of the Red Mountains remains in rubble. Its walls and supports have cracked and crumbled. A layer of pink snow rests on the walls and the ground with a howling whistle from the gust of the wind. Inside the main throne room remains a hole filled with bubbling water. Shabetha walks up to it – holding a black crooked staff with fragments of the shattered crystal ball that Prince Whitestone destroyed. She waves it over the pool to see the high school of Towns-end. She waves it again and changes the image to show Prince Whitestone standing among Xander and friends.

'So, Prince Whitestone is planning to restore the Hall of Heroes?' Shabetha looks over to the dark knight, Dragula, who is stuck to the wall like a frozen statue. 'I will destroy the heroes for you my Dark Lord.' She looks into the pool, her reflection bubbling in front of her. 'DRAGONHEAD,' she yells. 'RISE.' She plunges her staff into the pool which explodes into a magical red light.

In the town of Towns-end on a gloomy cloudy day – the large lake which had become a tourist spot was peaceful and still – until a rumble of thunder occurred from the sky and a bolt of lightning struck the waters. The water boiled and bubbled, then a green scaly hand came out of the water and reached up at the sky. A scaly green skinned body steps out of the lake. Its arms and legs – human looking but with the head of a green dragon. It looks up at the sky.

'What is your bidding, my Queen,' says Dragonhead in a deep beastly voice.

'Dragonhead – you will draw the Heroes out of hiding by attacking the school – once they appear you will destroy them.'

'At once, my Queen.'

6

The image of Dragonhead appears in the crystal ball. Prince Whitestone points to it to show the three students. 'His name is Dragonhead – his body is vulnerable to light attacks but his head is where his strength lies through the force of a beam of energy he can fire out.'

Xander holds up his hands. 'Wait – what are you talking about?'

'Is this a joke? – You've got someone to dress up in a dragon mask to try and scare us, right?' assumes Jessica.

Prince Whitestone is confused. 'Joke?'

'Humorous amusement,' confirms Cullum. 'Like a jester?'

Prince Whitestone realizes. Xander looks around the hall and inspects the metal cubicles. Each one has a different symbol on. A knight's helmet, a Japanese symbol, a plus symbol with a circle round it and a Norse Valkyrie symbol.

'What did you mean? The Hall of Heroes?'

'I come from a realm – parallel to this one. The realm of the Red Mountains. The Heroes are the protectors – sworn to defend against all enemies.'

'How did you end up here?' Cullum wonders.

'There was a war against the Dark Knight, Dragula – the heroes were defeated and he possessed the Princess I was going to marry – she joined his side, and now she has found me to destroy me and this world so the heroes can never rise again.'

Jessica looks at Cullum and Xander who seem to be drawn into the caretaker's story.

'Guys come on – do you really believe this crazy story?' A rumble above them causes them to look up. 'What was that?'

'We don't have much time,' insists Prince Whitestone. 'Step into the cubicles and receive your powers.'

'No one is stepping inside anything until you explain yourself better – what powers? – Why us?' says Xander, firmly.

'The heroes were chosen for their strength and special skills – you,

Cullum, are chosen to be the Mage – for your knowledge of science.' Prince Whitestone walks up to Jessica. 'You, Jessica, are the Ninja – through your athleticism, speed and agility.' He then turns to Xander. 'And you – the White Knight – through your courage and strength of leadership, and moral outlook on life – you three are the new Heroes.'

The three students look at each other. 'But we don't know how to fight?' insists Cullum.

'The powers of the Heroes combined with your heart and strength will guide your actions and will work together to protect this world from the enemies that come through from my realm.'

Another rumble occurs from above. The three students look up. Prince Whitestone insists for them to step into the cubicles.

The three students look at each other, then do as he says. As they approach them – the cubicles open up. They get inside and they close. Inside, a transformation begins to occur. In Cullum's cubicle medieval robes appear over his clothing. His hair changes from brown to white and his eyes glow with a white light. A staff appears in his hand with a crystal ball on top of it. In Jessica's cubicle – black leggings, belt, gauntlets, mask, hood, boots and socks appear over her body. Two batons appear in her hands. Her eyes are all that is seen of her face through the mask, and her mouth is covered. In Xander's cubicle – plates of armour clatter and clank onto his limbs and chest, covering his body in protection and chain mail. Gauntlets appear on his hands and a helmet surrounds his head – sealing it shut to cover his face. He holds a shield and a large sword in his hands. The three cubicles open and the three of them step out and stand in front of Prince Whitestone who looks proud of them.

7

Military Leader, John Crane, walks alongside Rachael, as she shows him around the school.

'I apologize,' said Rachael. 'It's unusual for Towns-end to get mild tremors.'

'No apology necessary.' John smiled. 'Nature and evolution are always changing.' He looks around. 'I must say that this is a really good school and if any of your students are interested in enlisting for a future military background...' But John is cut off by shouts and screams.

Chaos occurs in the school as the students are running for their life through the corridors. Dragonhead is giving chase; then corners three of the students. 'Where are the heroes?' They are too scared to answer. It opens its mouth and a glowing ball of energy charges up. It blasts out a beam which is then stopped from hitting the students and hits the shield of the White Knight as Xander crashes through the ceiling and lands in front of them.

'So, the heroes appear?' growls Dragonhead. 'Where are the others?'

The dragon is then hit by two batons, which causes the creature to be smashed through the wall. The ninja looks up at the White Knight. 'Let's do this'

Xander and Jessica join the fight outside as Dragonhead gets to its feet. Rachael and John appear at the window as they fight.

'What the hell is this?' said Rachael in disbelief.

John is mesmerized at what he is watching. This was not an act. This was the real world.

Dragonhead is struck down by a bolt of lightning.

Cullum stands on the roof holding a magical staff in the air. His mage cape flaps about in the air, before he leaps down and joins the side of the heroes. With all three united, they prepare to fight Dragonhead.

Before Jessica can attack – she is grabbed and thrown through the air. She lands on the ground with a thud.

Stunned. She looks up to see Bianca, who has transformed into a half human, half yellow and black striped hornet.

'The clue was in the name.' Bianca laughed. 'Bee-anca.'

Jessica gets to her feet and connects her batons together to form an energy staff that she twirls around herself.

Crane looks in awe at Bianca. The mixed evolution of human and insect was giving him ideas of his own. Rachael attempted to pull Crane away but he was adamant to stay and watch. He watched Jessica defend herself against the hornet's venomous stinger, until it was knocked out of her hands. She flipped back to escape Bianca's attack, but lost her footing and landed on the ground.

Bianca raised her stinger and flew straight to Jessica for a killing blow, but she didn't get that far, as she was sent spinning through the air by a shockwave that fired out of Cullum's staff.

Seeing where Bianca had been sent in the distance, Crane wasted no time and left immediately to confront her.

'Mr Crane?' Rachael called. 'Where are you going?'

Dragonhead charged up another attack. Cullum quickly created an energy shield around Xander and Jessica just as his deadly beam blasted towards them.

'You can't hide forever,' Dragonhead growled.

A bolt of lightning struck down from the sky and channelled its energy into the White Knight's sword bringing it to life. Xander was in disbelief at the electrical current he held in his hand. He spun around and threw it like a boomerang. It impaled Dragonhead and sent him flying. He then exploded into pieces of glass and the sword stuck in the ground.

Xander pulled the sword out of the ground. He couldn't believe what he had just done.

'We did it – we defeated him,' said Cullum.

'Look.' Jessica pointed to see the students staring at them, wondering who these three mysterious heroes were.

'First time the school has ever noticed us,' Xander pointed out. 'We are…' But he was cut off and sent flying across the school field with Jessica and Cullum.

A swirling black mist appears and Shabetha steps out from it holding her crooked staff tightly. 'Children,' she cackled.

'Shabetha,' Whitestone called.

Shabetha looked at Whitestone with curious eyes. There was something there – something familiar – like she knew him. But her mind was blocked with the darkness that Dragula had put inside her. As a sign, her staff glowed and shot a beam of purple energy at Whitestone, but it was returned to Shabetha by Xander defending him with his shield.

'Do you really think that these children will be the next Hall of Heroes?'

'They already are,' Whitestone replied.

'Then let's see what you've got.' Shabetha smiled, sinisterly, as the heroes charged towards her. She slammed her staff down into the grass and caused a shockwave to knock the heroes off their feet again. 'Moss Men – RISE.'

The damaged grass from the fight had begun to take on a life of its own. It started to reform and shape itself into the form of a person.

'Well, this is something new,' said Cullum.

Jessica pulls her staff apart revealing a strand of energy that is holding both batons together. She swings them around her like nunchucks.

The heroes charge and clash with the moss men.

Xander cuts the creatures to pieces with his sword. Cullum fights with his staff, hitting and striking the creatures with his magic. Jessica fights her way through and attacks Shabetha, but is quickly knocked to her feet when Shabetha creates a force field around her.

Xander throws his sword like a boomerang. It is deflected by the shield. Cullum unleashes bolts of energy from his staff but his powers are no good.

'Heroes,' Whitestone calls. 'Discard your weapons and call upon the power of the Dragon-Rider.'

The heroes throw their weapons into the sky. A look of dread filled Shabetha as she saw them disappear into the clouds.

'We call upon the power of the Dragon-Rider,' the heroes call out.

Dark clouds form in the sky. Rumbles of thunder and flashes of lightning. A roar of something big coming. The clouds part to see the golden dragon hovering in the sky. It charges up a beam of energy and fires it down to the ground. The energy explodes as it burns the force shield away. The power destroys Shabetha's staff, breaking Dragula's control over her.

'Well, that was easy,' Cullum joked.

Whitestone ran over to Shabetha. He held her in his arms as she struggled to catch her breath. 'My Prince'

'You're safe now, Shabetha – we will get you well again,' Whitestone promised.

'So, is that it? It's over?' Cullum questioned.

7

Meanwhile, far away from the school in a sand quarry, Bianca regains consciousness. 'My queen,' she buzzed, sensing that things had changed. Her left wing sprung to life, but her right wing was damaged. She then flinches. Electrocuted by a shot. She flops to the ground as two military figures approach her, their guns trained on her.

'What do you want us to do with it?'

'Far away from Towns-end is an island, where a biogenesis program has begun.' John Crane goes up to the hornet and smiles. 'I want to start a program. We'll call this one – Monster Zero.'

8

Inside the fallen castle of the red mountain. The pool is still. Not a ripple could stir it. Dragula's statue stood lifeless and still inside the walls of the castle. The new heroes had formed and his power over Shabetha had been broken. But a broken connection could only mean one thing. Dragula's eyes burned red and the rust in that infused him to the wall, melted. He pulled himself out and roared as loud as he could. He leapt into the air and disappeared into the pool.

On a desolate road of Towns-end, the road cracked and exploded. Dragula's feet landed on the ground. His burning eyes caught a glimpse of the school in the distance and step by step he marched towards his goal. The dark lord of Alcina, was back for war against the Hall of Heroes.

BRIDE

1

Elisabeth banged on the bedroom door, angry and frustrated at Christian who had locked himself in.

"Open the god damn door, Christian," she shouted with a strong British accent, "you have no choice and need to see this through." For a woman who was fifty-five, she looked gorgeous. Her figure was slender and was wearing a bright red dress while her long brunette hair hung past her breast. She punched the door hard and shouted, "Christian."

Christian sat on the edge of their king-sized bed. His hands shaking uncontrollably, scared that she was going to get in the room. He was forty-two, bald and muscular, but now he felt like a scared child.

"There's no running away from this you know," Elisabeth pointed out. "You promised me your love, your heart and soul."

"You lied to me," Christian shouted aggressively. "You didn't tell me who you truly were when we met, how can I marry you now?"

Elisabeth backed away from the door and gave a sinister smile. "Then don't."

Inside the bedroom, Christian began to smell smoke. He looked towards the door to see black smoke snaking in from under the door. As he reached for the lock to unlock it, the door burst into flames. He staggered back to stop himself from getting burned. Thinking quickly he hurried to the window. When he started to unlock the windows, the same thing happened. Fire burst up from the floor that stretched up to the ceiling. He was trapped. There was no way out of the room. His eyes were streaming while his lungs filled with the choking smoke.

Elisabeth stood in the corridor in front of the burning door. The fire spread into the hallway, burning the ceiling up above which began to fall around her while she stood and watched it. A large portion of the ceiling collapsed next to her, but she didn't move a muscle. The house then collapsed burying Elisabeth and Christian under the burning rubble.

But then something happened. The rubble started to move and, as it parted, Elisabeth emerged from the fire. She brushed off the soot marks from her dress and looked unscathed, then walked away from the home she knew.

2

The last yellow ball on the pool table went down the top right corner pocket. Mason smiled to himself as he lined up his next shot on the black ball. His opponent, Max, a man with long black hair and casual appearance, had a surprised look on his face from the conversation they had been having between shots in the bar.

"So, Billy shot Donna's father and the police shot him?"

"That's what happened," Mason confirmed.

Max shook his head. He couldn't believe it. As Mason had been a friend of Billy's for couple of years, he couldn't imagine how Mason felt.

"So, how did you feel when you found out your friend was dead?"

"Relieved," Mason replied. "Billy was a piece of shit. He treated me, his family and his girlfriends like we were trash. He got what was coming to him."

Their attention was then distracted by the sound of breaking glass. They looked up to see Father Thomas, from St Michael's Parish, staggering around drunk.

"It's all your fault, old man," Thomas slurred. Mr Geoffries and Mr Alan were sitting at the bar. Their attention turned to Thomas who was getting aggressive. "Yes – I'm talking to you."

Mason looked down the sight of his cue, then hit the white ball hard, potting the black in the bottom left corner pocket.

"I can't believe he had a girlfriend with a baby boy and another girlfriend on the side. Sick bastard."

"That's all in the past now – time to focus on the present." Mason hit the white ball. As it rolled to the right middle pocket, a woman put her hand on it to stop it going in. Mason and Max were stunned by how beautiful she was in her red dress that showed off her youthful looks.

"Hi – I'm Elisabeth," she introduced herself and held up the white ball in front of her face. "How about you play a game with me?"

"Sure, I'm up for that," Max insisted as he stepped forward to get closer to her. But to his annoyance she pushed him away as she set her eyes on Mason.

"Not you – he can play with me." As Elisabeth smiled sexily at Mason who couldn't believe that this woman who came out of nowhere had taken an interest in him. Max knew when he was wasn't wanted as Mason's eyes lit up with an attraction to the mysterious woman.

Max finished his drink and told Mason he would see him later. Elisabeth watched him walk out, then returned her attention to Mason raising her eyebrows. "Good – now we're alone." She set the pool game up, then took a cue and bent over the table to break. Mason couldn't help but check out her curvy butt. She smiled to herself knowing that he was checking her out. She broke the balls apart, then blew the top of her cue which lit up like a cigarette. Mason shook his head, after too much beer he thought he was seeing things.

"Open table – pick any colour."

Mason went to the nearest red and potted it into the left middle pocket.

"Red is my favourite colour," Elisabeth told him. "You naughty boy for stealing that from me."

Mason grinned to himself. "It's my favourite colour too."

As he walked around the table, he asked her a personal question. "So, what's a cougar like you doing picking up young men?"

"Cougar?" She laughs. "How old do you think I am?"

"With your youthful looks and no wedding ring on your finger, I would say fifties," Mason assumed.

"I am so much older than fifty."

"Really? How are old are you?" Mason asked surprisingly.

"Now, that is for you to find out."

"I got to admit, however old you are, you're looking good for it."

"Thank you," Elizabeth replied winking at him. But their flirty fun was interrupted by three muscular hoodies who looked to start some trouble between them.

"How about you give me and my boys a game?"

"We're already playing with each other?" Elisabeth explained.

"Well, there's plenty of us to play with."

"She said we're already playing a game," Mason retaliated.

The hoody chuckled to himself, then went over to Mason and pushed him back, trying to get him to start a fight with them. "Come on – me and my boys want a good night," he threatened.

"Boys – more like big babies." Elisabeth laughed. "Now why don't you leave us alone and go fuck each other as you want a good night."

"Oh you've got a big mouth on you, bitch."

"Leave her alone, you," Mason insisted. But the hoody went round the table and tried to punch him until his two friends stopped him telling him the barman was calling the police. The hoodies walked away causing Mason to snap his cue in half from how angry he was.

"Ooh – you have such fire inside you – it's turning me on."

"I'm sorry," Mason apologized. "I don't normally get this angry."

But Elisabeth assured Mason that he shouldn't be sorry.

She loved seeing the rage and aggression coming out of a man. The humanity that wasn't held back and hidden away.

She then handed him her cue and told him they could share to finish the game as, to her, things were getting interesting.

"So, no partner in your life? No boyfriend?"

Mason potted two more reds as Elisabeth confirmed that she was only recently single. She told him how she found Christian, a personal trainer at the Towns-end gym. The dates that they used to go out on. Then the time that he proposed to her after having too much red wine. Even with knowing Christian's secret, that he had a thing for pre-op transgenders ever since he tried to date one hoping he was going to have sex with Ana after the date.

"So, he had a fetish? He was gay?"

"Let's just say our relationship ended up where we both got burned."

Mason missed his shot then handed the cue back to Elisabeth. She potted yellow after yellow as she caught up with him. For her last shot she potted three yellows in the same shot. Mason was impressed. "Are you holding back on me – you're a professional aren't you?"

She looked up and grinned at him. "Oh, I'm so much more than you realize."

"I'd love to find out."

"Then I'll let you," Elisabeth replied as she lined up her next shot. "So, do you find it lonely being a single guy?"

Mason admitted that he did. He never had much luck when it came to women. They would see his nice side and dump him as they couldn't get used to it after being treated by awful men in their past. He had got to the point of giving up finding anyone.

384

"There's nothing wrong with a nice guy – maybe just a bad girl?" said Elisabeth as she put her lips together and blew him a kiss. Mason became aroused and couldn't help but stare at her. His heart raced as he thought about rushing over to her and kissing her passionately. But he wasn't the type to take advantage.

Elisabeth then did something random. She put the red and yellow balls in the pockets and placed the black ball towards the edge of the table. "Let's make this interesting – if you pot the black, you can give me a passionate kiss."

Mason was astounded by what she suggested, considering he was just thinking the same thing. "And if I miss?"

"If you miss – then you bind yourself into a contract with me and I get to take you home and do whatever I want with you." Elisabeth grinned.

Such a tempting offer got Mason excited. The kiss sounded great, but with Elisabeth's offer, it sounded like she was hinting she wanted to have sex with him. Mason swallowed hard as he approached the pool table. He leaned over and look down the cue to get the black ball in his sight. He paused, not knowing which he should choose.

"Well…" said Elisabeth tapping her foot impatiently. "I'm waiting."

Mason's heart was racing. A last minute decision. He held his breath pulled back and made his choice. The white ball hit the black as it spun towards the corner pocket and… hit the edge, causing it to spin away from the pocket, which Mason did deliberately.

"Good boy." Elisabeth smiled in delight. "I was hoping you would miss."

"So, what's this contract you were on about?"

Elisabeth took Mason's hand in hers and held it tightly. "Let's go back to yours and I will explain everything after I get to do what I want with you."

"Wait, I thought you said you would take me to your home and do that?"

"I will after I explain everything to you," Elisabeth insisted. "Come on."

3

When Mason and Elisabeth left the bar, they were confronted by the hoodies from earlier.

"You want a fight, you pieces of shit – you humiliated me," the hoody shouted. He took a swing at Mason knocking him down to the ground. Mason didn't take long to get back to his feet. His jaw hurt from the punch. The anger bottled up inside him, getting ready to retaliate. But Elisabeth pulled him away.

"No," Elisabeth demanded. "Not like that."

"Like what?"

"Like this." Elisabeth took Mason's hand in hers.

She took Mason's hand in hers, and put one of his fingers in her mouth and licked it with her tongue. Her warm moisture from her saliva started to feel hot. She then pulled him towards her and pressed her lips against his. His eyes widened as he didn't expect her do that, or slipping her tongue inside his mouth to massage his tongue with hers.

"Now you're ready," said Elisabeth, turning Mason around to face the hoodies. She got close, whispered in his ear to say, "Now just snap your fingers and you will win the fight."

Mason took a step towards the hoodies and snapped his fingers like Elisabeth suggested. But nothing happened.

The hoodies looked at each other and began to laugh. As they were mocking Mason, something strange began to form. The hoodies felt hot, and their clothes started to smoke like they were burning. Just then, they screamed and combusted into flames. Mason watched in horror as the flames died down, turning the hoodies into a pile of ashes.

"Now that's what I call a naughty boy," chuckled Elisabeth.

Mason looked at his fingers and then backed away from Elisabeth. "What the hell did you do to me?"

"You'll get all your answers when you take me to your bedroom," Elisabeth ordered. She leaned in close and whispered into Mason's ear, "I have such wicked secrets to show you."

4

The door to Mason's bedroom flung open with such force, it caused it to nearly come off its hinges. Elisabeth had her hands all over Mason, kissing and licking him all over his face. Mason was turned on to the point of ecstasy and couldn't wait to get his hands all over this mature woman's body.

Elisabeth pushed him down on the bed and got on top of him. She tore off his t-shirt and ripped his jeans until he was lying bare chested in his underwear. She then got off him and stood at the edge of his bed. His room was still like a typical teenager's. Sports posters all over the wall. Games consoles with gadgets and a picture of a topless woman on the ceiling.

Elisabeth undid her dress. As it flopped to the floor, she placed her hands on her hips revealing her mature naked body. Mason was aroused, he could feel the adrenaline pulsing through his body. For a man still living with his parents he didn't even think what they would think if they walked in on him having sex with an older woman who was about the same age as his mother. All he knew was he wanted Elisabeth, here and now.

Elisabeth got back on top of Mason and pulled his underwear off. "You won't be needing those." She then sat on top of his erection and gasped as it went inside her.

Mason couldn't believe how exciting and electrifying it felt. As he got lost in her gaze, he suddenly realized that something was missing.

"Wait – I need to get a condom."

"Oh fuck that," Elisabeth insisted. She grabbed hold of Mason's hands and pinned him down to the bed.

Thoughts flooded Mason's head, about what happened through the night with the hoodies, Elisabeth turning up out of nowhere.

"Who are you really, Elisabeth?"

Elisabeth brushed her lips over Mason's earlobe and whispered, "I'm the Devil's daughter." She let go of his hands and a transformation began turning Elizabeth's skin red and making her breasts swell up. From her bottom, a tail formed in the shape of a pitch fork. Her lips turned black, her eyes were fiery and black curly horns developed on her head. She grinned sinisterly and then kissed him passionately.

Elisabeth took his hands in hers and placed them on her ass – to his surprise he could feel the heat coming off her body like it was boiling. Elisabeth then took hold of Mason's manhood and put it inside her hot pussy. She pulled his face close to her chest and held up one of her breasts towards his mouth. Mason used his tongue to flick the pink nub of her nipple and then wrapped his lips around it, sucking it hard causing Elisabeth to gasp with pleasure.

She grabbed hold of his shoulders and thrusted at him, faster and faster. Mason couldn't believe he was having sexual intercourse with one of hell's demons. No matter how bizarre that sounded in his head, he never once stopped feeling aroused as she grinded and moaned on top of his groin. Elizabeth then came. Mason couldn't believe how it felt, it was like a hot sticky gooey juice inside of her. It tingled his genitals so much that he couldn't contain himself and ended up exploding inside of her.

Elisabeth screamed out with pleasure that it shook his bedroom to the core, knocking the possessions off his shelf, his TV exploding and the walls of his room cracked. She flopped on his hot and sweaty chest out of breath.

"You're so the one for me," Elisabeth panted. Her black eyes looked into his.

"I didn't think devils existed – I thought it was a made up."

"Well, you can see for yourself that it's real when you come home with me."

Mason looked worried. Home? Did she mean, hell? Elisabeth could read his thoughts. She put her clawed finger on his lips to put him at ease.

"Relax – it's not as bad as this world is going to become – that's why I'm here," Elisabeth explained.

Mason was puzzled at what she was on about, so Elisabeth explained her entire story.

Down in hell, she sat by her father's side to see what the world above was going to become. Her father told her to find a spouse to breed with and rule with down in hell. When she arrived out of the dust and ashes from below, she wandered like a lost lamb looking out for a man. That was when she bumped into Christian, the personal trainer who had just ended his date with Ana the transgender pre-op. As he was the first man that Elisabeth had set her eyes on, he was more than perfect for her. They talked until the early

388

hours and dated for a while but they never gave into their throbbing biological urges. Eventually she asked for his hand in marriage. He was surprised that she was the one asking. He naturally said yes, and to prove his love and loyalty, she agreed to make it a contract.

When the night came for them to make love, Christian witnessed Elizabeth's transformation and freaked out.

Elisabeth couldn't talk Christian round and, as he broke the contract, Elisabeth saw this as an end. So, she set the house on fire and trapped him inside to burn alive. After walking away from the fiery rubble, she went to a bar where she met Mason and Max.

Mason thought that was quite a story, but the only thing he didn't understand was what Elisabeth meant by hell not being as bad as the world is going to become.

Elisabeth smiled sexily at him. She leaned back and spread her legs apart revealing her juicy nether region.

"I can show you – one taste is all it will take."

She grabbed hold of Mason and pulled his head down between her legs. When he tasted her, he saw himself standing in the street. The ground was covered in pink snow which matched the colour of the sky above. All around him stood women. Some were clothed in fashionable dresses, while others were dressed in a leather dominatrix fetish. Mason looked up high to see a statue of a woman called Krista. A plaque under the statue read, *In memory of Krista Milburn, the woman with the vision that made the future*. The atmosphere around Mason attacked his emotions causing him to shed a tear. He was shaking with fear and had never been so frightened in his entire life. It was so strong that he began to have a panic attack.

"Mason," Elizabeth's voice echoed as she pulled him away from in between her legs. Mason felt dizzy. His surroundings began to change back to his bedroom, while Elisabeth tried to calm him down. "Breathe – you're back now."

"What…" Mason asked while trying to catch his breath. "What the hell was that?"

"The future," Elisabeth replied. "Thirty years from now."

"Is that what you and your father plan to do to the world when you get out of hell?"

"No – your world is going to do it itself," Elisabeth explained. "Now you can see why I want you to come back with me – I'm not killing you –

I'm saving you."

Mason buried his face in his hands. The image was now burned in the back of his mind of a terrifying future that was to come. He didn't understand how it was going to happen, but the emotions he felt made sure he didn't want to be around for when it was all going off.

"There have been whispers in the underworld that one day, love is going to die."

Mason looked up at Elisabeth when she said those words. This wasn't the first time he had heard this in his life. His ex-friend, Billy, who treated women badly and got himself killed said the same thing to him once on a drunken night out at the bar. Mason just thought it was because Billy had too much booze, but now this was too much of a coincidence. Mason then plucked up the courage to ask one simple question to Elisabeth that he hoped she could answer.

"How does all this begin?"

"It all begins, with a song," Elisabeth replied as she stroked the side of his face. "You're always forever in my heart."

"Do you mean me? Or is that what the song is called?"

"Both." Elisabeth smiled as she held onto him tightly.

Mason couldn't understand if all this hell was going to happen in the next thirty years, why was she ready to take him to hell? She explained it was her time, like an open window that would eventually close. As by the time she would be able to get out of hell again – it would be too late.

"When do you have to go back?" Mason asked.

"Midnight," Elisabeth replied.

Mason looked up at the clock to see it was five to twelve. There were only five minutes to go before Elisabeth would have to go. Mason knew he would have to make his decision quickly as he started to weigh up his life. He knew he hadn't been happy for a long time. Things between him and his parents had been rocky for a long time as he was staying under their roof and not looking for a better job so he could rent or buy a place of his own. He had no girlfriend or partner to call his own and yet Elisabeth was right in front of him wanting to be his spouse and being the best sex he had ever had. It was too good to pass up this opportunity.

"Okay – I'll go with and I'll marry you," Mason agreed.

Elisabeth gave a sinister grin. "I'm so happy – now close your eyes and kiss me."

Mason closed his eyes and leaned forward to press his lips against hers, but something was strangely odd. Elisabeth wasn't in front of him. Instead he felt heat and the smell of sulphur. When he opened his eyes he found himself looking up at a pit of fire, lava and brimstone. He then realized he wasn't looking up – he was looking down. His hands were cuffed and hanging down past his head. He was naked with chains wrapped around him, chained to a pentagram.

"It's going to be one, hell, of a life with the both of us." Elisabeth laughed.

Both? Mason thought. As he looked up, he could see Elisabeth in her demon form, three times bigger than when he was with her in his bedroom.

Elizabeth's red legs were spread apart. Her lower region was wide open. Mason thought it was like looking into a dark abyss. Her red boobs were ginormous, two red wings were now spread outwards from her back and she had grown another set of long horns that came out of her fiery long black hair. Her black eyes and sinister smile from her black lips hinted to Mason of what she was going to do to him.

"I'm looking forward to playing with you – it will help start my contractions."

Mason's eyes widened in horror when he noticed Elizabeth's big round red veiny pregnant belly. The child was clearly his from what he and her got up to in his room. Elisabeth's tail reached out to Mason as it pulled him towards her lower region, spreading her legs wide open and pushing him deep inside her.

ADOPTED

1

Not all stories have a happy ending. Some stories can end in tragedy. This was the test of recently married couple, Ana and Richie James.

One night after taking Ana out to dinner, they both went for a quiet evening walk. When they were alone, Richie got down on one knee and proposed to Ana. She couldn't believe her luck. She had seen so many of her friends get engaged and married that she never thought it would happen to her. Ana said yes instantly. She didn't hesitate for a second. When Richie put a diamond studded engagement ring on her finger, she grabbed hold of Richie and kissed him passionately while holding on to him tightly.

"Not that I'm complaining – but what is the real reason you proposed to me?" Ana asked with curiosity.

Richie explained that he didn't want to lose her. He loves her with all his heart. Their sex life was putting a strain on their relationship and he admitted it was his fault, so he thought it would help him by forcing him to go through with it on their wedding night as no one should ever miss that special night to make love.

Ana could tell that Richie had been frustrated with himself. She made it clear to him that he wasn't going to lose her as she would have persevered until they got things right. The proposal gesture was a sweet idea, but she didn't want to get married just so it was an excuse for them to have sex.

"The proposal wasn't a gesture, Ana, I meant it with all my heart – I want to marry you if you want to," Richie asked.

"Yes – I do," Ana replied by kissing Richie. "Don't worry okay, we won't have to tell anyone about our lack of a sex life and if anyone asks, we can have a bit of fun and joke about it." She smiled cheekily and winked at him.

"I love you," said Richie.

"I love you too," Ana replied.

Ana and Richie announced their engagement to Ana's close friend, Missy, just before Christmas. She admired Richie and was proud that Ana had finally met a decent guy. Ana asked if Missy would be her maid of honour and witness, but was disappointed when Missy turned her down.

Once the new year had rolled around, Richie found a place that would be legal for them to get married. They got married on a Saturday. Ana looked beautiful in her white wedding dress which aroused Richie.

That night came the honeymoon and this was the moment that Richie knew there was no turning back. He helped Ana out of her wedding dress until she was standing topless in front of him. He closed his eyes and took a deep breath and pulled down her underwear. When he opened his eyes, he saw it.

Ana grabbed hold of him and pulled him away. "Don't force yourself – it's okay if you can't – I love you and being married to you is more important than…" But she was cut off when Richie went through with it.

An hour later they were both lying in bed, hot, sweaty and out of breath. Ana cuddled up to Richie and grinning like a Cheshire cat. "Wow," she thought. "That was just…"

"I know – I did it." Richie smiled.

Months passed by and their married time together was magical. Richie would come home every week with a dozen roses for Ana, as a celebration of their love, and knowing that they had the weekend to be with each other. Ana would always make him a nice dinner when he got in and tidy the flat after getting home from working as an administrator at PharmCorp.

The repetitive routine eventually started to get stale, so one night she mentioned to Richie about adopting a child. Richie knew all too well that she couldn't have children as she was originally born a man, but to her surprise, he had been thinking the same thing.

"You surprise me every time," Ana said with excitement. "I thought you were going to say that you would prefer it to be just the two of us?"

Richie held her hand in his and assured her that he had always wanted kids and the sooner they put their names down on the adoption list, the sooner they would get the ball rolling. Richie knew it would take a long time before they got a child, so waiting to decide to go through with it would take longer. But to their surprise, it only took three weeks.

"Mr and Mrs James," said an attractive half cast woman. "Please come in."

Ana and Richie walked into the woman's office which had a vintage feel to it. Down to the varnished brown interior and desk, to the vintage flowery dress she was wearing.

"My name is Rosario Sinclair – please take a seat."

When they both sat down, Rosario showed them a picture and a file of a boy that they would be adopting. Ana read the details of the file and couldn't believe the back story of him.

The boy's name was Rick. He was five years old and had short brown fair hair. He had been abandoned by his mother called Marcy, who had been working as a prostitute. With the job she had, Rick hardly ever saw her and it wasn't until her latest client, she ended up getting arrested and Rick was moved to the boys home.

Her client was Missy. A woman who was engaged to a man called Will. But Missy struggled with her sexuality and was really a lesbian. Will had been tricked when Marcy took an interest in him and one day he caught the two of them having sex. The news about her secret escapades soon spread around Towns-end, forcing Marcy to work harder than ever. Eventually she couldn't cope and was never there for Rick. The neighbours got involved seeing her abandon her child on a daily and nightly basis and, before Marcy knew it, he was taken by social services. Knowing that she had lost her son, she did nothing to try and get him back and completely gave up on him.

Ana felt guilty. She was friends with the woman that Marcy had sex with which made things awkward. Richie could tell what Ana was thinking. To make things easier it would be better to see if they had another child they could foster with the colourful history that she had.

"Does the boy remember anything, about what happened?" Richie asked.

"No," Rosario replied. "And that's how it should be. He's a really happy child. I don't think it would be wise to tell him everything that happened and destroy that happiness that he's got inside him."

Richie felt Ana would be a bit more relieved, but secretly Ana was thinking they would be walking on egg shells for the rest of their life and living a lie, as one day their happy life would come crashing down as Rick would know the truth.

"Come – let me take you to him," said Rosario.

Inside a little art classroom, Rick was painting a picture. He picked up a brush and swiped it over some black paint and began to paint a night sky. Ana and Richie walked in with Rosario and wandered over to him.

"Rick," said Rosario.

Rick looked up at Ana and Richie and gave them a big smile. This sent

Ana's heart a flutter. She knew in her heart that this was the boy to adopt with their family and, by Richie's smile, she knew that he felt the same.

"This is Ana and Richie – they want to adopt you," Rosario explained.

But Rick's attention was on his painting. Ana kneeled down beside him to take a look at what he was painting. It showed a night sky and a woman standing on a platform surrounded by yellow stars.

"What are you painting, honey?" Ana asked. "Is that the night sky?"

"No – they're cameras," Rick spoke, softly.

Richie took a closer look at the picture. To him it looked like a music venue with a pop star standing on a platform singing out to the crowd while her fans took pictures.

"What's that next to the girl?" Richie asked.

"A chair." Rick looked up smiling.

Ana smiled at Richie and then smiled to Rosario and said, "He's perfect."

An hour later, after assisting Rick to pack and say goodbye to the orphanage, he soon found himself in the back seat of Richie and Ana's car.

Ana looked in the rear view mirror to see Rick smiling at the sights. It was going to be a new venture for him, one that would place his life in the right direction, Ana thought. Rick didn't talk much. He was too shy around being alone with his new foster family.

"Hey – that's Melissa." Ana pointed. "Pull over"

Richie pulled the car over to the side of the road and honked the horn to get her attention. Melissa wandered over not looking her best. Ana and Richie found out that Melissa had waited since the new year's ball to find the man for her ever since she was told by Mr Geoffries that he would find her. He never told her how long it would take but she always thought it would be soon.

"It's going to be a very lonely Christmas again this year at the cabin," said Melissa.

"Wait, you're going back?" Ana asked.

"Of course, it's tradition – but I won't be staying at the log cabin – there was an abandoned trailer that I'll stay in – besides I love the scenery."

"So, are your parents going?" Rick asked.

"I doubt it – not after what happened last Christmas, we haven't spoken since then," Melissa replied. "And who's this young man?"

"This is Rick – our foster son," said Ana, excitedly.

398

"It's nice to meet you." Melissa smiled. "I'm Melissa, the waitress at *Kays Coffee Shop*– I have a free piece of cake and a milkshake with your name on it, so stop by one time."

Rick smiled with joy. He had never had a free offer before and he liked Melissa straight away.

"Just so you know, I recommend you go home through the back streets," Melissa suggested.

"Why's that?" Ana asked.

"Because you won't get home the normal way. Everything is blocked off," Melissa replied.

"What happened?" Richie asked.

Melissa told them about Towns-end Heights. A four storey flat building that they had already heard about.

Melissa told them that the building had disappeared. Richie found it hard to believe that a building could just vanish. Melissa thought the same until she saw the site it used to stand on. The concrete looked like it had been ripped up and pulled out. But, for that to happen, someone would have obviously noticed. It was quite the mystery, one that she would be keeping a great interest on.

Ana and Richie then parted ways with Melissa and promised that they would see her again when they would pop into *Kays Coffee Shop* with Rick. They drove home through the back streets as Melissa suggested until they got to their flat.

Rick was a bit unsure of his new surroundings. The orphanage had become his home for a long time. He knew where everything was and how comfortable his bed was that he slept in. One thing he would miss was the paint room. He loved to paint pictures from his imagination which became the only thing he lived for. Ana promised Rick that they would go to town and get him some paints and paper. This made Rick excited and he couldn't wait for the next day to go out.

2

Years later, Rick now grown up was standing in front of the bathroom mirror dressed in a school uniform ready for his first day. Ana made him jump when she walked in on him not realizing he was in there.

"Oh god, sorry, Rick," Ana apologized.

"It's okay, Mum," Rick replied.

Ana crossed her arms and raised an eyebrow and said, "Wow – you look just as handsome, the day I met your dad." Ana straightened Rick's collar straightened up in the mirror. "You'll be fine – the first day of high school is always the scariest."

But Rick had something else on his mind, as the night before, he heard moaning noises coming from their bedroom and couldn't help but ask Ana if she and Richie were all right.

Ana was shocked. She felt embarrassed and didn't know what to tell him as she thought that the truth would be too humiliating for him. There was only one thing she could really say and that was "Your dad and I were… well…"

"I get it. You don't have to finish that sentence," Rick told her.

Ana felt more relaxed when Richie walked in and asked, "Have you two seen my watch?"

Ana reached over to the corner of the bath tub and picked up his gold Rolex. Richie complimented Rick on how he looked and told him to wait for him in the car. When Rick left the bathroom, Ana closed and locked the door.

"Really sweetie – here, now?" Richie joked.

"He knows. He heard us last night," Ana panicked. "If he knew the truth about me, it would humiliate him."

"Ana, stop it," Richie spoke firmly. "Rick's a grown man. He'd be able to handle it, okay? Do you really think it matters after all these years that we've been there for him, that you've been there for him – he loves us."

Richie held Ana in his arms to comfort her, but Ana was always constantly worried that something was going to burst their happy family bubble.

3

Rick walked through the gates of Towns-end High School with very little confidence. The place was bigger than his primary school with so many students crowding the place. Heads turned and followed the new stranger across the ground followed by whispers like a load of gossiping women.

Rick then bumped into a boy that looked the same age as he did. Sticky uppy fair hair and a smiley face greeted him.

"You must be the new boy. The name's Blue. What's yours?" Blue asked.

"Rick James," Rick replied.

"James? You the boy living with two guys?" Blue asked.

"No – I live with my mum and dad... well Foster mum and dad. I was adopted," Rick explained.

"Her name wouldn't be Ana by any chance?" said Blue. "She's a guy."

Rick was confused. He thought back to all the time he had spent with Ana. Even when he walked into the bedroom and she was topless, as he couldn't stop staring at her large breasts. She was all woman to him.

"Look Rick – you obviously haven't heard the word transgender. When a man wants to become a woman, but doesn't always have the surgery down below – they keep their boy parts."

"My mum is a woman," Rick argued.

"Are you a hundred per cent sure? Isn't there anything strange you've noticed about her and your dad?"

Rick thought back to the other night, when he heard moaning noises coming from their room.

"Oh, they were having sex then," said Blue, bluntly. "Your dad was probably being plugged by her."

"Plugged?" said Rick, puzzled.

"My dad takes my mum from behind, so Ana was probably doing the same with your dad." Rick was freaked out imagining what that could look like. "And the moaning was probably your dad from the pain and pleasure she was..."

"Shut up will you," Rick reacted. "God, What kind of home environment do you live in?"

"One that's not afraid to hide it," Blue admitted.

For Rick's first day, things didn't go as well as he had hoped. He sat in class with constant thoughts of what Blue had put into his head. All of the little subtle hidden things that Ana and Richie had been playing at all of his life had begun to make sense. Rick didn't want to believe it, but his gut instinct told him another story.

When it was time to go back home, Rick was quiet all the way. Richie noticed it when he drove him home. He didn't want to talk about his day or anything as it happened. Ana noticed the same thing when they were all sitting at the dinner table. Rick wanted to talk about what Blue had thought about them, but in his heart he couldn't bring himself to hurt his parents.

So, later that night as Rick laid in bed, he listened out for any unusual noise coming from his foster parents' room. To his surprise there wasn't any. Rick felt more relaxed than other nights and with his heavy eyes he tried to get off to sleep. But Rick's bladder stopped him from doing so and forced him to get out of bed.

Rick yawned as he made his way across the landing to the bathroom. When he opened the door, that's when his whole world around him came crashing down, when he saw Ana, standing at the toilet urinating from her penis.

Rick and Ana were both horrified. She was lost for words and didn't know how to explain.

"It's true, he was right." Rick freaked, as he backed into Richie who held him. Rick struggled to get out of Richie's grip, so he yelled, "Get off me."

Ana slammed the bathroom door shut in humiliation.

Richie could hear her sobbing from behind the door as Rick looked disgusted at the both of them.

Minutes later, after everyone had calmed down, Richie was sitting at the table with Rick, who he could see was mortified.

"This is the sort of thing we wanted to avoid, son," Richie explained.

"I'm not your son," Rick snapped. "How could you go through with this? How could you adopt me?"

"My name was Andy," Ana explained as she entered the room. "I may have been born a man, but I always felt like a woman, it's why I had

402

surgery. I was haunted and constantly stalked by the shadow of the man I was – it's how I met Richie."

"What she's saying is, it doesn't matter what she originally looked like on the outside – her warm heart on the inside has always been the same – we've loved you ever since we met you – why should all those years be a waste of time and we're still here for you, unlike your mother."

"Richie," Ana gasped.

The more and more Ana and Richie talked, the bigger the hole they dug themselves. "Wait – I thought you said that my mother had passed away to a better place?"

"Rick – it had only been a year since we adopted you. You were six and you were happy. A child at that age should be enjoying life, laughing and full of love, not thinking about depressing thoughts," Ana told him.

"See, Rick – she is your foster mother. We didn't tell you because you were a happy child. Why would we want to destroy you?"

But Rick had already made his decision by not speaking to them for the rest of the night and returned to his room.

As everything flooded in his head while he laid in bed, he could hear the raised voices of Ana and Richie downstairs.

Ana was yelling at Richie, why he mentioned that Rick's mother was still alive. Richie argued back saying that enough was enough. They had lied to Rick for too long and they were both to blame for wrecking what they had with him.

The very next day, Rick woke up and had breakfast with Ana and Richie, but an awkward silence between them all soiled the mood of the day. Each one didn't know what to say to each other to try and fix the damage of the night before.

"I'll give you a lift to school when you're ready," said Richie as he stood up to leave the table.

Rick was ready to leave straight away. Ana watched him grab his things and ignore her. He stopped and hesitated to leave. Ana hoped he would turn around to look at the mother who had brought him up and loved him. But he never did. Instead he walked away and made Ana sob the rest of the morning.

"You were right – she is a man," Rick told Blue as he sat on a bench on the school grounds.

"I knew it – how did you find out, they tell you?"

"I walked into the bathroom and saw my mum's penis... even that doesn't sound right, god," said Rick as he grabbed hold of his head with such frustration.

"At least you know now."

"I may have found out a bit too much. My mum is alive – I have been constantly thinking why she never came to find me."

"Families can be complicated. They're the biggest mystery of the world."

"I don't know what I'm going to do about my foster parents," said Rick, burying his head in his hands.

"Forgive them," said a female voice. Rick looked up to see a gorgeous looking short haired girl smiling at him. "Hi I'm Robyn – sorry to hear your bad news."

But Rick didn't know what to say. He was blown away how beautiful Robyn looked – considering she gave off that special tingle down below to him.

"You think I should forgive them?"

"Of course," replied Robyn. "Sounded to me that they must have loved you very much to keep their secret hidden from you and it doesn't change the fact that they spent all their years bringing you up."

Rick knew that they loved him and he loved them with all his heart. It upset him, sure, but inside him he didn't want to hate them. He just wanted things to be back the way they used to be. He needed them just like they needed him to complete their lives.

So, once school was over and Richie picked him up outside the gates, the first thing he did when he walked through the door was forgive Richie and Ana. Rick admitted it was going to take time for Rick to accept that Ana was born a man and to him he felt like he was living with two gay guys.

But as the years passed by, Rik's home life was fifty fifty. He found it easier when he was home with his foster parents, but never really wanted to be seen out with them. Richie and Ana began to feel frustrated with not being able to go out anywhere in public just so Rick didn't feel awkward with what people's opinions were of them.

Rick was now more comfortable with his life. He studied hard at school and became close friends with Blue and had a strong soft spot for Robyn. Rick felt he had an instant connection with her, but he soon felt she was quite a control freak. Most of the time he never had much say over what

404

they should do, eat, or where they should go. But he did find that when she made decisions it guided him to great memories and shaped his life.

Then one day they stopped being friends, when they were sitting near the lake at Towns-end's Park and shared their first kiss. With their relationship taken to the next level and college just round the corner, Rick was the happiest he had ever been in his life and he knew in his heart that one day he would ask Robyn to marry him.

Meanwhile, things between Richie and Ana had got more frustrating. Ana had been more horny than ever as she and Richie hadn't had sex for months. With Rick being home they avoided all intimate contact. Rick used to cringe every time they kissed, so they agreed they wouldn't do it in front of him.

Richie however had been working long hours and would get back not long after Ana had gone to bed. Ana felt that their marriage was falling apart.

So, on one Christmas Party, Richie had a bit too much to drink. With his drunk heavy eyes, he couldn't help but check out some of the hot women that were dancing on the dance floor. Richie felt turned on by his hard erection in his pants, so he staggered over to the dance floor and began to dance between them. Sure enough, the women danced around him, until they were grinding up and down him getting him extremely excited.

But Richie was a good man and wasn't the sort to cheat on Ana, so, he called it quits and went home.

The next morning, waking up to the god of all hangovers. Richie sat at the kitchen table with a handful of headache tables in one hand and a glass of water in the other. Ana walked in dressed in a silk dressing gown and quickly kissed him on the lips, before Rick came downstairs.

"Morning," said Ana. But Richie's mouth was dry and she could still smell the alcohol from the night before. "The party was good then?"

Ana turned the coffee machine on and got two mugs out.

"Could you please sit down – we need to talk," Richie insisted.

Ana was concerned. Did something happen at the party the night before? Richie couldn't have been unfaithful, surely. After all the years they had been together, she knew him too well. She sat down in front of him, where Richie said what he needed to say.

"I feel after all this time that we have grown apart. Our intimacy is dead. Because of Rick. I want my own children from my own seed. I feel like I don't have a connection with him – I'm unhappy."

Ana was upset. She tried to tried to think of ways they could repair their relationship. But the suggestions always came back the same, life would have to go back to the way it was without Rick and then Ana was told something she didn't want to hear.

"I'm still straight, Ana – I can't be with someone who isn't the opposite to me."

"No," said Ana wiping the tears from her eyes. "I thought you loved me with all your heart – we got married – I thought we were going to have a life with each other?"

"I'm sorry. But I made my choice. I'm moving out today. I want to be with a woman – the flat is yours and Rick's." said Richie as he stood up to leave.

A tear ran down Ana's face as she looked at her wedding ring on her finger.

4

Another year passed by and Ana felt like someone had hit the reset switch on her. She had felt more alone than ever. Her close friend Missy had moved away years ago and had made new friends. Rick and Robyn had become college sweethearts, where Rick had spent most of his time leaving Ana all alone in the flat.

So, one night Ana had opened a bottle of wine and looked over a box of happy memories that she had hidden away. There were photos of Ana and Richie enjoying a sunny holiday in a hotel by the beach and the gorgeous blue ocean. The photos of their wedding hit Ana hard and she didn't look at them for very long.

Weddings were a sore point to Ana. The year before Ana and Richie had divorced. Within a month, Richie had been dating another woman who was one of the women he had danced with at the Christmas Party and near the end of the year they were married with a child on the way. Richie had managed to achieve his dream and ambition. But for Ana she felt like she was the one suffering and didn't know why she was still alive as she felt she had nothing left to live for.

Ana put the photos aside. She then picked up some old paintings that Rick had done when he was younger. One painting showed a big house, like a mansion, and what looked like a woman holding a rifle. Ana thought it was weird that Rick would paint such a thing. It was that moment that Ana made a decision. A really difficult decision. But it was something that she would have to do to feel better.

When Rick came home and woke up the next day, he was greeted by Ana standing in the hallway with a big suitcase packed. She had packed her essential clothing and threw out what she didn't need the night before.

"What is this?" Rick asked.

Ana walked up to Rick and handed him the keys and said, "I can't do this any more. This was mine and Richie's home full of our memories and the life we built. Now it's yours to fill with new memories of you and Robyn."

Rick couldn't believe that Ana was giving up her home and most importantly on him. She told him that it would be the last time he would see her as she needed to move on.

She felt like she had done all that she could by bringing him up and now he could be free from the humiliation that she had given him.

"Where are you going to go?"

"Anywhere to be alone. I have come to accept that no one is ever going to accept me, let alone love me for who I am," Ana said as she picked up her suitcase. "Take my advice, marry Robyn, now. I know that you love her with all your heart and I know that she loves you – when a man loves a woman – how it always and should be it seems – goodbye, Rick."

And with that, Ana walked out of Rick's life.

At first Rick didn't know what to do with himself. The first few nights of sleeping in his flat alone was hard. Ana had been the longest one living with him and he found it hard to adjust.

Robyn was shocked when Rick told her the news in *The Open Bar*. She couldn't believe how unlucky he was by the amount of people that had walked out on his life. She assured Rick that she wouldn't be the next one to walk out and admitted that she loved him with all her heart and if he wanted to, then she would move in so they could live together.

As Robyn and Rick kissed, a woman approached them clapping their hands. "Beautiful – just beautiful – that's what I like to see – happiness in their life – something that I forgot…"

But the woman lost her balance and nearly fell flat on her face as Rick reacted and caught her. As he and Robyn helped her up, they both could smell the alcohol on her breath.

"Thank you, my handsome young man." The Woman smiled. "A grown man that started out as a boy."

Rick looked at Robyn thinking she was going to get annoyed by the way the woman was talking to him, but Robyn didn't let it get to her as the mature woman nearly looked in her fifties. Rick helped her sit at the bar.

"Thank you," the Woman complimented as Rick and Robyn began to walk away.

The woman looked up at Steve the barman who was standing in front of her. An average unshaven man in a vest and holey jeans.

"Why didn't you tell your son that you were his mother, Marcy?" Steve asked.

Marcy shrugged her shoulders and said, "What difference would it make? He's had enough pain and anguish without me coming along and causing more."

"Sounds to me like you need a change of scenery," said a woman who sat down next to her.

Marcy looked the woman up and down. She was quite young and looked like someone who was going to win a Miss World pageant.

"Who are you?" Marcy asked with curiosity.

"Madison Milburn." Madison offered her a hand out. "I can show you a better life than this. A life you'll never grow tired of. An exciting life for every day of the rest of your life if you come with me right now."

"Where is this place?" Marcy asked.

But Madison never told her. Instead she just bit her lip and smiled with excitement.

SEE

1

Samuel Stephens' social media account page appeared on the phone screen. Whoever was looking at it was scrolling through his information with great interest. They first tapped his profile picture, where it showed a medium built man with short dark hair with a slight smile and a visible scar on his forehead that he had recently sustained. They then scrolled through his information.

Samuel was born on the 26th of February, 1981. He was thirty-nine years old. Single and attended Towns-end High School from 1992–1997. They then scrolled through his common interests where he liked comic superheroes, science fiction TV and films, along with old sitcoms.

They then started looking through his photo albums. Each happy photo that had been posted of Samuel was being saved to the phone.

Once they had finished gathering information, they then pulled up the messenger and typed out a message.

It said, "Hi, Samuel – how are you? I hope you are well. I don't know if you remember me, but I went to Towns-end High School with you. I was in the same tutor group as you. It's Charlotte Graham."

When they sent the message, they waited for an eager response, but as the hours ticked away, they never got one. Charlotte became angry and would constantly check the status of the message. It was still unread.

At the point of giving up, Charlotte was about to get to sleep, but then her phone beeped. It was a message from Samuel. Charlotte got into bed and read his response.

"Hi, Charlotte, I'm sorry but I don't remember you. It's been a long time since high school, so I hope I haven't upset you by not remembering you. How have you been?"

Charlotte replied instantly to the message by telling Samuel that she had been through a right time since she left school and parted ways with everyone she knew. She had come down with a condition that stopped her from getting any sort of job. Her family didn't see or talk to her and had been lonely ever since.

Samuel messaged her back and told her that he was sorry to hear that she had been through a rough time. He then asked her what she looked like as he couldn't remember.

Charlotte had shoulder length brown hair. A medium built figure and acne when she was at school. She was the smartest girl, especially in science, but no one ever took any notice of her. She then suggested they meet up as it would be nice to reconnect. Samuel agreed and Charlotte sent him details of where she lived so they could meet up.

That evening, Samuel took a cab to the address that Charlotte gave him. When the cab arrived, he saw it was a grotty run down building that looked like it was about to fall to pieces. The paint was faded. The bricks were cracked and broken. Samuel couldn't believe that Charlotte lived in a place like this.

It was no better in the lobby. The smell of damp filled his nostrils. The plaster on the white walls was peeling and the floor was sticky with every step he took to the third floor where Charlotte was.

When Samuel knocked on the door he realized it was already ajar. The door squeaked open revealing a hallway with a flickering light. Something trouble him. It was quiet.

Too quiet. As he walked into the eerie flat, he called, "Charlotte – it's Samuel." But there was no reply.

All of a sudden, he jumped as the sound of footsteps startled him. He turned to leave but the door slammed shut. He tried to open it, only to discover it was locked.

"Samuel?" Charlotte called. "In here."

Samuel cautiously walked into the room at the far end where Charlotte's voice came from. The living room was smaller than he thought it would be. The walls were stained and the room was filled with a musty smell. To his surprise, the room was empty. There was no furniture which gave him the feeling that the flat was abandoned. But he swore to himself that he heard her voice.

"Charlotte?" he called, but there was no reply. He thought his mind was playing tricks on him. That's when he decided to leave.

"I'm glad you came," said Charlotte. Samuel turned around but there was no one else in the room.

"Where are you?" Samuel asked.

"Standing right in front of you," Charlotte replied. But Samuel didn't see her. The room was empty.

"Are you a ghost?" Samuel asked.

"No..." Charlotte replied. It was at the moment Samuel saw the room distort and something move in the corner of his eye "...I'm invisible."

2

"Are you sure you're right in front of me?" Samuel asked, unconvinced. He then fell back as if something pushed him. "So, you're the one that closed the door on me, I thought this place was haunted."

"Why don't we go to the bedroom and I'll explain."

Samuel watched his arm lift up by itself as Charlotte pulled him in the direction of her bedroom. He felt the touch of someone holding his hand, but as he couldn't see it, everything started to feel a bit surreal.

When Samuel walked into the bedroom, all he saw was a well-used mattress on the floor and a phone. The walls were cracked and dirty, with damp moisture making the room cold.

"How can you live like this?" Samuel asked Charlotte.

Charlotte explained that she had no choice. Her family had split. Father didn't want to know her. Her mother became an alcoholic and threw her out. She was the girl that literally had become invisible to the people around her. The interest in science was all that she had.

"Do you remember Jasper Long?"

"Our science teacher?" Samuel asked.

"He told me before our exams that I would never make a scientist – but I got straight As and proved him wrong. I experimented beyond my exams and discovered a formula where it could render the molecules of the human body, invisible."

Samuel was in disbelief. For someone to achieve invisibility was a breakthrough. "Why haven't you shared this with anyone? Why hide it? And what made me so special that you got in contact with me? Haven't you tried any of the others we used to go to school with?"

"I tried the girls. Some never replied, some blocked me. But there was one guy who responded. James Martin."

"I remember James. Used to go out with that Nikki," said Samuel. "Last I heard, Nikki got herself pregnant at that sex club called, Play 4 Real, before it was shut down."

Charlotte complimented Samuel and told him that it felt good talking to someone again and suggested that maybe next time she could go to his place and have a meal. But Samuel was a bit put off by Charlotte's urgency. "We'll see but I'll be in touch."

Charlotte went quiet. She didn't respond to him when he left the flat.

When Samuel got back to his home, he was a bit of mess. He fumbled with the keys as he tried to unlock the door in a hurry. He looked around at the empty street and the houses across the road. He started to become paranoid. He felt like he was being watched. With Charlotte being invisible, she could have followed him home and be watching every move that he made.

Samuel wasted no time and called his friend Ash, who he had kept in touch with after leaving high school. Ash didn't remember Charlotte at all. He had been focused on the popular girls like any predictable hormonal student, but Ash wasn't one to ignore his friends and offered to do a bit of investigating on Charlotte.

So, later that night, as Samuel laid in bed under his warm sheets, his mind began to play tricks on him. The moonlight caused the shadows to give his room a haunting feel to it. As his eyes focused through the darkness, it was then he spotted something. The outline of a figure stood by the end of his bed. He froze. His paranoid mind thought it was Charlotte. He kept his gaze locked on the figure while his hand reached for his light switch. The figure disappeared when the light came on. He looked around to see if he could see an outline, but there was nothing. When he turned the light off, he didn't see the figure. Samuel would never know if his mind was playing tricks on him as it took him half an hour to get to sleep. But when he did, his bedroom door slowly opened and closed by itself.

3

The next day, after a restless night's sleep, Samuel watched television while he ate his breakfast. He checked his phone constantly to see if he had any missed messages from Charlotte. He was relieved when he saw he had none. Samuel checked the messenger to see the last time Charlotte had been online. Each time he saw that it was the day before, making him more relaxed. As the day went on into the afternoon, he checked his messenger again only to wish that hadn't when he saw the status change to 'Online' and 'Typing'.

Samuel waited and waited for the inevitable beep to say that he had a new message, but it never came. All of a sudden he jumped when the phone rang. He was relieved to see it was Ash.

"Hey Ash," Samuel spoke into the phone. "Tell me you have some news, I've been at my wits' end."

Ash told Samuel all that he had discovered. He started with James Martin. He had spoken to James months back just for a catch up and to see how he was doing since leaving school. He had never mentioned Charlotte, but due to the lack of posts in his social media account, he started to become worried. He contacted some of his family and friends and that's when he wished he hadn't. He was told that James had disappeared and hadn't been seen for weeks.

Nobody knew about his whereabouts and there had been no messages or contacts to say where he was going.

Samuel had a feeling at the back of his mind that James may have been in danger. He could imagine that he had been killed. He then changed the subject and wondered if Ash had any luck with the girls.

Bringing up Charlotte's name started the girls off. They remembered her a lot as she was the easiest target to pick on through the school years. This confused Samuel after what Charlotte had told him that they ignored her, making her invisible to them.

"Look, Samuel, I understand how overwhelming this must be to you. Send me Charlotte's address and I'll take a look myself – I'll speak to her,"

Ash suggested.

But Samuel didn't think it was a good idea as he didn't want Ash to get himself into any danger. He didn't know how dangerous Charlotte could be and didn't want to find out.

"Okay – I'll keep you updated if I hear anything else," said Ash.

Samuel cut the call off and then typed out a message to Charlotte, suggesting that he was going to come round for another chat. Charlotte replied instantly, but suggested that she would make the effort and come to him if he would message his address to her.

He thought about things logically. He thought that he didn't need to send her his address as she may have already followed him home and know where he lived. But then again why would she be asking? Maybe she didn't know.

Everything rested on his decision. Samuel then decided to take a gamble and messaged his address to her. She replied back to him and told him that she would be round at seven.

For the rest of the day the time went slow for Samuel. He was anxious and nervous to meet Charlotte again. But her recent lies made him more curious to try and find the real truth behind her deceit.

The clock turned five past seven and still there was no sign of Charlotte. Samuel wondered if she wasn't going to show and began getting paranoid again that she was already there watching him.

"Charlotte," Samuel called. "Are you here?" But there was no reply. "Come on – stop playing games I know you're here." But again there was no reply. "Enough games okay – I know you're here – talk to me – say something."

The doorbell then startled him. Samuel realized that she was never in the room and felt like he was losing his mind more and more.

When he opened the door, no one was there until a voice spoke, "Sorry I'm late, Samuel – it was quite a way."

"I didn't think you were coming, Charlotte," said Samuel.

"You're kidding right," Charlotte replied surprised. "I would never stand you up, just like you wouldn't stand me up – I mean, you didn't when we met after all that time."

Samuel shivered in front of her and then invited her in.

"I'm already in," said Charlotte from behind Samuel. Samuel knowing that she slipped past him without him knowing, he began to regret his decision inviting her round.

"So, where are you?" Samuel asked in the living room.

"Sitting on your sofa," Charlotte replied.

Samuel saw the imprint on his two seated sofa that looked like someone was sitting on it. He sat next to Charlotte and felt stupid just looking at an empty space next to him.

"So, why did you really ask me over?" said Charlotte. "I'm not stupid, I know there's a reason."

Samuel confessed to her what Ash and he had been discussing. Ash asked others from the school if Charlotte had been in contact, but had confirmed they didn't remember who she was.

"Well, they would say that wouldn't they? I remember them too well and they look at me like someone that doesn't exist. Why do you think I did this to myself?"

"Hey don't have a go at me, Okay? I saved you tonight. Ash wanted me to give him your address so he could confront you," Samuel explained, but at the same time he realized he dropped himself in it.

Charlotte seemed distraught and upset. Living her life the way that she had, made her wish that she was dead.

Samuel didn't like to hear that sort of thing, as something in the back of his mind made him feel he had witnessed death before, but he couldn't remember all the details of who it was.

"I'm sorry, Samuel," Charlotte apologized. "I can imagine how hard it was for you to live with what you saw, did you have anyone else to talk to?"

Charlotte listened to Samuel tell her that she was the only person he had ever told. He had lived his life full of regret. He stayed in most of the day as going out and seeing people didn't interest him.

"Look, Samuel, you are the only one out of the entire school that has responded to my messages. You're the only one that talks to me and you're the only one that can see me... even if I am invisible," said Charlotte. "Follow me."

Samuel watched footsteps appear on the carpet that led out into the hallway. When he got out into the hall, he saw his bedroom door open by itself. Samuel went to his room to see the quilt cover pulled back and a dip in the bedsheets.

"I know you want this as much as I do," Charlotte insisted. "How long has it been since you were intimate with anyone?"

"Before I witnessed death," Samuel replied.

"Then you don't have to wait any longer," said Charlotte, seductively. "Take me."

Samuel's mind was confused. His urges were telling him to go for it as it had been a long time since he had sex, but on the other hand he couldn't get his head round to having sex with someone he couldn't see.

He then felt his hand being held and pulled towards the bed. When he was helped on, the dent in the bed next to him appeared which told him that Charlotte was next to him. "Get on top of me," she ordered. Samuel did as he was told and to his surprise, he felt like he was on top of someone.

He felt Charlotte's legs spread apart even though he couldn't see anyone.

"Ah," Charlotte moaned as he inserted himself into her. Samuel's arms were then pulled out in front of him. They were then placed to where Charlotte's breasts were. He couldn't see them, but he could feel what were like breasts.

As Samuel bumped and grinded at the air, Charlotte moaned constantly until she climaxed. A wet patch formed out of thin air on Samuel's bed. He couldn't believe his eyes which made him lose his concentration.

"It's Okay, don't worry – we can try again," said Charlotte as she tried to convince him that it wasn't the end of the world. But Samuel was angry at himself, he felt like a failure and that she would hate him for it.

Samuel then jumped as a bang on the door startled him. He quickly got his clothes back on and went to see who it was. When he opened the door, he saw a slim looking woman standing in front of him.

"Yes?" Samuel asked.

The woman gave him a big smile while she flicked her long straight blonde hair back.

"It's Ellie – Ellie Stewart," said Ellie. "Remember me? I was short until I sprouted. How are you?"

"Fine," Samuel replied. "What are you doing here? How did you find me?"

But Ellie shivered and wrapped her arms around herself. "Can I come in, it's cold out here."

"Yes, of course, Sorry – come in."

Ellie walked in to what she could imagine Samuel's place to be like. A

421

typical man cave with computers, DVDs and no sign of what a woman would have.

"I received a message from Ash. He's worried about you, that you heard from Charlotte?"

"Well, you both shouldn't be – I'm fine," Samuel snapped.

Ellie could see Samuel was on the edge, like he was hiding something. Ellie told Samuel that Ash mentioned that Charlotte had messaged her regarding a reunion, but she never got a message from her. The message she had was from her girls.

"Really?" Samuel found it hard to believe.

"Yes," Ellie replied. "The last thing we heard was that Charlotte disappeared – no one ever saw her again and we don't know where she went."

"This coming from someone who ignored her in high school."

"We didn't ignore her – she just wasn't one of us," Ellie snapped.

"Well, of course, she disappeared – she was invisible to you all and now she is invisible – come with me, I'll prove it to you."

Samuel walked off to his bedroom with Ellie following behind. When Ellie entered his bedroom, she saw the sheets a mess and a wet patch on the bed. Ellie felt grossed out with what Samuel had been up to.

"Charlotte – you have an old face from the past that wants to see you."

But Charlotte didn't reply. Ellie thought that Samuel was unwell, especially when he suggested the notion that Charlotte was invisible.

"Answer me, Charlotte, you're among friends," Samuel ordered. But Charlotte still didn't speak a word. Samuel glared at Ellie and said, "It's your fault that Charlotte won't speak to you, especially the way you treated her – get the hell out of my home."

Ellie did as she was told, but before she left she turned to him and said, "You need help, Samuel, you really do." And with that Ellie walked away.

"Thank you, Samuel, for getting rid of her – I couldn't face bringing up the old memories with her."

"Don't worry – you're safe while I'm around," Samuel promised.

4

Meanwhile Ash had been delving more into the mystery of who Charlotte really was. He had surfed the Internet for hours, printing every piece of information he could find on her and piecing it together like a gigantic puzzle. As he waited for the final print outs, a knock at the door distracted him.

Ellie stood at the door when Ash opened it. She looked worried and concerned and told Ash what Samuel had been like towards her. Ash showed Ellie the evidence regarding Charlotte and photos that he had found.

"Oh my god," said Ellie. "All this time?"

"I know," Ash replied as he threw on his jacket. "That's why I'm going over there now. I need to show Samuel the truth about Charlotte."

Ellie dropped the papers to stop Ash from leaving. "No, don't – it could be dangerous, you could get yourself killed."

"I have to do this – he's one of us and he has to know," Ash explained, as he took one more look at Ellie and then walked away from her.

But back at Samuel's place, Samuel was lying on his bed shirtless, while staring up at the ceiling. He felt Charlotte's hand resting on his belly, wondering where their future was going to go.

"It's late – I should go home," said Charlotte.

"No – you can stay here for as long as you want. I don't want you living in that grotty place any more. You will stay with me."

"Thank you, Samuel – but I should really get going."

"I said, no," Samuel ordered trying to control the situation. Another knock from the door got Samuel more angry. "Fuck sake – who is it now?" Samuel got to his feet and ordered Charlotte to stay where she was.

When he opened the door he saw it was Ash. Samuel took a different attitude towards him than he did with Ellie. Ash was the closest of what he could call a friend. Before Ash could speak a word, Samuel told him to follow him to his room so he could see Charlotte.

Ash looked around the empty messy bedroom while Samuel ordered

Charlotte to speak. But to his disappointment she didn't. He thought it was because she was shy. Samuel started to act peculiar and began to touch the bed, wave his arms around like he was trying to find where Charlotte was. When he checked the whole room, he realized that Charlotte must've left.

"She must've gone back to her place," Samuel told Ash. "I told her not to."

"Then why don't we go to her place and bring her back?" suggested Ash.

5

Ash drove Samuel to where he was telling him to go.

The grotty torn neighbourhood was everything Ash expected. A place that no one would visit. The perfect place to disappear so no one could find you. To be invisible.

"Over there." Samuel pointed to the flat block. "That's where she lives."

As Ash pulled up outside the building. Samuel noticed that Ash didn't react the same as he did when he turned up to it. He began to suspect Ash knew more than he was letting on.

When they got inside, they climbed the stairs to Charlotte's flat. Samuel knocked on the door. They both waited for Charlotte to open it. But nobody came. Ash became more impatient and banged on the door furiously. That's when the door swung open but nobody was standing in front of them.

Ash peered inside, then held his nose. "Jesus – it smells foul in there."

"I can't smell anything," Samuel replied.

Ash followed his nose till the smell became stronger outside Charlotte's bedroom. When he opened the door, he swiped at the air as a swarm of flies flew towards him.

That's when he saw a bloodstained patch on the floor.

"Samuel?" Ash called as he joined his side. "I think this is the answer you're looking for."

Samuel stared at the blood. "That wasn't there before – whose blood is that?"

"Oh, I think you know," Ash replied.

But Samuel didn't. Instead he called for Charlotte multiple times, but she never answered.

"She's not, Samuel, and you know that," Ash insisted. "Remember."

Samuel strained his memory. He closed his eyes tightly and that's when his memory triggered. He saw himself looking at his phone. A message from someone called Charlotte who he had gone to school with was organizing a school reunion with everyone. Nobody had responded regarding the reunion, but Samuel decided he would and suggested that they meet up with each other, so Charlotte sent Samuel her address.

When Samuel turned up at the grotty estate that Charlotte lived in, he realized that he lived in a better place than she did. He was even more knocked back when she opened the door to him. A young woman with messy hair, no make-up and crumpled up clothes who looked like she had been living rough.

"Samuel Stephens, wow – you look good," Charlotte complimented.

"Thanks – you look good too," said Samuel.

But Charlotte didn't agree. Life had been hard to her since she had left school. The contact she used to have with the students was non-existent. She lived her life being the background girl, trying to blend in with the others and was bullied for her kindness she showed.

Samuel could see how distressed she was and gave her a cuddle. Charlotte burst into tears and felt happy with the first person that showed her kindness.

As the hours went by, they both had a drink and talked about their memories from school. Samuel had felt depressed through his school life. He had made only one friend called Ash, who he still kept in contact with. But he felt finding a girlfriend in school was impossible as he struggled to connect with them.

Charlotte had the same problem. When it came to finding a boyfriend, none of the boys took any notice of her. She was the smartest girl, not very popular and not very cool. She concentrated too much on her studies where she took an interest in cookery. Charlotte was eager to prove how much of a good cook she was and made Samuel dinner.

With good food and lots of alcohol in their systems, the affection between the two of them made them move to her bedroom where they made love to each other. Samuel was overwhelmed and felt the happiest he had ever been. As he cuddled up to Charlotte, things were not the same with her. Charlotte was a virgin; she had no sexual contact with a boy before. Even though it was good sex, she admitted that she didn't feel a strong emotional connection with Samuel as she confessed that she had a strong crush on Ash.

Samuel felt his heart break. His face went bright red. He felt used, a typical drunken mistake that he felt was a strong bond between the two of them. Charlotte's attitude had changed in the short space of time and she insisted that Samuel leave her home. But Samuel couldn't control his rage any longer and grabbed hold of Charlotte by the throat.

He strangled her tighter and tighter so she couldn't breathe a single breath in. Charlotte clawed at the air until she managed to scratch him across the cheek. He staggered back wiping the blood off him. Charlotte coughed, gasping, as the air breathed back into her lungs. As Samuel looked up with murderous rage, Charlotte knew that this was going to be it, so, to defend herself, she grabbed hold of her bedside lamp and smashed it over Samuel's head.

Samuel fell to the floor, stunned. His head splitting with pain. When he touched his head he felt that it was wet and then he saw the blood on his hand. She had cut him just above his eye. A struggle took place between them. Samuel pulled out the remains of the bedside lamp and smashed it over Charlotte's head multiple times until she was a bloody mess.

The shock of Charlotte's murder shocked Samuel to the core. Realizing it was too late to take it all back, he ran out of there, his heart and mind racing with the things he had done. He ran far away, then he felt his lungs tighten. He began to feel weak and dizzy and before he knew it, he had collapsed to the ground.

When he came to, he was dazed and confused. He didn't know where he had been or how he got his head wound. The doctors put his wound down to memory loss and that was the last it was talked about. Over time, Samuel had forgotten that he had been in hospital and how he got his scar. The only thing he could put it down to was that he got it when he was a child, but people around him never asked or even thought about it.

"Charlotte's death never made breaking news – she was pretty much forgotten about just like she was in school – you killed her, Samuel," Ash explained.

Before Samuel could speak a word, his eyes were stunned by the flashing of blue neon lights coming from the Police that had arrived on the scene outside.

"Sorry, Samuel – we had to," said Ash.

6

The very next day, the big iron gates of Marwood Asylum opened as a police car drove down the driveway to two men in white tunics waiting outside the entrance doors. They assisted Samuel out of the car, up the stairs and into the large grand hallway. Samuel looked down at the black and white checkered floor that looked like he was walking on the largest chess board he had ever seen. But a long blonde-haired nurse receptionist by the name of Lisa Garland caught his eye. Samuel always had a thing for women that dressed in nurse's uniforms, especially American ones that wore a white skirt and red cardigan.

Lisa looked over her glasses at Police Constable Sarah Williams who stood with Samuel at her side. "Yes, can I help you?" Lisa asked.

"Samuel Stephens, checking in," Sarah explained.

"Ah yes of course, these gentlemen will take Patient 26021981 to his room," Lisa told Sarah who started to take the handcuffs off.

The two orderlies escorted Samuel down the maze like corridors. Krista who was a big beautiful woman appeared at the window and took close interest of the new arrival.

One of the orderlies opened a door next to another room where Patient 10051982 was and then escorted Samuel inside before locking him in.

Samuel sat down with his back up to the white padded walls. It was at that moment he heard a man's voice speaking to him through the wall.

"So, they got you too, did they? Took them long enough."

"Had to happen eventually," Samuel explained. "Did you get the job done?"

"It's done. It's finally over. No one is taking back control ever again," Samuel smiled.

"Good. Now we can finally rest."

DISTANCE

1

Mother Sunshine fell down on her bed in the little cozy flat that wasn't hers. She was naked. Her perky small breasts were smooth. She opened her legs to reveal her sex area as a bare chested man got on top of her attempting to stroke her nipples. Mother Sunshine slapped his hand away and said, "No, that area is forbidden – no touching and no kissing, okay, Alex?"

"Sure – whatever you want, Mother Sunshine."

"No," said Mother Sunshine firmly. "Whatever you want down below."

"I just want to fuck you," Alex reassured.

Mother Sunshine smiled. "Then let's do it."

Alex took a condom off the bed and slipped it over his cock. Mother Sunshine moaned as he entered her and started to plough her.

Mary's eyes then snapped open. She found herself in bed, in the dark lying next to her husband, Nelson. She lay there, her past life and mistakes haunting her dream.

Mary hadn't thought about her prostitute life for over a year. She had concentrated on settling down with her husband and baby son, John.

Luckily for Mary, she heard John crying on the baby monitor to distract her train of thought. She threw the bed covers back and got out of bed, then slipped on a pink silk nightie over her white bra and panties.

Mary walked into John's blue room, stepping over some of the cuddly toys that were scattered over the floor. John was crying in his sleep. Mary spotted the dummy that had come out of his mouth and placed it back in. John became more settled as Mary stroked the side of his face.

"Night, night, my beautiful boy," Mary spoke softly.

Afterwards, Mary had gone to the bathroom and was standing in front of the mirror, watching her reflection stare back at her. Her dream had triggered lots of memories about her prostitute life. A lot of the memories she wished she hadn't remembered. But her dream about Alex made her turned on.

Mary opened her gown and pulled down her panties.

She spread her legs apart and then inserted two fingers into herself. As

431

she thought about her dream, her breathing became rapid with small quiet moans as she turned herself on more and more. Her legs began to shake as she came closer to orgasm while her moans became louder. But before she could cum, she was interrupted by a knock on the door.

"Mary? Are you okay in there?" Nelson called.

Mary took her moist fingers out and stood in front of the mirror looking disappointed and frustrated as she was so close to cumming.

"What's wrong?" said Nelson, concerned.

But Mary never answered him. Instead she placed her hands on his face and gave him a passionate kiss. She needed a release after building herself up to the point of ecstasy. Mary continued to seduce Nelson by licking the side of his neck and biting his ear lobe, something she had never done before. That's when Nelson reacted and pushed Mary away.

"Whoa, what was that? You've never done that before."

"Sure I have. Lots of times," Mary replied.

"Not to me you haven't," said Nelson.

He never said anything else the rest of the night.

Instead, Nelson left Mary standing in the bathroom doorway thinking about what she had just done.

When she returned to bed, she lay there in the darkness. She thought about what she did to Nelson and was sure she had done that before to him. But, as her eyes got heavier, she began to doubt herself and realized that she did it to her old clients. Her eyes became heavy and eventually she went back to sleep. But Mary's mind wanted to go back to her dream.

Alex appeared again, wearing different clothes. Her dream was about another meeting they had as her client. This time there was more passion as he undressed her and kissed her with more force. Mary got on all fours. Alex kissed her from her thigh all the way up to her bottom.

Mary gasped as he entered her taking hold of her by her hips. He started to grind her with medium force, not hard enough to hurt her, but to Mary it felt good.

"Wow," Mary panted. "Keep going, don't stop."

Alex didn't and couldn't control himself. Mary screamed, "I love you." As she and Alex came at the same time.

"HEY." Nelson nudged Mary causing her to open her eyes from her wet dream. "What the hell is wrong with you? Why were you masturbating?"

Mary couldn't hide it any more. Her strange behaviour and what was going through her head needed to be told.

So, Mary and Nelson sat at the kitchen table in the early hours. Mary couldn't find the right words to say without hurting Nelson. She was too scared how he would react.

Nelson was annoyed and frustrated that Mary was hiding a secret and couldn't be strong enough to say what it was.

Mary took a sip of her tea, took a deep breath and said what she had dreaded to say.

"I've been having dreams."

"Wet dreams obviously," Nelson said, firmly.

"Yes. About my old life and my clients. One in particular that's regular," Mary explained.

Nelson folded his arms. It made him sick to his stomach hearing about her prostitute life. The old feeling he hadn't felt since he discovered her shocking secret when Alex turned up and everything unfolded.

"You were dreaming about Alex?"

Mary was frightened to admit it, but Nelson could see it in her eyes that he had guessed it. "Mary, it's been a year since then. You have me. You have John, our baby. Why would you even dream about having sex with different men?"

"I'm not doing it on purpose, Nelson," Mary insisted. "You have no idea what type of effect that life has. The degrading and disgusting things I've done I have to live with every day."

Nelson could see where Mary was coming from. But at the same time, he didn't want to, especially as he could never understand. He suggested that Mary talk to a psychiatrist to talk about her problems.

"I have considered that. I'm still not well after the abuse I had – Lilith, said she would get Jin, to teach me a lesson and any of the girls that would leave."

"Jin, was arrested though. His family home was shut down. All those lobotomies. He isn't coming for you," said Nelson.

"But, Lilith, is still out there though."

Mary then heard John crying from the other room.

Nelson stopped Mary from going and suggested that he would talk to his mother to see if she could look after John, while they sort themselves out.

2

So, the next day, after they dropped John off to Nelson's Mother, Nelson accompanied Mary to see Dr Melvin Clarke, a youthful looking forty year old who was recommended by a Doctor Redma.

With how beautiful Mary looked, Melvin took an instant interest in her and told Nelson that he would have to leave as Mary was his patient, they would talk one to one to make the sessions go easier.

With Mary's history, Nelson found it difficult to leave her with another man. But Mary agreed and insisted that he go.

When Nelson left, Mary sat with her hands on her knees and took a deep breath.

"Well, Mary," said Melvin, "start when you're ready."

"My life's complicated."

Melvin showed a look of intrigue and rested his chin on his hand. "Talk about complicated."

Mary started at the beginning. She told Melvin the story of how she fell out with her family because of the life choices she had made. She poured her heart out by explaining that she got involved with some nasty people and was recruited to be a prostitute. Melvin raised an eyebrow and took considerable interest into wanting to hear her story.

"May I stop you right there," Melvin insisted, as he took out a tape recorder and began to record their session. "This is for feedback – so the next time you come in, I can assist in finding the answers you need."

Meanwhile in *The Open Door* bar, Nelson was sitting at the bar alone with a glass of whiskey in his hand. He swayed the glass left and right to see the liquid moving from one side to the other. He looked at it, thinking it was the same as his life. He didn't know which way it was going.

"I'll have whatever he's having, Steve," a woman's voice called out. "Get him another as well, looks like he needs it."

Nelson looked up to see an attractive woman giving him the eye. She was very fit with her tight jeans and open check shirt. She leaned forwards so that Nelson could get an eye of her cleavage.

434

"I've never seen you here before – why don't we get a table, so we can get to know each other?"

Nelson chuckled to himself. He was amused at how desperate the woman seemed. Nelson swallowed the whiskey hard and shook his head while holding his hand up in front of her, revealing his wedding ring.

"Don't you women check out the guy's fingers any more, just to see if they're wearing a wedding band, before you start flirting with them?" Nelson snapped.

"I apologize – I'm sorry – I meant no offence." But Nelson didn't acknowledge her. "Look, can we start over please, I'm Marcy."

Nelson's attitude became more aggressive, as she held her hand out in front of him. He had heard that name before from Mary. Could it be the same Marcy, he thought. The only way he was going to find out was to play it tactfully.

"Marcy, huh? You're not a friend of Mother Sunshine are you?" Nelson asked.

"Wow." Marcy laughed. "You're a married man and you know, Sunshine – before, after or during your marriage?"

"All of it." Nelson glared. "Mary's my wife and you're going to tell me everything I need to hear."

Nelson and Marcy moved over to a table in the corner. Nelson crossed his arms waiting for Marcy to tell her side of the story.

Mary was a young thing when Marcy met her. Being the girl in the city of Towns-end caught everyone's eye, especially when Mary walked into *The Open Bar* for a drink. Marcy took great interest in the stranger and offered her a drink. Mary was grateful and instantly struck up a conversation. Marcy discovered that she had just moved to Towns-end city with her parents and she was looking for a job to earn some money as she was currently residing at a bed and breakfast called, *The Age Old Inn*.

Marcy told Mary that she knew this woman who could supply a small flat to stay in for free and a job with a great income. Mary knew that she couldn't pass up the chance to see what it would be like before she made a final decision, so she agreed to go with Marcy to meet her.

Lilith stood tall before Mary and Marcy. Her seven foot posture with a busty cleavage bulged out of her white vest top while her long legs went all the way up to her short black skirt.

"Well, let's take a look at the new girl." Lilith smiled. She looked Mary up and down and smiled to herself. "My word, you are pretty."

Mary was shy at her kind words. Lilith offered her hand and invited her to take a seat. Mary said that it was nice to meet her, but all she could do was stare at Lilith's height. She explained that she had a medical condition. Being a woman of fifty and looking like a hot Victorian cougar, she still had growth spurts. She was six foot five, the month before, and was now seven foot tall.

Mary listened to Lilith explain what her and her girls that she employed do. They worked for a man called Jin who owns *The Family Home*, who was funded and contracted by Krista who owns the extreme dare sex club *Play 4 Real*. Mary would be employed and housed to entertain male and female clients for such things as candlelit dinners and more as a partner experience.

But Mary knew what Lilith was hinting at. This was an escort business with benefits. Lilith however was very abrupt and to the point. The position was a one time offer, she would have a home free of charge and earn eighty per cent of what she brought in with the clients. Mary was nervous. She knew she couldn't turn the offer down, but the warning signs were right in front of her.

Lilith was pleased Mary accepted and gave her the title of Mother Sunshine, as her smile seemed to fill the room with love and joy. She paired her up with Marcy to show her the ropes. It started with a casual dinner with two male clients. They paid in their hundreds and all they did was talk about their lives such as their occupations and who they were. Mary thought it was going to be this way all the time, but how wrong she was.

As the weeks passed by, she met new and colourful characters. Some married. Some not. Then one evening, to her surprise, Marcy and Mary had to meet two new clients.

But this time they were both women, their names were Missy and Chastity.

Mary found a friend in Chastity. They would talk about their lives and laugh at the things they had done. But Mary's concern was where this friendship was going as, at the end of the dinner, Marcy and Missy were all over each other as they couldn't stop kissing.

A week after that, Chastity met Mary at her flat. They had dinner together and some drinks until the effect of the alcohol got the better of them. It was that moment that Chastity made a move and kissed Mary on the lips. Mary pulled away quickly and explained that she wasn't a lesbian. Chastity felt embarrassed and left hastily.

The very next day, Mary was escorted by Marcy to see Lilith. She had heard about the night before when Chastity was upset and complained. Mary explained that she wasn't a lesbian and the thought of kissing another woman made her feel uneasy. But Lilith showed her true nature and shouted at Mary. Lilith explained in terms that Mary could understand that, if a female client wants a kiss, Mary must kiss her and, if they want sex, you give them what they want. That was how it went.

Before Mary could say anything else, they were interrupted by Andrea Charms, a petite girl, in her early twenties, with a happy smile on her baby face. But Mary noticed it wasn't happy this time. She looked furious and shouted at Lilith regarding the client she had just left.

Andrea was disgusted by her client's attitude. His name was Dennis, a man who was married, but went behind her back to get his sexual kicks elsewhere. Dennis wasn't satisfied with Andrea. She had small lips and tiny breasts. The thought of larger breasts and bigger lips got his motor running and wanted Andrea's lips and breasts to be the biggest in the entire world. He would pay a fortune just to get his fantasy fulfilled.

Lilith agreed with the client, as to her the client and the money always came first with whatever request they desired. She then phoned someone and told them that she wanted to arrange an operation for Andrea Charms. The operation would consist of twenty rounds of acid lip injections that would quadruple her lips in size and her breasts were requested to be a 102 ZZZ which would weigh three stone a boob.

Mary watched in horror as Andrea was dragged away kicking and screaming. She knew that she would get the same treatment if anyone crossed Lilith.

A few days after, Mary saw Andrea in the street.

Perverts were wolf whistling her and attempting to chat her up. Mary couldn't believe what Andrea looked like now.

Her breasts were huge just like her lips. She looked like a freak, her body changed and scarred by surgery. Mary didn't want the same thing to happen to her. She liked her beauty.

Mary became the best of the girls. The clients that she would service and give the girlfriend experience too. She would fuck. She would fuck women. She was an all-rounder and as time went on she began to doubt her sexuality, even though she was disgusted by the things she didn't want to do. Until Alex came along.

"I already know this part," Nelson interrupted.

"Hey, you wanted to know every detail – so just shut up and listen," Marcy ordered.

Alex was different at first. Every time he went to see Mother Sunshine, they would talk and get to know each other. He visited her five times without ever having sex with her. Mary enjoyed his company. To her he was human and not a sex mad pervert like most of her clients were.

The night they went the distance was a totally different experience for Mary. It wasn't hard fucking like it had been. It was intimate and passionate. Mary hadn't cum with her other clients, but she did with Alex. He became Mary's favourite client. She would think about him every day and feel excited knowing when she was going to see him again.

But then, there was a change in Alex. He wanted a relationship with her. Mary told him that it was impossible for them to be together. The passion between them soon died and Alex became rough and twisted just like her other clients.

Mary felt tired to the point of exhaustion. But then she perked up from a chance encounter in a coffee shop. The day, she met Nelson. Mary was happy. All she could think about was him. Mary had been scared of Lilith for a long time, but meeting Nelson and being invited for a date made her realise she needed to get out.

Lilith on the other hand had noticed a change in Mary's behaviour. So, on Mary's time off, she followed her to the park and watched her have her date with Nelson. This made Lilith mad, that Mary had never mentioned another man and the way he was sweet and innocent with her made Lilith jealous.

She then devised a scheme to get revenge on Mary. She invited Alex to meet her and gave him an offer that he couldn't refuse. In return Alex was given a lot of money by Lilith and was told that he should ask for the wife experience. This would mean that she would allow him to cum inside her without protection. An offer that Mary was too afraid to say no too.

When the deed was done, Lilith was satisfied, but every person that she came across, she had a devious deceitful side to. She had bribed the doctors surgery that Alex had gone to, to make up a story and say that he couldn't have children. This way the child that Mary would carry would have proof that it would be Nelson's. Additionally, when the deed was done, Lilith made sure Mary would feel like garbage, having her raped and dumped in a dumpster.

Nelson fell silent. He had wished that he hadn't known all the details of the story. This made him doubt his relationship with Mary. Was the child really his or was it Alex's? At this moment in time, he only had one objective left.

"Where is Lilith hiding?" Nelson snapped. "Take me to her."

"No." Marcy was firm. "You'll be giving her what she has always wanted. You. She's always wanted you to have in a relationship. Someone who understands her and could love her for her growing condition."

"Then let's give the bitch what she wants," Nelson retaliated. "This ends today."

3

Back with Mary, she had no idea what Nelson was up to. Instead, she was pouring her heart out with everything she had been through. Doctor Melvin Clarke, listened with great interest. The thing that Mary didn't realise that, as he listened, he was aroused and getting hot under the collar. As he looked at Mary's features, he then realized he had met her before. He had been one of Mother Sunshine's clients.

He stood up and walked around her. He then put his hands on her shoulders and began to massage her to comfort her "It's okay Mary, relax, what you have been through will haunt you – it's those memories that live forever."

"But I don't want to remember that life," Mary insisted.

"Surely you would want to remember the good times. The times that made you happy. Like the time you were with me."

Mary's eyes widened in shock the second those words left his mouth. She quickly stood up and backed away from Melvin.

"I was surprised that you didn't remember me, Mother Sunshine," Melvin remarked. "The massage I always used to give you before we had sex – I suppose I was just a number over the hundreds of men you had." He grabbed hold of her wrists and pulled her close. "It's interesting that you're paying to be with me this time."

Mary quickly pulled away and slapped him round the face, hard. "Get the hell away from me, I have a husband now."

Melvin smiled as his face stung from the slap. "I knew my dominatrix girl was still inside there."

Mary went for the door, but Melvin was too quick as he slammed it shut before she could get out. He grabbed Mary by both arms and pinned her up against the door.

"Let go of me," she screamed.

But Melvin went to kiss her. So, she spat in his face and kneed him in the chest. As she turned to open the door, he grabbed her again and threw her across to his desk. As she fell on the desk with her ass sticking up, Melvin began to undo his trousers. "You always did prefer it from behind."

As Melvin grabbed her by the waist, she reacted and grabbed the letter knife and stuck it into his neck. Both were shocked at what just occurred. Melvin staggered back, choking and coughing up blood. Mary freaked out. She had never attacked anyone in her life. Melvin dropped to the floor and didn't move a muscle. Mary felt sick. She was terrified. So, she grabbed her bag and ran out of the office.

4

A red pick-up truck pulled up outside a worn down warehouse. The exterior showed its age with it being rusty and faded. Nelson overlooked the place.

"You serious, this is where Lilith is?" Nelson asked.

"This is the place. She's been here years. She lives here. Hiding. Because of her condition," Marcy explained. "Come on – I'll take you to her."

A rusty squeak occurred when Marcy pulled open the door. They both walked in to a cold derelict large open area. The concrete floors were covered in small puddles of water from the drips that came from the rusted holes in the metal roof.

Nelson shivered as he walked through the cold damp place. It was creepy. What gave it the eerie feeling was there was a bed in the middle of the area with propane canisters next to it. Marcy escorted Nelson to a chair where someone was sitting with their back turned.

"Lilith – it's Marcy – I have brought you Nelson. Mary's partner."

"Well – it's about time we met," Lilith replied.

She stood up tall and looked down at Nelson. Marcy wasn't exaggerating. She was really tall. Nelson could tell she had grown since when Marcy had told him how tall she was. Now she looked like she was nearly nine foot high.

Lilith licked her lips as she looked Nelson up and down. "Well, I can see why Mother Sunshine took to you." She raised her eyebrows at him and smiled.

Nelson began to check her out. Lilith looked quite mature for her age a woman in her late forties. Her body showed the defects of her growth spurts, from her stretch marks at the top of her cleavage and over her face and hands. "Her name is Mary – get it right."

"Yummy," Lilith flirted. "You're a fiery one."

"What do you want, Lilith?" Nelson asked.

"I want to know what Mary sees in you, by taking you to my bed." Lilith smiled.

"That's not going to happen – I am loyal to my wife." Nelson snapped.

"But is she loyal to you?" Lilith smiled sinisterly.

"What's that supposed to mean?" Nelson argued.

"I take it while you are here, Mary is seeing Dr Melvin Clarke – as it has been so long, she would have forgotten that he used to be one of her clients she used to fuck." Lilith got off on seeing Nelson's face realize that he helped Mary get into the hands of another man. "Now, come to my bed, so I can be the best scx you will ever have in your life."

Nelson walked to her and took her hand in his. "You never will be the best."

"Insolent," Lilith screamed as she slapped him across the face. She picked him up and threw him into the bed. He bounced and fell on the floor knocking the propane canisters over. "I wasn't asking you to take yourself into my bed, I was ordering you," she screamed, as she picked him up by the throat and pinned him down onto the cold damp mattress.

Nelson quickly took a flick lighter out of his pocket and lit it. Lilith looked puzzled. "My hands are quicker than yours. Thanks for throwing me."

Lilith then smelt gas and realized he had opened one of the valves while she wasn't looking. To her horror, she watched as he flicked the lighter out of his hand. She tried to catch it, but it slipped through her fingers and hit the propane. BOOM, the canisters exploded with such force that it threw Lilith across the warehouse. Nelson grabbed the side of the bed frame and flipped it over to protect him from the explosive blast.

Debris from the metal room above fell like a rain shower, smashing down near Nelson and Lilith.

"What have you done?" Lilith screamed as she saw her home crumbling to pieces in front of her. Marcy helped Nelson to his feet as Lilith got to hers. "You've ruined everything," she screamed. She then took big strides towards the exit as the warehouse fell around her. Marcy assisted Nelson to leave just as the warehouse collapsed.

They ran up to the jeep, inhaling and coughing from the dust and debris that crept into their lungs. "Are you okay?" Marcy asked. But Nelson was too interested in Lilith who was escaping down the road.

"We've got to get after her and make sure she doesn't disappear," Nelson insisted as he pulled the vehicle door open. "I don't want her coming after Mary again."

Lilith was struggling to run. How tall she was made it difficult for her to move fast. At first, she constantly kept looking behind, to see if she was being followed.

Eventually, Marcy's vehicle came into view. Her eyes widened to know they were catching up to her. She took big strides to gain some distance from them and turn a corner.

"She went there." Nelson pointed.

Marcy swerved round the corner to a wide open space, but to their surprise, there was no sign of Lilith. She had disappeared. Both of them looked puzzled. There was nowhere for Lilith to hide, as they would have clearly seen her.

"Shit," Nelson swore.

"How could she have just vanished like that?" said Marcy.

"I don't know. But she's gone – hopefully for good," Nelson prayed. His phone then rang. Nelson answered it to hear a scared Mary on the other end. "Whoa, honey, slow down… what alley?"

5

Marcy pulled up outside a side alley. They both couldn't see Mary. Nelson stepped out of the vehicle. Marcy called out to him and asked, "Did you want me to come with me?"

"No. Thanks. Be on your way," Nelson acknowledged.

"Good luck," Marcy complimented, as she drove away leaving Nelson to fend for himself.

Nelson walked deeper into the alley. His footsteps knocked into empty beer bottles and stepped over smelly rubbish and rotten food that had been dumped there. As he passed a dumpster, he didn't notice Mary hiding behind it.

"Thank god you've come," Mary called out.

Nelson spun around to see Mary a mess. Her dress had been torn with dried blood on from the struggle, while her hands were also covered in blood.

"What the hell happened to you?"

"Nelson..." Mary struggled to get the words out. "...I didn't mean to."

Nelson reached out to stop Mary crashing to the floor.

She was a wreck. "Was it the psychiatrist? Did he do this to you?"

"He..." Mary tried to get her breath. "...he turned out or be an old client. I didn't even remember him – but he attacked me, so I... stabbed him. He's dead."

"Lilith told me the whole thing was a setup."

"Wait – you've seen her?" Mary freaked.

"Marcy helped me. You don't have to worry about Lilith. She's gone."

"Did you kill her?" Mary asked. "Because if you didn't, you can't say that she's gone. She'll come back."

"She won't. I burned her home down. She's homeless. Nowhere to go but far away. You're free."

But what Mary didn't know was that Nelson was telling her what she wanted to hear. At the same time, there was more of a serious matter of what they were going to do next.

445

"I have to turn myself in," Mary admitted.

"No. We'll get through this. Even if it means starting somewhere else," Nelson explained.

"When do we leave?" Mary asked.

"Soon. I just have to see Alex first."

Mary was surprised. She hadn't seen Alex since the hospital when she was admitted and discovered that she was pregnant. With the way Nelson and Alex ended their friendship, she assumed Nelson never wanted to see him again.

"Lilith told me something. She paid his doctor to say that he could never have kids. Turns out he always could."

"So, he could have got me pregnant after all? Does that mean, John, is his?"

Nelson swallowed hard. Secretly he didn't like the idea of finding out that his son wasn't really his. So, instead he said to Mary, "I would rather not find out. I think it best. We've been through too much. I don't think I could cope with my heart being broken again. It's only just been repaired."

"Then let's tell him the truth. He needs to know that he can have children," Mary agreed.

6

Before Mary and Nelson went to see Alex, they returned home to clean themselves up. Nelson distracted the babysitter while Mary snuck upstairs to wash the blood off her hands and to get changed out of her bloodstained dress.

She soon joined Nelson, where they explained they urgently needed to see an old friend and would return as soon as they could.

Mary and Nelson both walked into *Kays Coffee Shop*, hand in hand, to see Alex standing behind the counter. He looked surprised to see them both, but felt awkward at how things had been left.

"What are you two doing here?" Alex inquired.

But before Nelson could speak a word, Kay come out the back with an excited look on her face and interrupted him.

"Alex," said Kay. "Look at me."

When Alex turned around to see Kay, he too looked excited at the pregnancy test she was holding up in front of him. "I'm pregnant."

"But I was told that I couldn't have kids," Alex replied.

"I guess the doctors aren't always right, huh." Kay smiled with delight as Alex hugged her. "We're having a baby together – our baby."

Mary smiled at Nelson. They both thought the same thing, that there would be no need to mention what Lilith had done.

"Sorry, you two," Kay apologized. "What are you both doing here?"

"Two coffees, please." Mary smiled.

"No really – it looks like you had something to say," Alex assumed.

"Coffee was pretty much it," Nelson implied.

While Kay made them cups of coffee, Nelson noticed that Mary looked freaked out. She was staring at the news report that had appeared on the TV above. Melvin Clarke had been discovered in his office stabbed in the throat. He had lost a lot of blood, but he had survived and was on the way to recovery. Footage had been found of a woman defending herself against his malicious attack and once Clarke had recovered he would be trailed and sent to jail. Police wanted the woman to come forward to give her statement.

447

Nelson pulled Mary to one side and said to her quietly, "You're in the clear – you're going to be okay."

Mary hugged Nelson tightly and was grateful that she was free from this nightmare that she had lived with for so long.

"One day – years from now – we're going to have to tell John my secret. We shouldn't keep this from him, it would be wrong of us to."

"I understand," Nelson replied.

"I'm just wondering where Lilith is now," Mary whispered.

"Yes – I wonder that too," Nelson thought.

7

Lilith was struggling to run. How tall she was made it difficult for her to move fast. At first, she constantly kept looking behind, to see if she was being followed.

Eventually, Marcy's vehicle came into view. Her eyes widened to know they were catching up to her. She took big strides to gain some distance from them and turn a corner.

Instead of the open area that Marcy and Nelson saw, Lilith's surroundings changed to a deep dense forest. Lilith spun around at her surroundings, confused as to how she got there.

The rays of light cracked through the green leaves as they blew a gentle breeze. The snapping of a twig alerted Lilith, to know that something was close by. For the first time in her life, she was actually afraid of the unknown.

All of a sudden, she jolted and shook uncontrollably like she was having a seizure. Lilith dropped to the floor to see a sparking dart that had impaled her chest. She looked up to see the bushes being brushed aside and a figure dressed in military kevlar aiming an assault rifle at her as they crept up to her.

"She's just like Girl Zero, Mr Crane," a man's voice spoke into their radio.

"Good – put her in the Monster Girl Program," Mr Crane replied.

WIDOW

1

A pair of Iron gates swing open as a large crowd of people flock into the grand opening of the 'Exotic Desert Zoo'. People wander around looking at the animals – watching the shows and participating in feeds.

In the middle of the zoo – not far away from a large circus tent is the Spider farm, with various different species of spider from the huntsman, Tarantula to even the Black Widow. People flock inside a medium sized shed with an entrance and exit door. It's dimly lit, humid, filled with a musty smell of straw and dampness. Spiders are behind various small glass windows, with twigs and small pieces of branch inside them. A long length glass casket is in the centre of the room with even more spiders inside.

A woman in her late thirties stands behind it. She is dressed in a black and white top, wearing black leather pants. Slim. Attractive and has shoulder length brown hair. She is pretty, wearing lots of make up. A name badge is pinned to her top that reads *Beth Williams*.

She reaches into the casket and takes out a Black Widow spider while closing the casket back up so none of the spiders escape. The Black Widow sits in the palm of her hand. She holds it out in front of group of people for them all to see.

'The Black Widow,' explains Beth, 'the species vary widely in size. The females are darker and are identified by the red markings on their abdomens, which are shaped like an hourglass.' The spider then crawls over her hand and up her arm, causing people to back away slightly. Beth doesn't show any fear whatsoever. Instead she smiles as it tickles her.

'Don't be afraid, everyone,' she assures them, 'even though their bite is dangerously venomous because of the neurotoxin carried in their large glands which can be fatal and can cause severe muscle pain, cramps and muscle spasms – they won't harm me or you.' She picks up the spider and returns it to the palm of her hand. 'Now – who would like to hold her?' she asks. The people shake their heads, not wanting to risk it just in case they get bitten. 'No-one?' asks Beth, looking rather disappointed.

'I'll do it,' a Man's voice calls from the crowd. The crowd move aside and a man dressed in a three quarter length coat appears. Beth looks him up and down. She raises an eyebrow and a smile. The man's in his mid-thirties. Fit. Has a look of innocence about him. He approaches Beth and holds his hand out.

'A man who's not afraid – I like that – what's your name?' she asks.

'Detective James Blackwell,' he replies.

Beth puts her hand closer to his and edges the spider onto his. The spider crawls over to James's palm. He smiles. 'Are you okay?' she asks.

'I'm fine – it just tickles,' he replies as it begins to crawl over his palm and along his arm. Beth watches closer as the spider crawls up James's arm – around the back of his coat and onto his other arm.

'I think she likes you,' says Beth as she smiles at James then winks at him.

2

The minutes pass by and the show ends. Beth has put the spiders back in their cases and has left the spider farm. As she locks up, she notices James waiting outside.

'Can I help you, Detective?' asks Beth as she puts the padlock on the door.

'I was just going to say – they are amazing species you've got in there.'

Beth grins in delight. She has always loved spiders ever since she was little. The people around her thought she was strange as not many women like spiders, but it didn't stop her. James agreed – why should it stop her from liking something others don't? It's what makes us different from everyone else and that isn't a bad thing. She totally agreed with him, and at the same time admired him.

James's curiosity gets the better of him due to her last remark. He begins to wonder why she admitted it to him. Beth explains that she admired him because he stepped forward, didn't show an ounce of fear and wasn't afraid of them. She reminded him of her husband as he did the same thing.

'Oh... you're married?' he asks, surprisingly.

She holds her hand up revealing her wedding ring. She is surprised since, as a detective, he should've noticed that. She's sorry to disappoint him but she loves her husband and is happily married.

'My husband is waiting for me outside – you can meet him if you like?'

James holds his hands up. He feels a little embarrassed. Reassures her that it's very kind, but thinks it better that he leaves. As he walks away, he gets the feeling that Beth is watching him. He looks behind to see her still looking at him confirming his suspicions. He hurries along and leaves.

3

Beth comes out of the zoo. She feels that something isn't right. There is no sign of her husband. She waits, shivers, feeling the slight chill in the air. She takes her phone out and calls him. The phone rings but no one picks up on the other end. The call goes straight to voicemail.

She begins to wonder if he's all right. Has something happened to him?

'Hey – it's me. Where are you? Look if you're running late, and if you get this message – I'll meet you at home, okay? I love you.'

She puts her phone away and begins to make her way home. She wasn't that far away from the zoo. She lives about twenty minutes away – but this was only if she took a shortcut through the nearby woods. Without the shortcut it was double the time.

4

The woods are large and go on for miles. The surrounding trees, brushwood and bushes obscure what's in the distance. As Beth walks, her footsteps make a rustling sound of the leaves underneath her shoes. It's getting dark as the sun has finished setting. A slight breeze causes the tree branches to rustle, and apart from that there are no other sounds. It's dense and quiet. Beth was always creeped out by how desolate it was. She felt like someone or something was watching her.

The snapping of a twig then freaks her out. She stops. Breathing increasing. Heart racing. She looks around. She sees nothing. It's quiet again – until another sound of a twig snapping causes her to panic. She turns and runs through the woods – not risking to look back at what could be around. She brushes past the brushwood – scraping her skin on some thorns scratching herself. She then trips over something, falling flat on her face.

Pain shoots through her body as she hits the ground hard. She looks to see what she tripped over. Her eyes widen in horror – as she sees a body, covered in cobweb, its hand reaching out to her. She screams as she realizes, it's her husband.

5

*Mankind has always been interested in the research of different species –
but what happens to their interests when they discover a species, beyond
their imagination?*

James arrives in the dark woods which has now been turned into a
crime scene. Police tape covers the area where the body is. Beams of light
illuminate the area from police officers holding flashlights. James
approaches a young looking officer.

'What have we got?' asks James.

'You must be Detective Inspector Blackwell – I'm Officer Cross –
that's funny,' he says smiling in amusement.

James doesn't look amused – instead he just stares blank at Officer
Cross.

'Cross and Blackwell – get it?'

James doesn't see the funny side or the appropriate timing to make
jokes at a crime scene.

'Right,' says James, 'are you going to tell me what happened here?'

James walks with Officer Cross towards the scene of the crime while
Officer Cross explains what was reported.

'A woman was waiting for her husband to turn up at her work as he
was going to meet her there. He never showed so she took a shortcut
through the woods on her way home. She came across this body.'

James takes a closer look at the cobwebbed body. Hand reaching out
to him.

'Do we have any ID for the victim?' James asks, as he begins to
examine the body with his eyes to try and work out what happened.

'Yes – his name was Michael Williams. His wife is over with the other
officers,' says Cross, pointing over to the woman. James looks up –
recognizes her. It's Beth from the zoo.

'I know her – thank you Cross, I'll take it from here.'

James makes his way over to Beth – she recognizes him instantly. She
doesn't smile. Doesn't look happy to see him. Why would she be?

'Mrs Williams – I'm so sorry for your loss,' he says. 'I will make sure that we get the killer.'

'It's Miss Williams now – and I don't think you ever will get them.'

James understands her disbelief, that they may never find who did this to her husband. But, in himself, he knew he was going to prove to her that he will find the one that killed her husband.

6

As the weeks passed by – the investigations commenced. The results from the pathologist showed that Beth's husband was killed by spider bites. But they weren't ordinary spider bites. The wounds were far too big. James is stumped – this case is too confusing, as he's never come across anything like this before. It leaves him no other option, but to pay Beth a visit and talk to her, to find out if she could help with the investigation – to find out more of what happened that night.

7

Beth watches her spiders crawl around in a glass tank.

She smiles as they crawl around – making webs. The door to the spider farm opens. She looks up to see James enter.

'Miss Williams.'

'Detective,' says Beth, looking happy to see him, 'it's nice to see you. I have to apologize, for snapping at you – I know you're going to catch the killer – it was rude.'

'Please, you have nothing to apologize for – you were upset.'

Beth loves James's understanding and compassion. She has always had an attraction to nice, kind people.

'I see you have even more spiders now,' says James, taking a closer look at the spider tank.

'More have been delivered, yes,' says Beth. 'Is there something you wanted, Detective?'

James explains that he needs her help with the case. He has some pictures he'd like to show her, but he's worried that the images may upset her. She assures him that she's prepared to see them – anything to help in the case. James takes out his phone, shows her the picture of her husband's body and the bite marks. She looks away when she sees the state of the body, but returns her gaze to look hard at the picture.

'These marks were found all over his body – do you know what they are?' asks James.

'They look like a bite from spider,' says Beth, 'which is impossible, because there is no spider in the world as big as that – not even the huntsman and that's as big as your hand.'

James puts his phone away. He doesn't know what else to say to her now. With all the knowledge she knows about spiders, he knows that he can't help with anything else.

James thanks Beth for her help – he takes a step to leave when…

'You want to join me for a coffee?' asks Beth. He looks at her – doesn't hesitate in the slightest to take her up on her offer. He knew in himself that he liked her.

461

8

Beth walks over to a table in the zoo café holding two cups of coffee. James sits at the table looking around. The café isn't full – three quarters of the café is empty. There are families sitting in the café – their kids making a lot of noise which is getting on James's nerves. Beth sits down and passes James his coffee.

'Thank you.'

'So, Detective – are you married – are you an only child?' says Beth, curious to get to know who James is.

James begins to talk about his life. He's never been married, he never had time to think about it as he was always studying and working all the time. His mother and father emigrated. He has a sister called Allison who lived with him for a time until she got married to her husband, Matthew. Her marriage eventually turned to divorce when her husband went to write some TV episodes for a soap. He had assumed that she was cheating on him, but it turned out that he cheated on Allison with a Canadian woman. She was heartbroken and he was there for her to help her through her divorce.

Beth can see that James feels upset at what happened to his sister. She holds his hands and squeezes them lightly, showing that she cares about how he is feeling. She smiles at him. He smiles back at her – his heart flutters as he loves how beautiful she looks.

'Could you take me to the scene of the crime, Detective? I'd like to see it – I might be able to help you.'

'Please – call me James,' says James, 'are you sure you want to go back there?'

She suggests that looking around the area might lead to something, as there may be a new breed of spider that no one had ever discovered. James thinks that if there is a new spider out there it would be extremely dangerous and he wouldn't want Beth to go the same way as her husband.

But at the same time he is curious and it would help close the case. He agrees.

9

James and Beth walk through the woods. It's midday, so it's still nice and light. The area is quiet, apart from their footsteps making noise on the fallen leaves on the ground.

Beth sees the crime scene up ahead. The police tape remains over the area where Beth's husband was found. Beth ducks under the tape, kneels down to examine some of the remaining cobweb that the body was covered in. She feels it.

'Nothing unusual about it. It's sticky as normal, feels like any normal cobweb.'

Beth looks at James, suggests it might be a good idea for him to look around, to see if he can find any spider residue. It would lead him to where the spider is. James leaves Beth to continue to examine the scene. When James is out of sight, a noise startles Beth. A snapping of a twig. She stands up quick. Her heart races. She starts having déjà vu from what happened last time she was in the woods.

Her eyes look around the woods to see if she can see anything. She begins to shake with fear. She wants to call out for James but she feels paralyzed. She hears another snap of a twig followed by a noise that a reptile would make. A shadow then looms over her shoulder. She sees in the corner of her eye, a long leg of an insect. A giant spider's leg. She shakes with fear as it hooks onto her shoulder. It hisses. Beth feels scared.

'Beth? Beth?' calls James. The spider leg retracts and disappears. James spots Beth looking scared – body shaking, frozen on the spot. 'What is it?' he asks.

10

James has taken Beth back to her place. A small flat in a suburban area. Beth hasn't spoken a word ever since the woods. James is quite concerned the way she has been shaken up.

Beth sits on the sofa in the living room. James enters holding a glass of water. On the picture frames with spiders in. The wallpaper has spiders on too. The corners of the room have cobwebs – he can tell she's not the cleanest of women.

'Here, drink this,' says James, handing her the drink. She drinks some, then begins coughing. James panics – wonders what's wrong.

'Went down the wrong hole,' says Beth.

James is relieved that she is still talking. He asks her what happened in the woods. She confesses that she saw it. The biggest spider in the world. She saw its leg. It touched her shoulder. James is in disbelief. He doesn't know whether to believe her or not. He can't go to his superintendent and tell her that Beth's husband was killed by a giant spider. It would sound too crazy.

'James – I want to thank you, for looking after me, you've been so kind,' she says holding his hand.

He sits down next to her – telling her that all he wants to do is to make sure she's safe. She then makes a move, holds him by his waist and presses her lips against his. His eyes widen, he never expected that she'd do that. He closes his eyes and kisses her back. She then breaks this kiss.

'I'm sorry – I shouldn't have done that.'

He reassures her that if she hadn't have kissed him – he would've certainly kissed her as he's wanted to kiss her ever since he met her. She admits she always wanted to do the same since she met him. She thinks it's okay to kiss as she's single again but she also thinks it's too soon as it's only been a matter of weeks since she lost her husband.

James looks around the room, he looks at the spiders in the picture frames. He is surprised that after what happened that she would be put off by spiders. Especially seeing her still working in the spider farm. Even though her husband was found in cobwebs, it could never put her off spiders.

She still loves them. James thinks it's strange – he would easily be put off by them.

'Even though you've got a spider theme – this is a nice little home,' he says, 'cozy.'

'You like my parlour – do you?' says Beth smiling at the compliment.

'It's the prettiest little parlour.'

The hissing sound startles both of them. They look around – but see nothing. Beth tells James that's the noise she heard in the woods. They wait for the noise to sound again. It doesn't. After waiting a long time – James thinks it's gone. He looks at the time, it's late and he decides he should go. As he leaves, Beth gets up from sofa and grabs his arm.

'No – I don't want to be alone tonight,' says Beth. 'Stay – Stay with me.'

11

The door to Beth's bedroom opens. The light is turned on. As James walks in, his hand being held by Beth, he is surprised at what he's walked into. A large double bed is in the centre of the room. Two lamps on either side of the bed with two wooden bedside cabinets. The wallpaper is cobweb patterns. He thinks that she likes spiders a little too much. She kisses him passionately – he has his hands all over her body. He then feels something sticky on her shoulder – it's cobweb. She looks at her shoulder. She explains that's where that spider leg came down on her shoulder.

She kisses him again to distract him so it doesn't put him off her. She helps him get his clothes off then pushes him down on the bed. He lays there as she stands at the edge of the bed.

'I want you – do you want me?' says Beth smiling at him.

His heart races in anticipation. He couldn't wait to get his hands on her.

'I want you,' says James nodding.

Beth takes her top off – followed by her trousers. James's face shows an expression of confusion. Beth stands in front of him, naked. Her breasts are hidden by a bra completely made out of cobweb. Her nether region is hidden by underwear that's also made out of cobweb.

'What the hell?' says James, sitting up on the bed. Beth opens her mouth and a hissing noise comes out of it. Two long spider legs then burst out of her back and lunge towards James, grabbing his arms and pinning him down to the bed. The arms spin web, sticking his hands to the bed, so he can't escape or move.

'Oh, Detective – you should've pieced together the impossible,' says Beth, who begins to explain the puzzle. As Beth talks – James's memories begin flooding into his mind. Right from his very first meeting with her. She was always attracted to men who liked spiders just like her husband was. The extra deliveries of spiders that he saw in the case came from her. She had mated with her husband and delivered her baby spiders through her egg sack. Even when the spider's leg hung over her shoulder in the woods – it was her own leg, her transformation had started. Once she had mated with her husband, she killed him, as the clue was always in her name and it was all an act.

'Beth Williams,' says Beth. 'Black Widow.' Six more long spider legs come out of her back. Six more eyes appear on her forehead and fang teeth appear in her mouth. Her bottom morphs into a black spider's abdomen with a red mark that looks like an hour glass. He remembers that's how you know the difference between male and female Black Widows. The female has the red hour glass.

Beth pins and webs up James's legs. She steps onto the bed.

'I need to deliver more of my babies – I always hoped I would drag you up here to my dismal den,' says Beth. 'Have you ever been curious about what it's like to mate with a spider?' She sits on top of him – he screams.

12

Weeks pass by. In the café of the zoo, a man, Paranormal Investigator, Frank Mason, was watching the TV while drinking a bottle of water. His head is bandaged like he has been in an accident. A news reporter is on the TV.

'It's been two weeks since the discovery of Detective James Blackwell. His body was discovered in the woods with mysterious bites and covered in cobweb...'

13

Inside the spider farm, Beth holds a Black Widow spider in the palm of her hand in front of a crowd of people.

'Now – who would like to hold her?' says Beth. The people back away. 'No one?'

'I'll do it,' says Frank, appearing out of the crowd. He walks up to Beth and holds his hand out.

'A willing volunteer who's not afraid – I love that,' says Beth, placing the Black Widow on Frank's hand.

As the spider crawls along his hand, Beth noticed that Frank didn't react the same way as James did.

'Tickles doesn't it?'

'I haven't really noticed – I think she likes me.' Frank smiles at Beth. She likes this reaction. She smiles back and winks at him.

There is a poem from 1829 – that warns us of poor foolish things, cunning and being dragged to their dismal den. And as a lesson we take from this tale, as we heed these words as they lie. 'Will you walk into my parlour,' said the spider to the fly.

―――――――――――――

TWISTED

1

The college was surprising and new for Riley. For a nineteen year old girl's first day among the students didn't make Riley nervous or afraid of being surrounded by strangers. She waltzed in wearing casual clothes like American schools did blending in with everyone else causing their heads to turn to see this new girl among them.

One student in particular took a big interest in her. Emily was the Queen Bee of the College, dressed in a hoody and tracksuit bottoms wearing sunglasses like some sort of important celebrity. Girls loved her and became her followers. Emily crossed her arms and looked Riley up and down amused at herself thinking that this new girl was a threat and a potential rival. As Riley walked past, Emily tripped her up. "Walk much?" Emily and the girls giggled.

Riley glared as they walked away laughing, followed by a voice saying, "Just ignore them – they're just a bunch of tools – Hi, I'm Amber." Amber was pretty, with a slender figure and frizzy long brunette hair. "You must be Riley – the new girl."

"How do you know?" Riley asked her.

"Well, you're the only new girl here – so it's pretty obvious." Amber smiled, then complimented her by saying, "I love your bag – where did you get it, it's so posh?"

"Online – at Vanquish, see," Riley answered showing her the vanquish badge on the bag.

"Wow," Amber said excitedly. "They're so expensive, you're lucky."

"Actually, it was on sale – 75% off."

"Say, I hope you don't mind, but would you like me to show you around as you're new?" Amber asked her.

Riley didn't hesitate and accepted her offer. Being the new girl, she had no friends, and Amber was the first person she had met.

Amber took Riley around the College showing her all the classes, the canteen, the main hall, the gym and the grounds. Amber looked at Riley's schedule to see that she was studying drama with Simon Chambers and

History with JR. Amber praised Simon up as a lot of students took everything he said and made it stick. There hasn't been a single student that criticized his teaching abilities.

"Just so you know, Simon was the one who taught Jessica George a thing or two about acting."

"No way." Riley smiled. "Look how well she did – Towns-end's number one actress."

When Riley got to class, she descended the stairs that led down to a small platform where Simon stood at a desk with a projector propped up behind him. She sat down three rows away from Simon while all the other students that she didn't know took to their seats. While the teacher taught the class and other students answered, Riley just sat in silence, listening and keeping herself to herself, but something made her feel uneasy, like someone was watching her. She turned around to see the girl that tripped her up, glaring at her.

The time went quickly and, before Riley knew it, she was leaving the class with the other students. While they coerced with each other, Riley slipped outside to get some fresh air. She saw a bench under a tree and sat down to relax.

"Riley," Amber called.

She turned around to see her smiling. Riley felt more at ease now to see a familiar face. Amber sat closely next to her and asked, "So, how did drama go? What did you think of Simon?"

"You weren't wrong – he is a good teacher," Riley replied.

"So, who were you back in high school? Smart? Unpopular, Nerd?" said Amber who was curious to know the real Riley.

Riley told Amber that she was the Queen Bee of the high school. Girls wanted to be her. Guys wanted to be with her to adore her. It was the happiest time of her life being at high school, but it did have its downsides.

Keeping up an image was hard work and she was a bitch to others. She told Amber that there was one student called Annalisa. She was smart and witty but she constantly bullied her and made her life a living hell through the years. But then it all went horribly wrong. It was only in a matter of days that Annalisa took her own life. Riley couldn't believe it. After Riley was honest and told them of the bullying, they came to the conclusion as it was days after leaving school it happened then it wasn't Riley's fault and she shouldn't blame herself as if it was because of the bullying she would have done it when she was still in school.

Annalisa had a sister who had gone to another school and was on work experience in another country and had no idea of what transpired.

"I can relate," Amber replied. "I lost a sister too, not long ago. It still hurts, so, I can imagine what pain they are going through."

"Me too," Riley replied, quietly.

But their conversation was interrupted by Emily and another two girls, April and Taylor. Emily's eyes were like thunder as she fixed her eyes on Riley for a confrontation.

"So, bitch – you think you're funny coming onto my turf and trying to take everything away from me?"

"What are you talking about?" Riley replied, puzzled at Emily's outburst. She then noticed other students walk over to see what all the commotion was.

Emily walked around Riley, looking her up and down saying that as she's the new girl she must have been the popular one, the Queen Bee at her old school and no one would ever take her crown. Riley couldn't control herself as she giggled in amusement.

"You're funny." Riley laughed. "Why would you think I would want to take away anything from you?"

Emily put her hand on her hips and looked over her sunglasses. "Well, prove it – come to my place tonight – and I'll set you up a challenge like I do all my girls."

Riley Jennings misses the life she knew, where she would accept any challenge in life that was presented to her. But the challenge that she will be playing today is a challenge she didn't expect.

Riley wasn't one for backing down from a challenge. She got in Emily's face and accepted. Emily smiled and then took out a piece of paper with her address on. "Great –see you later, bitch – let's go girls." Emily and the girls walked away with their heads held high. The students began to gossip among themselves while Riley heard her name and Emily's being mentioned. A hot looking guy caught Riley's eye.

"Taking on the Queen Bee – hope you win," he said winking at her. Riley was stunned by how good looking he was. Brown sticky uppy hair and a muscular figure gave Riley that special tingle.

"Who was that?" Riley asked Amber.

"Oh that's Joe – one of Emily's exes and the hottest boy in college."

"Wow – you're not kidding," Riley agreed.

475

2

Later that day, when college was over and the students had left like a flock of seagulls – Riley went to Emily's place, she discovered that Emily and her girls were waiting at the door for her.

"Your girlfriend not joining us?" Emily mocked.

"Girlfriend?" said Riley confused. "You mean Amber? Ew, she's not my girlfriend."

"Really?" Emily puts her hands on her hips again. "The way she was hanging around you – we thought you might be a lesbian."

"I am not a lesbian, okay – I like boys," Riley insisted.

"Are you sure?" Emily asked "Okay, okay, I believe you." Who was not convinced.

"Look Emily, I need to know why you really invited me over – I mean it's not like we're friends or anything," said Riley. "You think I'm going to take your reputation away being the popular girl."

Emily glared at Riley. "Every girl wants to take away my reputation, every one of them has failed – but you're the first I've set my eyes upon that could actually achieve it, so I'm going to give you a chance to try – you up for the challenge?"

Riley sighed "What's the challenge?"

Emily took Riley to her bedroom and offered her a seat in front of her laptop. "Sit here," she insisted. Riley sat in front of the laptop. "I take it you've masturbated over porn before?"

"Who hasn't?" Riley asked.

Emily smiled. "Good – then your challenge is to have an orgasm over this." Riley was shocked to see the video was lesbian porn causing her to jump out of her seat.

"Whoa – I don't think so," Riley insisted, jumping to her feet, but Emily pushed Riley back down by her shoulders.

"What's the matter, Riley? Afraid of a little competition, I thought you wanted to take the crown away from me and become the popular girl again?"

"Not like this," Riley insisted.

"What's the big deal? Are you scared you'll enjoy it?" Emily asked.

"It's not going to happen," Riley snapped. "How am I going to get turned on and have an orgasm if I'm straight?"

"It's true – you are scared." Emily laughed. "Come on, girls, let's leave her be so she can go through with it, or she can leave and be pathetic."

Emily and the girls left the room. Riley sat in front of the laptop staring at the video. She had a choice, an easy choice for her to make. But why was it so hard? she thought.

Riley remembered some of the best times being the Queen Bee at her previous school. She missed the times of being surrounded by girls and boys admiring her, asking her out and wanting to spend time with her. And then she thought that it wouldn't mean anything if she went through with it. So, what if Emily said to others that she went all the way over porn, she would be the Queen Bee and have control.

Riley swallowed and hovered her hand over the play button. She pressed it and the video started.

Two naked women appeared, their hands caressing each other's bodies. Their lips smacking passionately as they kissed. Riley was freaked out seeing the images and was turned off rather than being turned on. Riley listened to the woman's voice as she talked over the different women that appeared on screen.

"You're just a normal woman, you secretly hide the real you, you want to releases the real you that's trapped inside, you want to be with a girl, you want to touch another girl, you want to explore the place that's in between their legs…"

Even though she was freaked out the more and more she watched. Riley soon found herself with her hand down her pants and stroking herself. It was like the video was hypnotic. The more she watched, the more she played until she began to get turned on. Her legs started to quiver while he breathing rate increased, until she gasped and gave out a screaming orgasm.

Riley sat in the chair out of breath with a wet hand down her pants. Emily came back in the room and went over to her phone that was hidden in the corner. Riley realized she had been recording her the entire time.

"Holy shit," Emily screamed excitedly. "I can't believe you went through with it."

Riley looked freaked out when she realized that Emily was recording her without her knowledge. She worried that Emily would end up showing the entire school the video as they would think that she really was a lesbian.

"I did your challenge, okay – so, now I'm the Queen Bee," Riley insisted.

Emily and the girls mocked her. All they could do was laugh at her.

"You really think you're the Queen Bee? Bitch, that was only the first challenge and you passed with flying colours," Emily explained.

"What do you mean the first challenge?" asked Riley.

She didn't like the way Emily's girls were giggling at her. Riley felt angry at herself that she had gone through with something she didn't feel comfortable with.

"You can get out of my home now – get a good night's sleep and prepare for your second challenge," said Emily.

Without hesitation, Riley left. She couldn't wait to get away from her. She was poison. Part of her didn't want to go through with what other challenges Emily had planned. But the other part of her wanted to show Emily up and take her reputation away for revenge.

3

The next day, after getting a restless night's sleep, with the thoughts that Emily was going to humiliate her in front of the whole College with the video she had taken, Riley walked into the grounds looking around for Emily and her girls.

"Hey – are you okay?" said Amber, creeping up behind Riley. Amber noticed the dark rings around Riley's eyes. "Okay, either that's badly applied make up, or you are tired."

"I didn't sleep that great, that's all," explained Riley.

Amber was curious to know why and then made a guess at the only thing it could be. "Was it Emily's challenge? – She set you a tough one to start with, don't worry the remaining two will only get worse."

"Worse? How is that not to worry?"

"Emily always starts with the easiest challenge, I'm still on my third and final one, I can't complete it just yet as it's not that easy, all about timing."

"How long have you waited, Amber?" Riley asked.

"Too long, but I can't tell you what they are as I'm not allowed to say and neither should you."

"But I need someone to talk to about this," Riley insisted.

"Don't you think I'm desperate to talk to someone about my challenges? – We can't as it's all part of Emily's rules," said Amber.

But before Riley could say anything else, Emily appeared like the smug looking bitch she was. "Amber's right, Riley – she knows the rules so abide by them or do you want me to show her that video?"

Riley looked scared and shook her head immediately. "No, I just want to know what my second challenge is."

"Okay bitch, I'll tell you," said Emily, glaring at Amber. "Scatter." Amber grabbed her bag and left hastily. "Okay, so your next challenge is to improve on the previous one."

"What do you mean?" Riley asked.

"You see Lisa over there?" Emily asked as she pointed to a fit slender girl with long dark hair. "She's the smartest girl in College, bright, fairly attractive, and straight."

"Okay," Riley thought, but she didn't really get what Emily was hinting at.

"Lisa looks down on a lot of non-straights, I want you to give Lisa a passionate sloppy wet kiss and you have to stick your tongue inside her mouth and massage it with hers, in front of the whole class."

Riley jumped up in outrage. "You're out of your fucking mind."

Emily stood up and got in Riley's face like she was about to explode. She could see that Emily was deadly serious.

"I'm out of here."

Emily grabbed hold of Riley's hair and pulled her back. "I don't think so, bitch, you have a choice to make. You could do all of these challenges and become the Queen Bee, or the Queen Bee will make you her bitch and you will wish that your life is over by overdosing on pills – do I make myself clear?"

Emily laughed as she walked away leaving Riley with a serious choice to make. Normally this sort of thing would be classed as harassment and bullying, but a Queen Bee would never resort to telling the head of the College or squealing.

As Riley walked back to class, Joe came running up behind her, urgently wanting to talk.

"Hey, Riley – you got a sec?" Joe asked.

Riley smiled with joy at the sight of seeing Joe. Ever since she laid her eyes on him, he had been the highlight of the College. "Hey, Joe, everything okay?"

"I was wondering, Riley, if you would like to be my date for the College dance this Friday?"

Riley couldn't believe it. Her first week, a dance and with the hottest boy in college. "Of course – I'd love to go."

"Great – I got sports now, I'll see you around," said Joe.

"Sure," said Riley, as Joe winked at her then walked away. Her heart felt a flutter as she made her way to class.

4

In the history class, JR, a teacher in his sixties, was discussing the subject of the nuclear disaster at Chernobyl in the eighties. Riley found this interesting as her previous history lessons in her old school were always about Henry the eighth or World War two.

When JR had his back turned to the class, Emily leaned towards Riley and whispered, "Okay, now's your chance."

Riley's heart was racing. She didn't want to go through with Emily's challenge, but she knew she had to do it.

Everything would change for the better when she became the Queen Bee. Everyone would all look up to her and respect her as the popular girl.

"Come on, bitch – or do you want me to show everyone in this class that you love to masturbate over lesbian porn?" Emily whispered.

Riley got up quietly out of her seat so that JR wouldn't notice. She crept over to the next two rows where Lisa was sitting. Lisa looked up to see Riley standing beside her and, before she knew it, Riley had grabbed hold of her and pressed her lips onto Lisa's. Lisa struggled against Riley as she slipped her tongue inside her mouth and massaged it with hers. The students were shocked, some of the boys looked excited and took their phones out to try and take pictures.

Lisa managed to get out of Riley's grip and then slapped her across the face.

"What the hell is wrong with you? You're sick," Lisa screamed.

Before the students could take any pictures they were startled by JR who slapped his hand down on his desk.

"What the hell is going on here?" JR shouted.

"This dyke just stuck her tongue down my throat," Lisa screamed as she spat Riley's taste out of her mouth.

"Riley – come with me to the headmasters office, now," JR ordered.

Riley hung her head in shame as she followed JR out of the classroom leaving the room in complete gossip and Emily laughing her head off.

5

When Riley sat down in Mr Richie's office, a middle aged African man stood with his back to her, staring out of the window. An awkward silence filled the air. Riley didn't speak a word as she didn't know who should speak first.

"So, it's not a very good start is it – you being the new girl and all?" said Mr Richie.

"No, sir," Riley spoke softly.

Mr Richie sat down at his desk and tried to understand why Riley did what she did. "Look – I get nowadays that a lot of people go through the frustration of their sexuality, being gay is who you are, but you can't go around kissing other girls whenever you feel like it."

"But I'm not gay, sir," said Riley.

"Well, than why did you do that?"

But Riley didn't answer. She knew she couldn't say anything about Emily's challenge. Not only would she be a grass, she would fail the challenge to become the Queen Bee. With Riley's silence, Mr Richie made Riley promise her this wouldn't happen again.

"Trust me, sir, it won't happen again," Riley insisted.

"Okay, go on."

And with that Riley left his office post haste but she had a horrible shock when she saw Emily waiting for her outside the office.

"You're doing better than I expected, I never thought you would go for it – so serious to be the Queen Bee of the College."

Riley was angry at the sick challenges Emily was giving her to do. She urgently wanted to complete this game of hers, so as she had done two challenges, she was eager to complete challenge three.

"This is the ultimate challenge – one I don't think you're going to go through with." Emily laughed.

"Try me," said Riley with so much confidence, it made Emily excited.

The college bell rang and students came out of the classrooms in a hurry to have lunch. Emily grabbed hold of Riley's hand and dragged her out of the building.

Emily hurried across the field with Riley in tow and met her girls waiting for her at the metal fence that surrounded the school area. Taylor and April held open the wire fence while Emily pushed Riley through then followed behind. They all gathered at a fire exit door behind the back of a building.

"What is this place?" asked Riley.

"It's the old Play 4 Real club," Emily replied. "It was originally closed down, but then someone else came along and changed it for the better"

"So, what is it now?"

6

Riley followed Emily through a dimly lit smoke filled club. Three semi naked muscly men were on podiums dancing up and down in front of drunk business women.

Riley's jaw dropped and she felt aroused at the strippers she had her eye on.

"This is a strip club? Jesus, Emily, we shouldn't be in a place like this," said Riley, firmly.

But Emily rolled her eyes like she was bored and wanted Riley to enjoy herself. She put her arm around Riley and told her that she knows someone that works at the club and he allows her to get in for free whenever she wants.

But Riley's attention was too engrossed in one of the muscly male strippers.

"You like him don't you? You want a lap dance?" Emily asked. Riley didn't answer. So, Emily dragged Riley over to a chair and sat her down. "April – go get your stripper."

April looked excited and hurried off to fetch the stripper. Riley was a bag of mixed emotions. She was nervous and scared but mostly excited as it was like going into the unknown. But her excitement soon changed when April brought a slender looking woman over wearing next to nothing apart from leather underwear, bra and strappy black stilettos.

"Riley – this is Chastity, she's going to give you a lap dance you'll never forget," laughed Emily.

"What?" Riley freaked as she hurried to get up, but Emily grabbed her by the shoulder and forced her back in the chair.

"You're right, Emily – she's gorgeous." Chastity smiled while licking her lips. She took hold of Riley's legs and spread them apart. "I'll take good care of you as long as you take care of me."

Chastity winked at Riley and then began to dance for her. With her arms raised and her body shimmering, she took her time to entice Riley. Chastity turned her back on her and looked over her shoulder with a cheeky grin.

"She wants you to undo her bra," Emily hinted.

Riley nervously leaned forwards and reached for the catch to Chastity's bra. When she unhooked it, the bra fell on the floor and caused Chastity's large breasts to flop out. Chastity faced Riley and from the heat of the lights inside the club it made Chastity's body glisten and drip. With sweat.

"Go on – touch them," Emily insisted.

But Riley hesitated causing Emily to roll her eyes in boredom. She grabbed Riley's hands and placed them on Chastity's sweaty wet breasts.

"That's it," said Chastity excited. "Play with them."

Riley flicked her hard erect nipples and squeezed them slightly but quickly stopped as it felt too weird. But Chastity was too turned on for Riley to stop and grabbed hold of her head and pulled her face towards her sweaty breasts and smothered it while she motorboated them. Riley struggled to pull away. When she did, her face was covered in Chastity's sweat and she could taste the salt on her lips.

Chastity continued to dance dirty for Riley. She turned around and then slipped off her panties. She placed them in her hands. Riley could feel the dampness of them and dropped them instantly. Chastity spread her legs and bent over so that her ass stuck up in the air. The smell of her lower region mixed with sweat was too overwhelming

Emily grabbed Riley's hands and placed them on Chastity's ass to give her cheeks a good grope.

"Ah," Chastity moaned. She faced Riley for the grand finale by bending backwards and revealed the pink glistening nether region. "Taste it."

Emily grabbed the back of Riley's head and forced her towards Chastity, but Riley fought back and couldn't go through with it.

"No – I can't," Riley screamed. "Get off me."

"Sorry, Chastity," Emily apologized. "I guess she's not ready yet."

Chastity placed her hands on her hips. "Shame – well, when she is, I would love it if she came back so I could show her the inside of my bed." Chastity winked at Riley who could tell this was all a flirting game to her. "She can keep my underwear for a souvenir – a good excuse for her to come back here and return them to me."

When Chastity walked away, Emily couldn't believe it. "Holy shit – you've pulled, Riley – you're a lucky girl."

"What the hell are you talking about?" Riley snapped.

"Guys have been asking her out for ages and she refused every one of them – I guess she just wanted a piece of female ass all the time." Emily giggled.

"I'm out of here and I'm done with this shit," Riley shouted as she stormed out of the strip club and felt humiliated. Emily picked up Chastity's underwear and bra and smiled to herself as she had a plan up her sleeve.

7

The next day, Riley looked more tired than ever. The afternoon and night before was rough. She was haunted by what went on in the strip club and couldn't get the image of Chastity's naked body out of her head. It was so bad that she started to feel turned on even though she knew it was wrong.

"Riley, are you up?" called her mother. "You've got a visitor."

"Tell them to wait – I need to take a shower," Riley called back.

Emily smiled to herself while she waited at the bottom of the stairs with her mother. "She shouldn't be too long, dear – can I get you anything?"

"No thanks – I'm good." Emily grinned.

"I'll be getting on then."

When Riley's mother left for the kitchen, Emily saw this as the perfect opportunity to execute her plan. She hurried up the stairs and quickly checked each room for Riley's room. When she passed the bathroom she could hear the sound of Riley humming to herself which was muffled due to the splashing of the water coming from the shower hose.

Emily spotted what was clearly Riley's room. She snuck past the bathroom quickly and walked in. The room wasn't to her liking. Its blue walls, posters of shirtless men and rock bands didn't give it the girly feel that she expected. Not like hers which had pink walls, surrounded with branded shoes, clothes and handbags. Emily even had a dressing table with every bit of make up that had more than the shops.

Emily went over to Riley's unmade bed. The sheets were creased and the duvet was screwed up in a ball. When her feet knocked into the dirty clothes that were scattered on the floor, this was the perfect moment to leave the contents of what she had in her bag.

When Riley returned to her room with a towel wrapped around her and wet skin, she saw Emily sitting on the edge of her bed. Emily greeted Riley with a big grin.

"Showering were we? Or doing something else in the shower?"

"What are you implying?" Riley asked.

Emily rolled her eyes. "Oh come on, Riley, what else do girls sometimes do with the shower head? – Are you sure you weren't, you know, playing with yourself while thinking about Chastity's erotic dance or were you thinking about when she spread her legs for you and wanted you to...?"

"You're disgusting," Riley snapped and stormed over to her wardrobe to get out her clothes that she was going to wear. "What are you even doing here anyway? We're not friends, Emily."

"I've still got to give you your last challenge – get dressed, I'll wait for you outside." Emily giggled.

When Emily left the room, Riley grabbed hold of the door and slammed it shut. Being angry was not the way she wanted to start her day. The door soon opened again when Riley's mother burst in looking angry.

"What the hell is going on? Why are you slamming doors?"

"Mum, I don't want any of those girls from that college to be invited into my house or my room," Riley shouted.

But Riley's mother took a different approach to how Riley felt. She told her that she needed to make friends as it wasn't healthy to be alone and that she didn't want her to grow up with no friends at all like she did. Her father, God rest his soul, was the only man in her life. She also thought that Emily was a nice sweet girl.

"Sweet?" Riley laughed. "You wouldn't say that if you knew her." Riley began to get a headache. All this was too much to deal with. She pushed her mother out of the way and left for the bathroom.

Riley's mother was annoyed at the attitude that Riley had. She looked around her bedroom and was disgraced at how untidy she had left it. She picked up Riley's clothes for the washing pile, but then came across a couple of bits of clothing that were bigger than Riley's clothing.

The bra cups were bigger than Riley's breasts and it was clearly someone else's bra, where a sweaty odour lingered. She then picked up the cold damp underwear that matched the bra. Odd thoughts entered her mother's head and worried her that Riley may have been keeping a secret.

Then something in the corner of her eye distracted her attention. Her mother saw the corner of a magazine poking out from under the duvet cover. When she pulled it out, she was horrified. The porno mag showed two naked women with the hands wrapped around each other kissing. Her mother opened the mag up to see one woman licking the other woman's nether region. She was going to turn the page over but discovered that the pages were stuck together. She sniffed the magazine and realized it was stuck together because of the smell of dry cum.

Her mother felt sick. She dropped the magazine and ran to the bathroom just as Riley was coming out. Her mother flipped the toilet seat up just in time as she vomited. Riley was concerned.

"Mum, are you okay – what's wrong?" But her mother ignored her like she didn't exist to her. Once she had finished being sick, she pushed Riley aside. "What? What have I done?"

Her mother stopped. A look of shame filled her face. "I found them in your room – when were you going to tell me?"

But Riley didn't know what she was on about. She grabbed her hand and took her to her bedroom. That was when Riley looked horrified when she saw Chastity's underwear on her bed with the porno. Riley pleaded with her mother and told her the truth about what Emily did when she took her to the strip club.

"Don't lie to me," her mother snapped. "Why didn't you just come out with it and tell me you were gay? I mean who is this woman? Why do you have her underwear? Have you had sex with her?"

But Riley failed to convince her mother that she wasn't a lesbian. Instead her mother told her to leave before she was late for College. She felt disgusted by even looking at her. And with that, Riley quickly got her clothes on and left the house.

Outside her home, Emily stood by her car, smiling at Riley as she came down the driveway. "Hey, lesbo," she called. "Get in, I'll give you a lift to college."

"Why did you do that?" Riley screamed. "Why did you leave those things in my room? Thanks to you, my mother thinks I've been having sex with girls."

"Sweetie – you can't deny who you really are inside." Emily laughed "Now get in the car and I'll tell you your last challenge, then I can pass the Queen Bee title over to you."

Emily got in her shiny pink convertible and waited patiently for Riley to do the same. Riley hesitated for a moment, but the thought that this game could be over soon forced her hand, so she got in the car, so Emily could drive away.

"First may I say, I'm extremely proud of you – I've never met an opponent who has played so well."

"Just get to the bloody point and tell me my last challenge already," Riley demanded.

"Okay – your last challenge is to take everything you've experienced in your last two challenges and this time go all the way." Emily pulled the

489

car over to stop at the curve. "Riley, for your last challenge, I want you to seduce Amber and have lesbian sex with her. It mustn't be quick. It must be romantic, passionate, like you were both in love, like a couple waiting for their special wedding night and you both have to orgasm to win the title for Queen Bee."

Riley could clearly see that Emily was like a disgusting psychopath. She didn't see Amber that way and she knew that Amber didn't see her in the same light. To have passionate love making with her and to both orgasm would convert Riley into a lesbian. She would never feel aroused when she saw a naked man again.

"You know what? You win. Torture me. Bully me. I'm not doing this," admitted Riley.

"So, you're saying that you would rather give up? When you're so close to winning. You would rather have the entire college know that you masturbate over lesbian porn and that you keep stripper's underwear?"

Riley realized how far Emily was willing to go. What she would have to do just to win her place as the Queen Bee. If she accepted and attempted the challenge she could make all of this torment go away. Riley never saw Amber as a romantic interest. She had already got her eye on Joe and already worried what he would think of her.

When Riley arrived at the college in Emily's car, heads turned as the students were confused why Riley was in Emily's car.

As Riley walked over to Amber who was sitting on a bench. Emily called, "See you later, lover." She blew Riley a kiss as all the students stared.

"I'm going to make sure you pay for this, bitch," Riley mumbled as she sat down next to Amber.

"What was that about? You look terrible," Amber asked.

"I'm just tired that's all," Riley replied. "What are you doing tonight?"

"Not a lot, why?"

"I was wondering if you wanted to hang out tonight that's all."

"Sure, I'd love to hang out with you," said Amber, excitedly. Riley was surprised that she was excited. They had hardly known each other for five minutes but she couldn't believe how easy it was. Amber suggested that Riley go to hers. This was perfect, with her mum assuming the worst from her, the last thing she wanted to do is bring a girl home to meet her mother and get the wrong idea.

8

So, later that evening, Riley turned up on Amber's doorstep wearing a tight top and pants. Amber opened the door in a dull tracksuit bottoms and jumper. She looked Riley up and down "Wow, look at you."

"You like what you see?" said Riley.

"Ah ha," Amber replied by biting her lip.

Amber showed Riley around her home. It was a mixture of small and large rooms. The living room was smaller than the kitchen. Her mother's bedroom was the same size as the bathroom. The spare room was slightly bigger which was fully furnished with a bed and girly posters. Riley didn't understand why it was furnished considering Amber was the only girl living there. Amber ended the tour with her bedroom which was the biggest in the house. She had a king-sized bed. A large dressing table and a walk-in built-in wardrobe.

"Wow – I love your room," said Riley, amazed. She went over to Amber's bed and felt the silk sheets. Amber had already sat down on her bed and took out a fashion magazine from her bedside cabinet. They both looked through the magazine, admiring the different outfits.

Riley was nervous. She had lots of different ideas of how she could try and seduce Amber. She thought about stroking her hair, down to her neck, softly and then leaning forward to kiss her soft lips. Another idea was just to kiss her passionately like she did with Lisa in class, but she thought that Amber might slap her too.

Amber looked into Riley's eyes. They both never spoke a word. Instead both their hearts were racing with anticipation. Riley thought this was the perfect opportunity. She placed her hands on Amber's face and pulled her towards her lips. When she pressed her lips against Amber's, she was surprised that Amber was kissing her back. She didn't pull away and didn't hesitate. To Riley, it was surprisingly nice. She didn't feel sick like she did when she tried it on with Lisa.

"Wow." Amber smiled. "Where did that come from?"

"I've been wanting to do that since I first saw you on the day I met

491

you."

"I never even assumed that you were a lesbian."

"I'm not really… but." Riley held Amber's hands in hers and then sucked her finger seductively. Amber closed her eyes, her legs quivered as she got more turned on and her breathing rapidly increased.

Amber pulled away to push Riley down on the bed. She got on top of her and pulled her top off revealing her bra.

She quickly unhooked her bra to reveal her perky breasts. Amber leaned over Riley's face knocking her boobs into her. She wanted Riley to kiss and lick them, so without hesitation, Riley did. She didn't find it odd in any way and enjoyed every minute playing.

Amber changed position by leaning back. Riley was about to get on top of Amber until she pushed Riley away.

"No," said Amber as she slipped her trousers off. She spread her legs wide to reveal her pink underwear. "Take them off." She giggled.

Riley had flashbacks of Chastity spreading her legs wide open and the porn she had watched. This was the real deal here and now. Riley pulled Amber's underwear off to reveal her pink region. Riley slowly put her face towards it. The smell of her was quite overwhelming which made her hesitate with palpitations. But before she knew it, Amber grabbed hold of Riley's hair and pulled her face into her.

Amber gasped as Riley got to work. Amber moaned with excitement as she couldn't believe this was happening.

Within a minute she let out a yelp and then relaxed. Riley sat up for her and wiped her wet mouth. Amber kissed her passionately forcing her to lie down beside her.

While Amber continued to kiss her, Riley felt Amber's hands slip inside her pants. Riley couldn't believe the excitable pleasure as Amber played with her. She knew that if she had an orgasm then her conversion would be complete and she would never be straight again. Riley struggled to fight it but the excitement got too much for her and she let out a scream while trying to catch her breath.

An hour later, Riley's eyes opened. She found herself staring at Amber who was completely naked next to her on Amber's bed. Riley turned over to look at the wall. She didn't know how she felt. A small feeling of doubt and regret plagued her.

Amber stirred and dropped her arm over Riley spooning up against her.

Amber was the happiest she had ever been as she played with Riley's breasts. But Riley removed her arm and turned over to look at her.

"That was amazing – I never even dreamed you felt that way about me – I loved it," Amber smiled. "I know that Joe has asked you to the dance and after what we've just done, would you go with me instead?"

Riley knew that she would have to give Joe the elbow.

Especially if he found out that she had just had sex with Amber. All Riley could do was play along. She had won every challenge that Emily had set her and now she was going to show the bitch what it was really like; what a Queen Bee really does.

"Of course I would love to go with you to the dance." Riley smiled.

"Good." Amber smiled back. "Because I wanted that night to be special so I can enjoy it with my girlfriend."

Riley took hold of Amber's hand and kissed it. "I'm happy that I'm going with my girlfriend – I have loved you since the first day I met you."

"I love you, too," said Amber as she hugged into Riley.

But Riley was smiling on the inside as her true feelings were just lies so she could change everything.

9

The very next day, Riley waltzed through the College gates looking around for Emily. She spotted Amber talking to Taylor and April who were laughing and giggling.

"Riley." Amber smiled. She went over to her and held her hand while giving her a kiss on the lips.

A round of applause from Emily made Riley spin around as she walked up to her. "Congratulations, you finally did the last challenge – not everyone has managed to conquer all three and take the title away from me."

But Riley realized Emily wasn't even looking at her.

She was looking at Amber.

"I announce to the whole College, that you are now the Queen Bee," Emily shouted as she, Taylor and April clapped their hands.

Riley remembered that Emily had mentioned that Amber didn't complete her last challenge and couldn't tell Riley what it was.

"Amber, what's going on? What was your last challenge?"

Amber smiled sinisterly. She kissed and cuddled Riley, then whispered into her ear, "To get a girlfriend."

Riley realized she had been played the entire time. She risked everything just so she could relive her glory days. Emily held up a porno mag of a man in front of her and then a naked woman. Riley's senses tingled when she saw the naked woman and felt nothing for the man.

"The straight innocent girl that I have made into a permanent lesbian – you'll never be able to love men again, I've destroyed you like you destroyed me."

Riley shed a tear as she looked up. She saw Joe walk past her in disgust. Riley went over to him, but he backed away. "Get away from me – why didn't you just tell me that you fancied girls?"

Riley glared in anger. "What the hell do you mean I destroyed you?"

"You killed my sister, it's your fault that she's dead. Just because you wanted power and control being the Queen Bee. My sister was, Annalisa."

The horror that had haunted Riley all that time, had now come back with a vengeance. Riley never even thought for one second that Amber could have been related. She had waited all that time for the perfect revenge plot – to destroy Riley's sexuality, to change her forever and the woman that she used to be. There is a time to play games and there is also a time to walk away.

TALENT

1

The flash of neon lights illuminated the night as Police Constable Hannah Havers sped to the scene that she had been called to. Apart from the light haze in the air, the night was cool and rather still. Hannah yawned as her eyes began to lay heavy. It was 3.15 a.m., when she glanced at the clock. She was supposed to finish her shift hours ago, but a backlog of calls had kept her working.

Hannah then saw the flashing lights of another police car in the distance. When she arrived at the scene, she saw her colleague, PC Veronica Freeman, leaning up against the car with her arms crossed.

"What have we got?" Hannah asked as she stepped out of her vehicle and made her way over to the crime scene.

"Nelson and Mary – both have been murdered, they have a boy called John," Veronica explained.

Hannah saw the horror that was before her. Nelson's body lay dead on the cold ground in a puddle of his own blood. From what Hannah could see, he had been shot in the head as there was a gaping hole in the back of his skull. She then turned her attention to Nelson's car. The driver's door was open where Nelson had got out. The windscreen was cracked and covered in blood from where Mary had been shot as she lay dead in the passenger side.

Veronica could see it in Hannah's expression. She knew something about the victims. "Do you know them?" she asked.

"Not the man. But Mary I knew," Hannah explained. "I arrested her a few times – prostitution. Always side by side with her friend."

"Marcy?" Veronica suggested.

"That would be her," Hannah agreed. "So, where's the boy?"

"He's been taken," Veronica replied. "Kidnapped."

"How do you know he's been kidnapped?" Hannah asked, curiously.

Veronica reached into her car and took out a plastic wallet that had maps inside and had been marked randomly.

2

The night turned into the morning as daylight shone through the cracks of the blinds of the police station.

Hannah yawned as she sat at her desk, staring at a whiteboard with all the maps pinned up. The random markings gave no indication as to where John was being held, which begged the question, what was the kidnapper trying to achieve?

"Haven't you got a home to go to?" Detective Christine Miller asked as she waltzed into the room.

"Actually, I thought I would stay on with the case," Hannah suggested.

"So, what do we have so far?" Christine enquired.

"These maps have markings on. It's like the kidnapper wants us to look in all these locations."

"Interesting deduction. One of these locations must be where John is being held," Christine assumed.

Hastily, Veronica walked in and interrupted them. "Excuse me, Hannah, you have a visitor – Scott's here."

A handsome man walked in. Smartly dressed.

Holding a bunch of flowers.

"Scott – what are you doing here?" Hannah asked. "You shouldn't be here – is everything okay?"

"I'm okay – I woke up alone though."

"I'm sorry about that," Hannah apologized. "Urgent call."

"Bad?" Scott asked.

Hannah looked at Christine and was hesitant to say anything.

"A couple have been murdered – their boy has been kidnapped," Christine explained.

"My god," Scott reacted.

"Oh, I think we want God on our side here," Christine replied.

Scott wandered over to a large board with hundreds of photos of women of different age, race and colour. His eyes scanned over each one and then he asked Hannah, "What's all this?"

Hannah wandered over and explained, "Missing persons. It's been building for years. Ages between thirty and fifty. Disappeared without a trace – never been seen since."

"No motive or evidence to suggest what might have happened?" Scott asked, curiously.

"Just one. An MGP van was spotted driving past," Hannah explained.

"Well, have you questioned their HQ?"

"Chance would be a fine thing," Christine interrupted. "There is no record of MGP – they don't seem to exist and we can never seem to find one. We've had patrols looking out for them, but nothing."

Something then distracted Scott's attention, four men were mixed in the pictures of the missing women.

"Who are they? They're not women."

"No. Mike Brian, aged seventy and Neil Bolton, forty, were last seen on the beach with this man, Doctor Husbondi – all three of them seem to have disappeared off the face of the earth."

"Where do you think they went?"

"Who knows?" Hannah replied.

Scott took a look at the other man and read, "Frank Mason – wasn't he that Paranormal Investigator who was involved in the Field Towers incident?"

"That's right," said Hannah. "His car was found at Faymill Farm. Abandoned. There was no sign of him – it was like he just disappeared off the face of the earth."

Scott then noticed a photograph of a graffiti logo that said *Residents of War*. "You investigated these vigilantes?"

"We arrested these vigilantes. The two ring leaders are currently being held in Marwood Asylum – especially after what they did," Hannah explained. "Their video went viral and caused this world to change."

Scott then turned his attention to the maps on the whiteboard. "Interesting," he murmured. More photos of women took his interest. Rows and rows of thirty looking Asian, Japanese and transgender women. "More MGP abductions?"

"No," Hannah corrected. "These are the biggest mystery of all. They just disappeared. There is no motive, it's like they've been hidden away."

"So, who is the kink?" Scott enquired as he took a closer look at a dominatrix wearing a red cape and rubber mask.

"They're called Domme – they stopped a bank robbery by dicing up the robbers."

"So, they're a superhero?" Scott smiled.

"Hardly – vigilantes don't get a free pass I'm afraid," Sarah described.

Scott took a closer look at a picture of a dead female who had been brutally slain. Next to her was a pocket watch with the time set at twelve. "This is different."

"Ah, our Hell-Streamer. Typical slasher that likes to kill their victims while live streaming. We have others on the outside working on it for us." Hannah turned Scott's attention onto her main case. "These were found at the kidnapper scene. They were left in the victim's car – we're trying to figure it out, but we can't make no head nor tail of it."

"It's because you're looking at it too close," Scott replied.

Hannah and Christine watched in amazement as Scott rearranged the drawings in a pattern – joining up the lines until it formed an X. Scott stepped away and said, "Okay – want to tell me what I'm looking at?"

"Woodcreek? X marks the spot – genius," Christine reacted and grabbed her things in a hurry to leave. "I'll get a team together to that location."

Hannah was delighted and impressed with how Scott solved the puzzle. "Well done." She kissed him. "Wait here and I'll be back soon."

3

The night was still as were the trees in the woods. Not a sound stirred from the insects and the wildlife that roamed there. A droplet of water fell from a still branch and then it happened. Lights from torches cracked through the foliage, followed by faint sounds of dogs barking and voices.

Hannah's breath floated in front of her face in the chilled air and droplets of rain fell from her face. "Spread out," she called to the other officers that were distanced from her. "He must be around here somewhere."

Christine joined Hannah's side. The two of them went deeper into the woods. Their footsteps crunched across the dirt and dead leaves and snapped the twigs beneath their feet.

"I find this quite ironic," Christine murmured.

"Why?" Hannah questioned.

"Because this is the second time I have been called to this place," Christine replied. "I met Detective James Blackwell at the scene of a murder. A body was found eaten and covered in cobwebs."

"James Blackwell? Wasn't he the detective that disappeared?"

"That would be him," said Christine.

Hannah then spotted something hidden behind some foliage. "What is that?" She aimed the flashlight to reveal something wooden. A casket. The wood looked rotten and damp. A faint murmur could be heard from inside.

Together, Hannah and Christine managed to pull open the casket and reveal John, tied up with dirt marks all over his skin.

"It's okay, honey, we've got you," Hannah assured him.

Later that morning, Hannah is asleep at her desk.

Christine wakes her up. "Come on, sleepy head – time to go home."

"What time is it?" Hannah yawned.

"A little after nine," said Christine. "Your man has been waiting for you." Hannah gets out from behind her desk. "You did good work today."

"If you remember – it was Scott that worked it out. Thanks to him the boy was saved."

"Indeed," Christine agreed. "He's got talent – if he's interested, there is an opening for a new PC. He works the way he's going – he could work his way up to detective."

"I'll tell him." Hannah smiled as she left the office to meet Scott.

Outside, it's a bright sunny morning. Scott is sitting on a bench outside the station, smiling to himself. He turns his head to see Hannah walking towards him.

"Home?" Scott suggested.

Hannah looked across the street and noticed *Kays Coffee Shop.* "Coffee first."

"Coffee it is," Scott agreed.

As they walked across the street, Hannah mentioned, "There is a job vacancy going for a new PC. Detective Miller thinks you should go for it and so do I – with what you did today – you're guaranteed the job."

"I'd love to." Scott nodded. "I can see why you like it. You're doing something good for the community." Hannah opened the door. Scott hesitated to go in with her. "I've just got to make a phone call."

Hannah kisses and him and goes inside. Scott takes his phone out. It rings and he waits for someone to pick up. While he waits he overhears two men talking about recent events.

"I can't believe the police found that boy already."

"All that planning was for nothing," mumbled the other.

Overhearing their conversation, Scott put his phone away and at a distance began to follow the two men. One was bald and skinny with tattoos on his arms, while the other was masculine and rough looking. The two men turned down a side alley.

The two men approach the back of an abandoned building. The skinny one looks down the alley and sees Scott walk past.

"What's wrong?"

"It's nothing – I thought he was following us," said the skinny man. "Come on, let's get inside."

When they went inside, Scott peered round the corner of a wall to see that the coast was clear. He hurried over to the door and waited a couple of minutes, before slowly opening it and slipping inside.

He crept along a long hallway, overhearing a conversation going on between the two men.

"So, have you heard from him?"

"No, not a thing," replied the skinny man. "I thought we might have, considering he planned it all."

Behind the two men, Scott snuck into the room and hid behind a stone pillar.

"We should go – he's not going to show," said the muscular man. He then spotted a shoe behind the stone pillar. "Son of a bitch – there's someone here."

Scott looked down at his footwear and realized they could see it. He attempts to run for the door, but is grabbed by the two men. The skinny man pins Scott up against the wall. "Well, what do we have here?"

He didn't know how to react, so Scott said the only thing that he could think of. "I've been offered a position to join the police force." Both men look at each other and are confused by his statement. "I've always wanted to join the police force and am now helping the case with the missing boy. I finally got my wish." He pushed the men off him. "Thanks for helping me hide him."

"It was easy – we just had to kill the parents to get him," the skinny man boasted.

"Now you can help me – become a detective." Scott smiled.

We all have talents. But sometimes the real talent we can have, can be the most manipulative and deceitful.

———————————

SONGBIRD

1

Alison Chance's head flooded with thoughts while she stood in the darkness, waiting for her cue. She saw her childhood flash before her eyes. While other kids of her age were interested in dolls and playing outside, she was more interested in staying indoors playing with a xylophone that her parents had got her for her birthday.

For the entire year she played with it every day. It got to the point where her parents regretted getting it for her, but then they saw something. She started to make her own tunes with it. By Christmas they bought her a toy piano which expanded her creative flare. From a karaoke machine to a keyboard, Alison made music her life. She got straight As in music class. She won first prize in the talent contest. Then one day, on a night out with a friend, she was spotted by a talent scout who wanted to represent her. His name was Tyrone who had represented pop sensation Megan May.

She thought a lot about her journey that got her to where she was now. From all the hard work she had put in, to the sacrifices she had made. She missed out on the prom. She had neglected friends to go out with after school. Her music became an obsession. She had lost hours of sleep and eventually became ill.

Alison was taken to a doctor who prescribed her some medication. The pink pills she had been prescribed, gave her the buzz she wanted, making her more relaxed so she could switch off from everything she had built up inside herself.

Now she was standing on a platform, hearing the roar of a hundred thousand people inside the stadium. The platform ascended as she rose up on stage to see and feel the heat of the blinding spotlights. As she approached the edge of the stage, her black sparkly dress twinkled like a thousand stars in the night sky. Her pouted red lips and curly long blonde hair made her look like a model on a catwalk. The crowd went wild, giving her screams and whistles making her feel a buzz down her lower region, which made her feel wanted and adored. She gave them a sexy grin as she held the microphone to her lips.

"Good evening, Towns-end," she shouted as the fans gave a deafening roar back to her. "I am so happy to see so many dedicated fans here tonight – so let's not waste any time and get the ball rolling."

A great darkness filled the stadium as the spotlights dimmed. Alison arched her back as the green, red and blue lights surrounded her. She placed the mic near her lips and sang into it. An explosion of fireworks brightened up the arena causing fans to go wild as Alison professionally danced sexily around the stage while blowing kisses and winking to her fans.

After a couple of hours, the platform descended under the stage, where Tyrone was waiting for her with a towel and a bottle of water. Alison grabbed the towel off of Tyrone. Never had she been so happy to wipe the sweat off her forehead.

"Great show, Alison," Tyrone complimented. "That's my girl – now you can relax for a couple of days before the last show."

"Water." Alison snatched it off Tyrone and guzzled it down.

"The fans are waiting out the back for photos and signings – don't want to disappoint them."

"Did they pay good money to see me?" Alison asked.

"Yes – the VIP treatment," Tyrone explained.

"Good – as long as we get that money that's all that matters and they can wait as long as they like." Alison laughed as she walked away from Tyrone, but he was too quick and grabbed her arm to stop her.

"Now wait just a minute, Alison – Megan would never take that attitude towards her fans."

"Well, Megan isn't here – I am – and you've got to be pissing in the wind for me to waste my time with selfish people who want to see more of me – they've got what they wanted in the concert and that's where it ends." She smiled and lightly tapped Tyrone on the cheek. "Now why don't you deal with them while I have a shower and freshen up?"

Tyrone was furious as he watched Alison walk away from him. Of all the talent he had found, she was the first he began to regret signing up. A hateful dislike for her began to build up inside him.

Alison emerged out of the backstage door. She strutted like she was the most important woman in the world.

Nothing was going to get in her way, she was determined of that.

"You are walking on thin ice, Alison," Tyrone warned her. "Your fans have been tweeting and posting on social media how they didn't get the VIP

510

treatment they paid for."

"I've learned how to swim, thin ice doesn't bother me, they're just comments I won't take seriously." She laughed.

When Alison emerged out on to the main street, the media were already looking around for her. She hastily decided to cross the street, hoping they wouldn't see her, but as she took a step out onto the road, a parked car on the side of the road blinded her with their headlights. As she shielded herself from the beams, the car's engine came to life and sped straight towards her.

Tyrone emerged out onto the street and saw Alison standing in the middle of the road and the car coming straight for her. "Alison," he screamed.

As Alison staggered back to get out of the way of the incoming vehicle, she lost her footing and fell, but a stranger coming out of nowhere caught her. They pushed her out of the way as the car hit them and then sped away from the scene.

Tyrone and random strangers went over to help Alison as she sat on the cold concrete ground.

"Alison, are you okay?" Tyrone asked, but all his words did was faintly echo through Alison's hearing as she wasn't paying attention. Instead, all she could do was stare at the stranger who saved her life. Who was he? She wondered. Where did he come from? Random strangers checked him over and called an ambulance as Alison watched.

An hour later, Alison was sitting in her dressing room holding a glass of water. She was staring into space looking back on her life, realizing how she had wasted it. Feeling the loneliness hurt her. She knew she should be dead if it hadn't been for the random guy that came out and saved her life.

Alison was startled when Tyrone walked into the room.

After the way she had treated him, he still stood by her side.

"How are you feeling?" Tyrone asked.

"To hell with how I'm feeling. How is that guy that saved me?"

Tyrone felt proud of Alison for thinking about someone else's feelings than herself. "He lives to tell the tale. He was pretty banged up, but luckily there were no life--threatening injuries."

Alison sat back down relieved. "Who was he? Did you get his name?"

"No, sorry," Tyrone replied. "I've given a statement to the press. They're going to be following this story for a while. I suggest you lay low for a week to be safe."

As the week passed, Alison kept herself busy.

Practicing for her upcoming performance, exercising on her treadmill and writing new material for ideas of her next album. But as she was doing all these things, she kept reliving that night over and over in her head. She was eager to know who the stranger that saved her life was.

When Tyrone checked on her, he could see something different in her. She was full of stress and frustration and suggested to him that he take her to the hospital to go and see the man that saved her life.

Tyrone was reluctant to do so and explained to her that it had been over a week and he would have been discharged by now.

"I don't care – take me there now," Alison yelled at him. "I'm going to find out who he is no matter what."

"Why is this so important to you?" Tyrone asked.

"Please, I need this for closure – the media didn't even mention who he was, just some random stranger and focused more about me."

By midday, a limo had pulled up outside the hospital that Alison's hero had been taken to. She strolled in all glammed up in a white dress and wearing a pair of sunglasses. The air was a mixture of disinfectant and floor wax which caused her to lose her balance as she approached the reception desk.

"Excuse me…" Alison asked a black lady sitting at the desk wearing a name tag. "…Tiffany – I'm…"

But Tiffany recognized who she was and smiled with excitement. "You're Alison Chance, oh my god, I'm a huge fan."

"Like I've never heard that before," sighed Alison.

"I apologize, Miss Chance – how can I be of assistance?"

Alison explained the details of the situation to Tiffany and told her that she was eager to see the man that had saved her life. Tiffany looked up the details on the system, then gave Alison the bad news that he had already been discharged in the week.

"What was his name?" asked Alison.

"I'm sorry – he wanted to stay anonymous," explained Tiffany.

"Look, Tiffany – I understand about patient confidentiality, but this is driving me out of my mind, no one is telling me who my hero was – I need this for closure, surely you can understand where I'm coming from?" yelled Alison.

Tiffany shuddered at Alison's outburst. The singer she admired had a side that she had never seen before. With Alison's demand she agreed to share the name. "His name is, Rick James."

When Alison heard the name she felt warm, tingly and excited inside. "Rick is my favourite name – it's what I would call my son if I ever had a baby."

Tiffany looked at Tyrone as Alison just stood still with a creepy big grin on her face. They began to suspect that Alison wasn't well, that the effects of what happened had made her ill.

All of a sudden they both jumped as Alison startled them by snapping out of it and yelling, "What's his address?"

Tiffany shook her head and was reluctant to share the details. She had already broken the rules by sharing his name and didn't want to lose her job.

Alison chuckled. "Tiffany, I have a shit load of money and I could buy your job out from under you – the address, now."

It wasn't long after the visit to the hospital, Alison's limo pulled up outside a grotty beaten down three-storey flat building. The window to the limo had lowered. Alison stuck her head out and lowered her sunglasses looking unimpressed.

"This is where Rick lives – boy, what a shit hole," Alison mumbled.

"You've got to realize, Alison, not everyone lives the glamorous life."

Alison glared at Tyrone and told him, "I just feel sorry for the poor bastard, a hero shouldn't have to live like this."

"What are you going to do?"

"Make him a better offer, Ty."

Alison left the car and walked over to a set of mail boxes; they were the near the door buzzers. She looked for Rick's surname and was about to call it when someone came out of the building nearly knocking into her. Alison barged past them and entered the building.

The interior smelled terrible with dirty marks spread over the cracked faded cream coloured walls. The hallways echoed with the sound of rap music coming from the rooms. She climbed the stairs to the next two floors then found the flat Rick lived in. Impatiently, she rung the doorbell and banged on the door, so Rick would hurry to answer it. But nobody came. Alison clenched her fist tightly in anger and was about to give it all she had on the door, when it opened and a woman stood in front of her.

"Who the fuck are you?" Alison reacted.

The woman looked Alison up and down. She thought she looked familiar but wasn't too sure. "I'm Robyn James, I live here – who do you think you are talking to me like that?"

"I'm Alison Chance, you can't tell me you haven't heard of me?" Robyn's chin dropped. The fact that a celebrity she was a fan of was standing at her door was the biggest surprise she ever had. "Where's Rick? You his sister?"

"I'm his wife," Robyn snapped. "Look, Miss Chance, it's great to see you here but would you mind telling what you want with my husband?"

"I will when you invite me in," ordered Alison.

Robyn opened the door and Alison stepped in. She looked around the cramped little flat and felt uncomfortable as there were boxes of junk scattered everywhere. It wasn't the tidiest of places she had been to.

"Sorry, about the mess," Robyn apologized.

"Does he always live like this? How can you put up with that?"

"Actually, we're always rowing about this constantly," Robyn explained. "He's got bad OCD and is always moaning at me to keep the flat tidy, I can't help it, I always lived like this."

"Oh, so you're the messy one and he's the tidy, hmm, a man after my own heart," smiled Alison.

"So, what do you want with my husband? Are you going to tell me or not?" Robyn sat on the sofa and put her feet up while Alison looked around the living room.

"I wanted to thank him for saving my life," Alison told her. Robyn looked surprised like she didn't know what she was talking about. "He hasn't told you, has he?"

"No, I think I would have remembered something like that if he told me."

While Alison explained that Rick wanted to remain anonymous, she picked up a photo of Robyn with three other women and examined it closely. Robyn told Alison that Rick had been secretive through the week. She had come back to him from her forty-eight hour shift at the local hospital as she worked there as a nurse. Rick had been cagy when he showered and changed his clothes and they hadn't had sex in the week, like he didn't want Robyn to see his body. Now she knew why, to hide the bruises he had sustained from the hit and run.

Once Robyn had stopped talking, she noticed that Alison wasn't paying

514

attention to her, as she was more interested in the photo she had in her hand.

"That's the ladies, as we like to call ourselves. I've known my friends for years since high school, we've always kept in touch and met up regularly, apart from now as I'm always busy and can't afford it."

"It must be nice to have friends," said Alison, jealously.

She put the photo down and abruptly asked, "So, where does Rick work?"

Alison's limo left the estate and made its way across town towards the industrial estate where lots of factories occupied the area. The limo pulled up outside a large building made of glass and steel. Alison got out of the limo and looked in awe at the building.

"Well, isn't this fucking posh?" Alison thought as she walked over to a set of doors that lead to the reception.

When she went inside she was greeted by a blast of cool air from the air conditioner and the smell of polish. The floor was covered in grey tiles and had two leather sofas near the doors. She took a closer look at the awards on the wall which the company had won every year.

The reception desk was curved with the logo 'CL Petra'. As she stood in front of the desk, the receptionist was nowhere to be seen, until a young woman came to the desk and asked, "Can I help... you're not are you?"

"Yes," sighed Alison. "I'm Alison fucking Chance."

"Wow – we hear your songs everyday."

"I don't care, where's Rick?" Alison ordered. "I demand I see him now."

"It's okay, Ellie," Rick called. "I'll handle this."

Rick placed his hands on the desk as he stood in front of Alison, smartly dressed in a shirt and tie. It sent Alison's heart a flutter, something she had never felt in her entire life.

2

"Can I help you?" Rick asked Alison, who stood in front of him like a frozen statue. He waved his hand in front of her face trying to get her attention, but instead caused her to start panting. "Miss Chance?"

She then shuddered, snapping herself out of the trance like state she had put herself in.

"Rick." She smiled with excitement. "How are you? Are you okay?"

"Fine," Rick replied. "What exactly are you doing here?"

"I wanted to see you, to thank you for saving my life."

"What's she talking about, Rick?" Ellie interrupted.

Alison raised an eyebrow, then shook her head and told Ellie, "You're receptionist is a hero, he saved my life a week ago and he obviously didn't tell anyone."

"Because I didn't want to make a big deal about it – anyone would have saved your life, Miss Chance."

"I'm not so sure about that," she mumbled. "And it's Alison."

"Well, Alison, you've seen me and thanked me, are we done here?" Rick asked her.

"No, we're not – I didn't track you down just to thank you. I want to take you out to lunch, as I feel that a simple thank you isn't enough."

Rick held his hand up and showed Alison his wedding ring and told her that he was already taken.

"I've met your wife, I know you're married, I don't think she would care about taking the man who saved my life out for a free lunch."

"I'll go if you want someone to take," said Ellie.

Alison glared at Ellie, who backed down and walked away knowing that she had outstayed her welcome.

"One thing you should know about me, Rick, is I never take no for an answer – so get your things and join me in the limo," insisted Alison, as she turned her back on him and left the building feeling proud of herself.

Minutes later Alison was sitting in the limo waiting for Rick to appear. She began to clench her fists, getting agitated as time went by.

"I'm telling you, Alison, from what you've told me about him, he doesn't sound keen – let's just go," Tyrone urged.

"No," she yelled. "He'll fucking be here if I have to drag him out of that building myself."

Tyrone then spotted Rick walking over to the limo. He turned to Alison and said, "Heads up." Alison fixed her clothing and her hair to make herself look a bit tidier. She leaned forward, opened the door and told Rick to get in.

Rick sat down in the limo and closed the door. Alison moved closer to him and drooped her arm round the back of his neck and leaned closer to him so that he would smell the scent of her perfume and see her cleavage. "So, where would you like to go for a bite?"

Rick removed her arm as he felt uncomfortable at how close she was getting to him. He then told her about a café just down at the end of the industrial estate he liked to go in. Alison didn't look impressed. "A café? Surely you'd like to go somewhere a bit posher than that." She then reached for a glass and a bottle of champagne. "Here, have some champagne to start off with." But Rick refused.

"I don't drink when I'm at work," Rick explained.

"Then take the rest of the day off and enjoy yourself," Alison insisted.

"Maybe this was a mistake," Rick realized.

As he went to leave, Alison grabbed hold of Rick to stop him. "Take me to the café down at the end of the industrial estate," she told her driver. "I'm sorry, Rick, please forgive me, we'll do what you want."

Tyrone introduced himself to Rick who shook his hand. Rick instantly recognized him and struck up a conversation with him about his two former singers, Megan May and Clarice. This annoyed Alison as she always felt she was living in the shadows of his two successful clients.

Alison felt uncomfortable in 'The Greasy Spoon, Café' as she sat at a little table, cramped with lots of sweaty workers from the industrial estate wearing hi-vis and dirty clothing. She stood out like a sore thumb and caused everyone to turn their heads and notice her. She hated the atmosphere, a combination of noise, body odour and greasy cooking that filled the air.

"God, how can you like this shit?" Alison moaned.

Rick looked up from his menu and explained, "That's the honest smell of hard work – not everyone lives the glamorous celebrity life you know?"

517

"You sound like my fucking manager."

"Well, maybe they're right – they must have worked hard and struggled to get where they are, just like yourself to get noticed."

"Not really, I had a lucky break using YouTube to get noticed."

"Well, I'm sure that ginger haired singer had to work hard to get where he was," Rick explained.

"You mean Ed Sheeran?"

"No, Mick Hucknell from Simply Red."

"Who?" asked Alison.

A waitress called Leanne walked over to the table with a pen and pad at the ready. Alison noticed a big grin on her face and could see that Leanne was nervous.

"We're not ready to order yet," said Alison.

"I could see that…" Leanne paused. "…could I please get an autograph, I'm a huge fan?"

Alison smiled smugly at Leanne. "Did you buy my latest album?"

"Not yet," Leanne replied.

"Fuck off then," snapped Alison.

Rick could see the hurt and disappointment in Leanne's eyes from Alison's behaviour. He closed the menu shut and stood up to leave.

"So, is that what your mother and father wanted you to become – a stuck up bitch?" Rick snapped.

"And your mother and father wanted you to become a receptionist, huh?" argued Alison.

Alison's retaliation hit Rick hard causing him to lose his temper with her. He went on about how she shouldn't judge a person who had no parents. Rick sternly explained that he was given up by his mother, Marcy, and adopted by a man called Richie James prompting Rick to take up the James surname. His mother, if he could call her that, was Ana, who was a pre-op transgender. Life was strange living with them, even if everyone in the flat he lived in left the toilet seat up. As the years passed things got tough between Ana and Richie and eventually their marriage was torn apart. Richie confirmed that he was still a straight man and preferred women and wanted a child of his own, so he walked out and left Ana and Rick behind.

Ana was heartbroken and never fully recovered. She found life hard with Rick. She couldn't connect with him properly and the love she started with, faded. Rick became a constant reminder of the life she used to have

518

with Richie. So, one day out of the blue, she packed her bags and told Rick that the flat that her and Richie once had was now his own. And with that, Ana left and he never saw her again.

Alison sat quietly, she knew she had been put in her place with Rick's life story who she had clearly judged.

"You may have the money, the glamour and the lifestyle but there's one thing you don't have."

"And what's that?" Alison snapped.

"The real you," said Rick. "And, honestly, I don't care for your music." As he walked away and left her sitting in the café looking embarrassed in front of all the eyes that were watching her.

Later that night, Alison was tossing and turning with what Rick had told her. She was mumbling in her sleep like she was upset. But things soon turned into an erotic twist. Alison was dreaming that Rick was kissing her passionately, ravaging her on her silk sheets and she was loving every minute of it. She began moaning in her sleep and panting while her hands were creeping between her legs. She gasped while she rubbed herself, turning herself on more and more as she dreamed of Rick making passionate love to her. Before she knew it she let out a scream when she had her orgasm.

Her eyes snapped open from her dream. Her hands were wet and sticky and she felt clammy while she tried to catch her breath. It was that moment she realized she liked Rick and she would do anything to make up for her behaviour.

She wanted to show Rick the real Alison and no one would stop her getting what she wanted.

When morning broke, Alison was up at the crack of dawn. Tyrone was already in the kitchen, drinking a coffee and reading the paper. When Alison walked into the kitchen, dressed in her gym gear, she had a gleaming smile on her face that got him worried.

"Good morning, Ty, such a beautiful morning," said Alison enthusiastically.

Tyrone couldn't believe it, gone was the selfish foul mouthed bitch he had come to know and now this nice pleasant girl was in front of him. While Alison filled up her water bottle, Tyrone was curious at her change. She wasn't on drugs, he knew that, so he asked her, "Are you feeling okay?"

"Never better – I finally feel happy."

"What? Did you wake up and have an orgasm or something?" Tyrone joked.

"Sort of the other way around," Alison explained.

Tyrone wished he hadn't got an answer to the visual he just got in his head. "I can't explain it, Ty, but I do feel good about myself."

"Are you sure it wasn't because that guy said a few home truths that hurt?"

"I think it was, yes," said Alison. "I think I needed to hear it and find the real me that I used to be."

"Great," Tyrone agreed. "Maybe after your run we can go through your next tour dates."

"No, what I'm going to do is go back to Rick's company and make it up to him for what happened at lunch, the man saved my life, I can't leave it there," Alison insisted.

After her morning exercise, Alison got her driver to take her back to Rick's company. She was greeted by a mixed reception when she walked through the doors as the employees glared at her after what happened the day before. Alison once again found the reception desk empty and no sign of Rick which disappointed her.

She then saw Ellie look up from her desk and waved at her to acknowledge her. Ellie sighed, she was reluctant to go over to her after the hostility she had received from the day before.

"Excuse me – can I have a little service, please?" Alison called.

All eyes turned to Ellie as no one else volunteered to serve Alison. Ellie got up from her desk and walked over to serve her.

"Hello – how can I help?" Ellie asked.

"Hello again – I was looking for Rick."

"He's currently on lunch at the moment."

"At the café?" Alison asked.

"Yes," said Ellie, bluntly.

Alison took out an envelope from her bag and handed it to Ellie. "This is for you."

Ellie looked puzzled. She opened the envelope in front of Alison and took out a ticket to her next concert.

"It's a back stage pass – it's an apology that I didn't sign my autograph and thought it would mean more that you come to my next concert – I'm going to perform one of my songs and you could join the VIPs on stage with me."

Ellie couldn't believe it. She was excited that it would make up for the day before. It changed her attitude towards Alison completely.

"How about a selfie?" Alison suggested.

"Wait right there," said Ellie as she rushed off to get her phone. Alison stood there smiling, she felt good about herself that she made up for what she did and felt even better to see someone happy.

Ellie came running back. Alison put her arm around her and took the phone off her. Ellie hugged into her while Alison took the photo.

"That will make your Instagram and Facebook friends jealous." Alison laughed.

"Thank you," Ellie replied.

"I'll see you at the concert – till then." Alison walked out, leaving Ellie admiring her new photo.

Leanne took an all-day breakfast over to Rick who was sitting at the table reading a newspaper. When she put it on the table, she saw Alison walk in.

"Holy shit – she's back," said Leanne.

Rick put his paper down to see Alison waving at him. "You've got to be kidding me."

"You've certainly made an impression on her, Rick," Leanne mumbled.

As Alison walked over, Leanne walked away. Rick stood up and told her, "Look, Alison, I just want to eat my lunch in peace."

"That's sweet, but I'm after Leanne," Alison replied.

Leanne overheard and stopped in her tracks. Alison took out a VIP ticket and handed it to her. Just like Ellie, Leanne was excited and was jumping for joy and hugged Alison in appreciation.

Rick watched and found it hard to believe and thought that this was some sort of an act.

"I'll see you tomorrow evening, okay?" said Alison.

"I'll be there," replied Leanne as she left for the kitchen.

Alison then went over to Rick who had thrown down the paper on his table. "A bit coy isn't it?"

"I don't understand."

"One minute you're an utter bitch and now you're playing Miss kind celebrity?"

"Well, that's your fault," argued Alison.

"My fault? How is it my fault?" Rick snapped.

"I'll tell you if you sit down, please."

Rick gave Alison the benefit of the doubt and the chance to explain herself. She told Rick that he was the reason she had a change of heart. Ever since he told her a little home truth, she laid in bed and thought about all the wrong things she had done in her life and meeting Rick was the best thing that could have happened to her.

Alison held Ricks hands. "It's you Rick, you're my hero, that's why I've decided that all the VIPs I wronged, along with Leanne and Ellie, I want to make up for it – that's why I want to invite you to my concert tomorrow night."

"Does it feel good? Not to be selfish and to do the right thing?" Rick asked.

Alison smiled with delight. "It does – It feels good to be the real me, something you wanted me to be."

As Rick ate his all-day breakfast, Alison just sat in front of him not speaking a word. Rick began to feel a little uncomfortable, until he asked, "Not being rude, I thought we were done here."

"You haven't given me an answer."

"Answer to what?" Rick asked.

"I've invited you to my concert as a thank you for saving my life – front row."

"Okay, Alison – you remember I told you that I'm not keen on your music, right?"

"You did," Alison held Rick's hands again. "Come to my concert, you may have a change of heart and like what you see."

Rick squeezed Alison's hands and told her, "I can't – I'm spending time with my wife."

"Think about it," said Alison as she pulled her hands away from Rick and stood up to leave. "Just think about it, please – I hope to see you there."

Alison walked out of the café, leaving Rick with a decision to make.

When Rick got home later that evening, he walked into the living room to see Robyn on the phone in front of a reality program.

"Yes – that was her." Robyn laughed hysterically. Rick kissed her on the cheek then sat down next to her "Okay, I've got to go, Rick's just come home – See you later." Robyn ended the call and felt that Rick was a little

522

different than normal. "Everything okay?"

"No, not really," said Rick.

"Do you want me to pour you a drink?" Robyn asked.

"Please."

Robyn got up and went over to the drinks counter to pour Rick a single malt scotch. When she handed it to him, she kissed him then sat on the arm of the chair.

Rick told Robyn that Alison came to see him again and had invited him to her concert tomorrow night as a thank you for making up for saving her life and what happened the day before. Rick made sure that he wasn't going to go as he had Robyn to spend his time with.

"Oh, honey – that's so sweet," said Robyn as she kissed him again. "You should go – I won't be here tomorrow night."

"Really? Where are you going?" Rick acted surprised.

"Out with the girls – it's been ages – that was them on the phone and the best part is, it's not going to cost me a penny – they're paying," Robyn explained.

"So, it doesn't bother you – me going to Alison's concert?" Rick asked.

"Of course, not – you don't think I trust you?"

"I didn't mean it like that, Robyn."

Robyn put her arms around Rick's neck and pulled him close to her. "Look, you're a hero, you're my hero in fact – I am so lucky to have you – so go to her silly little concert it's not like you're going to cheat on me with her, she's a big celebrity and I know you're not a cheater, you're a good man."

"I love you," said Rick.

"I love you, too," Robyn replied.

The Open Door bar was in full swing by the time Robyn arrived. People were dancing on the black and white checkered dance floor, while others were sitting at tables and in booths drinking and laughing. Robyn looked around for Anita, Lindsey and Chloe to see if they had arrived.

"Robyn," Chloe shouted, waving from a corner booth. "Over here."

Robyn was delighted to see her girls after being away from them for so long. She walked over to them with a big grin on her face.

"Hey – it's so good to see you," said Lindsey, as she exchanged hugs and kisses. "It's been too long."

Robyn sat and joined the girls with glasses and bottles of wine that were already flowing.

"So, aren't you going to tell us all about it?" asked Anita.

Robyn was puzzled to know what Anita was on about. "I'm confused – what?"

Anita elbowed Robyn in the ribs. "Rick of course – it must be great being married to a hero."

"Wait – how do you know about that?" asked Robyn.

"Alison Chance of course – she came to see each one of us," Chloe explained. "She told us that you haven't seen us in a long while and gave us a load of money to treat you to this girls night out – this night is on her."

Robyn went all quiet. Thoughts flooded through her paranoid mind that this was a hidden agenda.

"So, as you're out tonight, what's Rick doing?" Lindsey asked.

"He's at Alison's concert," said Robyn as she crossed her arms with an annoyed expression on her face.

All three girls looked at each other with a jealous expression. They would have done anything to go to one of her concerts as they always missed out to get tickets.

"Are you shitting me? How did he get tickets?" said Chloe.

"Alison offered him a VIP spot."

"And you chose to spend the night with us instead of going to the concert – that's sweet." Lindsey smiled.

"I wasn't invited – it was just Rick," Robyn explained.

"Sounds to me like Alison wanted him all to herself," Anita suggested.

"That would explain why she gave you a load of money to get me out the way," Robyn implied. "That bitch is trying it on with my husband."

3

Robyn paced up and down in the cold night air with her phone pressed against her ear. Ring after ring the phone rang. She became agitated as Rick never answered. When it went straight to voice mail, she redialled and called him again.

"Come on, Rick, pick up," Robyn panicked.

Anita, Chloe and Lindsey stood outside vaping while Robyn continued to pace. Eventually Anita stopped Robyn and said, "Could you stop? – You're making me dizzy."

Chloe put herself forward to try and help Robyn calm down. "Robyn – I think you're looking too much into this."

"What do you mean?" said Robyn, who didn't like Chloe's attitude to the situation.

"I mean, she's a big celebrity pop star – I don't think she would take that much interest in Rick as he's just a receptionist," Chloe explained. "Celebrities don't go for that."

Robyn shook her head in disgust at Chloe's shallow attitude. "And this is why you're still single."

Anita stepped in between them before things got too heated "Okay, stop – just calm down."

Robyn always looked up to Anita. She was the favourite out of her three girlies. She had done everything right. Got a good education, a loving and loyal husband and a daughter. Robyn was envious at times but she never let it get to her too much.

"Look – why don't we just go back inside and have a drink – save something of this night as we haven't seen in each other in a long time?" Anita suggested.

"Agreed," said Chloe and Lindsey.

"Robyn – call Rick again – leave him a voicemail and a text message. Get him to call you, so you can stop worrying over nothing – we'll see you inside."

The three girls left Robyn calling Rick one more time.

Even with Anita's advice, she couldn't stop pacing and worrying herself silly. "Come on, pick up, pick up."

Meanwhile, Rick had joined the VIP queue. Halfway up he saw Leanne talking with Ellie. He waved to get their attention but they didn't spot him as they were too engrossed, gossiping about Alison.

"Rick James, right?" said Tyrone, distracting Rick from his train of thought. "I remember you – if you'd like to follow me."

Tyrone took Rick past the security checks and then to the backstage where Alison was preparing herself for the show.

Alison wore long black see through stockings that showed off her smooth legs, while her top was black and sparkly which pushed up the top half of her cleavage. Her long blonde hair and pouty red lips would make any man want to kiss her, but Rick was different. He didn't feel anything like that towards her as he was faithful to his wife.

Alison was delighted when she saw Rick standing with Tyrone. "You came." Alison threw her arms around Rick and squeezed him tightly. "I'm so glad you did – I would've been disappointed if you didn't."

"You're in the front row centre, Rick," Tyrone explained. "Come, I'll show you."

Alison could tell that Tyrone urgently wanted to get Rick away from her. But she was too demanding and pulled Rick towards her. "Wait – I haven't had time to explain everything to you – why don't we go to my dressing room?"

"Alison – you're on in ten minutes – there's no time for that," Tyrone explained.

When Rick left with Tyrone, Alison sighed with lust filled eyes. "See you soon," she called.

The stadium was plunged into darkness. The bass of the music built up getting the fans excited until an explosion of coloured lights filled up the stadium followed by pyrotechnics. The crowd went wild when Alison walked out with her backup dancers and started to perform.

Rick was looking at the crowd around him. He was the only one who was the odd one out that wasn't going crazy over her. All he could think about was Robyn.

Rick took out his phone to text her and noticed all the missed calls. He was about to message her back, but one of the crowd next to him barged him and knocked it out of his hand, causing it to break. He picked it up, but there was no power to it and the screen was smashed.

Alison danced her way to the front of the stage where Rick was standing. She bent over, wiggled her bum and made her boobs jiggle while staring at him with lustful eyes. She blew him a kiss, then walked away to join her dancers.

Once her introduction performance was over, Alison called out to all the VIP girls to join her on stage. Her security escorted a lot of excited girls to the stage where Alison explained what was about to happen.

"First, I would like to thank you all for coming tonight it means a lot to me," said Alison speaking into the microphone while the crowd cheered. "As some of you missed out on the VIP treatment at my last concert, I would like to ask all my VIPs to dance alongside me to my cover song, 'I Was Born to Love You'."

Rick couldn't believe how wild the crowd went over Alison, when the song started. It proved to him that she was definitely a crowd puller and they all loved her music and performance. Deep inside, he admired how well she worked with the crowd. He was even more surprised when he saw Alison go up to Ellie who mimicked her dance moves perfectly. He could see that Alison was impressed with her. Little did Alison know, as Ellie was a fan, she had danced to her song so many times that she practically memorized the whole routine.

As the song came to an end, all her VIPs were hyped beyond belief that they had been part of her concert and danced with her on stage. They were then even more surprised when Alison told one of her professional dancers to take a photo of her and her VIPs. In a big girl group hug, the photo was taken and as the VIPs walked off stage feeling it was the happiest night of their lives, Alison told them, "I'll tag you all into the upload – thanks for coming."

In the line-up of her concert she would have started her next song straight away, but she had waited for this moment to interrupt the night and talk to the crowd.

"Before I carry on – I would like to be serious for a moment," said Alison as she walked to the front of the stage. "A week ago, there was an attempt on my life, I could have been killed, that was, until this man saved my life."

The spotlight hit Rick who looked rather embarrassed.

"Rick James, everyone, someone who wanted to remain anonymous, but, Rick, I think people want to know who my hero is and to stop you being modest – come join me on stage. Rick James, everyone."

The crowd cheered and applauded Rick, as he was escorted onto the stage by one of the security. One of the dancers came out from backstage and placed a chair in the centre of the stage. Rick was puzzled why they did that and was a little annoyed at what Alison just did.

"Sit down, please," Alison ordered.

When Rick sat down, Alison stretched her leg out so it was over his legs.

"Rick – as a big thank you for what you did for me, I am going to perform my hit number one song, 'Naughty Bad Girl'."

Rick knew this wasn't good. The music video of "Naughty Bad Girl", was exactly what it sounded like. It was one of Alison's raunchier sexy songs that had complaints from parents of the kids that had watched it.

The lights went down and plunged the stadium into darkness. All Rick could see was the twinkling of the lights coming from people's camera phones. When the spotlights hit the stage, Alison stood in front of Rick giving him a sinister smile. The bass of the music built up to the intro of the song, making Alison put the microphone to her lips and sing her heart out in front of him.

Alison walked around Rick making sure she didn't break eye contact with him. The crowd roared; they were loving her performance, but Rick was feeling uncomfortable.

Meanwhile in *the Open Door* bar, Robyn had given up calling Rick and had finally relaxed for the night. The drinks had flown well between her and the girls, with empty wine bottles and glasses occupying their table.

Chloe was already drunk. Her eyes had been heavy most of the night and she had constantly been yawning. When she looked up at the TV, she saw the concert of Alison Chance, being aired live. She was even more surprised when she saw Alison dancing around Rick.

"Jesus, I must be totally wasted," Chloe mumbled.

Anita, Lindsey and Robyn laughed in amusement. They thought she was joking, until Robyn looked up at the TV and dropped her wine glass.

"Rick," Robyn screamed. She stood up and rushed over to the TV and was horrified to see Alison's performance on her husband.

Alison spread her legs apart. She placed her hand on her neck and ran it down past her cleavage, all the way down to her belly and finishing between her legs. She then stretched her leg out and rested it on Rick's legs. She bent forward while singing into the microphone and then kissed him on his cheek.

Rick wanted to run away. But in front of a crowded stadium and the cameras, he was scared to move and make a scene. He wanted the night to be over quickly, as it turned into a night of regret.

Alison pulled her leg away and danced around him one more time. She then stood in front of him so she was facing the stage. Alison bent over so her cleavage looked like it was going to fall out in front of the crowd. She wiggled her butt in front of Rick, then fell backwards landing in his lap and wiggled her butt into his groin while she put her arm around the back of his neck and lightly brushed her wet lips over his.

Her performance wasn't that of a pop star. Alison's performance was more like a sexy lap dancer that couldn't wait to get her hands on him.

When the song was over, Alison got off Rick and lightly touched the bulge in his trousers. She looked at him and smiled cheekily to him, knowing that he was aroused at her dance. The crowd roared as Alison bowed. They thought it was all staged and innocent, but what they didn't know was the truth that Rick had a wife and there would be consequences.

Robyn had her hands over her mouth. She was shocked at what she had seen Alison do to her husband on TV. Her eyes flooded with tears, she felt betrayed and broken. Anita ran over to Robyn to help her while snapping at the barman, "Will you turn that shit off, please?"

Instead of turning the TV off, the barman changed the channel while Anita took Robyn over to their table.

Chloe could see how distraught Robyn was and tried to comfort her by telling her, "It's not his fault, he did nothing wrong, it was all her doing."

"Chloe's right, Robyn," Lindsey assured. "You've told us many times that Rick is faithful to you and would never cheat."

"This is harassment – technically you could sue her," said Anita.

But Robyn knew it would be pointless to drag Alison to court. Robyn and Rick struggled with money at the best of times. Alison had it all and could easily destroy them financially by twisting the facts.

"What do you want to do, Robyn?" asked Chloe.

"I want to go home," Robyn replied.

When Alison walked off the stage after finishing her encore, the lights came on and the crowd began to leave the stadium.

Ellie and Leanne had their eyes on Rick the rest of the night after the sexualized performance. They pushed themselves through the crowd and made their way down to the front to see how humiliated he looked.

"Rick," Ellie called "Are you Okay?"

"What do you think?" Rick mumbled. "I can't go home. If Robyn saw that, then…"

Just as Ellie was about to say something to comfort him, Tyrone had interrupted them by saying, "Sorry, girls, but Rick needs to come with me."

Tyrone pulled Rick away from the girls as they made their way backstage. It was then Rick made a decision and pulled himself away.

"Look enough is enough," Rick insisted. "I can't do this, I'm going home."

But Tyrone stopped Rick from leaving. "Look, I can understand how uncomfortable this is making you feel and that performance back there, I don't know what's wrong with Alison, she's acting weird, but she has one more thing you need to attend and I promise you, I'll make sure she leaves you alone."

Rick knew inside that all this was a mistake. With Tyrone's strong advice, and a promise it would end, well he had made it this far and this was the final hurdle. He hesitantly agreed and followed Tyrone to the backstage room.

When Rick walked in, the room was dimly lit. There was a table set out for a candlelit dinner for two. Rick couldn't see what was under the plates but it smelt delightful and slightly familiar to him.

"Hi," Alison spoke, softly.

Alison stood in front of Rick dressed in a white floral party prom dress. Her hair had been done up like she was about to attend a high school prom.

Rick didn't know what to say. Sure, she looked stunning but there was something about her that started to give him the creeps.

"I hope you are hungry; I got your favourite delivered to me." Alison smiled. "Please, sit down."

Favourite? Rick thought as he sat down at the table. Alison removed the cover of the plate to reveal a piping hot, all day breakfast.

"It's from the café that Leanne works at."

For once, Rick saw for the first time that Alison had taken notice of something he liked, which made her more human in his eyes. Alison sat down in front of Rick and revealed her plate to be the same.

"Wait – I thought you didn't agree with all this unhealthy food?" Rick assumed.

"I guess you don't know me the way think you do," smiled Alison, as some egg yolk dripped down her chin. She wiped it away then sucked her fingers in front of him. She could tell that Rick had something on his mind "Care to share what you're thinking about."

"Robyn hates me having this sort of food. She doesn't know I go to the café."

Alison put her knife and fork down and couldn't believe that Rick had to sneak around to have food that he wanted. "Rick, you're married, you shouldn't keep secrets from your wife – tell her."

"I have done in the past. That's what caused the rows."

"Sounds like you're not happy in your marriage?" Alison assumed.

"It's complicated. Robyn was a party animal before I met her. Her energy was what drew me to her. Then when we got married, jobs got in the way. She worked long hours and didn't have the money to do that any more. I saw a change in her and she seemed more miserable."

Alison was loving hearing the story. In her mind, this was a perfect opportunity to reveal something she had been keeping from him.

"What about kids? I'm surprised you and her haven't had any."

"I did. She made it very clear to me that she never wanted kids as she didn't want the responsibility to look after them as it would stop her going out partying."

"That's ridiculous, Rick," said Alison. "Did you ever consider that she wasn't the one for you? Why did you marry her and give up on what your wanted'?

"I don't know," Rick replied.

Alison got out of her chair and stood before him. "I have a confession – ever since you came out of the blue and saved my life, you're all I've thought about. You're honest. You tell me the truth that I need to hear. I want you."

Rick didn't know what to say. He was dumbfounded and couldn't think straight.

"I wore this dress for a reason, as I missed out on my prom and was hoping that I could pretend I had you as my prom date," Alison explained. "I wore this dress, so you could take it off me."

But Rick couldn't get any words out. He couldn't move or believe what he was hearing. Alison waited for him to make a move. She was hoping he was going to get up and undress her. Eventually she got tired of waiting and decided she would do it herself. She removed both the shoulder straps and let her dress flop to the floor. She placed her hands on her hips and stood naked in front of him. She placed her hands on her perky large breasts and played with them.

"Do you like what you see, Rick?"

Rick swallowed hard. He wanted to run out the door and never look back, but for some unknown reason he couldn't look away. He was so hard and aroused that he couldn't control himself.

Alison took her chair, pulled it further away and sat down in front of him with her legs spread apart while she stroked herself. "I know what I want, I want a husband, I want babies and most importantly, I want you."

The more Alison stroked herself, the more she was turning herself on. She stared at him while her breathing increased and she began to moan out loud.

Even though the temptress was right in front of him, Rick finally found the strength to get out and leave her to it. Alison would have reacted angrily for him to leave her there like that, but she didn't. She was too far gone to stop, she carried on keeping the image of him, playing with herself until she came.

Her orgasm had gone straight to her head. Feeling dizzy, warm and wet, she regained her breath and felt satisfied. "You can run, but you'll never get away from me, I will own you, Rick James."

When Rick got home late, he walked through the door to find Anita comforting Robyn, who he could see was clearly upset. The look on Robyn's face said it all, she saw Alison's performance and was now questioning their marriage.

"Can I say something, please?" Rick asked. He could tell that Robyn didn't want to hear anything that came out of his mouth, but Anita gave Rick the benefit of the doubt.

Rick came clean and told them what happened after the concert. He mentioned that her manager escorted him to a backstage room where a meal was waiting for him and the promise that Alison would never bug him again after this night. He then admitted that it was all a plan to get him alone, as Alison stripped off in front of him and wanted him to take her.

"Jesus." Anita was shocked. "That's sexual harassment, Rick – you should go to the police and you could sue her for this."

"I plan to," Rick agreed.

"Why?" Robyn asked. "What's the point? Isn't our marriage over?"

"Robyn, you can't think like that," said Anita. "Rick's innocent in this – he saved her life and she's obsessed with him – it needs to stop and be exposed."

But Robyn couldn't think straight. All she saw was the worst which made her sick to her stomach and with that she left for the bedroom and didn't speak to him for the rest of the night.

Back at Alison's home, things were getting heated in the kitchen. Alison's face was red, filled with anger like she was about to explode. She held a red apple in her hand that she had taken from a glass fruit bowl in front of her and felt her hand crushing the apple with pressure as Tyrone shouted and hollered at her about her actions she took at the concert.

"That's the last time, you hear me," Tyrone shouted. "You stay away from Rick James."

"You can't tell me what to do," Alison snapped.

"Oh yes I can – you're contracted under me," Tyrone referred. "The man is married and I promised him that it would be the last time you contact him – you leave him alone – he can sue you for harassment, have you even thought about that?"

"Really? If that's true, then why hasn't he done that already? I don't think he minded, when I got naked and started masturbating in front of him," said Alison, smiling. "Besides, he isn't a happily married man, but I could make him happy."

And from that moment, Tyrone made a final decision. He couldn't believe what he was hearing coming out of her dirty mouth. He knew he couldn't represent her any more. "Okay then fine, we're done, I'm terminating your contract."

With that, Alison knew that he was bluffing, that he wouldn't really do that. She was his star. He needed her. She turned her back on him and left the room.

The next day, after having a rough night on the sofa, Rick got ready for work. Normally he would see Robyn doing the same thing, but this time there was no sign of her. Rick checked the bedroom and saw Robyn laying on her side. Her red tearful eyes stared at him as if they were dead.

"You're going to be late," Rick spoke, softly.

"I'm not going – I don't feel well," Robyn whispered.

"Don't you think we need to talk?" asked Rick, but she never answered him, causing Rick to leave for work with their unresolved issues.

But it wasn't just Rick who had a bad night's sleep. Alison was lying in bed while her head flooded with Tyrone's outburst. With all the humiliation she did to Rick, her guilt began to sink in. Alison wanted to make things right and decided to get in touch with Tyrone, just in case he did terminate her contract.

She got out of bed and threw on her pink robe over her white silk nighty, then made her way downstairs and into the kitchen.

"Ow," said Alison, as pain shot through her foot. When she checked what she stepped on, she discovered a small fragment of glass was in the bottom of her foot. She took it out, causing it to bleed and then noticed a trail of glass that lead to a trail of blood which was coming from Tyrone's dead body.

4

Ellie was browsing for shoes while she took her lunch break. Most of the morning she had constantly looked over at Rick who had been keeping himself to himself. Ellie knew this wasn't the normal Rick she knew, all happy and bubbly which was what she liked about him, but now he was in a world of his own and hadn't even said good morning to her like he always did.

Ellie continued to surf the Internet and then came across something shocking. The news about Tyrone had hit the Internet. She got up out of her chair and walked over to Rick to tell him about it.

"He's dead," said Ellie, bluntly.

Rick looked at Ellie blankly, not knowing what she was on about. "Who's dead?"

"Tyrone, Alison's manager," Ellie explained. She took over his computer and brought the news article up. Rick couldn't believe it as he was only talking to him the night before. Rick read the details that Tyrone was found dead in Alison's kitchen.

Just then they were interrupted by Robyn who was standing at the desk. She asked Rick if they could have a private moment to talk. Rick agreed and took Robyn into a small meeting room next to the board room.

Robyn admitted she had given things a lot of thought and came to a decision that Anita was right. Rick wasn't to blame and it was time to go to the police and sue Alison. Rick didn't think it was a good idea, what with the current news that had transpired. He assured Robyn that Alison wouldn't be contacting him as she would be focusing on the loss of her manager.

Three weeks later, everyone was gathered to say goodbye to Tyrone. His former stars, Clarice and Megan May, had turned up to say goodbye to their dear friend. Megan, with her husband Jason and son Mark, arrived and caused the media to go crazy with her arrival.

Inside the dimly lit church, Jason and Mark sat among the friends and family of Tyrone while Megan got reacquainted with Clarice who she hadn't seen in years. Her head soon turned when Alison walked in, dressed in a long black dress and wearing a dark pair of sunglasses. She didn't say a word as she made her way over to Tyrone's coffin.

"They'll get whoever did this to you – I promise," Alison whispered.

She sat down at the front as the vicar began to talk about Tyrone. Alison was silent the whole way through, she was too upset to speak. She thought how kind he was to her and how much of a bitch she was to him. She felt bad for the way things had ended between them.

The doors to the church distracted everyone inside as Rick walked in. He sat at the back to hide from drawing too much attention, but Alison had already spotted him. To his surprise, she didn't smile or acknowledge him. She ignored the fact he was there and focused on thinking about Tyrone. Alison couldn't hold her emotions in any more and began to weep in front of everyone.

Once Tyrone's body was laid to rest, everyone began to mingle. Rick helped himself to a few rolls at the buffet. He didn't realize that a famous face was trying to get to where he was standing.

"Excuse me, can I get there, please?" Megan asked.

Rick stepped aside and was surprised to see Megan standing in front of him. "Sorry, Miss May."

"I'm sorry, I haven't seen you, before have I? Were you close to Tyrone?"

"Not really? I met him a couple of times. Last time I saw him was at Alison's concert – he was a good man."

"He was my close friend, we had a lot of good years together and to correct you, it's Mrs May, my husband and son are over there." Megan pointed as they were talking to Clarice.

"My wife, Robyn, was a big fan of yours when she was a girl – she always wanted to meet you," Rick explained.

Megan smiled and a thought popped into her head. Megan took a napkin and her lipstick out of her bag and wrote, 'To Robyn – Megan May'. She then handed the napkin to Rick. "This is for her."

"Wow – thank you," said Rick. "She's going to love this." He then noticed Megan's small bump.

"Congratulations by the way."

Megan looked down at her belly and smiled. "Thank you – we've just had the twenty week scan, it's a girl, we're going to call her, Taylor."

536

Just then, Rick felt uncomfortable when Alison walked over to him. But that feeling soon went away when he saw a change in her.

"What are you doing here?" said Alison.

"Just thought I would come by and pay my respects," Rick explained. "How are you?"

"Shit – I feel like shit," said Alison. "I am so sorry, for everything that I did – I wasn't myself – I just wish the police would catch the person that killed him."

Rick being the man he was, always thought that when you get an apology, all you have to do is forgive them and that's what he did. Alison was grateful. She didn't' want to feel terrible any more. She wanted to feel happy, but knew it wouldn't happen for a long time.

"Thank you for coming." Alison smiled and walked away, but she wanted to know something and looked back to see Rick looking at her. When she looked away, she smiled to herself.

Later that evening, Alison sat on a white fluffy sofa in front of a roaring fire. Alison pulled up the strap to her blue silk nighty, covering her right breast that was hanging out. She then placed a glass of whiskey to her lips as the fire reflected in her eyes. The memory of Rick watching her as she walked away was all she thought about. She was delusional. She thought that Rick had feelings for her and wanted to be with her.

Alison rubbed herself and felt the wetness between her legs. She closed her eyes and pictured Rick making love to her and letting out a loud passionate gasp as he impregnated her.

It was then that Alison made a final decision and knew what she wanted to do. She finished her drink, got changed, grabbed her bag and met her driver outside, ready to take her to where she wanted to go.

Meanwhile, Robyn was sitting on the sofa with her legs up watching TV. The news was reporting from the red carpet at the movie awards where a man had got down on one knee, onto the red carpet, and proposed to, movie sensation, Jessica George.

A knock at the door distracted Robyn. She sighed at the thought of getting up and missing the identity of who was proposing.

When she answered the door, she saw the one person who she never thought she would see again.

"Hi," Alison whispered. "I'm sorry to bother you like this late."

"Ricks not here – he's out with his work colleagues," Robyn explained.

"I'm not here to talk to Rick," Alison replied. "I'm here to talk to you, please."

But Robyn was looking at Alison with daggers, as her hatred for the girl hadn't changed.

"I would like to apologize for my behaviour and the way I hurt you – could you ever forgive me?"

Robyn thought about what Rick would do. Rick was kind and forgiving. He wasn't the type to hold a grudge. She nodded and then added, "I'm sorry to hear about your manager."

"Thank you," spoke Alison, softly.

It was then that Robyn decided to do the right thing and allowed Alison inside.

Once Alison had sat down, Robyn asked her if she wanted a drink. Alison refused her offer and got to the point of the real reason why she was there.

She made an offer to Robyn of 6.6 million dollars that she could transfer to her bank account immediately, enough money for her to enjoy her life and go out partying like the party girl she used to be and in return Alison would buy Rick off her. Her point was simple, when Rick told her that he wanted kids and Robyn didn't, Alison could give him children and the life he deserved as he wanted a family of her own.

Robyn's face was bright red as she exploded in front of Alison. "Who the fuck do you think you are? Is that what you do? Just because you have a load of fucking money – you think you can buy love and not earn it?"

Alison leapt off the sofa and followed Robyn who had stormed off into the kitchen. Robyn grabbed her phone off of the kitchen counter.

"What do you think you're doing?" Alison asked. "Doesn't it make more sense for Rick to be with me?"

"I'm calling the Police, bitch," Robyn screamed. "This is sexual harassment and when we get a lawyer, we're going to sue the living backside off of you."

Before Robyn could finish dialling the number, Alison had already seen something in the corner of her eye on the draining board. Alison grabbed hold of a kitchen knife and plunged it into Robyn's gut.

Alison twisted the knife, causing Robyn to scream and drop the phone.

"You lot are so hellbent on stopping me and him from being together – I have always got what I wanted one way or another."

Alison pulled the bloody knife out of Robyn and then cut her throat. Robyn collapsed to the floor, covering her hands in the blood as she held her throat while she gargled and spat it out.

"This was a lot more graphic than what I did weeks back." Alison smiled. She then confessed to Alison that she had returned to the kitchen when Tyrone had threatened to terminate her contract. Alison was still wearing long black silk prom gloves, so that she didn't get fingerprints on the glass fruit bowl that she picked up and smashed over Tyrone's head. "What do you think of that?"

But Robyn had died before she could give Alison an answer to that question. Alison smiled to herself that everything was beginning to fall into place and she could continue the next part of her plan.

An hour later, Rick came home. He had had too much booze and was feeling rather mellow.

"Robyn?" Rick called. He was surprised to not see her. It wasn't late and the TV was still on. "Where are you? I'm home."

Rick was concerned when she didn't answer him. When he got to the kitchen it was dark. As he stepped in the kitchen and reached out to turn the light on, he slipped and fell to the floor with a loud thump.

"God damn it," Rick mumbled.

Rick got to his feet and flicked the light on. It was then a look of horror filled his face when he discovered that his hands and clothes were covered in blood. Robyn's blood.

Weeks had passed by since Rick found Robyn's body.

He had been taken to the police station, asked constant questions and breathalysed as a suspect for Robyn's murder. After his colleagues testified to his whereabouts as witnesses and insisted that Rick loved Robyn and would never have hurt her, let alone kill her, Rick was off the suspect list and now was standing in a church staring at the coffin that Robyn was in.

Rick was an emotional wreck that day. He didn't speak to anyone that came up to him giving their repetitive condolences.

Once Robyn had been buried, Rick stood at her graveside for over an hour. His attention hadn't been distracted till one person who he never thought he would see stood by his side.

"What are you doing here, Alison?"

"I'm returning the favour – you came to Tyrone's funeral when you hardly knew him – I hardly knew your wife – so, I'm doing this out of respect."

"Thank you – it was a nice thought."

Alison smiled slightly at Rick as she stared into his eyes. She wanted to hold him and look after him, but in her mind, she knew it was the wrong time to do such a thing.

All of a sudden, they were bombarded by the media. They came in droves, like it was a Black Friday sale. One man holding a small recorder waved it in front of Rick's face, shouting, "Rick – Rick – what did it feel like to be a suspect to your wife's murder?"

Alison could see that Rick wanted to burst into tears. So, to protect him, she stepped forward and thumped the reporter hard in the face.

"For god's sake – what the fuck is wrong with you people – the man is saying goodbye to his wife you fucking ghouls," Alison screamed, as she helped Rick get away from the crowd and took him to her limo.

Minutes later, Rick was staring out the window. Alison never spoke a word. She thought it would be best to leave Rick with his thoughts and talk to him when he was ready.

After driving around in circles for fifteen minutes, Rick finally spoke. "Thank you, Alison, for doing that – for helping me – and you've got one hell of right hook."

"Don't mention it." Alison smiled.

"You don't have a lot to say? I thought you were quite the chatterbox," Rick mentioned.

"After what you've been through, I thought I would just let you be – there's nothing like having someone talk and talk while you're not really paying attention to what they're saying."

"True," Rick agreed.

Alison ordered her driver to drop Rick off at home, but Rick admitted that he was staying in a Holiday Inn as it was too painful to stay at home, what with everything that happened and the constant memories that haunted him.

When the limo arrived at the Holiday Inn, Alison asked Rick for his phone. She stored her number and told him if he ever needed a friend to talk to, she would make time for him. Rick was appreciative of the offer, but assured her that he had his close friends. Alison didn't argue, she accepted his decision and said goodbye to him before the limo drove away.

Another week had passed by and Rick had returned to his home. His first night was an uneasy one. He had stored the photos away of him and Robyn as a constant reminder of who he lost. He spent a sleepless night and called in sick because of his tiredness, they understood what he was going through.

The next night he called Ellie, but there was no answer. He messaged Leanne on Facebook, but she never replied. His mum and dad were the last he called, only to discover that they were away on holiday. Of course, the last person he would think about calling was Alison, who picked up instantly.

"Rick, are you okay?"

Clearly, he wasn't. He was lonely and upset and was hoping they could talk.

"Why don't you come to my place? I'll send my driver to collect you," Alison insisted.

Before Rick knew it, he was in the back of the limo being driven to Alison's home. It didn't take too much imagination to think of the type of place she lived in.

The limo pulled up outside a large set of iron gates.

They followed a trail of lights down a long-stretched road with acres of land surrounding it until it pulled up outside the doors of a mansion. The driver got out and opened the door for Rick.

When Rick stepped out, Alison was standing at the top of the steps looking rather glamorous. Her hair had been done up, while dark mascara and red lipstick had been applied. To Rick it looked like she had lost weight as her see through silk black dress made her figure look so slender and her large earrings hung from her ears like a pair of chandeliers.

Alison gave Rick a gentle hug and stroked his back. She took his hand and led him inside while her driver closed the front door for her.

Rick stood in a grand hallway with doors leading off to different rooms on either side. A large sweeping staircase led up to the upper floors. Rick couldn't believe the size and scale of the place.

"Wow, that's impressive." Rick's voice echoed.

"This is what made my buy the place – it's perfect to practice my acoustics – come on through."

Rick followed Alison though the doors to the left of him and entered a large living room. There wasn't any furniture to the first half of the room, but there was in the second half. Alison sat down on a white fluffy sofa. A glass coffee table was in front of her which sat on a large white fluffy rug that led towards a roaring fire place. To the right of her was a bookcase with various novels and music related books.

"Wow – that's posh," said Rick, pointing over to the grand piano that was near the window.

"I spent years trying to find one and it had to be the right one, the one that sounded right to me."

"But don't they all sound the same?" Rick asked.

"I mean the one that sounded right in my heart," Alison explained. She patted the empty seat next to her. "Sit down beside me."

When Rick sat down, he couldn't help but wonder why the other half of the room wasn't furnished. Alison told him that she used that space to practice her dance routines. On the coffee table was a bottle of red wine, two glasses and a plate of cheese and crackers.

"Wine?" Alison offered.

Rick didn't have to hesitate. The way he had been feeling, he knew he needed a drink to dull the pain. As Alison poured the wine into the glasses, Rick kept on looking over at the piano.

"Is it all right if I have a look at that?"

"Of course," Alison replied.

Rick wandered over to the piano. He was fascinated how smooth and polished it felt. It looked brand new and he could see himself in the reflection. But what Rick didn't know, as his attention was distracted, was Alison had taken a small plastic pouch out of her pocket with pink powder in and tipped it into his wine. She stuffed the empty pouch down the side of the sofa, then swirled his wine around so the powder would mix. She then grabbed both glasses and handed Rick his.

"Cheers," said Alison.

Instead of toasting their glasses, Rick had already downed half of his drink. Alison was sipping hers slowly. She was pleased that he was eager to drink as she couldn't wait for the substance to get to work on Rick's insides.

"So, you like my piano?"

"It's great," Rick replied.

"Would you like me to play something for you?" Alison asked.

"Please."

"Well, drink up then and I'll play for you," Alison ordered.

Alison gulped down her wine until her glass was empty.

Rick was slow at drinking, so Alison lifted the bottom of his glass, so he would drink it faster. When the glass was empty, Alison took both glasses back to the coffee table, then sat down at her piano, moving aside so Rick could sit next to her.

"This is actually a new song, I wrote – called 'You're always forever in my heart'."

Alison sang the slow ballad with such powerful emotion while staring into Rick's eyes. For the first time in his life, he actually had a song that he liked of hers and thought she should do this sort of music more often as he could see her career improve. She stopped halfway and told him that the song wasn't finished.

"Wow – no one has ever written a song for me before."

"Oh – you're mistaken," Alison explained. "It's not for you... well it is, but it's dedicated to your wife, as I know how much you loved her and she will always be forever in your heart."

Rick began to tear up as her words touched his hurt. He began to feel hot and flustered like he was having an adrenaline rush. He wasn't sure, but he began to think that he started to have feelings for Alison. For someone to understand what he's going through and write a dedicated song to his lost wife showed a kindness he had never seen before in Alison.

Whatever Alison put into his drink, began to work a little too well. Rick's eyes became heavy and he looked hot in the face. Rick closed his eyes and leaned towards Alison to kiss her on the lips, but Alison backed away and stopped him.

"Wait – what are you doing?" said Alison. "No, Rick – you're confused. You've just lost your wife, remember?"

Rick backed down. He was confused and wasn't thinking straight. Alison held Rick's hands in hers and said, "Look, I more than like you – I think you know that – but I don't want to be the woman that takes advantage of a man who has just lost the love of his life when he's vulnerable – you understand, right...? Oh... I see."

Alison could clearly see that Rick had an erection when his trousers stood to attention. Rick grabbed hold of Alison and pressed his lips on hers. Alison pulled away and screamed at him, "Stop – please stop."

But Rick didn't. He got Alison to her feet and kissed her passionately. Alison gasped as he ran his wet tongue up the side of her neck. She then threw him down on the sofa and took his clothes off. Alison wasted no time; she pulled and tore her dress open to get out of it and sat on top of Rick while he lay on the sofa. Rick's eyes were so heavy that he was barely conscious. Everything was vague to him. Alison's blurred image changed into Robyn's and his sounds were ringing and muffled.

Alison screamed her lungs out as she inserted Rick inside of her. It was like an explosion of ecstasy. She gripped his shoulders tightly as she rocked herself back and forth. She had waited for this moment so long and now it was the most exciting moment in her life as she came three times until he finally exploded his load inside her. She placed her hand on her womb, trying to catch her breath.

"I love you," said Alison, but Rick never heard her as he had passed out just before things had really got going.

The next morning, Rick awoke with a blanket over him on Alison's sofa. He had the mother fucker of all headaches as well as a semi hard on. Rick pulled the blanket back, only to discover that he was naked. He noticed his clothes on the stool of the piano that had been neatly folded. He then saw something that made him really worried. On the white fluffy rug was a used condom.

"Oh shit," Rick worried.

Just then a memory popped into his head. It was Robyn on top of him, moaning and panting excitedly. In his mind Robyn changed into Alison on top of him.

"Good morning," Alison spoke softly. She could see the look of worry and a guilty conscience. "I think we need to talk."

Rick rubbed his heavy eyes and remembered something else. He remembered attempting to kiss Alison and her saying, *"Wait – what are you doing? No, Rick – you're confused. You've just lost your wife, remember?"*

Alison had tried to stop him, but Rick was too forceful. "We did, didn't we?" he asked her.

"We did – I did try and…"

"I know you tried to stop me – it's not your fault," said Rick.

"Do you regret it? Because I think if I was you, I think I would as I had only just lost the love of my life." But Rick was too confused to pay any attention to Alison. "I'll get my driver to take you back home."

Alison left Rick to get dressed and think about the night before. What he didn't see was Alison grinning with amusement,

One month later, Rick's life had gone back to normal.

He had returned to work as his normal cheery self. Ellie loved seeing the old Rick back as she had missed him and was pleased that he had started to go out for drinks again instead of being cooped up inside living with the heartbreak of losing Robyn.

Alison, on the other hand, had been working nonstop.

She had worked hard to finish her work on her latest single, 'You're always forever in my heart', which went straight to number one upon release. Alison had made it clear that the record was a dedication to a friend who had lost his wife.

From signings to charity events, Alison was busy. But one day, Alison didn't feel well and collapsed in the street through sickness and dizziness.

Once the doctor had told her what was wrong, she had no choice but to take things easy. So, one day, she walked into an old familiar reception area and waited to be served by the receptionist.

"Alison?" said Rick. He couldn't believe that she was standing in front of him. "What are you doing here?"

"Erm... I need to talk to you – can we go outside?"

"Okay."

Rick got up from behind the desk and went outside with Alison. Before she could say anything, Rick told her that it wasn't a bad thing that she had turned up. He had been thinking of her and was grateful for the dedicated song.

"I've been thinking about you too and I was wondering if you fancied going out on a date with me?"

"Wow – really? You're asking me out on a date?"

"I think a date would be better than having a one nighter, eh?" Alison winked.

Rick agreed after what happened a month back and was ready to give Alison a chance.

"I've got something to tell you anyway," said Alison, shyly.

Before she could get the words out, the media came rushing up to the both of them and hounded them with constant questions.

"Alison, Alison – is it true that this is who you're dating now?"

"Well, we are going on a date, yes," Alison explained as she smiled and held Rick's hand. "And also... we're having a baby together."

5

Once the media had vacated the premises, Rick and Alison sat in the small meeting room. Loads of thoughts were buzzing around Rick's head, like a busy crowded motorway. He hadn't spoken to her for ten minutes and she was worried that he would never speak to her again.

Eventually, Alison made a decision. "I should go."

But Rick stopped her. "You're sure you're pregnant?" he asked.

Alison told him that she collapsed in the street and was told by the Doctor she had been pregnant for at least three weeks.

"But I thought that I wore a condom, didn't I?" said Rick, confused.

"It must have broken and leaked," Alison explained.

Rick buried his face in his hands. He knew Alison wasn't to blame as she tried to stop him, but what was done was done. "It's my fault."

Alison got on her knees and held him. "No – we're both to blame – I should have been stricter and stopped you – I let this happen too."

She could see Rick was at a loss. He didn't know what to do. "Look – I know this wasn't exactly how things should've happened – ideally you would've preferred to have a child with Robyn, even though she didn't want kids… but I do and I know you do, so we can work this out together."

"Is there anything you want me to do?" Rick asked.

"I just want us to be there for each other," Alison replied as she rubbed her belly. "For our baby – and for you to be available so we can attend the scans together."

"I meant financially."

"Money isn't an issue; you should know that – I don't expect a penny – all I want is our baby to have a mother and father that's together and would never leave them."

As Alison left the room, she bumped into Ellie. Alison glared at Ellie, hung her head up high like a typical snob and left the building.

Ellie attended to Rick. She couldn't believe what she had overheard Alison tell Rick. Ellie was unsure if it was true. She brought up about how obsessed she had been with Rick and she knew Rick wouldn't be that

546

careless. Ellie tried to jog Rick's memory into what happened on the night with Alison.

The details were still very vague. He strained to try and remember only to give himself a headache. Ellie suggested that he go and see a doctor and get tested to make sure there wasn't anything wrong with his brain. Memory loss and blacking out was just too suspicious.

"What are you saying? You think Alison did something to me? Don't be silly? She was the one trying to stop me from having sex with her?" explained Rick.

"But she didn't stop you. She still let it happen, didn't she?" Ellie insisted. "Please Rick, I don't trust her."

Rick had taken Ellie's advice. He sat in his doctor's office and told him everything that happened. Doctor Evans was concerned as he had never heard of anyone having acute memory loss from having a glass of wine before.

What was strange to Rick was the praise he got from Doctor Evans when he congratulated him for his and Alison's pregnancy and bagging a celebrity. Rick thought it odd as it wasn't very professional for a doctor to say that sort of thing. Doctor Evans checked Rick over and took a blood sample. He told Rick to give it a couple of weeks for the results to come through.

In the meantime, Rick's mind flooded with ideas, fears and worries. Even though Alison had assured him that everything was going to be fine from a financial perspective, he didn't feel right. As a man and a father, he now had a responsibility for someone more important than him.

Was the baby going to be healthy? Was it a boy or a girl? And then there was Alison. Was he ready to start a relationship and settle down with a woman he was unsure of? Someone that he didn't really love. Could he learn to love her? He felt trapped in one of those escape rooms and couldn't find a way out.

Before Rick knew it, two weeks had passed. Not once had he contacted Alison, but then again, she had never contacted him which surprised him.

Rick went to the Doctor, as he never heard any updates to say that his blood test results had come in. Receptionist Paula checked with the Nurse practitioner, who confirmed that Doctor Evans had received them but was not in the surgery at the time and suggested they would call him to tell him the results.

Rick returned home and waited most of the day to hear from his doctor. Then a call occurred an hour before closing. It was Receptionist Paula, who had some bad news. Doctor Evans had confirmed that the blood test had failed and had asked Rick to come in to have another test. By this time Rick had refused to, as he thought it was a waste of time as whatever had been wrong with him would have left his system and the test would be clear.

It was by this point Rick had made a decision to step up and see Alison. The baby was his and would need support from its father, so Rick took a taxi to where Alison lived.

When Rick arrived outside the large iron gates, he pressed the button on the intercom and waited for Alison to respond. But nobody did. Instead the gates opened and he was free to enter her estate.

As Rick walked up the long driveway, he heard noises that echoed like a rocket whizzing through the air. Rick couldn't place what those noises could be and as he arrived at the steps of the front door, he was surprised to see Alison's driver waiting for him.

"Miss Chance is on the fields – If you would like to follow me."

Rick was escorted across the green acres by the driver.

As they passed a row of trees which opened out into a wider field, the noise that Rick had heard all became clear to him.

Alison was dressed in trainers, jeans and a polo shirt.

Ear defenders covered over a baseball cap she was wearing while she stood some distance away from her horse while aiming up at the sky with her clay shooting rifle. She focused as the clay came into view. She applied pressure to the trigger and blew the clay pigeon to pieces. She smiled to herself, not because she hit her target, but it was because she saw Rick in the corner of her eye.

"Are you going to stand over their all day?" Alison asked. "Why don't you come over here and give us a kiss?"

Rick reluctantly walked over to her and did as she asked and gave her a kiss… on the cheek.

"Not like that," said Alison. She pulled Rick towards her and kissed him passionately. When she stopped, Rick was about to speak, but she silenced him by placing her finger on his lips. "No – I said why don't you give, us, a kiss?"

Rick realized that Alison wanted him to kiss her belly with their baby inside. Rick got down on one knee and took hold of her by her hips and pressed his lips on her belly.

"Our baby likes that." Alison giggled as she held onto Rick's head tightly. She then pulled him up and asked him, "Have you ever tried clay pigeon shooting before?"

"No – I never thought I'd be any good at it," Rick replied. "Besides, should you be even doing that as you're pregnant?"

"I know how to handle a gun. The baby is protected well enough from the noise and as long as the gun doesn't recoil into my belly, we'll be fine." Alison chuckled and then insisted, "Go on – give it a go."

Alison handed the gun to Rick. To him it was quite weighty as he had never held a weapon before. Alison instructed him to get a firm grip, look and don't aim, pressing the butt of the gun into his shoulder to compensate for the recoil.

"Pull," Alison shouted. The clay flew off into the distance. Rick concentrated really hard, then pulled the trigger. He missed. Rick looked disappointed. "Okay – try again, remember, look don't aim."

Another clay flew out into the distance. Rick looked and went with his gut instinct. When he pulled the trigger, he missed again. Rick gave up and passed the gun back to Alison.

"Told you I wouldn't be very good at it," said Rick.

"It just takes a lot of practice." Alison handed the gun to an older man with a tweed jacket and peaked cap. "Thank you, Terry."

Rick followed Alison over to her horse and asked her, "Who's Terry? This horse yours?"

Terry was Alison's ground keeper. He tended the grounds and looked after Alison's horse. She trusted him with everything and set him up with anything he needed.

"Yes, I bought her from a lady called Donna from a ranch just on the outskirts of Towns-end – I paid a very reasonable price for her, more than she was worth. Donna's father was shot down dead – that money will help her and her husband out, financially."

"Donna? Her husband isn't Zac by any chance?" Rick asked.

"You know him?" said Alison who looked surprised.

"He's an old work colleague," Rick replied.

"How about that? Small world," said Alison, amused. "So, is everything okay? It's really good to see you."

Rick admitted that he had been thinking about Alison and their baby.

He was always a man who wanted to do the right thing and over the last two weeks since he last saw her, he had started to feel guilty.

Alison was quite sympathetic. She acted like she didn't want Rick to be forced into anything as it would be his choice and he didn't have to feel guilty. She could look after herself but hoped that Rick would support her to get through the pregnancy.

Rick agreed that he would be there for her and would attend the twenty week scan. Alison was the happiest she had ever been. Everything she had wanted was all starting to fall into place. Her hormones were turning her on making her want to take advantage of Rick again. She couldn't resist and lost control by grabbing him and pulling him into the back of the limo.

As she sat down with legs spread apart she asked Rick, "Kiss us again." Rick didn't hesitate and leaned towards her to give her a soft kiss on her lips and then a kiss on her belly. As she grabbed the top of his head, she then asked him something he wasn't expecting. "While you're down there."

Rick was surprised that she wanted him to give her oral sex – to explore the inside of her body with his tongue. He slowly pulled her trousers down followed by her black silk lingerie. Alison grabbed Rick's head and pulled him closer.

She gasped the second that his wet tongue touched her.

As he got to work, her breathing increased and it wasn't long before she came. Rick thought it was over but Alison continued to hold him so he would keep giving her orgasms.

Normally Alison would have grabbed Rick and hurried to her bedroom so he could make love to her, but she began to have better ideas for him which turned her on even more.

Rick was frustrated but he was too polite to take advantage of her and preferred to wait his turn as he was scared that if he attempted to make love to her, it would be a failure as he still loved Robyn with all his heart. He didn't know if one day he could say those three words to her. I love you, was only meant for ones with a strong connection to each other.

The day of the twenty week scan soon came around. Rick and Alison had seen each other more regularly. Rick started by seeing her two times a week, which soon developed into four times a week. As they built up to the scan they discussed their plans.

Alison was understanding. She never expected Rick to be with her twenty four seven when their baby was born and wanted to take the pressure away from him, just in case it became too overwhelming. All she hoped was that one day they would all be together like a family.

Rick didn't mind. He agreed that he would try living with them when their baby was born instead of visiting. Their baby would need stability as he didn't want to be a part time father. Alison loved him for that. He was coming round and getting closer to her. It had been a long time coming, but her plan was nearly complete.

When Alison and Rick arrived at the ultrasound department at Townsend General, they waited outside the consulting room. It was at that point they both mutually decided that they wanted to find out the sex of their baby.

Rick was breathing heavily. That nervous tension of realizing that this was actually happening. Alison reached for Rick's hand and held it in hers.

"It'll be okay," smiled Alison.

Alison began to fidget. She had downed two pints of water and was desperate for a wee.

When they were called into the consulting room, Alison laid back and lifted her top up to reveal her bump. Jelly was applied and the sonographer brought up the baby on the screen and explained that she had taken the measurements of the baby's body and checked the heart, kidneys and bladder. They asked Rick and Alison if they would like to know the sex of their baby. Naturally, they both agreed.

"It's a boy."

"A boy," Alison screamed with delight.

"I'm going to have a son," said Rick in disbelief. For once he felt happy that this was all coming true.

Later that afternoon, after parting ways from Alison, Rick returned to his flat overwhelmed with joy, that he was going to have a son. He sat down in front of the TV and was about to turn it on, when a knock at the door distracted him. Rick got up and answered the door. When he opened it, he saw a woman standing in front of him who looked familiar.

"Rick James?" she asked.

"Do I know you?" Rick asked.

"I'm Paula, the receptionist… well former receptionist, at your local surgery under Doctor Evans – can I come in? I have something to show you," Paula insisted.

Once Paula was invited in and offered a seat, she took out a folder from her bag with printed documents in.

"So, what did you mean by former receptionist?" Rick asked.

Paula told him that she had been fired for coming across a folder in Doctor Evans' office that he was hiding. What Doctor Evans didn't know was she had taken photos of the contents of the folder that was linked to Rick and printed them out so he could see.

It was then that Rick could see the truth and why Paula had been dismissed. The evidence that she had got hold of, was proof that money had changed hands to buy an experimental drug called Dadiya, which was being produced by PharmCorp. The drug itself was like a sedative mixed with a strong viagra and the side effects of the drug could cause memory loss.

Rick couldn't believe the results of the test, that showed this drug in his system. As it was months ago, the drug would have disappeared but he couldn't remember taking such a drug.

"Doctor Evans kept your results hidden so his involvement wouldn't come out to the person who bought the drug," Paula explained.

"Who bought it?"

"I know this is probably hard to believe, but it was Towns-end's biggest star... Alison Chance."

Rick felt a cold shiver down his spine when he heard that name. It was then he realized the truth that everything that Alison did and told him was a lie. They hadn't had sex, she had raped him to get pregnant.

"I'm sorry – but I thought it best you know."

Rick looked up at Paula with eyes like thunder. There was only one thing on his mind now. A confrontation. He stood up and told Paula to show herself out, and with that, he grabbed his keys and left his flat.

When he left the flat, he hurried to the stairwell but bumped into Caroline, his next-door neighbour who he had known for six years.

"Sorry, Caroline," Rick apologized. But Caroline blanked him. Rick didn't understand why she did that as they had been close neighbours. "Caroline? What's wrong? Why are you ignoring me?"

Caroline had been fumbling with her keys like she was in a hurry to get inside. Knowing that she couldn't hide the fact she didn't want to talk to him, she gave in and snapped at Rick.

"You've got a lot of nerve, you know that – how could you?"

"What are you talking about?" said Rick, confused.

"Cheat on Robyn – what's the matter, you got amnesia or something?"

"Whoa, I did not cheat on Robyn."

Caroline dug into Rick really hard. On the night she was going away to stay with her friend, she heard raised voices coming from Robyn's flat. Caroline overheard the conversation where another woman was trying to buy Rick off her as she loved him more. Robyn lost it, then all of a sudden it went quiet. Minutes later Caroline left her flat and saw the other woman coming out and she couldn't believe who it was. It wasn't till two days after she saw the news that Robyn had been killed.

"Wait." Rick stopped Caroline in mid conversation. "You saw Robyn's murderer – who was she?"

"It was the pop star, Alison Chance."

6

Rick stood like a statue piecing together every bit of information he gathered. It all made sense now. The way things had been manipulated over the course of time ever since he saved Alison's life. A murderous rage began to bubble inside him.

"Rick – Rick," Caroline's voice echoed around him. She waved her hand in front of his face. He didn't flinch. "What is wrong with you?"

"It's not his fault," Paula interrupted. "He just found out that Alison had drugged him into giving her a baby. Rick's innocent in all of this."

Caroline could see how broken Rick looked. His whole world had been brought crashing down by a obsessed celebrity

Paula suggested to Caroline to call the police. They would get justice for Robyn's murder and hand over the evidence of Rick's rape. But what Paula and Caroline didn't know was that Rick had slipped away. There was only one thing he could think of. Even though Alison was carrying his child, he knew he had to kill her. The child wasn't conceived out of love. Rick was about it turn into a monster.

Alison stared out at the acres of land, thinking to herself that everything had worked out the way she wanted. She had never felt so happy in her entire life. Not even becoming a pop star was enough to make her feel satisfied as there was always something else in the back of her mind she needed. And now she had it. She placed her hand on her belly. She was in love with her baby boy that was yet to be born.

"Are you finished, Miss Chance?" Terry asked as he grabbed hold of the rifle.

"Yes, Terry, thank you." Alison smiled.

Terry walked off towards the estate to put the rifle away. But as he passed a tree, he got clobbered from behind by someone holding a thick branch. Terry fell to the ground. He was unconscious. Rick looked satisfied as he swapped the tree branch for the rifle.

As he saw Alison in the distance, he checked the rifle over. It was empty. Rick quickly checked the bag that Terry was carrying. Only two shells remained. Rick didn't care, in his mind he thought it would be enough to kill Alison.

As Alison rubbed her belly, she had no idea that Rick was creeping up on her. Rick then stopped some distance apart from her. He raised the gun and focused her in his sights while his finger applied light pressure to the trigger.

"So, when were you going to tell the truth?" Rick shouted causing Alison to jump. "That you killed my wife."

Alison closed her eyes in regret. Rick had finally worked out what she had done and now there was no running from it. Her eyes snapped open as she turned around to face him while her hands rubbed her belly. She stared at the barrel of the gun while Rick's hands shook nervously.

Alison explained to Rick that what she did, she did for them. Her offer of money would've set Robyn up for life where she could have the life she always wanted and in return Rick could have the same, a family with his own children and a wife that loved him. Alison didn't think that was unreasonable, but Robyn was evil and preferred to keep Rick – not wanting his dreams to come true – that's why Robyn had to die, just like Tyrone who wanted to stop her and Rick from being together.

"So, you killed Tyrone too? What the fuck is wrong with you?"

Alison began to walk towards him. Rick's hands were shaking even more now. He could easily pull the trigger now, but as he kept looking at her belly with his baby inside, he just couldn't do it.

"I love you, Rick – we both do – put the gun down and let's go to bed."

"You're crazy, Alison, obsessed – our baby wasn't even conceived through love – it was rape," Rick screamed.

Before Rick could do anything, Alison seized her chance and grabbed hold of the barrel of the rifle. Both of them struggled against each other to pull the gun out of each other's hands. Alison got more angry and punched Rick in the face pulling the gun out of his hands and falling to the floor.

Rick ran for his life, just as Alison raised the gun and pulled the trigger. Rick ducked to avoid the shot as Alison got to her feet. She opened the gun to see she only had one shot left.

"More – I need more," she murmured.

Rick's chest hurt as he began to get out of breath. He was so unfit as he was a man who never did any proper exercise. He ran across the open acres to see the Manor in the distance. As he brushed past the trees, the branches scratched his arm. When he climbed over a fence, he looked back to see no sign of Alison. But Rick didn't think he was in the clear as that was too easy.

The limo was parked outside the Manor entrance. He tried every door only to discover that the car was locked. He had to think quickly. What was he going to do? He needed to escape as she was hunting him. Rick thought about elbowing the driver's window, but even if he got in the limo he had no keys. He didn't know how to hot wire a car, so that was no good.

Alison's horse? But he didn't know how to ride. The only other option he had was to hide inside the Manor or find the driver and get the keys off him. He needed a weapon to defend himself so the kitchen was the best place he could start with.

Rick ran across the main hall towards the kitchen in the back. It was large in scale, with its white tiled floor, kitchen utensils and knife rack. Rick pulled out the largest knife he could find followed by a smaller knife that he tucked in the inside of his sock. He then returned to the hall, only to see Alison climbing the stairs with the gun in her hand.

Too early for a confrontation, Rick ran up the stairs. As Alison entered the hall, she saw him run across the stairwell. She quickly took aim and fired. The shot chipped the wall that Rick ran past. She lowered the gun with a disappointing look. She wanted to shoot him, but not enough to kill him as she had plans for him. The hunt was on.

When Alison climbed the stairs, she checked room after room. She began with the bathroom. As she thought, the shower curtain was pulled across like a typical horror cliché, she smiled with delight, poking the gun outwards so she could push the shower curtain open with the barrel of the gun. When she did, Rick wasn't there.

Just then a slight breeze made her shiver. There was an open window nearby. She left the bathroom and went into the next room. It was her bedroom. When she caught a glimpse of her bed, she could see in her mind, Rick tied up while she took advantage of him against his will. It gave her that excited sexual tingle she had always been looking for. But then her eyes wandered to the open window.

"Shit," Alison mumbled to herself. She looked out over the grounds but didn't see any sign that Rick could've gotten out at that height. Something didn't feel right. She turned back round to look at the bottom of the bed and smiled to herself. "Oh, Ricky – come out, come out wherever you are." She crept over to the bed aiming the gun low with her finger resting lightly on the trigger. She knelt down, then pulled the bed covers up to look under the bed, but there was no sign of Rick. She then noticed the bed cover move.

When she looked up, Rick had crawled out from under the bed just in time to make his escape.

Alison fired another shot, blowing a hole in the wall as Rick darted out of the room. Alison opened up the gun and loaded some more shells into it. When she left the room, Rick emerged from the side and stabbed Alison in the arm causing her to drop the gun. Rick pulled the knife out then kicked the gun away. Alison backed away as Rick slashed at her. She screamed at him, then charged towards him and grabbed hold of his arm. She clawed at his hand causing him to drop the knife. Alison grabbed Rick's head and forced him towards her bleeding arm.

"Drink my blood – taste it," Alison screamed. She then tried to force his head down between her legs. "Lick me out, you belong down there forever – it's what you were born for."

Rick struggled to get out of Alison's grip. He tried so hard, that there was only one other way to do it. He reached down for the small knife and pulled it out from his sock.

"Screw you, you crazy bitch." Rick plugged the knife into her leg causing her to scream. When she slumped to the floor, Rick kicked her in the face, but it wasn't enough to stop her, as when she stood upright, she clawed his face with her finger nails. Rick staggered back, the blood was in his eyes and he couldn't see clearly. Alison charged at him, grabbing hold of him tightly, then fell over the banister, causing them both to roll down the stairs. Luckily Alison never rolled or landed on her belly. It was the one thing she was worried about, the safety of their child.

Rick got to his feet and retreated into the living room. Alison limped after him. She reached out and wrapped her hands around Rick's throat tightly. Rick began to choke.

She was surprisingly strong. Rick grabbed hold of her head and pressed his thumbs on her eyes. Alison let go and let out a loud scream. With her partly blinded, Rick saw an opportunity and grabbed her by her blonde hair and tried to push her over the sofa, but she grabbed hold of him and caused them both to go over and smash onto the glass coffee table.

Their fight stopped. They both lay on the fragments of glass, weakened, in pain and out of breath. Rick looked at Alison, her blonde hair and clothes were now bloodstained. Alison rested her hands on her belly as she lay next to the crackling log fire. Rick forced himself to get to his feet. This had to end, right now. He staggered over to Alison and grabbed her arm and dragged her towards the fireplace. He propped her up and pushed the back of her head so her face was pushed into the roaring fire. Alison got aggressive, she pushed back enough to get out of his grip, so she could grip his hand tightly.

"Let's burn together." Alison giggled. Rick was horrified when she pulled his arm in and held it in the fire so their flesh burnt together.

They both screamed as their skin blistered. Rick punched Alison in the face forcing her to let go. Rick could see her sanity was too far gone as all she could do was laugh hysterically. Rick staggered out of the living room to make his way upstairs where the gun was left. The pain and the loss of blood made Rick feel weak.

When he got to the top he saw the gun. As he reached for it, he was pushed out of the way by Alison who picked up the gun and aimed it at him.

"Haven't you worked it out yet, Rick – I own you, I'll never let you go," Alison threatened. "Now tell me you love me."

Rick had no choice but to say the words that played on his mind, "I… Love…" He paused and then smiled with joy. "…Robyn."

Alison's face filled with thunder. Her insides burned with such rage. Her hands trembled as she wanted to pull the trigger but couldn't find it in her heart to.

"I have never and could never love you, Alison," Rick insisted. "I'm not the man for you – I guess you're going to have to find the one man who will love you and tell you you're insane."

The words that Alison never wanted to hear all became clear to her. Rick was right all along. She had followed her heart blindly and now was the time to stop wasting her life with the wrong man for her.

"You're right," Alison mumbled. "You're not the man for me – there is someone else who will love me and make love to every inch of my body."

"Do you even hear yourself? Your thoughts on how a relationship should go? It's all about real love, giving not just taking, about being fair…"

Alison was bored hearing Rick talk about the moral values of a relationship. "Shut up," she yelled, so instead she aimed the gun and pulled the trigger. The shot was powerful enough to blow his throat apart causing his blood to hit her face. She licked the blood off the side of her face and felt excited. She watched as Rick put his hands over the gaping wound as he choked on his own blood.

"Sorry, Rick – it's such a shame our song had to end." And with that, Alison used her last shot to shoot Rick in the face, ending his life.

With the gun now empty, Alison stood over Rick's body like an emotionless zombie. She didn't even notice the blue neon flashing lights and sirens coming from outside.

Months had passed since that night. It plagued Alison's mind – replaying the events over and again while she sat near a window looking out the at the bright sunny day that shined down on the communal garden outside.

Patients and orderlies occupied the room she was in. The floor was paved with black and white tiles. Female patients sat at tables and on a small leather sofa watching the TV while orderlies kept a close eye on them to make sure they didn't misbehave or start trouble. One lad sat in a corner on his own. Alison recognized him from the news that she had seen a year ago. Tom was a bright kind teen, now a man, but when his mother's boyfriend put her into hospital he turned to murder to save his mother.

Just then a large woman who looked like she was three hundred pounds sat down in front of Alison. She smiled as her eyes scanned Alison up and down. Her behaviour made Alison feel uncomfortable.

"Well, who would have thought that Alison Chance would be the newest patient of Marwood Asylum – I'm Krista."

"I've been here months, your face looks familiar and I haven't seen you around – you're new?"

"No – I've been here eighteen years – most of the time I spend in Isolation, keep me hidden away next to patient 10051982."

"And who's that?" said Alison with an intriguing tone.

"Somebody that's going to set things in motion – once you're in here you never leave. I'm just waiting for a special sort of girl to come here," Krista explained. "So, what did you do to end up here?"

Alison told Krista her story of Rick, her life. Being saved and his wife that she killed. She went about how she had such plans and ideas for Rick that turned her on to the extreme, but she had to kill Rick as there was another man that she would want to do these plans on. This sparked Krista's interest, she urgently wanted to know what plans she had. Alison looked around as the orderlies walked past. She then leaned towards Krista and whispered into her ear.

Krista gasped at what Alison told her. "Wow – that's quite a plan, but can I suggest you make a little change to make your plan even better?"

When Krista whispered into Alison's ear, she nearly wet herself in excitement. Her legs trembled enough for her to rub herself.

"I bet you can't wait to set your plan in motion now." Krista giggled. "I just wish I still had my club to try it out – what a challenge it would be."

Alison then realized who Krista was. She used to be the owner of a sex club called *Play 4 Real*. It got closed down after Krista was arrested from a pregnancy dare challenge.

"My sister Lily came to visit me. I was surprised considering what I did to her boyfriend – my club was shut down and now stands as a strip club near Towns-end College."

Their conversation was then interrupted by a female orderly who came to take Alison back to her room. The orderly helped Alison to her feet as she struggled with her nine-month pregnant belly.

"I'll see you around, Alison Chance." Krista smiled.

Alison thought about all the wonderful ideas that Krista had planted in her head. She had been the happiest she had been for a long time and now all she could see was an exciting future ahead. Her legs were trembling as she was escorted along the corridor of the asylum. The excitement of finding herself another man made her wet, but not in a way she thought as she realized her feet were now wet.

"Oh my god," Alison panicked. "My waters just broke." She felt weak at the knees and nearly collapsed to the floor when she started to have a panic attack.

The female orderly helped her sit down. "Somebody help, quickly – she's gone into labour," they shouted. The orderly held Alison's hand tightly and made her look at her. They then asked Alison if she was having a boy or a girl to calm her down from her panic attack.

"A…" said Alison who struggled to catch her breath "A boy."

"That's great." The orderly smiled. "And what are you going to call him?"

Alison turned her head and smiled sinisterly saying the only name she could think of "…Rick."

#JESSICAGEORGE

1

'It' s over,' Jessica George told me bluntly.

My heart dropped the second she said that. I stood in front of her not knowing how to react. I held my pendant tightly in my hand. Made of white gold with a single crystal of yellow, purple and green. It was like a comfort blanket as I was found with it when I was abandoned as a baby. I never knew my mother or father. From an orphanage I lived my life the best I could. I thought I had the best thing in the world, Towns-end's sweetheart, but now I was back to square one.

'It's not you okay, it's me – you're perfect,' Jessica reassured me. I had heard a lot of people use that same excuse. If I was perfect, why was she breaking up with me? All the time we had been together, I knew she had a past, but she never explained what it was, until now.

She started by touching on the finer parts of when we first crossed paths at the high school prom. Jessica didn't have a date for the prom after breaking up with her boyfriend two days prior. I was in the same boat. I didn't have a date as no one wanted to go with me, but it didn't stop me as I didn't want to miss out on an important event.

She had seen my kindness, when I asked Miss Gunn, our teacher who had celebrated her fiftieth birthday, to dance. Jessica was a little bit jealous as she wished her ex-boyfriend would have showed the same kindness.

When I crossed the dance floor to get some drinks for Miss Gunn. It was that moment I bumped into Jessica. All we could do was stare into each other's eyes. She was so beautiful. That sparkly cream-coloured dress and that long brunette hair hung past her shoulders.

I took her hand in mine. Not once did she pull or look away from my gaze. As the song, 'Bad Liar' by Imagine Dragons, played, I spun her around and we both danced like professionals. The students had spread out and focused their attention on the two of us. Jessica danced in close. She felt like and we both felt like nothing else mattered. Her dress sparkled like diamonds from the lights that reflected from the disco ball.

When I spun her around again, she noticed another girl with long brunette hair, dressed in a red dress, looking jealous. Miss Gunn was unhappy as we danced, which caused Jessica to suspect something about her. I had no idea what.

After that magical moment, we had both gone our separate ways. I didn't go to college. Instead I focused on getting a job in an office with my A-Level business study. Jessica however, had gone to college to focus on her drama studies and become an actress.

Jessica's drama teacher, Simon Stewart, saw potential in her. She had put tons of emotion in when she acted out scenes, that looked so believable. Simon was in his forties and Jessica was eighteen.

One day he asked her to meet up with him for some extra rehearsing. Being so young, Jessica didn't think anything of it and agreed. Her sister, Kayleena, who was five years younger, found out and she was horrified as it sounded dangerous. She urged Jessica to tell her mum and dad, but she couldn't bring herself to, as she trusted her teacher.

Later that evening, Jessica took a taxi to the address that Simon had given her. The taxi pulled up outside an old derelict warehouse. The outside was old and rusted. The door looked like it was hanging off its hinges.

'Are you sure you want to get out of here, girl?' the taxi driver warned. 'I mean, look at this place.'

Jessica wasn't worried and assured the driver not to worry. She thanked him and paid him, then stepped out into the cold night air. When the taxi pulled away, Jessica wrapped her arms around herself to protect her from the cold.

When she pulled the door open, the rust and damp caused it to squeak as it scraped across the ground. She stepped inside and was greeted by the smell of damp which caused the warehouse to stink. She shivered as it was colder inside than outside. She looked up at the ceiling to see the constant drops of water splashing on the ground from the holes in the ceiling.

'Jessica?' Simon called. Jessica noticed he was standing next to an old rusty metal framed single bed with a dirty damp mattress with holes in. On the floor were two champagne flutes and a bottle of champagne.

"What's all this?" Jessica asked cautiously.

Simon revealed a script for Jessica to look over and then explained that it was all props for the scene that they were going to act out. Jessica stepped back from Simon and then scanned through the script. What she read was innocent which relaxed her.

"Sweet?" said Simon as he held out a small sweet tin with pink looking pills in. "Don't worry it's cherry."

Jessica took the pill and popped it into her mouth at the same time Simon did. The strong flavour of cherry felt electric to her as it dissolved extremely fast. But what Jessica didn't see was when Simon turned his back on her, he quickly took the sweet out of his mouth and slipped it into his pocket.

Jessica and Simon began rehearsing the script. Their first scene was their characters having an argument. Jessica gave everything she got as she yelled at him with as much anger as she could muster. Simon applauded her for strong acting and then offered her another sweet which she put in her mouth and gave Simon a smug smile, but it was Simon who was smiling on the inside.

The next scene they acted out was an apology scene. Simon cracked open the bottle of champagne and filled up each flute a quarter of the way. Small quantities of champagne worked best during the scenes so they didn't get drunk. Jessica agreed, but then she admitted that she didn't like champagne as it was too bitter and gassy. Simon then slipped one of the pills into the champagne.

"Try it now with extra flavour, Jessica."

Jessica took hold of the glass and necked the champagne like a shot. The strong cherry flavour that had dissolved was certainly more pleasant as Jessica licked her lips with pleasure. Her insides heated up as the alcohol took an instant effect.

Simon poured half a glass and then added two pink pills to it. Jessica grabbed the glass to act out the scene. It was an emotional apology which she passed with flying colours. As she necked the drink, she began to feel light headed. Her temperature rose. Her eyes felt heavy. She felt a buzz in her loins and excitement between her legs.

This was the moment that Simon took advantage of her.

He held her close by the waist while his hands got busy feeling all over her body. Jessica felt his hot breath on her face as he went down and began to kiss her, under her neck. She closed her eyes as the electrifying tension began to take effect. Simon then licked her neck like a dog slobbering over her. He pressed his lips on her, while he kissed her and massaged her tongue with his.

His hands moved down past her waist. She was too far gone to even stop him as the room started spinning.

Simon lifted Jessica's vintage flowery dress over her head until she was standing in front of him just in her bra and underwear. She looked down to see his hard on bulging out of his trousers.

Simon unclipped Jessica's bra so it flopped to the ground revealing her perky breasts. Her nipples were already hard and erect from the cold air. He wasted no time groping them with his warm hands, sucking on then and flicking her nipples with his wet tongue.

Jessica closed her eyes. Her breathing increased rapidly while she bit her finger, while Simon got on his knees and pulled her underwear down. He parted her legs and got to work orally. Jessica gasped and her legs quivered as she felt the sexual electricity fly through her body while letting out a slight moan. With the pink pill working more and more sending her hormones into overdrive, she was desperate for release. As Jessica was close, Simon deliberately stopped.

"No," Jessica screamed, "don't stop."

That's when Simon seized that moment he had been longing for. He grabbed the smelly damp mattress and popped it on to the rusty wire framed bed. He grabbed her hard from round the back of the neck and pushed her down. Her mouth got the taste of the dampness which she spat out. Simon parted her legs and inserted himself into her from behind. He fucked her harder and harder while her face was getting soaked from the dampness being squeezed out of the mattress. She coughed and spluttered while the vile damp taste went into her mouth and down her throat.

Simon got more brutal. Jessica knew that it started to hurt but the pills told her otherwise. She couldn't control herself. She wanted this. Simon tugged at her hair while he humped her harder. Her face bashed into the rusty wire frame headboard causing bruises and cuts that bled. Jessica screamed her lungs out from the mixture of pain and orgasms she was having as Simon came inside her, unprotected.

I stood in front of Jessica, horrified at what she had told me. Jessica continued her story saying that it was all a blur after she came as she must have passed out, because when she woke up, she found herself naked and bleeding down below inside a dumpster. She had been dumped there like a piece of rubbish.

She was rushed to hospital when she was discovered by a woman. She never did find who discovered her but she was grateful to her for saving her life. Her sister told her that it took her weeks to recover from the trauma and for her vagina to heal. Jessica was ill a majority of the time from all the germs she had ingested from the dirty mattress water.

"What happened to Simon? Did the police arrest him?" I asked aggressively.

"No – my statement and a semen sample of his wasn't enough to convict him," said Jessica with a crack in her voice.

"Is he still around?"

"No – he disappeared, once everything was dropped," Jessica explained.

"Why didn't you tell me this before, Jessica?"

"If I had – do you think you could ever touch me or look at me the same way?" said Jessica wiping a tear from her eye. "Besides, I'm a murderer."

"What do you mean?"

Jessica told me that after the weeks passed by and the illness had faded, she still had constant vomiting, so her physician, Doctor Evans, congratulated her for the baby she was having.

"You were pregnant?" I said, in disbelief.

Jessica thought that she should know better than to think if she had unprotected sex with someone, chances are they would get pregnant. Jessica became distraught. She hated the idea of having a baby by someone that she despised by raping her. So, she thought that the solution was to get an abortion.

"I killed that baby." Jessica burst into tears. I hurried over to her with open arms, but instead of letting me comfort her, she backed away from me. "Don't – I don't want your pity – I don't want you to hold on for me."

"Jessica, I love you – I would do anything for you. I would hold on till the end of love – we can face these problems together."

"You can't, okay? I'm going away for a bit – I need help and I can't drag you down with me. I don't want you to wait." But I didn't know what she meant by waiting. "I'm going to the other end of Towns-end, back to my mum, Dad and sister and then I'm going to commit myself to Marwood Asylum so I can get the help I need."

"For how long?" I asked.

"For however long it takes," Jessica explained.

2

Those were the last words that Jessica said to me, that repeatedly went around my head as I sat at my desk, outside the office of the CEO, Tracy Luna, in Foptix Industries.

"Good morning," said Tracy as she walked up to my desk looking like some important celebrity dressed in a dark fur coat. But instead of going straight to her office, she could see that something was wrong. "What's the matter and don't tell me there isn't anything wrong, I can see it in your teary eyes."

I wiped the tears from his eyes and replied, "It's Jessica, she broke up with me."

"I'm sorry to hear that," said Tracy. "What happened? Why did she break up with you? I thought you were both happy."

"So, did I – but it's complicated, more for her. I can't really say why. She told me I did nothing wrong."

Tracy stood beside me and put her arm around me to comfort me. She didn't like to see me upset and, being an older single woman herself, she always had a soft spot for me. When I applied for a position as an admin assistant after leaving college, she saw something she had never seen in her previous employees. Newcomers always had a nervous tension, they wouldn't ask questions or take the training in which would lead to constant mistakes.

But I was different. I showed a willingness to learn. I showed strength and wasn't afraid to take on new tasks. Between Tracy and me, we sparked up a good team work, which lead to her promoting me to her assistant. Tracy was proud of herself for making the best decision for her and her company, which showed up a lot of the employees who were slacking.

As time passed we both became friends. I would always have a coffee, black, no sugar, ready for her when she walked in and tell a joke to make her laugh. To Tracy it was always the highlight of the day which made every day worth living for. But, deep inside, Tracy wanted a bit more. She was in her fifties and I was in my early twenties which was a large age gap between us. She had a problem that she found hard to resolve.

She was desperate to ask me out on a date. She had let her feelings for me get the better of her, but she was too afraid, as she was my boss and the other employees would clearly see how I got to be her assistant. But there was one time that she put all that aside and didn't care what people thought, so upon asking me out for a drink, I had come in the happiest I had ever looked. That's when Tracy found out that I had met my old high school flame, Jessica George, that I had danced with at the prom and we were going out on a date that very night.

Tracy's heart sank when I told her that. She felt like she had waited too long and missed her chance. But now, as Jessica had broken up with me, there was an opening. But she couldn't do it, as I had my heart crushed it was too soon to ask me out.

"Look at me," said Tracy. I looked up wiping the tears from my red stinging eyes. "I can't say that I understand how you're feeling and what you're going through – I never had anybody in my life to love, so I never got hurt. But you're a special man. So, I suggest tonight that we make a deal and you and I…"

But Tracy never got to finish that sentence as we were interrupted by the phone. I answered the call, "Tracy Luna's office, how can I help?" I paused for a moment and then said, "Okay – send her up."

"Who was that?" Tracy asked.

"Your nine o clock with PharmCorp," I replied.

"Ah of course." Tracy realized. "The business world never sleeps."

As Tracy went to her office, I was curious at what she was going to say to me before we were interrupted. Being a busy time. I never asked. It was just something I was always going to think about and never get the answer to.

While Tracy prepared everything for her meeting, I quickly tidied up my desk. As I put some of my belongings into the desk, I heard the lift down the end of the corridor, being followed by high heeled footsteps.

Liz Cooper came waltzing through the door looking like some fashion model in her sunglasses, red high heels and green business dress. Liz walked over to the reception desk and said, "Liz Cooper to see Tracy Luna."

I looked up and smiled. I nodded and then got on the phone to let Tracy know her meeting had arrived. But there was something off with Liz and I could see it as I ended the call.

"Miss Luna will be with you shortly – if you would like to take a seat, Miss Cooper." Liz sat down on a comfy red two seated sofa. "Would you like a tea or coffee?" Liz shook her head.

I returned to my work doing my daily paperwork and booking schedules to try and get the constant memory of Jessica out of my head. Every now and then I would look up at Liz to see her staring at me. This made me feel uncomfortable and gave me the creeps. But from Liz's perspective, she stared at me, because she thought I looked familiar, like she knew me. And then it happened. It was that moment she realized who I was.

"It's you isn't it?" Liz asked. "High School prom?" Liz walked over to me. "Holy shit, it is you isn't it? I was standing next to Miss Gunn our teacher while you were dancing with Jessica George."

Liz went behind the reception desk and gave me a cuddle. She then complimented me for how well I had done since leaving school. She was impressed and always thought that I would do better than the other students.

"So, how are you? We've got so much catching up to do? I bet you're happily settled right?" Liz assumed.

But my sad face said it all. "I was, till Jessica broke up with me."

"Jessica George? So, you both got together after the prom?" said Liz stating the obvious, but even she realized what she was saying. "I mean… I'm sorry to hear that."

Even though she clearly wasn't and was glad that I was single and back on the market.

"This way, Miss Cooper," Tracy insisted.

But Liz's train of thought was too focused on me. She wasn't really bothered with the meeting as she wanted to talk to me more and catch up. "We will catch up after, okay?" She smiled. "It's really great to see you."

Liz reluctantly followed Tracy into her office. I noticed that Liz kept on looking back at me until the office door was closed by Tracy.

As the time ticked by, Tracy did all the talking about the current situation with her company. Liz's mind however was in a different place and she had not listened to a single word Tracy had said.

"Miss Cooper? Miss Cooper?" Tracy's voice echoed. "Liz!"

Liz looked up at a concerned Tracy. "Have you been even listening to a word I've said?"

"Sorry, I haven't," Liz confessed.

"I thought you came here to make a deal?" Tracy asked, but then realized that Liz kept on looking at the doors like she wanted to leave. But it wasn't that. It was me. "He's going to okay you know – the pain of losing Jessica will heal."

"I think I can heal that pain," Liz suggested. "I've always had a soft spot for him ever since high school."

"Please, don't hurt him," said Tracy.

"Hurt? What, are you in love or something?" Liz chuckled. But she could clearly see a look of concern on Tracy's face which confirmed her suggestion. "Oh… really?"

The cat was out of the bag. Tracy couldn't hide it from Liz. Even though I was half her age, Tracy had never felt love or kindness like I had shown her and she had imagined that one day I would be hers, living a love life together for the rest of our lives.

"I would never hurt him, Tracy," said Liz, firmly. "But my life philosophy has always been, I see, I take, I get."

"That's a very selfish philosophy, Miss Cooper."

Liz got to the point and proposed her business proposal to Tracy. A Frenchman by the name of Pierre was looking for companies to invest in a project that would focus on the study of dreams. The company, Oslow Corp, would delve into the minds of the individuals to unlock the power that causes people to dream.

'So, you think this would benefit my company?' Tracy questioned.

'I don't like to see companies collapse and fail, Miss Luna,' Liz snapped.

"You say about the collapse of companies – but if I'm not mistaken, yours nearly took a turn for the worst am I not mistaken – the whole thing with the pink snow that fell and wiped out a population of ten thousand – the Silent Village as they call it now."

"Those pills were hijacked. It was not our company's fault or any of my employees. Every company has a security breach," Liz explained.

"Well, we are secure here," Tracy assured.

"One day it will happen to you," Liz insisted.

"We are doing excellent work here. Our robotics program is in full swing – soon we will have created our first realistic prototype then people not be able to tell the difference between person and machine."

"What about the baby program? Three babies? There are rumours going around."

"Liz…" Tracy paused. "…You know better than to listen to rumours."

"Look." Liz sighed. "My journey here isn't wasted today. I will be meeting Pierre tomorrow night at the vintage ball. Big business names and celebrities go to this every year – I suggest you go too and hear him out."

"I don't go to these events," Tracy insisted.

"How about your assistant? Why don't you send them to represent you. He can listen to what Pierre has to say and get back to you on it – then you make a decision whether you want to invest?" Liz suggested.

Tracy chuckled. "Are you sure that this isn't just a way to go on a date with my assistant?"

"Would that really be an issue?"

"Very well – it better be good," Tracy agreed.

"Don't worry, Miss Luna – I'll take good care of them for you." Liz smiled.

3

After work, I went to get myself some formal wear for the vintage ball. As my mind was all over the place in the busy city centre, I bumped into a woman who looked vaguely familiar.

"Oh my god – it's you." She smiled. "Teresa – Teresa Gunn – I was your teacher for two years."

Wow, I thought. She looked amazing. Her long blonde wavy hair and slender figure made her look younger than she gave her credit for. She complimented me by saying how well I looked and rather handsome. I could tell she was coming on to me. We talked for quite a while. She was impressed how well I had done since leaving high school and was proud that I was able to use my full potential.

Life for her however had taken a rough turn. Teresa was always hard on us as students. Not because she was being harsh, but to push us in the right direction and use all our skills that we could to better our education that would help us through the rest of our life. She explained that she was a pusher and as she pushed so hard, she pushed her husband away.

I couldn't help but feel sorry for her. She had a heart of gold and I was proud to know her in my life.

"Your girlfriend must be so proud of you."

I didn't lie to her. I told her what had happened with Jessica and me. Teresa had an understanding. "It sucks being us – the nice ones." I couldn't agree more. I suggested that she should get out there. Go out for a meal and have some her time to heal.

"Is that an invite?"

"Whoa. I didn't mean it like that."

"I'm kidding – you're half my age. The whole Toy boy, cougar thing."

Age never bothered me though. It was just a number. It was the person's heart and soul that mattered the most to me. So, I agreed and suggested we get a bite to eat right away.

We went to *The Chunky Pie*. It was the best place to go, run by Will Williams, who had built it from the ground up.

Their signature dish was the burger pie. Two beef burgers, with mushrooms, cheese, onion and gravy encased in short-crust pastry served with green beans and creamy mash potato. It was making my mouth watering just thinking about it.

We had finished our dinner in the first half hour, but talked about life and our futures for the next three. Before I knew it, it was closing time. I had gone to the restroom while Teresa paid the bill. I had offered to pay but she wasn't having any of it. When I returned she told me that she had just seen Jessica who had seen both of us sitting at the table together.

"She said we make a great couple."

Couple? Before I could say anything else, Teresa leaned in and kissed me on the lips. Her kiss was soft and she tasted amazing.

"Thank you – but this is as far as it goes. I liked you from the first moment you walked over to me at the prom – held my hand and took me over to the dance floor. I always hoped that one day I would find someone like you." Teresa smiled. "I wanted to kiss you that night – it was so romantic but I was kidding myself – age differences never really work out, now I should go before I drag you to my apartment and make love to you in my bed – take care of yourself."

She was upset. Trying to fight against the tears that were building up in her eyes. I didn't know how to react. If I went after her, then we would end up in bed together. For her age her body was amazing. But what kind of future would we have? Age gaps can work, but the end of their life can come quicker.

The very next day, I talked with Tracy about what happened between me and Teresa. She was shocked beyond belief but admitted that I was a catch and anyone would be happy to have me in their life. If that was true then why didn't Jessica want me? Was it because of my youthful looks, my boyish girlish haircut and slim figure. I looked like a boy who could get with a girl and I looked like a girl who could get with a boy. When it came to my gender, who knows what I really was?

Before I knew it I was sitting in the back of the limo, clinging onto my necklace. Nervous. Liz sat next to me in a lime green business suit and feather boa. She raised a glass of champagne to her lips. "Relax – it's not just business – have fun – let your hair down." That was easier said than done I thought as I was still thinking about what happened with Teresa and Jessica saying that we made a good couple. Why was Jessica still here? She told me that she was going to commit herself to Marwood Asylum.

Something didn't add up. Was there another reason why she broke up with me?

The air turned warm from the cold air as we entered a large grand lobby. Two men in suits stood by a pair of doors. One stood with a tablet to check if we were on the list, while the other collected our coats.

"Liz Cooper, from PharmCorp, plus one." Liz smiled.

The guy ticked us off the list and Liz held onto my arm tightly as we walked into the large hall that had tables and chairs scattered around. The place had a fifties and sixties vibe with a live band playing classic hits of old. Liz pointed out our table that we would be sitting at. Pierre was already sitting talking to Towns-end's young pop sensation, Megan May, who had just started out.

I listened to Pierre's proposal for Oslow Corps dream project and took everything into consideration. Some of the ideas he had made sense, but some sounded dangerous and could put the health of the individual at risk. This was something I couldn't agree with. Pierre was disappointed, but it didn't stop him from giving up as he was determined to try again and speak to Tracy personally.

Liz was impressed and a little turned on. She thought that me being an assistant was the wrong position for me to be in. She saw me as a natural born negotiator and offered me a position in her company. She thought we would make an amazing team and told me to consider the deal she was offering.

"Pierre – I get that you want to pursue Foptix for funding. I would be more than happy than to put some funding towards your project," Liz suggested.

"That's very noble of you, Miss Cooper – you're only twenty one – a young thing – Tracy Luna is experienced in the business world."

"Right." Liz chuckled. "I'm the CEO of PharmCorp – I'm twenty one – rich as fuck and I can have anything I want." Liz then stroked my hand and winked at me. "Or anyone I want."

"What about your former employee? Simon Stewart. That shipment of pink pills that went missing. A supposed hijack am I mistaken?"

"No one knows where Simon disappeared to," Liz explained.

A cold shiver ran down my spine when Simon's name came up. What he did to Jessica using pink pills. It was Liz's company that made them and destroyed Jessica's life. I pulled Liz aside and told her everything that Jessica had told me.

"I need some air." Liz hurried. She was in shock. I needed to talk to her more, so I followed her outside. "You're not kidding are you?"

I assured her that I wasn't. The look on her face said it all. The thought that the pills her company created destroyed a life more than helped it. It was a female Viagra pill that had been tampered with. Liz felt sick. I held her in my arms as she sobbed. She didn't know what to do and how she could make things better. She blamed herself for letting this happen. But it wasn't her fault. It was her employee that did the damage.

I escorted her back inside and returned to our table. As we sat down, people's heads turned to see Jessica George walk into the hall. I couldn't believe it. She looked amazing in her white vintage flowery dress. Liz looked away and kept her head down. She didn't want to be seen by Jessica, knowing what she knew now. I sat next to Liz and held her hands to comfort her.

"Hi," Jessica spoke softly. "Are you okay? I didn't think I would see you here."

"He's representing his company he works for." Liz stood up and offered her hand. "Liz Cooper – CEO of PharmCorp." Jessica shook her hand. "You need no introduction – Jessica George, Towns-end's sweetheart and film actress." Jessica looked embarrassed. "You've come a long way from working in *The Chunky Pie*."

Huh? This was something I didn't know.

"That was a long time ago – when I was still in high school," Jessica explained. "I sucked at it."

"They still have your picture up in the best employees. You can't have sucked at it that much," Liz joked.

"Liz Cooper?" Jessica asked. "Now I remember you. You were at the prom – standing next to Miss Gunn watching us dance."

"Just like everyone else was."

Jessica looked at me. "Can we talk?" We couldn't. I made it clear to Jessica that I needed to stay with Liz. She needed me to stay by her side. "Of course – have a good night."

Jessica walked away. I could tell she was disappointed.

But Liz wasn't. She was happy. "Why don't you get us some drinks?"

As I made my way across the dance floor, Jessica deliberately cut across my path just as the song "Run-around Sue" which was originally sung by Dion played. Talk about history repeating itself. But this time it was Jessica who was mesmerized. I don't know why, but we took each-other's hands and started dancing. Spinning her around and jigging to the song. As we danced, I caught a glimpse of Liz looking disappointed. So, I stopped and told Jessica I couldn't and continued to get the drinks. Jessica followed me, prompting Liz to come over to us.

"Jessica," Liz called. "I'm sorry, okay?"

"Sorry? For what?" Jessica was puzzled.

"For what happened to you. With Simon."

Jessica looked at me with daggers. That I told Liz all the personal stuff that had happened in her past.

"He was an employee of mine. He stole a consignment of pink pills which he used on you," Liz told her. "The pills were never meant to be a weapon – they were meant to help women with low sex drives."

Jessica took a step back from us. Not knowing what to say. "I... I need..." She struggled to get to the words out. "I need to go."

Jessica left the hall in the hurry. The information that had haunted her caused the memories and the truth to come flooding back. I didn't hate Liz for telling her the truth, instead I admired her honesty.

We didn't speak in the back of the limo. All Liz wanted to do was rest her head on my shoulders, cuddled up to me and held my hand all the way home. To my surprise, the limo pulled up outside a pair of iron gates that automatically opened for us. The driver took us down the driveway, that led to a large posh house.

Liz preferred to live far away from work as she wanted to keep her work and personal life separate. The driver opened the door for Liz and took her hand to help her out.

"Thank you, Barnes – I'll see you in the morning."

We went up a small set of steps and stood at the front door. Liz fumbled about in her bag to get her key. She unlocked it and we walked into a large hall with two stairwells on either side. The hall was lit up brightly by a crystal chandelier and it was surprisingly warm inside.

"This way," Liz told me. She slid a pair of doors open to the left of us and we entered a large living room with a roaring open fire. The walls were white with what looked like a seventy-inch TV on the wall. A bookshelf was in the corner and two white corner sofas were angled in towards the fireplace. In the opposite corner was a grand piano. "I don't play – it's just for decoration." Liz laughed.

She took two glasses of champagne that were already left out on a glass coffee table. She handed me one as she sat down next to me on the sofa.

"You're quiet – are you okay?"

I didn't really know what I was doing in her home.

Especially after everything that had happened.

"Look I'm sorry about earlier – but I had to be honest with Jessica and tell her the truth." I couldn't hate Liz for that. It's what everyone wants in a partner. Honesty, as there is no future in deceit. "You know, business would be so much better if I had a man by my side – someone to call my own."

Liz put her glass down on the coffee table and then left the room. Minutes later she returned, now dressed in a silk see through robe. She stood in front of me and opened the robe to let it slip off her body and flop to the floor. She placed her hands on her naked posterior.

"I know I'm not perfect," she said with a crack in her voice. "I know I have flaws and can come off selfish – but I am kind, I'm understanding and I can love. I know I may not be someone you would fall in love with and it doesn't have to mean anything to you, but this would be a perfect end to a perfect evening."

I picked up the robe and handed it back to her. I told her I was sorry but I couldn't make love to her without feeling anything. I preferred it to be an emotional connection.

"I want that too," Liz replied. "I want someone that I can love and they can love me for who I am. I want us to get married, have a family together and I want it to be you." She took hold of my hands. "I am not Jessica George – but I want to fall in love and be loved – I am real and I am here."

I took hold of Liz and kissed her softly on the lips, which soon became passionate. She began to pull my clothes off until I was naked and then she dragged me upstairs to her bedroom.

She sat down in front of me on her four poster bed. Her legs were spread and hung over the edge of the bed as she reached out to pull me down to her knees where everything was exposed. She took my hands and placed them on her cold breasts. I massaged her erect nipples while she guided my mouth to her nether region.

She gasped and moaned as I pleasured her. Her body shook with

578

excitement leading her ever closer to cumming. I wanted to tease, so I pulled away.

"No," she panted. "Don't stop."

My hands played with her while I lay next to her. The sensual feeling of my fingertips caressing her skin made her become uncontrollable. She took hold of me making me stop. I started to thrust her in a scissoring position. She became louder and her body quivered like it was going to explode. She let out a yelp as I felt her wet orgasm. We both tried to catch our breath for a second. She kept eye contact with me the entire time we did it. We were hot, sweaty and exhausted by the time we finished and it didn't take us long till we both fell asleep in each other's arms.

4

The next morning, I woke up in Liz's bed, alone. I got dressed and went looking for her but she was nowhere to be seen. When I went downstairs, her driver, Barnes, was waiting by the door. He handed me a note, which said:

I'm sorry I wasn't there next to you when you woke up.

By now, Barnes will have given you this note as there are some things I can't say to your face. Last night was amazing, truly amazing. But it can never happen again. Because it wasn't real. I know where your heart truly lies. It will always beat for Jessica George. You will always love her no matter who you are with. So, let's not kid ourselves. You know what you have to do.

I was truly lost for words. How could others see this and not myself? Jessica was my one true love. There was a spark when we first crossed paths. I knew she was the one that I wanted to spend the rest of my life with and see her develop into the woman she was always going to be.

"I'll take you back to the city," Barnes urged.

I read the note over and over again, while Barnes drove me back to the city. I was taking Liz's words into consideration. I knew I had to find Jessica and there was only one person I could think of that could help me.

I walked into Tracy's office only to see her talking to a young girl. Her wavy long blonde hair made her look very pretty and she looked identical to Jessica.

"This is my personal assistant. This is Kayleena George; she's here for a job interview."

Kayleena got out of her chair, open mouthed like she had seen a ghost. "It's you, isn't it? Jessica always talked about you – she showed me photos." She gave me a hug and then apologized. "Jessica was a fool to let you go – she hasn't been happy since she broke up with you – how are you doing?"

Heartbroken, upset and confused was the obvious answer to give. Everything was happening way too fast and my heart felt like it was burning. I just wanted everything to go back to the way it was.

"Well, maybe you're about to get your wish," Kayleena suggested. "Jessica has never stopped talking about you. Every night I heard her crying – regretting what she did to you and then seeing you with someone else made it worse."

I made it perfectly clear to her that there is nothing between me and Liz as she made sure of that by using me. I couldn't help but notice Tracy's reaction when I mentioned Liz's name. She had a face like thunder.

"Tonight is the gala. Jessica will be attending the premiere of, *His Last Story*, that will be your opportunity."

The movie adaptation of Towns-end's most popular book.

With stars and the media attending the event. I knew what I was going to do and one place I needed to go first.

When the evening arrived, I dressed in my grey suit and attended the event early. Staying out of sight I saw hundreds of people arrive, waiting behind the barriers waiting to catch a glimpse or a photo with their latest celebrity.

Sure, enough it got loud when they started to arrive in limos, waving at their fans and being blinded by the continuous flashes of cameras.

All of a sudden, the crowd went wild as a limo pulled up. The door was opened and Jessica stepped out. It was a deafening roar of screams. She looked amazing. Her brunette hair was tied back and she wore a pink dress. She turned to her fans and started waving at them. Some fans wanted personal selfies, which she happily gave them.

This was my moment to act. I wouldn't get another chance. I came out of hiding and quickly jumped the barrier, approaching Jessica on the red carpet. I stood there, scratching the back of my hand, thinking how I'm going to open up what I was about to say. The barrage of lights soon came to a stop as the crowd stared at me wondering who this mysterious stranger was in front of them.

Jessica turned around. We gazed at each other like we always did when we saw each other. "Why are you here?" she asked.

I got down on one knee and took a ring box out of my pocket. I opened it up to reveal a purple diamond ring. The crowd gasped and began taking photos to post on their social media accounts before Jessica could say anything.

Will you marry me? The predictable question that everyone asks when they get down on one knee and present a ring.

"Yes," Jessica spoke softly, "I'll marry you."

5

The happy ending that everyone searches for was in sight as I stood at the window watching everyone arrive down a long winding road in their formal wear. The sun was shining and the grass looked fresh for its countryside look. Jessica hadn't arrived yet, but I knew she was on her way. The doors behind me burst open. Kayleena looked me up and down, wondering why I was dressed in my grey suit.

"Why are you up here?"

It was where I had to be, was the only answer that I could give. Any moment now, he's coming.

"Who's coming?" Kayleena asked.

The one she loves.

"You," Kayleena whispered. "You are the one she loves."

Yes, I agreed, as my pendant glowed brightly causing my chest to burn. I always would be the one she loved, but her heart changes and I must die.

Not long after my proposal, planning the wedding took a step back. Jessica was too busy to focus on it. As time went by, I wondered if we were ever going to get married. Then, one day, she met Miss Towns-end, who had won the Towns-end beauty pageant and introduced her to Jamie, a screenplay writer. With Jessica being a well-known actress, she and Jamie both clicked and could talk for hours.

Then, the day came that Jessica admitted that she loved Jamie more than me. Her heart had changed and she knew she wanted to be married to him and spend the rest of her life with him. And that was it. I loved her enough to let her go. I'll always remember, for one brief moment, how Jessica always made me feel.

The memories flashed before my eyes. The dance at the school we had shared on our first meeting. The time we sat out in the park cuddled up while we had our picnic. The first kiss we shared. My proposal to her at the film Gala.

And now I see the most heart-breaking moment of all. The doors to the church open, revealing Jessica dressed in an elegant white wedding dress.

She's smiling. Happy.

Because her life was going to change for the better. "No – please don't go," Kayleena weeps.

I stepped out as my hand exploded into the three colours of my pendant. They crept all over my body. I felt numb.

What the hell was happening to me? I didn't understand what this pendant really was. I took a deep breath and closed my eyes.

6

When I opened my eyes, all I could see was nothing.

An endless, blackness was everywhere. There was no sound. No smell. No taste. It felt like, it was something more than that.

The blackness seemed to open up and reveal an office. It was PharmCorp. Liz sat with her back to the desk staring out at the city. The doors behind her opened. Tracy walked in and spoke her mind.

"Why did you do it?" Tracy snapped.

Liz turned round. "I had to make the most difficult choice of my life after we made love." Tracy turned her nose up at Liz. "I let go. You and I both know that Jessica George was the one true love."

"Obviously not. Jessica married someone else. Someone called Jamie and now my assistant has disappeared off the face of the earth," Tracy argued.

"I would have married. We would have been happy. But there are some things that just aren't meant to be – now why don't you sit down and listen to a proposal I have for you?"

Tracy sat down and listened to what Liz had to say.

"I am the daughter of Elizabeth Cooper. The CEO of Vision Electrics – she wanted me to be the one to take over her company, but I had bigger ideas."

"Such as?" Tracy enquired.

"All the companies in Towns-end are in agreement to put money into a project that will take years to go into effect. A new energy source for Towns-end. Lifewell Nuclear Power Station – bringing jobs and cheaper energy to the consumer."

Tracy smiled. She agreed to put money into the investment. Their companies would keep trading as normal, all the time putting small amounts of money to build the station.

They soon faded before my eyes. I was in the dark again, but I heard the faint sound of an engine. I then saw a car. Jamie was driving, while Jessica George sat in the passenger seat holding his hand. She smiled at him.

"I can't believe we did it," said Jessica.

"Now we have the rest of our lives to focus on," Jamie suggested.

"Where I can reach my full potential and live the way I was born for," she said, excitedly.

Bang. The car is hit by another car, causing them to flip over and come to a sudden halt. The bonnet smokes and hisses. The windows are shattered and glass is all over the ground. Jamie hangs upside down. Bloody. Dead. Jessica was more lucky. She was conscious. Her face and arms were covered in scratches.

The car door was then ripped open and she was pulled out just as the scene faded to black. She was missing.

Assumed dead. She was alive all this time. Taken by... I don't know. But I intended to find out.

The blackness opened up to show Matthew Cornwall speaking to Madison. She was offering him a writing job. The beginning of the story. So, that's what happened.

That's how I came to Towns-end to observe everything. I had forgotten. But now was the opportunity to tie up the loose ends. To uncover the truth and end this story. The only place to begin, was Marwood Asylum.

LEGACY

1

I sat in the back of a police car while Hannah Havers was driving. I hadn't been arrested, just the opposite, she was escorting me to Marwood Asylum. Everything I had observed and every piece of information I had gathered was all going to make sense to end this long game that had begun with Jessica George. There were only two people I needed to talk to, that predated Jessica. The vigilante team that had changed this place forever.

The tall iron gates squeaked open as Hannah drove us down a long winding lane. Green fields surrounded us.

Patients wearing white robes were staggering around like a load of zombies. Whatever medication they had been given had certainly mellowed them out.

When Hannah pulled up outside, we were greeted by two orderlies who wore white guarding the entrance. Their blank expressions made me uneasy, like they were a bunch of emotional robots. They reminded me of the family home where people were lobotomized.

Our footsteps echoed across a large reception area. The floor was tiled black and white, like a large chessboard. We approached the receptionist who was sitting behind a desk. She looked more like a nurse from the way she was dressed. White mini skirt. White blouse with a red cardigan over it with a name badge that said, *Lisa*. Her pretty eyes looked over her glasses as she asked, "Can I help you?"

"We have an appointment to see, Doctor Redma," Hannah explained.

"That's okay, Lisa," a man's voice called out. "I'll take it from here."

Doctor Redma looked like the actor Richard Dreyfuss, in a grey suit with a small white beard. We followed him down a long corridor, passing rooms with patients locked inside, until we reached his small office. It was a simple little place. The light from outside cracked through the blinds making it dimly lit. A filing cabinet, bookshelf and desk with chairs were all that were inside. We sat down and listened to what he had to say.

"You are lucky you got to see me today. I have been rather busy lately. I've been with a patient. Her name is Vikki. She has a dream complex you could say."

That was fascinating but highly irrelevant to what I was there to find out.

"Doctor Redma – we're here to see the two patients. The vigilantes," Hannah told him.

"Not possible," said Redma, bluntly. "They are to be kept locked up until the end of their days."

I had to insist. This was important. Time was running out for the world. Love had begun to die all over Towns-end and if there was any chance of saving it, then these two patients were our only hope.

I could see that he didn't like the idea. But he came around and agreed that we could briefly see them. We followed him to a small room. A table and three chairs with one of those two-way mirrors was all that was in the room.

I waited for about five minutes, while Redma and Hannah were watching from the other side of the two-way mirror. Eventually Justin Richards and Samuel Stephens were brought in, both in straight jackets unable to move.

They stared at me with envious eyes. It was like there was darkness in their souls. I made my intentions perfectly clear to them.

"Good luck with that." Samuel sniggered.

"He says that a lot." Justin smiled. "So, you want to know what we did to end up in this place? How we were wrongfully put away for doing the right thing?"

I told them how it would be a start. I didn't expect them to be cooperative, but to my surprise, they told me their story.

2

The streets of the city were crowded with people gathered outside the government peninsula building. Anger had erupted, with the people shouting abusive threatening language holding up signs that read *No More* and *Enough*. Police stood outside the Peninsula, blocking and attempting to stop the protesters. On a nearby path a reporter holding a microphone stood in front of a camera.

"Chaos, outside the Peninsula today – as the Government have confirmed there will be price hikes and a wage freeze."

The scene then paused, as Adam hit the pause button on a laptop in the spare room of his flat. He selects a live feed, adjusts the camera, which blurs then changes as a man comes into focus.

"Is this thing on?" said Adam, as he continued to tweak the image making sure the microphone was working.

Satisfied that everything was right – Adam began to talk in front of the camera using the video that he was just watching as an example of his opinion and what he wants to say.

He begins with the obvious, pointing out the government's flaws and lies they had told the people. From having secret parties, giving themselves pay rises and spending health and school funds on themselves.

Aggressively he used the media as an example. Fake news. Negative depressing reports and plenty of injustice where criminals were having their sentences reduced to pretty much nothing. There was only so much we could all take.

"If that is the way they want things – then they can guarantee that there will be a civil war," Adam suggested. "There are a hundred and fifty thousand police all over Towns-end. All it takes is two hundred thousand of the millions that live here to rise up and take it all back. Sure, they'd get their martial law out and threaten us with guns, but that will only show everyone who the real monsters are that try and stop our freedom of speech."

Adam grasped his head feeling his stress levels building. "I don't know how long this video will be kept up for before they get scared. My previous posts have already been taken down."

Adam stops the recording. Hovers the mouse arrow over the upload button and presses it. As the video uploads and shares to multiple social media sites, Adam lies back on the bed feeling satisfied with himself and shuts his eyes. As he sleeps through the night – the video gets hundreds of positive comments, likes, loves and shares. It goes viral, spreading like wildfire.

The next day – Adam's wife, Kate, comes down the hallway yawning looking heavy eyed like she had a terrible night's sleep. Her long hair is messy and hangs over the top of her gown. Kate knocks on the spare room door.

"Wakey, Wakey." Kate waits, but there is no reply. "Look I'm sorry about last night, you didn't have to sleep in here." But still there is nothing. Kate is concerned and enters the room. She gasps, with a look of horror on her face as she sees blood on the wall – blood on the floor – the window smashed and no sign of Adam's body. All she can do is, scream.

We have always been fascinated by secrets and conspiracies. But how far would we go to uncover the truth? Would we put ourselves in danger? Or the ones that we love?

Half an hour had passed after Kate had discovered Adam gone. She panicked when she saw the damage and the blood on the floor, and was a wreck when she called the police.

When the police arrived they tended to Kate while Detective Jameson and a forensics team looked over the scene of the crime. Kate's friend Rachael sat with her arm round her for comfort – while Police Constable, Sarah Williams questioned Kate.

"So, you heard no sounds coming from the other room?"

"I told you, no," Kate snaps, "we had a row last night and we slept apart."

"And what was the row about?" Sarah asks.

"The government, his social media posts had been taken down. But our row escalated when he insisted he was going to post a video." Kate sighs and buries her face in her hands feeling stressed.

Rachael rubs her back and snaps at Sarah. "Don't you think Kate's been through enough?"

But before Sarah could answer, Kate yelled, "He was right – he said that the government would make him disappear because of his freedom of speech. The government doesn't want the truth to come out so they make people disappear."

"I don't believe that the government would go that far," Sarah insists.

"Well, you would say that wouldn't you? – After all you work for them." Rachael tries to calm Kate down seeing how angry she gets. Sarah doesn't know what to say but understands why she was reacting the way she was. She notices Detective Jameson coming down the stairs and hastily joins him.

"Well, Williams – what have you got?"

Sarah shows Jameson what she wrote down. As he reads it, she can tell that a look of disgust is beginning to form. He shakes his head then throws the pad at her and leaves. She chases after him wondering why he was angry. He sternly tells her that he won't believe the ramblings of a distraught woman.

"Sir, there's a reason why she's distraught – how can you just dismiss that?" Sarah snaps.

Jameson wags his finger in front of her and warns her that she's treading dangerous ground and needs to keep her opinions to herself. Sarah felt angry as he walked away from her. She looked over at Kate feeling sorry for her and made a promise to herself to find out anything she could about what happened to her husband. She watches Rachael hold Kate's hand talking to Kate before inevitably walking away.

"I can't believe this happened," mumbles Rachael.

"Neither can I," Kate replies. "It just goes to prove one thing – the government really are dictating monsters – say something out of line or get close to a truthful theory, and they will do whatever it takes to keep it hidden." She pauses. "I just wonder how long it will be until it's my turn."

Rachael couldn't believe that Kate would say such things, but Kate believed it with all her heart. What her husband said and warned her about was all true – and now he was gone. Kate told Rachael that no one really knew what goes on behind closed doors. We are told something – but unless we see it with our own eyes – that's the only way you can believe in anything.

"So, what you're saying that they have a curtain over the country? When we pull it back we can see what they've been really doing? Like a distraction?" Rachael assumes.

"That's exactly what I'm saying," Kate assures.

Rachael's phone vibrates interrupting them in the middle of their conversation. She apologized to Kate and took the call. "Yes... yes, sure... okay... I'll be there soon."

Rachael stood and apologized to Kate again and told her that she had to leave and pick up her son from school.

"Of course, Rachael – go."

"I'll come back – check up on you," Rachael assures.

"Thank you."

Rachael left. Kate rested her head on the cushions of the sofa. Her eyes were red, stinging and felt heavy from all the crying she had done. She struggled to keep them open – but couldn't fight to stay awake and eventually closed them to go to sleep.

But it wasn't for too long – as Kate's eyes were snapped open by a sound that startled her. She sat up quick, dazed and confused, thinking that she may have dreamed it. She listens hard but all there is, is silence. She relaxes, realizing that there wasn't anything to worry about. That her mind was playing tricks. She grabs her phone from the coffee table to look at the time. She had been asleep for about an hour.

Kate then gasps – letting her phone slip out of her hand when she hears a noise coming from upstairs. Her heart races – she is frozen to the spot and her body is shaking.

She looked over to the kitchen, then heard the noise again like furniture was being moved around. She leapt off the sofa and ran to the kitchen taking out a large kitchen knife from the cutlery drawer for protection.

She stood still – listening for another noise to follow. Kate waited for a good couple of minutes but all she heard was silence. She then made a bold decision and cautiously made her way up the stairs – her heart still pounding through fear and adrenaline.

Kate crept along the hallway – making her way to the spare room. The door is closed – covered by police tape. She stretched her hand out and grabbed hold of the handle. As she turned it – her other hand gripped the knife tightly as she didn't know what was waiting for her on the other side of the door. As she swung open the door – she dropped the knife and screamed.

3

An hour later – Rachael's blue car pulls up outside Kate's house.

"Why are we here?" Xander asked.

"It's complicated – I just need to see if Kate is okay," Rachael told him.

Rachael stepped out of the car. Xander watched her walk up to the front door and press the doorbell. Xander found it strange that Kate didn't answer the door. Rachael pressed the bell again, but still Kate didn't come. He stepped out of the car and joined his mum's side.

"She's not in, Mum."

"That's impossible – she was a wreck – she wouldn't leave the house." Rachael knocked on the door – but she found it already ajar. Xander assumed that maybe Kate forgot to lock the door. "Stay here, Xander."

Rachael walked into Kate's house and began to look around. The living room was immaculate – like Kate had tidied up the mess that was left from the investigation. She called for Kate but there was no reply. Once she checked the kitchen and the back yard, she made her way upstairs. But she didn't have to go very far when she saw fresh blood on the walls and the floor – and no sign of Kate.

4

Rachael's hands held a polystyrene cup in her hands which shook with the shock of what she discovered in Kate's house. Xander helped Rachael steady her hands. The door to an office in the police station opened as Sarah Williams entered and took a seat in front of her.

"I'm sorry to keep you waiting – are you okay to answer some questions?" Sarah asked Rachael who nodded. "So, you left Kate's house around lunch time?"

"Later in the afternoon – I went to the school to pick Xander up," Rachael told her. "Is there any point to these questions, Miss Williams?"

"Any information is required to assist in the investigation of her disappearance." Sarah explains.

Rachael shook her head and laughed at Sarah's comment. She thought that it was ironic that her husband, Adam, went missing and then his wife after he uploaded a video just because of his opinion on the government.

"Now, Miss Bendon – you can't jump to conclusions like that," Sarah demanded. But Rachael remembered talking to Kate – convincing her that there was something strange going on. Rachael thought that the justice system had got to her and was now protecting their precious government.

Sarah wanted to react from Rachael's harsh outburst – but she knew it wasn't professional and felt there was more to this than she realized.

Rachael stood up and told Xander that they were leaving – that they couldn't be around the police. Sarah pleaded with Rachael to sit down as she hadn't finished questioning her, but Rachael insisted that she needed to leave, so she could get back home and share the video on social media so everyone should know the truth about what was happening.

"Miss Bendon – do you hear yourself – if this is true – you are putting yourself and your son in danger," Sarah insists. Rachael looks up at her, glaring in anger.

"Then I hope that the people will see that the government are monsters."

5

Later that evening – Rachael was sitting in her living room pouring herself a glass of wine. She had a headache – overthinking about the events of the day – and knew all too well that the wine wasn't going to help.

Upstairs – Xander was sitting at his computer, flicking through the videos on YouTube. He finished watching a *Fortnite* streaming video and then decided to look up Adam's video that was causing all the trouble.

He was then interrupted by Cullum who was calling him on his phone.

"Cullum, what's up?"

"Xander, Whitestone wants us to see him immediately. Heroes Assemble," Cullum explained.

"I'll be there as soon as I can. I'm busy at the moment. People we know are disappearing."

"Sounds like we should assemble the Hall of Heroes."

"No. This isn't something that the Heroes should get involved in – I'll be in touch when I can." Xander hung up, then turned his attention to Adam giving his opinion about the government, little knowing that something was happening downstairs.

Once Rachael had finished her glass of wine – she went to the kitchen and started to wash the dishes. She placed some plates on the drainer and then went to get a tea towel. She jumped when a noise startled her from outside. She looked closely through the window but it was too dark to see anything. Once she felt everything was all right again – she picked up a plate to dry – but then someone grabbed her from behind – covering her mouth with their hand so she couldn't scream.

As Xander finished watching the video, he heard a smash from downstairs. "Mum," he yelled, but there was no answer – all he heard was footsteps coming up the stairs. "Mum," he called, but still there was no reply. He began to panic feeling that someone else was in the house. He moved some of his furniture in front of the door to make a small barricade and then returned to his computer to broadcast a live video.

"It's true," Xander panicked. "I have just watched the video. The government did make Adam and Kate disappear and now they're coming for us." He looks away to see the furniture pushed aside. "HELP," he yelled. "See the truth of the Government."

Xander falls back onto the computer which falls on the floor. The image from the camera shows the floor and doesn't show who enters the room. All the camera was recording was Xander screaming and being dragged away.

6

The video then stops. John Alan looks horrified to see the video that had been sent to him through his email as he sits at his computer on a reception desk at *See through Windows Installations*. Being a man in his late sixties, John had seen a lot of things through his life and worked many different jobs, but nothing like what he had just seen in the video.

"Carole?" John calls across from his desk. "Was this a joke?" Carole didn't understand what John implied until she watched the video for herself. She began to get paranoid and called Rachael's number immediately, but to her surprise Rachael's number was no longer in service.

"What the hell's going on?" John asked. Before Carole could say anything, two men in suits walked through the door. John gets up out of his chair and stands at the desk. John notices the name badges on their suits 'Mick Cook' and 'Matt Greenway' both are government MPs.

"Are you Mr John Alan?" Mick asks.

"You should know that shouldn't you? Being Government officials and all."

"It has come to our attention that you received a video from a Xander Bendon – we would like to see it," Mick insists.

John laughs to himself – just because they have a status as an MP it doesn't give them the authority to barge into a business and demand anything they want. John turns his back on them and returns to his desk.

"What are you doing? We haven't finished talking to you," Matt snaps.

"I have." John sits down. "I'm working – which is more than can be said for what you're doing."

"We want to confirm it you have this video," Mick insists.

John stands up urgently and aggressively says, "Or what? You're going to make me disappear too?" He kicks his chair out from under him and flings his arms out. "Go on then – kill me – in front of everyone here," he yells. "Do it – come on just do it – do it." Screaming at the top of his voice banging his fists on his chest like a gorilla. Matt shows aggression to John's behaviour but Carole reacts and grabs her scissors to use as a weapon to defend John. Mick stops Matt from going any further.

"You want a war – well this is it," John warns. Matt and Mick look at each other but don't say anything. As they leave the building, John goes over to Carole who is still holding the scissors. John holds her shaking hands then takes the scissors away from her. "Don't worry – all we have to do is share the video – the more people see it – the more they will realize the truth."

7

The news spread quickly about the government conspiracy. Videos of Adam's message turned up on social media pages and adverts as more and more people shared it. The footage of the two MPs harassing John was recorded on Carole's phone and uploaded to YouTube and shared on multiple media sites. It became so big it ended up on the news and in the papers.

Mark sits on the sofa in his second floor flat watching the video. He shook his head in disgust. He then looks up from the video as the doorbell sounds. Mark answered the door and saw the same two MPs standing in the stairwell.

"Mark May?" Mick asked.

"What the hell do you want?" Mark replied.

"We've had reports that you have been sharing a particular video to stir up trouble – we'd like to check out your computer"

"And that's all it takes is it? No warrant or police escort? Just thinking you have the authority of God to do whatever you want," Mark snaps. "You've accused me – so – when you find out that I haven't been doing what you think I have – I'm going to have you for false accusations."

"Is that a threat?" Matt insisted.

Mark sighs and holds his hand up in surrender. "No – I'm sorry." Mark asked for Mick's forgiveness then put his arm around him and explained that he had watched the video which made him angry – and with them being there, it proved that the video was right.

Mark grabbed Mick and pushed him down the stairs. His body tumbled hard causing him to bleed and suffer considerable pain. Matt rushed to help him while Mark warned them both never to return.

Matt helped Mick to his feet then they left the building.

Mark returned to his computer and took out a hidden camera which was disguised as one of the buttons on his shirt. He connected it to his computer and played the footage back he recorded. He then uploaded it to multiple websites and linked it to the video that was taken at *See Through Windows*.

601

8

Inside the Government Peninsula building, an uproar debate is occurring. The MPs of different parties cause a deafening noise through constant rowing over the poison that the videos were causing among Towns-end.

"This video has caused gossip – rumours and panic in the streets – and the people are starting to believe these false claims – the video should be taken down and the one responsible prosecuted," the MP demands.

The MPs squabble amongst themselves like children in a playground. The Prime Minister stands in front of the MP on the opposite side and interrupts, "Even though this video has been shared thousands of times it would be impossible to stop it. This is just trolling and unacceptable behaviour."

"How can you justify that this cannot be stopped? – The people of Towns-end are believing in false accusations that the government are making people disappear for using their freedom of speech," the MP retaliates.

All of a sudden – the room shakes. Everyone looks around to feel the rumble. Outside, the chaos has begun. The police are forced back by violent people throwing flammable bottles and attacking them with weapons. The police begin to fall like dominoes, being stabbed and beaten by angry rioters. A policeman staggers around burning to death until they drop to their knees with no one to help them.

Vans of riot police turn up at the scene – rushing out of the vans holding riot shields to defend themselves with, but more civilians join the crowds of rioters and overpower them.

Eventually the rioters break into the peninsula and begin to attack the MPs. The Prime Minister and MPs inside the room barricade the doors and are deafened by the sounds of screams from the other side.

"Everyone remain calm – we have been made out to be the bad people – and the people on the other side of that door think we won't be safe," the Prime Minister argued.

"And yet… it is true," a man's voice speaks through the a speaker. All the MPs look around wondering where the voice came from. The Prime Minister walked around the room as the voice said what they had to say.

They started by stating that the government had controlled people's lives by telling them what to do and how to live. Throwing everything in reverse where wrong was right. Corrupted bent laws where criminals and people that don't work get rewarded while the hard working person suffered. They controlled the media using fake and negative news to keep people scared. Fake reality TV that brainwashed the public and prompted suicide. People's taxes that benefited the government's own personal bank accounts. And, finally, getting people thrown in prison or making them disappear for using their freedom of speech.

"Here is a message to the government," the man's voice threatens. "This is not a story – this is the real world."

"But we haven't done anything wrong – we have never killed anyone or made them disappear – these are false accusations," the Prime Minister insists.

"You forgot – all the years you have been in power that there are millions of ordinary people that outnumber the government and police – you have no power over us any more and the people now know that."

The room begins to fill with smoke from all sides. MPs eyes begin to sting and their lungs fill with the burning fumes that cause them to choke.

"How does it feel to have your own brainwashed corrupted system that your created – turned against you…?"

9

Mark stands on a rooftop from afar to see the Peninsula on fire while he has his phone to his ear.

"…to realize that some of us can still break your rules we have been waiting for the world to know that we exist." Mark puts the call on hold, then two men join his side. "I hope I didn't hurt you too much."

"Just a few bruises – no serious injuries," Mick said amused.

"The others are on their way," Matt told Mark.

"Would you look at the sight of that?" Adam smiles, as his wife Kate and friends Rachael and Xander stand by his side all safe and sound.

"You did a good job," Mark praised. "You all managed to fool an entire country through a fake disappearance and murder – Bravo."

"Just playing the government at their own game," said Adam remembering the plan.

Adam uploaded the video and lay back on the bed closing his eyes. The door to the spare room opened and Kate stood in front of him holding a bottle with red liquid inside. She put the blood on the carpet while Adam smashed the window.

After Rachael had left to see Xander at the school – Kate had fallen asleep. She woke up to a noise coming from upstairs. When she went up the stairs, Adam was waiting for her, with another bottle of fake blood. "You ready for this?" he asked her. She nodded and smiled.

Rachael and Xander walk into their house after leaving the police station. "Do you want to go upstairs and get that video ready to be made?" she asked.

"Okay, Mum," Xander said enthusiastically as he rushed up the stairs to his room. Rachael pretends to hear a noise in the kitchen then is grabbed from behind by... Kate.

Upstairs in Xander's bedroom, he has barricaded the door as someone forces their way in. The barricade gives way knocking the camera to the floor. Xander just stands there screaming like he's being grabbed. But Adam walks past him and stamps on the camera. "Good job, Xander,"

Adam compliments.

John met his two colleagues Mick and Matt in the pub with Mark sitting at the table. John went through the plan that they should dress up as MPs so they can give the illusion that they are working for the government and are ordering people to take down Adam's video.

Adam hears them coughing as the fire rages even higher outside the Peninsula. "Know this – you got your wish – the country is united in equality. People from all backgrounds, a mixture of foreign citizens and religious backgrounds, straights, gay, lesbian, trans. They're all burning the government down to the ground.

A loud explosion occurs. They all watch from the rooftop as the clock face flies off, while the entire tower crumbles.

"A world without government? Life will be so much better without them." Matt smiles.

"There's one more left," Samuel interrupted. "The government's powers would have been passed on, if anything happened to them. Luckily I know Charlotte."

"Then you should go." Everyone, including Samuel turned around to see Justin Richards, dressed in a black leather jacket. "This was all my plan and now you should all go and carry on living your lives without the consequences."

Everyone pattered Justin on the shoulder, wishing him luck. Rachael noticed that Xander held back from leaving.

"What is it?" Rachael asked.

"I need to see Cullum and Jessica – they need me."

"Now is not a good time," Rachael explained.

"It's the perfect time – we're the heroes, Mum, the ones who defended the school."

"What?" said Rachael in disbelief.

With Justin and Samuel watching the two of them, they decided to leave and take their conversation away from all the chaos that was occurring, leaving the two remaining ring leaders to discuss their final moments.

"You're giving yourself up?" Samuel asked.

"I'm distracting them, so you can get the job done," Justin explained. "I go on the run and they eventually catch me, I should have bought you enough time."

"That is one hell of a gamble." Samuel placed his hand on Justin's shoulder. "Good luck with that."

"You too." Justin smiled. When Samuel walked away, Justin took one last look at the destroyed government. "The world has changed."

10

From there on it all made sense. Why Samuel killed Charlotte and was haunted by what he did. The government's plans had been left for her to carry on and it was the only way to stop the government once and for all.

What they didn't take into account, was that they changed the world… forever.

"You got all your information you need," said Samuel, sarcastically. "What's the real reason why you came here?"

I told them everything that I had observed. That there was an even bigger threat than the government. I feared that what was prophesized was all going to come true. The day love will die.

"Bull shit," said Justin, bluntly. "Love never dies."

The lights then shut off. Plunging us all into darkness.

The emergency red lighting kicked in and an alarm sounded.

"Didn't they pay the electric bill to vision electrics?" Samuel joked.

"It wasn't us," Justin insisted.

"Nobody panic – we have an intruder," Redma's voice, came out of a speaker in the room.

Both Justin and Samuel stood up, they realized they were being watched by the two-way mirror. They were smart. They couldn't be fooled. They began to wriggle, like they wanted to break free from their restraints. It took them a while, but they didn't give up and eventually their strait jackets fell to the floor. They were free.

They both grabbed a chair each and threw it at the mirror, shattering it, into pieces. Before Redma and Hannah knew it, they were inside the room with them focusing their attention onto a monitor that showed various areas of the asylum.

An aged woman, wearing a funeral dress and black hat was waltzing through the hallway. Not a single one knew who she was. But I did. I recognized her from a long time ago. It was Madison. Madison Milburn, who bought Charlie Bradshaw and then cut off his manhood. Why she was here was a mystery. I couldn't work out what reason she had after observing what I had seen her do.

The orderlies stood in her way. Blocking off her path to wherever she was going. She stood there. Smiling like some sadistic psychopath.

BANG, BANG, BANG. We watched in horror as she shot the orderlies stone dead on the spot. She then turned her attention to the camera in the ceiling.

"I know you can see me. Open up all the cells. There's one patient I need to see," Madison insisted. "Or I'll kill you all, if you dare get the police involved."

Hannah was about to radio in to send back up, but after Madison's statement, she hesitated and turned off her radio. Redma's interest in Justin and Samuel had already sparked an idea.

"You could help us. Do what you do and take her out," Redma suggested.

"What for? A meal?" Samuel replied sarcastically.

"And what happens to us after that? You gonna lock us away for another fifteen years?" Richard snapped.

"This is serious, gentlemen – you're the Residents of War – you help people – that's what you do," Hannah explained.

"Did, love – not any more – this is your domestic," Samuel referred.

"I can't let these patients out," said Redma.

"Oh, you can't," Justin replied, as he pushed him out of the way. "Watch me." And with that the cell doors all opened.

One by one. Each of the patients exited their cells. They looked puzzled. Wondering what was going on. I noticed three familiar faces. The first was a man, formerly a boy who went by the name of Tom. He was the boy that Ashley the vampire had met. The boy that killed his abusive stepfather. The other was Alison Chance, the psychotic singer who was obsessed with Rick, who killed him when he rejected her and had her baby taken away. And last, but not least, a three hundred-pound woman by the name of Krista. The one that created the Play 4 Real club. The life destroyer.

We watched on the monitor as Madison walked into the cell area. Tom approached and asked her, "Are you the one that let us out?" But Madison's only reply was to blow his brains out.

"I'm only here for the women." Madison smiled. "Like you Alison – I'm impressed with what you did. Would you like another chance to do it all over again?"

"I need to find the man that I'm supposed to torment and be with forever." Alison giggled.

"Then come with me and I'll make your dream come true."

Alison joined Madison's side. Krista attempted to approach her, but found herself held at gunpoint.

"Why not me?" Krista enquired.

"Because you're not the real Krista. The real Krista is my daughter. You've tried to take credit for the legacy I have been building for her. This is where your story ends." Madison unloaded bullet after bullet until the gun was empty and Krista was a dead bloody mess. She then offered her hand out to Kate. "Come with me – you have such a gift that should not be wasted."

Kate smiled deliciously and took hold of Madison's hand. They all walked together like an army down the corridors of the asylum. When they got to the reception, the receptionist, Lisa, joined them and together they left the building.

When all was clear we left the asylum too. Her little murder spree was traumatic to see all the orderlies' bodies that had been killed by Madison. When we got outside, Justin grabbed hold of Redma and swiped his car keys from inside his jacket pocket.

"This is Police Constable Hannah Havers, we have escaped patients and a murder suspect at Marwood Asylum – I need back up, now," Hannah ordered into her radio.

"What about patient 10051982?" said the man on the other line.

Justin and Samuel, looked at Hannah with anticipation at what she was going to say. "They're dead – send back up as fast as you can."

"Thank you." Samuel nodded.

I tried to make them stay. Pleaded with them to help me. One last hope.

"Word of advice," Samuel referred. "Retrace your steps to the beginning and you'll find your answers."

And with that, they drove off, to make up for all the lost time.

To retrace my steps I started at the first place I could think of. A small house at the top of a hill. Madison's place. It was exactly how I remembered it, with a few faded colours and rotted walls. Time hadn't been kind to it. From the top of the hill I could see my goal. Pentemy Village was in sight. But facing Madison was the first thing I had to do.

When I knocked on the door, it creaked open. It was already ajar. She wasn't very security conscious. I called out, but no one answered. She wasn't home. I had a feeling that the place had been abandoned for a long time.

As I took a look around, layers of dust and musty smells made it clear that it hadn't been lived in since I last observed it. Flies buzzed around the mouldy food that had been left from Charlie and Madison's meal and his chair hadn't been picked up from when he passed out from when she drugged him.

My curiosity took me to the basement. It was the last time I saw Charlie and I wondered if his body had been left there. The infamous red door squeaked open and there it was. The guillotine that chopped his manhood off with dried blood on the floor. There was no sign of his penis or his body as the drag marks on the floor made it obvious what happened to it.

When I returned to the living room I took a look around. Looking in cupboards and drawers for any clues that could help me. I didn't find anything of interest. Just cupboards full of cleaning and table mats.

I moved onto her bedroom. A place I should have started with. Madison's clothes had been left in her drawers and her wardrobe was filled with long colourful dresses. But wait. Behind the dresses was a cardboard box filled to the brim with newspaper cuttings.

When I spilled the contents on the floor, I spotted an old faded photo of Madison. She looked like she was a high school girl. But it was the boy that she was in the photo with that sent a shiver down my spine. It was Matthew Cornwall.

As I looked through the scattered contents of the box, I found more pictures of familiar faces. Ana and a dark haired man. Dennis. The police woman's boyfriend, Scott. What really got my attention was a baby scan. The same year that Madison and Matthew had been together. I thought back to what Madison had told Charles, about her abuse that she had sustained that left her pregnant. What I found hard to believe was that Matthew was that monstrous.

With this evidence in my possession, it was time to piece all this together. So, I retraced my steps to the first faces that I had seen. Allison and Matthew.

By this point, the two of them had been happily remarried and were more in love than ever before. Matthew had given up on the idea of being a writer, considering that it was the thing that caused a dent in his marriage.

When I turned up at their door, they welcomed me with ease, like there was some sort of trust. I asked them questions about their past that involved Madison Milburn. It was a question that Matthew regretted to hear. While Matthew told me his past, Allison held his hand and was supportive.

"It was on the night of the school prom. We were young. She was such a wildcat and rather scary," Matthew explained. "After a great night – she wanted sex. But not normal sex. She demanded it rough. Sex that would make her scream from behind." Matthew paused, I could see it in his eyes that he didn't want to tell me any more. "I broke up with her after that night, as the way she behaved scared me. It was a month later that our paths crossed, the day after I met Allison. Madison told me she was pregnant, she showed me the scan and then admitted she was going to terminate the baby, as I met someone else."

Sometimes in our life we have to decide if doing the right thing is always the best thing. I could have told him the truth. That Madison kept the baby and left her in Pentemy Village to grow up without her real parents. After everything that Matthew and Allison had been through, I knew this was the right time to walk away and let them discover the truth for themselves.

My checklist made me skip Megan May as there was no evidence to suggest that she was involved in Madison's box of tricks. Nelson and Mary were both dead, so the next face I went to find was Missy. When I got to her apartment, I discovered that she had moved and Will was still working at his *Chunky Pie* restaurant.

Will wasn't very cooperative at first. He didn't want to be reminded of

Missy and Marcy. It turned out that Missy hadn't seen Marcy since that day after upsetting Will and that she had moved out and met someone else, a few blocks away.

After getting the details of where she had moved to, I set out to find her. She opened the door and wondered what I wanted.

"Who is it, hun?" a female voice called out.

Evelyn walked up to us. She stood behind Missy and wrapped her arms around her. The twinkle of her wedding ring said it all. They were married. They had met not long after Will had seen Marcy with Missy. Evelyn found a friend in Missy as they shared a drink together after she had moved from Pentemy and poured her heart out how she had been deceived by Matthew. With the amount of men that had been unfaithful to Evelyn, she turned and discovered true love with Missy and couldn't have been happier.

When I showed them the picture of Madison, Missy knew very little about her. But Evelyn on the other hand told me plenty of info on her. After winning Miss Towns-end, she became quite the leader of Pentemy Village. But her hatred of men began to rub off on its population and spread outwards. Evelyn shared her experiences with men and could relate. She was obsessed with Matthew and wanted him back in her life. But when she couldn't get him she began to go out with some of the worst men she could find.

The first was a man named Gordon. He was an abusive bastard, who I remembered very well. He was the man that Tom killed after witnessing him abuse his mother. The second man was Dennis. Married and quite the unfaithful pervert that loved to destroy relationships. The last man was Scott. The one who was hell bent on becoming a detective. It was his one goal in life. Madison was jealous as she wanted herself to be his goal. But it never happened.

As I was about to move on, Evelyn remembered one more man that she wanted to have a relationship with. The last man that made her turn crazy. He was a priest. Father Thomas of St Michael's Church. She had been seductive towards him, but his religion was something that she just couldn't get in the way of.

What was even more bizarre was Evelyn knew about Matthew before she had even met him due to Madison talking about him. She confessed that when she saw him and how nice he was, it was then that Evelyn could see that Madison was nuts, all in the sake of revenge for what happened to her mother.

I remembered PharmCorp's involvement in her mother, so that was where I went next. I had no time to wait around for appointments, so barging in was the only way to get what I wanted as time was running out.

Running away from the security wasn't on my agenda, but I had no other choice. I burst into Liz Cooper's office, but found out that Liz wasn't there. Tracy Luna from Foptix was sitting in her chair, with Harry and Cynthia in front of her. They smiled at me, like they knew me but they didn't. The security guards burst in to apprehend me, but Tracy stopped them. "No – it's okay – you can go."

The security acknowledged her and left us to it. Cynthia took great interest in me. She scanned me and knew that I wasn't normal. An unknown entity that was created from that pendant that I was found with when I was a baby.

"You're called The Observer – you've been watching us – following all of our stories," Cynthia confirmed.

I apologised for the interruption. Told Harry that I was sorry for his loss of Jennifer. I asked Tracy where Liz was as I needed to know more info about Madison Milburn's mother, Leighanne.

Tracy couldn't help me as Liz was out. She pointed to a live broadcast on the TV that showed Liz in front of a camera and speaking into a microphone, live.

"It is a great honour and a historic moment for me to be here today. It has taken years, time and money for all of Towns-end's companies to achieve this goal. With the financial aid from PharmCorp, Foptix Industries, Vision Electrics, See Through Windows Installations, Curly Cables Ltd and CL Petra – I am proud to announce the opening of, Lifewell Nuclear Power station – supplying energy and jobs for the whole of Towns-end."

The crowd applauded. Liz had finally achieved her goal.

"Miss Cooper," a journalist interrupted. "What are your next plans for the future of Towns-end?"

"I'm sorry – who are you?" Liz enquired.

"India Johnson – Towns-end Gazette," India replied.

"Well, Miss Johnson – if everyone looks up, that's our next step." Liz grinned with delight. "We will be starting a space program to explore what's out there. With the aid of Foptix Industries, a team are currently working on producing the engine for the starship, swift-shift."

"How long will this take?" India questioned.

"A very long time." Liz chuckled. "I doubt we will get to see it in our lifetime."

Space exploration? Liz was always ambitious but I never imagined how far she was planning to go with her wild ideas.

12

Mr Alan was next on my list. The natural history museum was about to close, so I needed to hurry along and talk to him before it was too late.

I made my way past the glass cabinets of old dinosaur fossil bones and items of historical value until I found Mr Alan's office. When I walked in, the office was a mess and there was no sign of him. Books were scattered around in a circle. Upon closer inspection, it was a book on a stone circle, just on the outskirts of Towns-end, but one of the carved stones was missing from it as there was talk of a guardian demon that was inside it. Another book showed a supernatural entity called, Shadye.

"Doesn't anyone have manners and knock any more?" an elderly voice called out. The desk chair span around revealing Mr Alan. Time had been unkind to him as he looked rather frail.

I was surprised he was still working on cases of possible hauntings. I checked out the books that were on his desk that were separate from the pile on the floor. The Timeless Woods, Destination X, The Chamber of Horrors and the Silent Village incident, that Liz Cooper was responsible for.

"Those cases are ones I won't touch. Not even the Abandoned Ghost Hunters will investigate them, especially what lives in the Silent Village. They're off limits to everyone – classified as the most dangerous areas in Towns-end – now tell me, why are you here?"

I got to the point and showed him Madison's picture, but he had no idea who she was. I told him that I needed to find Frank Mason as he may be able to help.

"Frank Mason disappeared a long time ago," Alan explained. "His car was found abandoned near Faymill Farm – but he was never found. I wish I knew what happened there."

As he didn't know I filled in the blanks. I told him that he had been contacted by Sharon who had changed her name from Lilly after what her fat sister, Krista, did to her.

Together they uncovered the mystery of Faymill, but the biggest mystery turned out to be Lilly. Her body was discovered by Frank and that was when he disappeared.

"There was always something special between Lilly and Frank. It made sense. Losing her would make him want to disappear. That explains why he was talking to himself – he was talking to her."

Mr Alan was smart. He seemed smarter than me. A man that could piece a puzzle together with ease. I needed him to come with me. Together we could conclude all this.

"Well, that's rather tempting. But I don't really know you. Convince me." His reaction to when I said the words *He Will Die in Pentemy*, was proof that I meant business. "With dangerous words like that, the words that threatened my brother, Mr Geoffries, how can I trust you?"

There was only one thing I could think of. Fourteen words I could use to convince him. *LOVE ISN'T A WEAPON; LOVE IS AN EMOTION THAT WE WILL ALL USE. FOREVER.*

Mr Alan smiled. The key words that had been set up since the beginning had a reason to be used. He was convinced and agreed to help me find Mr Geoffries before it was too late.

"I'll find him for you – in the meantime, I suggest you go to Faymill Farm. You might find some clue that will lead you to Frank."

13

Faymill looked like it was about to fall down when I arrived. The wooden farmhouse was rotted and decaying before me. Frank's old car was still there. Rusted and faded over time.

The front door swung open when I tried it. It hung on one hinge, with it nearly falling off. The floorboards creaked as I wandered through the dimly lit hallways and my lungs started to get blocked with all the dust floating in the air, which made me cough.

The floorboards above me creaked. I thought it was because of the age of the farmhouse, but a thud told me otherwise. There was someone else in the house with me. I called out to see if anyone would answer me. Predictably they didn't. It made me tense as I stood at the bottom of the stairs and slowly made my way up step by step.

I held my nose when I got to the top. A foul smell filled the air from one of the open rooms. As I approached, the sound of buzzing flies grew louder and when I entered the room, they were buzzing around filthy bedsheets. This was the room that Sharon's body was in. But the body was gone. It was good in a way as the last thing I wanted to see was a decaying corpse.

Just then, a shiver was sent down my spine as a cold draft hit the back of my neck. Was there something behind me? From the reflection of myself in the window, there clearly wasn't. When I turned around, I jumped out of my skin to see a short haired pale woman standing before me. I looked at the window again only to see myself. She was still there when I looked back at her. I then realized who she was. She hadn't aged a day since I last saw her. It was Ashley, the vampire who got with Tom then ran away when she discovered he killed his step dad.

"I haven't seen anyone in years. Why have you come to this place?" Ashley asked. Her eyes stared at me with lustful intent. Not to make out, but to bite my neck.

I told her who I was and everything I had observed. She relaxed more as I showed that I could be someone she could trust. I couldn't help but wonder why she was held up in this old farmhouse.

"Because of the MGP." Ashley sighed.

I had heard that name once before. But I never understood what it meant.

"Their vans are everywhere. They have an interest in people like us. Surely, you've seen them around. Haven't you noticed how many women have disappeared?"

I thought back to Hannah. When she was in the police station showing Scott a board of missing people. Hundreds of women that were missing. The only thing Ashley didn't know was what the letters stood for. The full name. For all I knew, it could have been something that I had observed in front of me this entire time.

I was curious, how it was possible that Ashley was a vampire, so she told me her story and where she came from.

"We all come from Alcina Castle – on the edge of Towns-end in the North. There were four of us – all girls. The tall lady, Lilith, who was queen of the castle was scooped up by a cloud and taken from her kingdom and King Dragula. The cloud had made her grow over time. She never stopped growing. She made us all walk into the cloud which ignited our blood lust."

I remembered the story of the kingdom of Alcina. Dragula's Queen and Castle that had disappeared that sparked the war between Princess Shabetha of the red mountains and her Hall of Heroes. I never realized that Lilith was Dragula's Queen. But now I could understand how vampires were made. I couldn't help but wonder where the other three vampires were.

I asked Ashley if she could help me track down Frank Mason. Ashley didn't want to leave, due to the MGP, but she did point me in the direction of his scent that led to a zoo. Where he went after abandoning the farmhouse.

As I drove down a long and lonely road, I soon came across the entrance to the zoo. It wasn't busy as it was out of season. The place felt eerie. Not many animals were outside.

"Can I help you?" a woman's voice called out.

I turned around to see Beth Williams looking at me with such delight. Dinner and breeding was on her mind, as I remembered what she could turn into. A giant black widow spider.

I got straight to the point. That I was looking for Frank and I needed to see him urgently.

618

"Ah yes, the man who could handle my spiders," Beth remembered. "I didn't eat him if that's what you're thinking. Besides, how would you know what I really am? Are you from the MGP?"

It turned out that Beth had escaped the MGP and found the heart of her husband, but what the MGP did to her caused her to change and become the freak that she was. A test subject.

Beth told me to follow to the back gates of the zoo. She pointed in the direction of the large woods. I remembered it well, as this was where the remains of her husband were found. She suggested it was best to go on foot and walk ten miles. There I would find Frank. I couldn't help but wonder why she wasn't attacking me. "Because I'm not supposed to. Let's just say I have to let you go, so you can see how this is going to end." And with that, I walked away.

14

The woods seemed to go on forever as my footsteps crunched the leaves and twigs snapped beneath my feet. The cool air had turned colder, making me shiver and I could see my smoky breath. I eventually came to a clearing and found myself standing in front of a familiar location.

The log cabin that Melissa and her family used over Christmas. Flakes of snow floated in front of my face, so to get out of the cold, I quickly went inside.

It was dark in the hallway, except from a flickering light coming from the nearby living room. The fireplace was crackling away and I could see that the wall still had a hole in it from Melissa's dad's shotgun that he fired.

"You're the first person I have seen in over... however many years," Frank said, as he turned on the light to reveal he was sitting in an armchair in the corner holding a whisky glass.

Frank Mason had a long beard. He hadn't bothered shaving in all the years he had been in the cabin. He remembered Melissa revisiting the cabin. She never went inside, instead went on in the woods to see the abandoned trailer that she found Mr Geoffries in.

I told him what I knew about him. That he investigated Field Towers, with Lilly and Mr Alan. The truth about Lilly and meeting journalist Sasha Dawson.

"And that is the one statement that makes me not trust you," Frank chuckled. "I've never met any Sasha Dawson."

Of course, he hadn't. I realized that when it was too late. Sasha never became a journalist after using Ben's time travel watch. When she got her fortune, she didn't bother going for a journalist job, so instead her rival would have got that position. India Johnson. Frank's timeline had changed slightly. I could see Frank's eyes light up at the mention of India Johnson.

"You seem well informed. But I don't investigate Paranormal activity any more – I gave that up after I lost Lilly at Faymill," Frank mumbled.

He was my only hope. So, I had to convince him that we were running out of time and running out of ideas. Mr Geoffries had been threatened. He will die in Pentemy.

Frank closed his eyes and shook his head. "Mr Alan's brother." He got up and went over to the window to stare out of it. "I swore that I would never use my ability after I lost Lilly – to put all this behind me – but that man has done more good over the years than any one of us put together. He needs his friends and family by his side."

Frank closed his eyes again and began to strain. I don't know what he was trying to do. But it looked like he was channelling something through him. "He is at Pentemy – the old man is on his way," Lilly's voice spoke through Frank.

I thanked both of them for the assistance and left straight away for Pentemy Village. The snow by now had started to fall heavier and thicker. The cold was already at freezing level. I passed the old trailer where Melissa and Father Thomas had made out and continued my journey through the woods until it came out onto the open road.

I walked and walked, what seemed like miles, not seeing any sign of any other vehicles or life. When I was about to give up all hope, I saw the last piece of salvation. A ranch.

Through the snowfall I could see someone. "Mum," they called. "There's someone out here."

Their mother joined them and called out to me, urging me to join them. "What are you doing out here? Come inside."

The cold disappeared quickly when I went inside. I brushed the snow off my coat and could feel my hands regaining their senses again. When the mother lowered her hood, I quickly remembered who they were. It was Donna. She lost her father to her psycho boyfriend Billy. Zac stood by her side and their son, now all grown up, was Henry.

"Have you got a death wish or something?" Donna asked.

I hadn't, but a good man was about to die. It turned out that Pentemy wasn't too far away, by vehicle, and with Henry convincing them to do something good, we all got in their truck and made our way through the snow.

We didn't talk a lot. I felt awkward being a stranger that wanted help. They had no reason to really believe me, but something told me that this was meant to be, that their path intertwined with mine.

After what felt like half an hour, Zac pulled up outside Pentemy Graveyard. The snow had died down by then, and with a thank you, I hurried through the gates of the cemetery.

The place seems to go for miles. Hundreds upon hundreds of

gravestones. A shallow place of death. But then, there was someone there. Someone dressed in a hoody. A slender looking figure. It wasn't Mr Geoffries. I decided to follow them, keep my distance so they didn't know I was there.

They walked up to a grave. Their hands in their pockets to keep them warm from the cold. "I'm so sorry I wasn't there for you – I should never have left you." That voice.

Why did I remember that voice?

They lowered their hoody and that is when it all made sense. That long blonde hair was something I never forgot. It was Ana.

"It's not your fault," Mr Geoffries called out, as he approached.

"How can you say that? Of course, it was my fault. I abandoned Rick. If I had stayed to look after him, that crazy pop star, Alison Chance, wouldn't have killed him."

"Whether you were there or not – some things are just meant to happen," Mr Geoffries comforted.

Ana looked at Mr Geoffries curiously. There was a memory that Ana remembered. "You wouldn't be the man that talked to a Richie James, would you?"

Mr Geoffries chuckled. "A name I haven't heard in a long time. Yes. I was that man."

"You convinced him to give me a chance. Thank you for that." Ana paused. "But things didn't work out in the end. He left me and Rick on our own."

"I'm sorry," Mr Geoffries apologized. His attention became distracted. Father Thomas had arrived and was standing at the back end of the cemetery that led to an old warehouse. "Stay here – I have someone I need to see."

He took a deep breath, knowing that this was it. He couldn't deny his inevitable fate. He then looked at me. He knew I was there all along and called out, "Are you coming?"

I followed him to the warehouse and entered to see Father Thomas standing in the centre of the building. The place was cold and abandoned. Rust covered the walls. Droplets of water fell from the holes in the ceiling. Light-stands surrounded Father Thomas. We entered the circle and I listened to what Mr Geoffries and Thomas had to say.

"So, it's finally come down to this," Thomas threatened.

Mr Geoffries held his hands up in surrender. He clearly didn't want a fight. He was a good kind man. "Father Thomas – please listen – I know you blame me for Melissa's death, but we all know I had nothing to do with it. What's happened to your faith?"

"Fuck my faith," Thomas snapped. "Love is dead. We all knew that this day was coming." He began to walk around us. "Take a look around you – are you so blind that you can't see the truth?"

"What truth?" Geoffries replied.

"Towns-end of course. Ask yourself, are we all that's in this damn world? Are there any other countries? Is there any other life? Name another town? Another place in this world?"

Mr Geoffries was at a loss. He didn't know what to say. He couldn't answer the question, which made me believe that he started to see the truth, as did I.

"You gullible old fool. If you look up Towns-end – there are no results. It's like this place doesn't really exist. This place was grown from those yellow, purple and green tears that have been left behind."

Yellow, purple and green tears? I went to grab my pendant that had a crystal of the same colour but I realized it was no longer there. Was my pendant responsible for creating them?

"What tears?" Geoffries questioned.

"The tears in reality. People have been talking. Lots of people. They're saying that this place was created out of three elements. That we are the only life there is. The three elements are the tears. And people go missing."

"Missing?" Geoffries is intrigued. "Example?"

"There was this tall lady. Lilith was her name. She got into some trouble. People chased her round a corner and just like that she vanished."

"And you're suggesting she went through one of these tears? To where?"

"If I knew that, I would tell you," Thomas snapped. "And then there was that Alcina Castle – the one that appeared out of thin air – do you think it was a coincidence?"

Geoffries shook his head at the ramblings of his delusion. "Look – I'm a simple man – I just want to rest in front of a roaring fire, with a glass of whiskey in my hand, listening to my old records while I watch the snow fall. Just listen and think. What would Melissa and your baby think of you now? You are not the man she fell in love with."

Thomas's expression dropped. Geoffries' words had hit him in a way that he never thought of. He began to see Melissa's face in front of him. The look of disappointment said it all. Thomas hesitated for a few seconds and then glared in anger at Geoffries, but before he could do anything, Thomas fell to the floor when his leg was shot out.

Scott stepped out of the shadows holding a pistol in his hand. Madison followed behind clapping her hands. "I thought the old fool would never stop rambling," she stood in front of Geoffries. "So, we finally meet."

Ana came rushing into the warehouse to see what all the commotion was. She turned to leave. "No, stay," Madison ordered. Ana joined Geoffries' side.

I explained to Mr Geoffries who she was. The truth about her. The plans that she had and how she had manipulated everything to kill love off.

"I thought Father Thomas was the one that was going to do that?" Geoffries assumed.

"Oh no, this is my legacy that I will leave for my daughter to finish off what I started," Madison chuckled.

"Mind telling me, why you have a detective on your side?" Geoffries questioned.

"Scott," PC Hannah Havers, reacted, as she arrived at the scene. "What are you doing?"

"What's the matter? Scott never told you, his history?" Madison chuckled. "The story begins with his girlfriend, Lilly."

Frank Mason's old flame. There was something. A memory of when Sharon was telling Frank about her history with her boyfriend and her sister, Krista, the one that ended up in Marwood insane asylum for creating the Play 4 Real club.

"Lilly caught Scott being teased by Krista in her bedroom. She was teasing him by threatening to chop his penis off. I, however, threatened to do it for a real when I intervened after Krista was locked up in Marwood. I had plans that only with the help of him, I could make happen," Madison explained.

"The pink pills? You were behind the hijack of PharmCorp's container? You're the reason why Jessica George was sexually abused?" Geoffries snapped.

"Towns-end's sweetheart had it coming. The innocence of youth. The heart of a saint. The hijack of PharmCorp couldn't succeed without someone who was working there."

"That company should have treated me and Simon better," Scott argued.

"And then there was Jamie – the perfect way to manipulate her into the direction I needed her to go in," Madison chuckled.

So, she was the one that came between me and Jessica. The one that changed her mind to marry Jamie instead of me. She had seen me on TV – proposing to her at the Gala event.

"That's why Jamie had to die. I had to crash my car into theirs after they were married. I convinced her that she would reach her full potential – just what my auntie would say."

Full potential. I had heard those words before. Think.

Where was it? Of course, our former teacher – Teresa Gunn. This was not just a coincidence. This was all a plan. Leighanne, Madison's mother, was Teresa's sister; this was a revenge plot.

"I took her away to a place no one would find her. And now she is happy being who she was always supposed to be." Madison giggled. "Not even the Residents of War could find her and they tried so hard to before they toppled Towns-end's government."

I knew that Jessica was still alive. I felt it within my heart.

"Anyway, enough talk," Madison snapped. "It's time for him to die in Pentemy." She glared into Geoffries' eyes. "All alone."

"I'm ready." Geoffries closed his eyes and took a deep breath as Madison aimed the gun at him and applied pressure to the trigger.

The lights around her blinded her as they all came on at once. She put her hand in front of her face as she could see Allison and Matthew join Mr Geoffries' side.

Missy and Evelyn appear on a balcony above followed by Frank Mason. Donna, Zac and Henry enter the warehouse to support Geoffries with Mr Alan, Shane and Michelle. Madison couldn't believe the support that had turned up.

"He had more…" Thomas struggled to breathe. "…support than you have ever had in your life."

"No matter." Madison lowered the gun. "He will still die in Pentemy – in front of everyone."

As Madison raised the gun, Ana grabbed hold of Geoffries, as Madison pulled the trigger. Hannah seized the opportunity to pull her pistol out and fire, blowing Madison's brains out. As Scott trained the gun on Hannah, Father Thomas kicked his legs out from under him, giving Hannah an opportunity to shoot Scott, dead.

Hannah got to her knees as Mr Geoffries lay lifeless.

She spoke into her radio for assistance.

Mr Geoffries gave his life to stop love dying out. The ones he had touched, had shown that love could never die between two people. The strength and determination he had all those years, those wasted days thinking about others was more important to him than living his own life. Madison's plans had faded away and her manipulation over Towns-end had resulted in her own demise. Love was alive. I hoped we had all done the right thing, as I placed flowers on the grave and read the name on the headstone, one last time. Ana.

Mr Alan stood next to me with his hands in his pockets to protect them from the cold of the snow. "After everything that we have been through – it still ended the way it was predicted."

I didn't get what he meant. We had stopped love from dying and Mr Geoffries didn't die in Pentemy. It hadn't come true. That was when Mr Alan told me otherwise.

"But it did. Had you forgotten. Ana was born a man. Her name was Andy. A woman in a man's body. A transgender. He will die in Pentemy."

It was something I never saw coming. The trick, the prediction that was in front of my face the entire time. There had been too many twists and turns through everything I had observed. But, as a result, I had failed to do one simple thing. I never found Jessica George.

"Did you fail? Really?" Mr Alan questioned. "Who is to say, that you are the one that finds Jessica George? I have a feeling that you never would be the one to do that. That there are others who are supposed to find her and you are the one that has to observe them in the right direction."

He was right, my time in Towns-end had come to an end. But one final thing I did wonder, was if we were going to see Mr Geoffries again.

"No," said Mr Alan, bluntly. "Mr Geoffries…" He paused. "Is tired. He needs to live. He can finally have what he always wanted."

Far away, in the trailer that Melissa and Shane had come across, Mr Geoffries sat in an armchair, in front of a little fire with a glass of whisky in his hand, listening to old vinyl records and watching the snow fall.

THE END

Epilogue

Liam Brixton's eyes snapped open like he had woken from a nightmare. In fact, he had. The nightmare in question was a memory of his past that he never shared with his wife or four-year-old daughter.

His wife, Maria snuggled up to him, smiling, happy and so in love. But what she didn't see was Liam's unhappy expression.

"Mummy? – Mummy?"

"Can you see to Anna, babe?"

Liam threw the bed covers back and sat over the edge. His heavy eyes showed how exhausted he looked. Without speaking a word, he sighed as he got up and went next door to his daughter's room.

Getting up at five in the morning wasn't exactly how he wanted to start his weekend while his wife laid in. Sorting out Anna, dressing her and getting her breakfast ready became too much of a chore.

Later that morning – Liam went for a drive just to get a get away for a short period. It was that exact moment he knew that today was the day that all the stress of his life was going to disappear.

He drove over the high bridge that showed Townsend City in all its glory, under the bright blue sunny sky. He then slammed on the brakes and turned the engine off. He sat there for a minute. Angry drivers honking their horns wondering what he was doing. So, to show them he meant business – he opened the door and got out the car. He stared at the drivers who were miming foul language in their vehicles. He then walked over to the side of the bridge and climbed over the railings. The constant sound of horns soon faded due to the drivers looking more concerned at what Liam was doing. Some just watched. Others took out their phones to report an attempted suicidal jumper.

Liam looked down at the drop. The water was deep enough for him to possibly survive as he wasn't too sure it was enough to kill him. He then spotted a concrete platform to the left of him. He side shifted so he was in line with it. This was what was going to end his misery.

627

"Stop – don't do it," a woman called out.

Liam looked around. She was gorgeous. A sweet innocent face. Slender figure and soft spoken. "Who are you?"

"Sasha Dawson," she replied as she stood next to her car with her little boy in his toddlers seat she reaches out for Liam's hand. "Why don't you come back over the railings?"

"No – it has to end," Liam replied.

Sasha stepped closer. As she got a better view of the jumper she then realised something important "Oh my god – it's you isn't it? You're the guy that worked at Vision Electrics. James somebody wasn't it?"

"Richie James – yes," he confirmed. "But now I go by the name of Liam Brixton – because the Richie James destroyed so many lives. You think you can move on – but how wrong I was."

"What do you mean? Destroyed so many lives?"

"Ana," he paused. "Who was originally Andy Mancini – I thought I could really love someone who was a transgender – but I couldn't. We adopted a boy called Rick. I walked out on them both. And now they're both dead because of me."

Sasha slowly creeped towards him.

"I thought moving on was the right thing. I got a wife and child. But I'm still not happy. 2004 was the happiest I ever was. One mistake set me on this path and I won't have it any more."

"Look – I know something about mistakes, but I corrected them and found my happy ending." Sasha looked at her son then back at Liam. "I'm sure your wife and daughter love you very much so why throw all that away?"

"Because I'm doing all the work and feel emotionally exhausted," Liam sighed. He leant over the edge – his arms held onto the railings like he was about to let go."

"Wait," Sasha interrupted. "If you really hate your life that much – there is a way to change it." She revealed her smart watch and took it off. "This watch can control time."

"Bull shit," Liam thought she was crazy.

"I'll prove it," Sasha clicked the button on her smart watch causing time around her to freeze. She walked over to his side then resumed time.

Liam blinked to see no sign of Sasha. When he turned, he nearly fell when he saw her at his side. She grabbed hold of him to stop him. "But…but that's not possible."

"I told you." Sasha placed the watch in his hand. "Tell me what happened in 2004 – where, when, who?"

"My first girlfriend. I met her in a shop just before Christmas. She played me. Messed around with my emotions and my head. Then other girlfriends came along – the cheater – the user who didn't know what she really wanted – the depressive – the misery – the single mother who wanted me just to be a parent so she didn't have to be – all those wasted years of hurt scars after a while and I always thought what if I hadn't had met my first girl and avoided it so I went on a different path."

"Well, now you have the chance – I don't need this watch any more I got everything I need – now come over the railings – please."

Liam did as he was told. He held onto Sasha as she assisted him to safety. She then helped him put the watch onto his wrist.

"Thank you," said Liam. He twisted the watch and disappeared in front of her.

It all went quiet. Sasha looked to see the bright day turn darker as the rumble of storm clouds covered the sky. A slow clapping came from behind her. When she turned around she saw a woman with long blonde hair and a slender but sinister looking face – with someone else standing behind them in a hoody – their identity hidden.

"Bravo – Sasha Dawson."

"Do I know you?" asked Sasha.

"We know you – Ben Parsons sends his regards – he gave you up."

"But that's impossible – he never met me."

"He did – in an alternative time."

"Who are you?"

"You should know who I am. My mother recently died after all. I'm the real Krista Milburn," Krista smiled.

Krista told Sasha what connection she had with Ben Parsons. It started when he was found sneaking in to her home looking for food. Her daughter had freaked out when she saw the Intruder. So, Krista's people took him to Doctor Husbondi to experiment on. He had a talent for unlocking the secrets of the human mind, but what he didn't expect was to uncover a wonderful discovery.

Husbondi's assistant, Linsey who was a large breasted lady stood by his side and watched in awe at the memories that were extracted from his mind. She saw that she was part of his memory. She was in a casino bar in Bright Light City. She took an interest in his wealth, married him and cheated on him.

"But I've never met him before?" Linsey questioned.

Husbondi hushed her. He was too interested in what happened next. They both witnessed the time travel by his watch and his alternative time line with Sasha – where she ended up with the watch to change her life that Ben had manipulated and destroyed.

When they informed Krista – it became part of her legacy to track Sasha down and find a way to get the watch – using the only person that she shared a past with.

"Richie James was my daughter's father. History repeats itself. Just like my mother was abused – knocked up and I was the result. I'm glad that Richie didn't go back too far as me and my daughter wouldn't exist and the residents of War wouldn't have stopped a government. With no power like that – he has made sure that I win after all our planning"

"What do you mean? Our planning?"

The figure behind Krista lowered their hood and revealed themselves to the people on the bridge who were astonished.

"Jessica George," said Sasha. "You've been with these people all this time?"

"They saved me," Jessica replied, "and what a vision they have had for me. And our new life is about to begin."

"Townsend City has hidden so many secrets from the public eye," Krista cackled.

"What secrets?" Sasha yelled.

"Foptix Industries had been keeping a secret in their lab. It was at a time when their prototype, Jennifer, was destroyed. They were experimenting with three babies. Someone stole them. The babies had names, Xander, Jessica and Cullum."

"Wait – they were students at Townsend High School," Sasha remembered, "my friend Rachael's students."

"The three mysterious heroes that fought an insect woman that my benefactor – John Crane – a paramilitary politician who survived the governments downfall, captured her and formed the MGP. The monster girl program. Over the years he took and experimented"

"All those missing people that the police were looking for," Sasha

630

realised.

Krista and Jessica raise their arms in the air like a lunatic cult, "This is our world now."

Sasha runs to her car only to discover that her son is nowhere to be seen. She breaks. Knows that Richie going back in time had erased him from existence. People and vehicles around her faded before her eyes. Buildings and companies disappeared like they had never existed.

Krista and Jessica faded until Sasha was the only one left standing – desolate and alone in a world of nothing.

The concept of changing one's timeline to erase the mistakes and improve our life is the biggest wish anyone wants to come true. But when we get our wish to come true we don't think about the changes that affect the lives and the world around us.

What new world replaced the one we knew? What experiences did the people go through. Where was it set? Well...that is a story...for another time.